Time Benders and the Two Promises

Book II

JB Yanni

Time Benders and the Two Promises

For my parents, who have loved and supported me throughout my life. They have set the standard on which I judge myself, and strive for each day. I know, if I am half the kind, loving, strong, honorable people they are, no matter what else I have accomplished in life, I can count it as a success. It is my sincerest hope that they know how much they have given to their children, grandchildren, and great grandchildren. Plus, I hope they have some understanding of how nothing in my life has been possible without them as parents.

Acknowledgement

I need to provide a special thanks to someone for the aid provided for this book as it stretched my scientific knowledge to its limits several times. Without the help of my much smarter son, Tyler, the ideas in this book would seem more fanciful than I intended. I want this story to seem just plausible enough, just close enough to actual history as possible. He always hated movies and stories that had totally impossible story lines, especially as it relates to physics and space. Hopefully, he doesn't find fault with my interpretation of his wealth of facts.

Deb and Ken practically dragged Joe back to campus. After Deb questioned Joe for the first few minutes and Joe didn't answer any of her questions, everyone was silent. Ken couldn't believe this was happening. After all the agreements they had made, all the discussions after they first tried the time machine, today of all days, when he was graduating from high school, Joe went and did the unthinkable. Kim was crying for most of the walk back and finally Ken picked her up and whispered to her that everything was going to be alright. He would make sure. Kim smiled at Ken and was able to calm down just in time for them to get to the girls' dorm.

Aunt Alicia was looking very alarmed as she talked excitedly to the staff because the kids were not there. She turned and saw them coming toward her, and just walked away from the staff person. "Where have you been?" she asked.

Deb, who had apparently come up with something, replied, "We're so sorry. We realized after we were done talking to our friends that we hadn't said goodbye to one of the staff here that had been really helpful to us when we first arrived. Looking for him meant we had to walk across campus to where he lives. Hopefully, you understand. We just couldn't have left today without saying goodbye to him, but then we realized we must be taking too long, so we practically ran back here. Aunt Alicia and Mr. Reynolds, we didn't mean to worry you."

Mr. Reynolds jumped in at that point to calm things down. "No harm done. Kim, are you ready to go with the McGowans? They're waiting for you, dear."

Kim turned to her brothers and sister to say goodbye. She was going to spend the next two weeks with her friend Amy. She hugged Deb and Ken and then went to hug Joe. When she wrapped her arms around Joe's neck, she whispered to him, "Joe, it'll be alright. I know they're mad at you, but talk to them and fix this. I don't want us to be mad at each other all summer."

Then Kim left with Mr. Reynolds to go to where Amy's family waited. While Kim was getting settled, Ken and Joe loaded all the luggage into the car that Michael, the butler from Mr. Reynold's Hampton house. He had driven to carry all their things home for the summer. When Mr. Reynolds returned, Deb, Joe and Ken, along with Aunt Alicia, got into the other car. Mr. Reynolds was driving, with Aunt Alicia in the front seat and Joe, Deb and Ken in the back seat. Ken asked Deb to sit in the middle, not because she was smaller, but because he didn't want to sit next to Joe. He was still so angry at what Joe had done; he couldn't spend the next few hours sitting next to him.

Joe spent most of the ride looking out the window, trying to figure out what everyone was so mad at him about. Sure, he took off in the machine on his own, but he was trying to do what he thought was right. He went over everything he had done, and nothing seemed to be something that should make Deb and Ken this angry. It all seemed right. He figured he'd hear about it soon. He just sat there quietly.

Deb spent the trip going over what she remembered, and what she had read in the note from her mother. In the note, her mother had asked her to not blame Joe, and to be sure to help him get over what had happened in their family. She also asked her not to blame their father. What on earth had Joe done? She remembered things, things that didn't seem possible, but also wisps of memories of other things. What was going on?

Ken was so angry he was steaming, like literally steam was coming off his body as the window fogged up some. Not only had Joe gone into the machine alone, with no help, and telling no one what he was doing, he had really made things worse this time. He remembered this morning that his parents had separated about six months before their father died in a plane crash. He was on his way to a business meeting. They separated because one day in the fall of 1973, Joe supposedly told their father a fantastical tale about time travel. Of course, their mother disagreed totally because she said she spent the day with Joe at Harvard. This caused so many arguments. Their mother even thought something terrible was happening to Joe. The arguments kept up and got worse, and ended in a blowout just before school started that fall. Their father had moved out. Then, their father was in a plane crash and their mother, racing to the hospital to see him, was in a car accident. She survived for a few days and then died from her injuries.

Ken couldn't believe that once again, an effort to stop the accidents had not prevented his parents from dying. He knew Joe had done something, even if he couldn't remember exactly what Joe did. This didn't stop his parents from dying. It had just changed the circumstances around their death. This time, putting the death back to the same weekend they originally remembered. Ken had to face the reality staring him in the face: they couldn't change their parents' deaths. Mary and Deb, and perhaps Ryan, were all right. There was a plan, and they couldn't really escape it. He found a seat and looked out over the water as the ferry made its way across the river, thinking about what his grandfather had taught for years in church. Sitting there, he remembered the lessons when he was a child about how God loved everyone, and how the Lord wanted only good for everyone. He remembered feeling totally safe in church and at home, knowing that nothing bad would happen to him as long as he tried to be good and was in these places of love. Then his parents died, and he questioned all of this. How could a Lord that loved him take the two people he trusted to care for him? How could His plan include such pain and loss?

Deb came over at that moment and told him they were arriving soon and he needed to come back to the car. They all got back into the car and Ken sat quietly with his thoughts for the quick trip to the Hampton house. Michael arrived with the other car full of luggage and things, and Ken started helping unload it and take things into the house. Joe helped, but they didn't speak. As Ken entered the house, he heard Aunt Alicia ask Deb what was going on between them, as they had not spoken at all in the car. Deb replied that Ken and Joe must have had a minor argument, but she doubted it would last past dinner. Aunt Alicia seemed satisfied with this, but Ken saw Mr. Reynolds turn and look at him as he entered the house.

Deb spent the next couple of hours unpacking her things and Kim's things and putting them away. She heard nothing coming out of the room next door. Then she heard a door open and close and she looked out to see Ken holding Joe's arm and heading for the back stairs. She quietly followed. They all ended up down on the beach. When Deb got down the stairs to where Ken was, he was shoving Joe as he let go of his arm. Joe fell to the sand, but got up and brushed off the sand. Ken said only one thing, "Why?"

Joe looked between Ken and Deb and then replied, "I had to. I had to fix what I messed up. If I hadn't talked to Dad about the computer ideas, he would never have been on that trip, and they would not have been caught in that avalanche."

Deb started before Ken could get up the steam he was obviously feeling. "Joe, we agreed we would wait and discuss it. Why did you feel you had to go alone? Do you know how risky that was? What if something had happened to you? No one would be able to save you. And what if something had happened to the machine? No one was there for that either. And we sat here for nearly twenty-four hours wondering where you were and if you were OK."

"I know, but I had to chance it. I was sure none of you wanted to try again to save Mom and Dad. No one wanted to get back into the machine, anyway."

Ken yelled, "That is not the point!"

"How is that not the point? You weren't going to let me try again. I knew that. Mary was putting pressure on you, Deb and Ryan were putting pressure on you, and I knew you would end up siding with them and say we would never make another trip."

"Joe, you're my brother, my only brother, and I'm not prepared to lose you, too. Don't you ever do such a fool thing again, you hear me?"

"I'm here, aren't I? Nothing happened to me."

"Yes, but Joe, you really messed our family up," Deb said.

"How? I don't know what happened. I can't figure that out, but I don't know what the result of my trip was."

"Isn't that what we've been talking about since we first discussed using the time machine? How you can impact other people's lives without even realizing what you did. In this case, you went back and created a real rift between our parents," Deb said.

"I just wanted to keep them from being in an accident. I was very careful. See, I remembered a day when Dad was talking about having a whole day to get things done around the house because we were all going to be gone. Coordinating my location at the Cambridge Highlands near Fresh Pond, I made my way down to our house. When I got home, I spent a couple of hours talking to Dad. He believed me. I showed him the printouts from the machine, and some of the formulas, and he believed me. I told him I had to get back. Then I made my way back to where I left the machine, but there were some men around Fresh Pond, and all over the Highlands there were people hiking, and I had to hide out until nightfall. That's why I was gone so long. I expected to be back before the graduation dinner that Aunt Alicia planned for you, or maybe even get there and need Mr. Brewster to help me get home if it had worked."

Ken stepped toward Joe. "What you ended up doing was driving a wedge between our parents so wide they couldn't overcome it. Instead of spending my last years of high school worrying about my friends and my girlfriend, I spent it worrying about my parents. I spent each game looking up into the stands to see them sitting far apart, and never having dinner together. Kim missing out on all the times and memories we were lucky enough to have with both our parents. That's all you accomplished. Oh, that and having our parents die in two separate accidents over a few days. Proud of yourself?"

"What do you mean, two separate accidents?" Joe asked.

"Joe, why don't you know this? Wait a minute. I remember when we got back from the Dallas trip. All the new memories didn't sink in until the next day. Is that what's happening to you? I had weird memories too today, like some of the old timeline was kind of there, wispy or foggy. As the day wore on and by the time we got here, all I can really remember are new memories of what you did," Deb said as she tried to think this all through.

"I guess so. Listen, I'm not trying to make you madder; I really don't know."

"Well, he had to go on a trip, and even though he promised you not to fly, he flew and the plane crashed. Then Mom went racing to the hospital where they brought him and someone hit her. She hung on for a few days and then she died. That's what happened," Ken blasted.

"I never intended for any of that to happen. I just wanted to save our parents. That's all I've wanted since we got home from the camping trip. Why can't you see that?" Joe pleaded.

"What I see, Joe, is that you're grieving and making poor decisions because of that grief. You have two sisters and a brother who love and need you. And every time we have used that machine, we have messed up our memories of mom and dad. Do you realize that? If we keep this up, one of these times, one of us is going to say we are glad our parents died. Perhaps we're going to get back here one of these times and step out of that machine to find Kim not having been born or something. Is that what you want?" Ken asked as he threw his hands up and turned away from them both.

"No, that's never what I wanted. I just want them back," Joe said to Ken's back.

"I think it's about time you accept the fact that nothing we do is going to bring our parents back. Regardless of the significant discovery you have made, you can't bring them back. In fact, you wouldn't have made this discovery if they hadn't died, and you wouldn't have siblings that care about you the way we do," Ken said as he turned around.

Deb quietly raised her hand to get their attention and said, "Joe, I know you've been hurting. I know that for whatever reason, what happened to our parents has hit you harder, or lasted longer, than it has for the rest of us. But, Joe, the fact is that we lost our parents. We can't bring them back, and whatever you were intended to discover and do with your life should happen without them."

Joe dropped to the sand and lowered his head. He began to cry and shake. Deb sank down and put her arm around him. Ken was still standing there, looking out over the water. He said, "Joe, you have to face this, and stop trying to push us all into dealing with this loss repeatedly. You're not just keeping you from getting better, you are keeping Deb and Kim from getting past it too, and that is something I'm just not going to allow anymore."

"You're not in charge of all of us!"

"Yes, I am in charge of all of you for all intents and purposes. And I have had enough of this."

At that point, Ken stalked off and headed back to the house. Deb sat with Joe on the beach for a long time. He cried for most of that time but refused efforts from Deb to comfort him. After what seemed like an hour, Joe looked up and said, "I suppose you're mad at me, too?"

"I was very mad at what you did when we discovered it. Mostly, I was angry because of the risk you took. You remember when you were about nine years old and you were determined to climb that tree in our backyard that overhung into the yard of the row houses behind us? You fell out of that tree and into that yard, and we couldn't find you until after dark. Mom and Dad were so worried. We were all frantically looking for you and calling out to you. Mom, at one point, said she would be so very mad at you for what you put her through, once she knew you were alright. I didn't understand what she meant then, but I do now."

"Do you think Ken is only mad because of the worrying?"

"No, I think Ken is mad about more than just that. He was furious this morning when we discovered what the outcome of your trip was. Mom and Dad separating really hit Ken hard. Just think for a minute. You're having a really hard time accepting that our parents died, and all you succeeded in doing was making it harder for Ken. And there is the fact that you did all this on the day Ken graduated from high school. You kind of took all the fun out of what was to be a big day for him. "

"I didn't really think about how this might impact the rest of you. My plan was to just go back for a few hours, convince Dad not to travel, and then I would come back and our parents would be OK. I thought this was so much simpler than trying to get Dad to change his business or something. And I really didn't expect to be gone so long and impact Ken's graduation."

"Listen to yourself. You didn't think about anyone but yourself and what you wanted. Not only did you put yourself at risk, you acted very selfishly. I never expected you to act this way. You were always the careful one, the one who considered all angles before you acted. Like everything was a scientific experiment or a math problem."

Joe hung his head again. Deb stood up and said, "I guess I'm very disappointed in what you did. We're a team. We're supposed to be there for each other and help each other. It's just the four of us. Your actions showed me you don't care about Kim and Ken and I very much."

"That's not true. I just miss Mom and Dad so much."

"I miss them too. Every day there is something that happens that I wish I could tell Mom or Dad about. I think I will always miss them. But Joe, it's time to face the fact that they are gone, and move on, and help us all do that."

Deb waited, but Joe said nothing. She turned to head back to the house but looked back at Joe and said, "Are you coming up? It's almost dinnertime."

"No, tell them I'm down here and I won't be eating dinner tonight."

Deb walked up the stairs and into the house. Aunt Alicia was coming down the stairs and asked Deb where she had been and where her brothers were. Deb indicated Joe was dealing with missing their parents and wanted some time alone, and he was at the beach. As she said that, Ken came around the corner from the den, and they went into the dining room and sat down. Aunt Alicia was a little surprised at the setup in the dining room, but Mr. Reynolds had them all seated at one end of the table. Mr. Reynolds talked to Ken about his preparation for Harvard and what he wanted to do with his summer. When Ken said he wanted to go into the city soon and talk to Mr. Davis about possibly doing some work with the company over the summers, Aunt Alicia looked up from her dinner and said, "Why would you want to involve yourself in the workings of your father's company after what he did to your mother?"

"Aunt Alicia, I know you were very supportive of our mother when they separated, and I really appreciate all you did for her. Regardless of what happened between them, he's still my father, and I want to learn more about his business. I want to see what engineering they have going on that I might want to be involved in."

"Alicia, I don't see any harm in Ken taking advantage of this opportunity. He might decide he wants to do something else, or he might decide this is what he wants, and there is no better time for that to begin than this summer," Mr. Reynolds said in support of Ken.

"Well, I was hoping he might want to see what you do on Wall Street this summer, Darrick."

"That's a good idea. I would like to see what your business is like, Mr. Reynolds, if you're willing to arrange that," Ken said, trying to avoid further argument.

"I would be happy to do that. Why don't you visit with Mr. Davis and we'll talk afterward? You don't want to be too busy this summer. It should be a little bit of a celebration of your success in high school. Maybe look to start internship work next summer."

Ken smiled but thought to himself, *Thanks to Joe, there is no chance of celebration this summer.*

They all sat at the table after they finished eating, discussing plans to shop for the things Ken would need in college. Ken said he had a letter from Harvard saying he would receive a package in the next couple of weeks with his dorm assignment and a checklist of items to bring. He also thought he would have to go up to Harvard to take some exams for placement in classes, but he was still waiting for that information to be mailed. With all the shopping and going to the city plans arranged, they got up from the table. It was getting dark outside and Mr. Reynolds said he would go down and check on Joe.

Mr. Reynolds found Joe standing in the surf, looking out over the ocean. He walked up to Joe and asked what was going on.

"Just needed some time. You know, sometimes it still bugs me about my parents."

"Yeah, my parents divorced when I was your age. It was hard dealing with that, and more so when my mother contacted me when my father was ill. But Joe, what triggered it today?"

"It wasn't today, it was yesterday, when I was talking to friends after the graduation."

"Is that why you didn't want to go with us to dinner and went out with a friend's family?"

Joe thought for a second and realized that this must be what the others told Mr. Reynolds and Aunt Alicia when he was gone. He answered only, "Yes."

"You want to talk about it?"

"I don't know. Did you feel like your parents getting divorced was your fault?"

"When it happened, I thought it must have been my fault. You see, my parents both came from very wealthy families. Their marriage was something each of their parents had wanted. By the time I was your age, my parents were each doing their own things. They rarely went to social events together, and they were rarely in the same place together for very long. That was because they realized too late that they had very little in common. For a young boy, I was sure I had done something, or not done something I should have, that made them argue and not want to be together. As a result, they didn't really want to be with me. At fourteen, it was hard for anyone to convince me otherwise. So, I carried that around for a long time. Feeling unworthy of love and the cause of my parents' breakup has made me very sensitive to what you all are going through. Even though I now understand that children are not responsible for their parents' relationship, I know it might be hard to see that from your vantage point."

"Yeah, but in my case, I know I caused it. I convinced my father of something, and he and my mother fought about it because my mother disagreed, and that's what caused them to split up."

"Joe, even if you said something to your father, your parents' splitting was because they couldn't work through their issues. It wasn't about you; it was about the relationship between a man and woman who were married."

"Yeah, but if I hadn't tried so hard to convince my father, they wouldn't have argued."

"Eventually, something might have come between them anyway, even if that's true."

"Also, it's something else I talked to my dad about that caused his plane crash."

"Joe, nothing you could tell your father would cause a plane to crash."

"No, listen, I talked to him about my ideas for computers, and he went off to start that business. They always had little getaway meetings for new businesses, and while my dad was getting to that meeting, his plane crashed. If I hadn't told him about this idea, there would not have been a meeting, so no plane crash."

"As I understand it, your father and Mr. Davis had several business lines and had started new businesses every few years for the past decade. Again, Joe, nothing you said to your father could have caused this. He likely would have had a planning meeting, anyway. It just might have been about something else."

"You're just trying to make me not feel so guilty."

"No, I'm trying to help you see that there is no need for you to feel any of this guilt."

They both stood there in the surf for a few minutes. Joe wanted to believe that Mr. Reynolds was right, that none of this was his fault, but he was sure both Ken and Deb would disagree on that point.

"Mr. Reynolds, is that why you're trying to take care of us? Because of what you went through when you were a kid?"

"Yes, that and the fact that I care very much about your aunt and want to help her."

"That's cool."

"Yeah, I suppose it is cool."

"That's funny, you saying cool!"

"Are we finished with the serious talk now?"

"I think so."

"Shall we go up then?"

"Yeah, I guess."

They both walked slowly back up to the house, and then Mr. Reynolds took Joe into the kitchen and made him a sandwich. He left Joe there to eat and went looking for Ken. When he discovered that both Ken and Deb had already gone up to their rooms, Mr. Reynolds went to sit with Aunt Alicia. A short time later, Joe called from the hall that he was going up and Mr. Reynolds called out goodnight.

2

That Monday morning, Ken got up and left the house with Aunt Alicia and Mr. Reynolds to go into the city, as they had arranged for him to meet with Mr. Davis. Just before graduation, Ken had contacted Mr. Davis, asking if he could come down and meet with him. Mr. Davis had extended an open door and said he would be in the office most days through the remainder of June. So, Ken was ready to get excited about something else as he entered the building where his father had gone each day to work.

When Ken asked for Mr. Davis and gave his name, the receptionist quickly ushered him into his father's old office. The furnishings had not changed and someone had been watering the plants that Deb and Kim had gotten their father for his last birthday. He sat down facing the desk and waited. A few minutes later, Mr. Davis walked through the door and Ken stood up to shake his hand.

Mr. Davis said, smiling, "Look at you, Ken, all grown up and graduated. And what exactly are you doing in front of that desk? Perhaps you should try it from the other side."

"Oh, Mr. Davis, I'm not sure I'm ready for that side of the desk just yet."

"Ok, shall we sit over here, then? We can talk more casually."

"Sure."

The two walked over to the sitting area of the office, where there were two chairs, a small sofa, and a few tables. Ken sat down on the sofa and Mr. Davis sat in a chair.

"How was graduation?"

"It was great, Mr. Davis. It feels good to be done with high school. I just wish my parents could've seen it."

"Yes, well, your father spoke of it often, and I know he was very proud of what you have accomplished so far."

"I hope so."

"And what are your plans now?"

"Well Mr. Davis, I've been accepted into Harvard and start there in the fall. I plan to pursue an engineering degree."

"Just like your father, I see."

"Yes, I believe I might be interested more in mechanical engineering, though. I know we have some business to discuss from reading my father's will."

"Ken, your father was very clear with me. He didn't want you to just move into his office if you were not ready for it, or if you had other ideas about what you wanted to do. However, I can't think of anything better to solidify your father's legacy with this company than for you to work here after you're done at Harvard."

"Mr. Davis, I admit there is a part of me that wants to come here so that I can have my father's work live on. However, I'm not totally sure yet. Would it be too uncertain or hard for you to wait for me to decide this in the next four years? I mean, you have a business to run here, and I don't want my indecision to stand in your way."

"The mere fact that you are saying this tells me you're already mature enough to do the job. Your interest in the business will stand until you are ready to decide. That is how your father set the terms in his will, and with the board here. Until you make a decision, or no later than your twenty-second birthday, your interest remains the same. However, Ken, I have to ask, how do you plan to make this decision? It won't be something you can decide sitting in classrooms at Harvard, you know."

"I was thinking about that very thing today driving into the city. What do you think about this plan, Mr. Davis: I will start working the summers in some internship capacity after my first year at Harvard? I would like to learn the different aspects of the product offerings and how you've organized things and run day to day. But I feel like I should get a year of college under my belt first. Then, at the end of that last summer, I can sit down with you, and we can make a better decision You would be able to judge my worthiness as partner, if that is what I choose, and I can have something sounder to make my decision on."

"I think that is an excellent plan, Ken. How about if I work up a schedule for next summer for you to learn the various product lines and send that you just before your Christmas break? We can meet over break and complete a plan; then we can start you working as soon as finals are over in the spring."

"That sounds great. I was hoping you could take the lead in setting up where I should be. I have to admit, I was always interested in what my father did, but was generally too busy with football and friends to ask much about it."

"Oh, so fun and games are over now? Time to get serious about your life?"

"Yes, it's turned serious quickly this year."

"I don't mean to pry Ken, but have you taken custody of your siblings? Is that why it's so serious now?"

"No, I've followed my parents' advice and wait on that until I have graduated from college. However, that doesn't change the enormous sense of responsibility I feel for them."

"As I said, you are already showing such maturity, but isn't your aunt providing for Joe, Deb, and Kim?"

"There's a trust that is providing for them, and Aunt Alicia has access to that trust to pay for things they need, but that is not really what I'm talking about."

"No, parenting is so much more than writing a check."

"Yes, it is. Especially when one of your siblings is doing something you don't agree with."

"Is that possible? Your father always spoke of all of you children as so talented."

"Joe has really struggled with the loss of our parents and has had some issues this year. Right now, he and I disagree over the best way to work through that, and he has done some things that have made it harder on Deb and Kim. I'm sure if it were about anything else but losing our parents, we would probably label this a little sibling dispute, but everything has been so amplified this year by their deaths."

"I'm sure this has been hard on all of you. Just remember that you have people around you that will help. Ann and I both are more than ready to lend any assistance you all might need. Do you think it would be good for Ann or I to talk to Joe?"

"I know we can count on you, Mr. Davis, and Mrs. Davis. It's actually kind of funny, but the four of us have grown much closer this past school year than I ever thought possible. We rely on each other in a way that I know we never would have if circumstances had been different. I appreciate the offer, but I think Deb and I can straighten Joe out this summer."

"I really like your take charge attitude, Ken. I'm looking forward to convincing you of your need for a partner over the next three years. Now, let me show you around the office."

"That sounds great. I need to be downtown by eleven-thirty, though. I'm meeting Mr. Reynolds for lunch before I head back to the Hamptons."

As they walked out of the office, Mr. Davis asked about Mr. Reynolds and Aunt Alicia. Mr. Davis introduced Ken to several of the other executives and showed him the product line display room. Ken asked many questions about the different products and prototypes and Mr. Davis said he was impressed with Ken's understanding. They shook hands as Ken was boarding the elevator to the main floor.

Ken made his way down, hailed a cab, and met Mr. Reynolds for lunch. They talked about Ken's visit and his plans for the summers, and then Mr. Reynolds brought up Joe.

"So, Joe told me last night that he feels very guilty about your parents' split and their accidents. Are you aware of this?"

"Yeah, we've been dealing with this the whole time we were at boarding school. I feel bad for Joe, but some of this he has brought on himself. He can't seem to let go of the idea that if something had been different, our parents would be here today."

"Ken, I think it might feel different for you than it does for Joe. Remember, you have something that none of your siblings have. You had both of your parents for the entire time you were growing up. They will never have all the time you did."

"Yeah, I get that. But Joe has made it so that Deb and Kim have struggled to move on as well. I have to look out for all of them, Mr. Reynolds."

"I thought we had dispensed with the Mr. Reynolds thing?"

"Sorry, that dad we were just talking about. He taught me to always respect those that are older than I am. I can't help it. It just feels wrong to call you Darrick."

"Even though you graduated, and I have asked?"

"I will try."

"Ok, back to Joe. He's in a very precarious place right now. Boys his age really need their father to show them how to transition to being men instead of boys. That's probably why he is having a harder time."

"Just because Deb, Kim and I are not carrying on about losing our parents doesn't mean we are not upset about it. I think about it every day. Every time I look at Deb and Kim, I think about it. Graduation was hard for me because all I could think as I was walking up to get my diploma is how wrong it felt to be doing that without my parents there."

"I'm sorry. I wasn't trying to imply that none of the rest of you were having any difficulty over the loss of your parents. What Joe is experiencing is different, and you need to respect that and help him see that none of this is his fault."

"I see what you mean and I'm trying. Joe doesn't exactly make it easy, but believe me, I understand my responsibility to my siblings."

"Now don't get angry with me. I'm also not trying to imply that you are not doing a stellar job taking care of your younger siblings. Aren't you the one that sacrificed your time and money to get your sister a dress? Aren't you the one I saw playing on the beach with your ten-year-old sister? You have been very responsible for them all."

"Yeah, well, if I don't do it, who will?"

"You could ask for help from your aunt, or from me, you know."

"I don't want to sound rude or anything, but Aunt Alicia doesn't exactly immerse herself into our lives."

"I have noticed that she doesn't quite know how to deal with any of you. Do you have any idea why that might be?"

"I don't, really. When we were growing up, Aunt Alicia breezed in and out of our lives infrequently. She was always talking about how busy she was. Then, when our parents split, she was around a lot more, but she seemed to really be more interested in supporting our mother than in anything we were doing. Maybe she doesn't know how to deal with kids?"

"I've seen her with other people's children, and she seems warmer than I've seen her with you four. I don't understand it. Perhaps I should just speak to her about it."

"It's Ok really, you don't have to do that on my account. This entire life change has really made my siblings and I much closer and I'm glad about that. It's just right now, Joe is kind of pushing the limits of my patience. As an only child, I don't expect you to understand, so maybe this is just a sibling thing."

"Perhaps. Just remember, I'm here for you, regardless of how un-involved your aunt may seem."

"Thanks, but I think I see Michael in the car out there. I should probably get going so he doesn't have to find a place to park."

"Good idea. I'll see you tonight."

With that, Ken left the restaurant and went out to flag down Michael. Mr. Reynolds paid the lunch bill and left in time to send Ken off in the car.

Meanwhile, back at the Hamptons, Deb spent the morning reading the book assigned for summer reading. Joe found her on the back porch doing that after he had finished eating breakfast. He sat down in a lounge chair and looked at Deb until she finally glanced up from her book.

"What do you want, Joe?"

"Are you going to be mad at me all summer?"

"First of all, this is the first day of summer. Second, I'm trying to read."

"You sound mad."

"Well, you've interrupted my reading, and yes, I decided last night that I'm, in fact, still angry with what you did."

"What made you decide that?"

"You risked your life, you upset Ken's graduation, you messed up our family, and you won't consider anyone else's feelings in any of this."

"Ok, fine, be mad."

Joe stalked off toward the beach and Deb returned to her reading. About an hour later, the cook came out to tell Deb that she had a phone call. Deb went into the den and picked up the phone.

"Hello."

"Hi babe, are you ok to talk now?"

"Oh Ryan, I'm so glad you called me."

"Me too. I've been so worried about you, but I had a big family dinner with all kinds of relatives and then a conference with Mother about the year. It's a thing she does at the end of every school year."

"To do what, exactly?"

"She wants to know what I learned about myself; what growth I think I've made. I think it's her way of analyzing me or something. I tolerate it, but I was about ready to jump out of my skin all weekend thinking about you and what happened with Joe."

"I wanted to call you too, but I was so angry and confused that I've been pacing and reading and thinking and am just exhausted."

"So, I'm kind of dying here."

"Well, he came back, but we had only enough time to drag him back to campus to get into the car with Aunt Alicia and Mr. Reynolds. When we got here, we unloaded everything, and I was unpacking Kim's and my things, and then I heard Ken drag Joe down the hall. I followed, and we went down to the beach. We confronted Joe, and he told us what he did, but he didn't have any knowledge of our parents separating. He decided we were all ganging up on him, and he was determined to either fix what had happened or, better yet, stop the accidents. So, he went back to Cambridge on a Saturday that he remembered my dad was alone in the house because of everyone's plans. He arrived in Cambridge that Saturday morning and went home, and spent a couple of hours explaining everything to our dad. He took papers, and the formula, and prints, and drawings of the machine, and showed them all to our dad."

"Where was he able to land—or whatever—the machine so no one would see him?"

"There's this pond not too far from our house and a forest-like area around it. He landed there and then walked to the house."

"What was your father's reaction to what Joe told and showed him?"

"Apparently, my father believed him. He wanted to come and see the machine, but Joe said that was a bad idea. Joe pleaded with him to not travel any time in the fall, so there was no accident."

"So that seems pretty harmless. What was the issue?"

"Well, my mother spent the day at Harvard with Joe. When they got home and my father talked to my mother, she didn't believe him. In fact, it caused a lot of arguments between them. They spent the next few weeks deciding what to do. They even took Joe to some doctor to be examined. In the end, my mother and father argued so much that they split up. My father moved out of the house and they stopped talking."

"Really? I only remember you telling me your parents had split up, not any of the details. It always upset you to talk about it. What is the original timeline like?"

"Well, the only reason I remember any of the original timeline is because Ken and I wrote some things down. I guess in the original timeline, they died together, and they never split up."

"Wow, what else did Joe say?"

"Well, he said in the fall my father called to tell us he had to go meet with some clients and there was a plane crash. When we got the call at the house late that night, my mother took off to go to the hospital where they had taken my father. She was in a terrible car accident on the way. She lived for another few days and then she died from her injuries."

"Oh Deb, I'm so sorry about all of this. You must be so upset. It's kind of like reliving it again, isn't it? You told me about this at school, but now you have to deal with it again. Were their deaths different in your notes, too?"

"Yeah, so, the night before we left campus, I went to Ken's room, and we wrote notes of what we remembered. I just had this feeling that something was going to shift by morning. Then the next morning, I knew it felt strange to remember my parents dying separately. So, I got out my notes and the letters from our parents from the will and it all seemed so strange. As the day went on, my memories from before seemed to just disappear and now all I have are the notes to remember the previous timeline. In my notes, they died in an avalanche crash in a car, but they were together."

"I just remember you telling me about your parents' split and the accidents, sweetheart. I don't remember any other details."

"No, you wouldn't, and I think that's why I only still remember a little, because of my notes, but the things I wrote seem vague and like a dream. I can't explain it."

"How angry was Ken?"

"Well, he was mad, really mad. I was too. Joe really took too big of a risk doing this. He could have been hurt, or found out, or something could have happened to the machine. We would have never known what happened. And more importantly, Joe said he was feeling really weird the whole day, and it got worse and worse. He barely made it back because when he got into the machine, his vision was getting cloudy and he was dizzy and sick to his stomach."

"Oh my gosh, why?"

"He said it must be because he existed in that time and place. He and Mr. Brewster are probably going to have to research that before we know for sure."

"Hey, wait a minute. If Joe only spent a couple of hours with your father, why wasn't he back sooner?"

"He said he went back to where the machine was and found people on the lake and then some men camping and hunting and he had to hide out for the night."

"Even more risky."

"Yes."

"Ken was also really mad at Joe for not being able to let this go about my parents, and how it could hurt Kim and me with his continued antics. He yelled at Joe. Ken declared no one was ever getting in the machine again. Oh, then he added he's starting to believe we can't change the plan set for us and clearly, we can't have what we have now and go on with our parents here, so Joe needs to accept it."

"Wow, that's a big shift for Ken."

"Yeah, our parents being separated and Joe's action really shook him."

"That's not good. Ken has told me he's really thankful about how close you all are now and he's so grateful he has you all. I know it must be hard for him to say those things to Joe."

"I'm really mad too. I told Joe I didn't want to talk to him right now."

"I think it's ok for the two of you to be angry, but remember you're talking about your brother. You have to find a way to work this out, Deb. You and Ken both."

"I know, I just need to calm down before I can talk to him again."

Ryan saw that as a clue to change the subject, so they spent the next few minutes talking about plans they had for the summer. Ryan said his mother had given him permission to come out to see Deb at the end of the week, if it was OK with her aunt. Deb said she would check and call back tomorrow. They hung up and Deb went back to her book for the rest of the afternoon.

Joe had stalked off to the beach. He sat back from the water's edge, as there were quite a few people out today to enjoy the water and weather. Sitting in the sand, he started digging in it with his feet as he looked out at the waves. His mind was reeling over his parents and what a mess he made of things. He alone could remember what had happened in all three histories, the first original one, the one they changed by the trip to Dallas and now this really messed up one from his trip to Cambridge. Perhaps, he wondered, if he should have figured out a way to tell his mother what he told his father. Shifting to current issues, he thought about what Ken and Deb had said to him yesterday. Was he being selfish? Could it be the way Ken said? His stomach growling interrupted his thoughts, and he got up and headed back to the house. While he was in the kitchen having a sandwich, Michael found him and said he had a phone call. He went into the den and picked up the phone.

"Hello."

"Joe, this is Mr. Brewster."

"Oh, hi Mr. Brewster. How're you doing?"

"I'm ok, Joe. The bigger question is, how are you?"

"Well, both Ken and Deb are ready to kill me, and I really made a mess of things."

"It was a pretty foolish thing to make a trip in the machine, making no one aware of your plans. What if something had happened to you while you were wherever you went?"

"Yeah, I know it wasn't a smart thing to do. I just had to save my parents. The others were going to say we couldn't make trips anymore, and I just wanted to try."

"I know losing your parents has been so hard on you, but you terrified us all. That's probably the basis of the anger you're getting from Ken and Deb. They were just distraught over you while you were gone."

"I went to Cambridge on a Saturday when I knew my dad would be alone at the house. I convinced him I had come back from the future and showed him the formula and some other papers and he believed me. He and my mother argued for weeks over whether to believe me, and then they split up. They died anyway. My father in a plane crash and my mother in a car accident."

"Oh Joe, this must be so hard on you. I wish there was something I could say to help you here. I have been through this, but I know it's not the same. Losing parents is not the same as losing a wife."

"I'm not trying to upset you. I know you've had a hard time as well. Maybe Ken is right; maybe I was just being selfish."

"It's hard to put that label on a boy who just wants his parents back, and has found a way to make it happen."

"But I haven't found a way. Every time I step into that machine, I make it worse."

At that moment, Ken came into the house. He noticed Joe on the phone and went onto the porch to speak to Deb.

"Mr. Brewster, I'm sorry, but I have to go. Ken is home."

"That's fine. You hang in there. We'll figure this out."

"I'll call you tomorrow."

"Good. Looking forward to it. Miss having you all here already and it's only been one day."

"Bye Mr. Brewster."

"Bye Joe."

They all sat together that night at dinner. Ken and Mr. Reynolds spoke about plans for tomorrow, as Ken was spending the day at Mr. Reynolds' office. Deb then asked if she could spend the day with Aunt Alicia. The request pleased Aunt Alicia, and she said yes. She checked her schedule and told Deb a photoshoot on location was on the books. Deb said she loved that from the spring trip. Aunt Alicia suggested she wear something she had picked out from her birthday shopping spree. After dinner, Mr. Reynolds asked Joe and Ken if they wanted to play a game and they went into the den for a game of Monopoly. Deb went up to her room to read.

The game got interrupted when Mary called for Ken. Joe sat with Mr. Reynolds and talked while Ken spoke to Mary in the other room. Ken told Mary about what had happened, about the notes he and Deb had written, and how angry he was. Mary was, as usual, very supportive and listened to all Ken had to say. She said she was glad nothing bad had happened to Joe while he went on this trip, and understood how angry Ken must be feeling. Ken wasn't ready to discuss his changing thoughts on his spiritual issues and the idea there was a plan for everyone. He left out that he had told Joe he believed they couldn't change their parents' deaths, and maybe the loss of their parents was necessary for them to have a better life. They talked about his meeting with Mr. Davis and that he would spend the day with Mr. Reynolds the next day. Ken left Mary with word that he would call her tomorrow evening and that he loved her.

While all the calls and games were being played, Aunt Alicia was filling out the paperwork required for her to get funds from the trust. She would send them over via messenger to the lawyer tomorrow when she and Deb got back to her office. Aunt Alicia thought about how angry it made her. She had to ask for funds to raise these children, why? Sometimes, she still felt such anger at her sister's husband because she was sure he had basically abandoned his family and, prior to his abandonment, kept her from seeing her sister.

3

The next day, Ken and Deb left with Aunt Alicia and Mr. Reynolds in the morning, leaving Joe alone in the house. He spent most of the day going over the printouts from the machine when he went back to Cambridge. Then he spent time working on the calculations to nail down the time passage issue. He also spent some time documenting all the physical symptoms he had had so that he could share those with Mr. Brewster. The three trips were not consistent in the way time passed for those that left in the machine, nor for those that stayed behind. He was going to have to call Mr. Brewster to discuss this. He tried Mr. Brewster several times but did not get an answer when he called, so Joe went down to the beach.

Ken really enjoyed the day with Mr. Reynolds. He learned how companies use stock to raise capital for their research and development or to grow their business. He learned how a trade was made through calls and messages to a runner on the New York Stock Exchange floor, and he learned about some tools that the investment team used to determine which stocks to recommend to their clients. Mr. Reynolds handled a group of clients that he referred to as "high wealth individuals." Ken didn't understand the difference between individual and institutional trading, but he enjoyed all he learned. They went out to lunch with a group of very important men from various investment firms like Mr. Reynolds'. It was interesting listening to them discuss politics and business people.

Deb spent the day with Aunt Alicia at a location shooting. Like last spring when she did this on her birthday, the people that surrounded the shoots were considerably more interesting to Deb than the models. The models seemed aloof and somewhat pretentious, while the people doing make-up, hair, clothing, taking pictures and setting up around the location seemed like normal people trying to make a living. They moved around like a choreographed dance. When Deb mentioned this to Aunt Alicia at lunch, she laughed, but then thought about it. After lunch when they went back to the shoot, Aunt Alicia found her in a corner, watching everything and leaned over to say conspiratorially that Deb was right. It looked like a dance from a distance. They laughed and watched for a bit before someone from her office approached Aunt Alicia.

"Miss Swanson, they asked me to come and get a package that you needed delivered today," said the assistant.

"Yes, it's with my things over by the trailer. Follow me, and I will get it for you, and the address it needs to be delivered to," replied Aunt Alicia.

Aunt Alicia told Deb she would right back. The two of them walked off to the trailer and Deb saw the assistant leaving with a large envelope as Aunt Alicia walked back to her.

"Apparently Darrick and Ken are ready to go, and I'm pretty much finished up here, so we're going to head back to the Hamptons."

"Ok, I have nothing except this bag right here, so I'm ready."

"Great, I have some things to gather up at the trailer. Why don't you come with me, and then we can meet Darrick?"

With that, Deb and Aunt Alicia gathered up her things and walked to the intersection close to the park where they were doing the photo-shoot. On the way back in the car, Ken told Deb about the day he had and Deb talked about the shoot. They laughed to themselves about the people who were so very important, or at least those that thought they were, like the investment men and the models.

After dinner, Deb went to call Ryan and then Kim to see how she was doing at her friend's house. Ken was watching a ball game with Joe when Deb came into the den and sat down to read. Just as she sat down, Michael came in and said Joe had a phone call. Joe went into the other room and picked up the phone.

"Hello, this is Joe."

"Joe, this is Mr. Brewster. How are you doing today?"

"Ok. How are you doing?"

"Had a long day of maintenance around campus today."

"Oh, that's why you didn't answer when I tried to call you this afternoon."

"I'm sorry. I didn't mention that I'm working for the next month, until July fourth, on maintenance around campus. Then I have July and some of August off, and then back to it before you all come back here."

"I see."

"What were you calling about? Is everything OK?"

"Yeah, I was working on the time passage calculations and had some issues. Also, I had a lot of strange physical symptoms on this trip that I've never had, and I wrote everything down and mailed it off to you today. You should have it by the end of the week or so. Maybe you could look at what I did and where I noted my questions and get back to me?"

"Sure, I'll take a look. What physical symptoms did you have?"

"As soon as I got to our house in Cambridge, I got this terrible headache. A couple of times I felt kind of dizzy. That persisted until I got back to the forested area where the machine was. By then I was also feeling very sick to my stomach. I had to hide out because there were people around, and I started feeling really weak and disoriented. I had some trouble getting back to the machine and once I was inside, I had blurry vision and it was hard to start things up."

"Good Lord, Joe, I'm surprised now you made it back! What are your assumptions about these symptoms?"

"I think it must be because I existed in that time and space already. I mean, I've read some theory about the fact that there is a finite amount of energy in the universe and my being there twice was double the energy and the universe had to reconcile that. When the symptoms got worse later in the day, I think it might have been because I had arrived home with my mother by then, and while I was not face to face with myself, we were within a few miles of each other."

"Well, that sounds reasonable. I've read some of this theory as well over the years. Not sure if I agree with it, but then I didn't think time travel was possible a year ago either. I don't think we can run more tests to prove it—that sounds dangerous—but when we started this conversation, I was asking how you are doing, not what you are doing."

"I know. Both Ken and Deb were gone today with Mr. Reynolds and Aunt Alicia, so I didn't talk to either of them. I think they're both still mad. I've been thinking a lot today about what Ken said to me and what you said to me. Haven't figured anything out yet."

"Can I help?"

"Not right now, but thanks. You've been such a help to me all this time. I don't know what I would've done if I'd not started talking to you. I'll let you know if I want to talk this through. Is that ok?"

"Certainly. I'm here for you."

"Thanks a bunch."

"How about if I call you once I get your letter and we can go over it?"

"That would be great."

"Take care, Joe."

"Thanks again, Mr. Brewster."

Joe went back into the den just as the Boston Red Sox were executing a double play. He cheered and sat down. Neither Deb nor Ken commented, so Joe figured he was right about them still being mad. Ken got up at that point and said he was going to go call Mary. Aunt Alicia asked if she could speak to Mr. Reynolds and he left too. When it was just Deb and Joe in the room, Joe asked if she was still angry with him. She said she was calming down, and he would have to give her a few more days.

Out on the porch, Aunt Alicia was lamenting the issues with driving back and forth to the city each day for work from the Hamptons. She said it took too much of her time, and she had to leave too early and got back so late. She could not do this all summer long.

"Sweetheart, the kids will be off with their friends off and on all summer. Perhaps you can stay in the city on weeks when they are all gone?"

"Yes, but I have just looked at the calendar Deb put together of all these comings and goings and whenever Deb or Ken are gone, Kim is here. I would rather be in the city unless Kim is here. Although I don't know how much good I will be to her if I have to leave at five in the morning and don't get home until after six at night."

"So, what would you like to do, Alicia?"

"I want to go to the city tomorrow and stay through next week. There are some important parties this weekend that I need to attend. Kim will be back next weekend and we can spend the weekend with her, and then I can be in the city during the week."

"I suppose we can hire a nanny to be here for the summer to make sure the children have supervision outside of Michael when you have to be in the city. Would that be better for you?"

"Yes, that would really help me out. Of course, we don't need a nanny for Ken or Deb or Joe, but that would be helpful for Kim."

"I will ask Michael to arrange for some interviews."

"Can you handle the interviews? I mean, you had nannies growing up, and I didn't, and I need to be in the city for the rest of the week."

"I will handle it, Alicia."

"Thank you. I knew you would understand."

So, the next day when Mr. Reynolds and Aunt Alicia left for the city, they were not coming back until the next weekend when Kim returned. Mr. Reynolds said he would call each night and check in with them. He left Ken with money so they could do things for the next week. Deb was not too upset that they would be left alone. Plus, Ryan was coming out Saturday for the day to see her, so she was fine with her aunt and

Mr. Reynolds being gone. Ken took off mid-morning to go into the village nearby. Joe sat down in the office to write to Becky, the girl he had started talking with just before the end of the school year. She was in his math class, and Joe thought he might like her. She lived in Fairfax, Virginia. Deb sat on the back porch and looked out over the ocean and read the book that Ryan had given her for her birthday.

Friday night, just after Deb, Ken, and Joe had finished dinner, Aunt Alicia and Mr. Reynolds arrived at the house. Deb said it surprised her to see them, as the plan was for them to be gone until the next weekend. Aunt Alicia looked furious as she said she had come back to see Ken. Mr. Reynolds steered Ken and Aunt Alicia into the office and closed the door.

"What's this all about?" Ken asked as he turned to face Aunt Alicia and Mr. Reynolds.

"What is this all about? You tell me what this is all about. Apparently, you went behind my back to the lawyer and placed yourself between the trust and me. Me, who is supposed to care for all of you all summer and all year, every year until Kim is eighteen? Why did you do this, Ken? You're just like your father!"

Ken was stunned by Aunt Alicia's outburst. He wanted to remain calm, but something inside him just broke as he said, "First of all, Aunt Alicia, I didn't go behind your back. It's my feeling, in fact, that you kept something very important from me for months after our parents died for no good reason. I simply went to the lawyer to ask to read the wills of my parents since you wouldn't let me. It was a big surprise to me he expected to see me, and that we had some forms to sign now that I was eighteen years old."

"What made you decide you needed to leave school to go see the lawyer and not tell me? I demand an answer right now, Kenneth!"

"I went to see the lawyer because when I asked you to bring me to the will reading, you refused. When I asked you later what they said in my parents' wills, you wouldn't answer me. Why would I ask you again after you had refused me twice already? I went to the lawyer because, as an eighteen-year-old, I'm no longer under your guardianship and do not require your permission to do anything!"

"Now, let's not get so out of control that we say things we don't mean," Mr. Reynolds tried to reason with both of them.

"Don't need my permission? I suppose that's true, you don't need my permission, but there were secrets kept at that will reading. There were things I couldn't see. What about the letters that your parents wrote to you all? You know I wasn't allowed to even see them, don't you? And by the way, you live here, right? You are here by the good graces of Darrick and only because I'm with him."

"Those letters were from my parents to each of us. Private notes from a mother to her child and father to his child. They were intended for each of us only, and really none of your business! And, if you want me to go, Aunt Alicia, I will leave. But I'm taking my siblings with me if you do this. I will get custody of them. I can do that, and you will never see them or get any of the money. So whatever plan you have to take my parents' money, it's over if you push me right now."

Mr. Reynolds then put his hand on Ken's shoulder and asked if Ken could give him just a minute to talk to Aunt Alicia. Ken nodded, but did not speak, and went out the French door to the patio. Mr. Reynolds turned to Aunt Alicia and said, "Alicia, what's going on? You cannot force Ken to leave until we sort this out. Do you understand this will have some lifelong, profound consequences? I've been in this kind of conversation, and trust me, it takes decades to come back from these kinds of words, and you do not want that. You don't understand what that kind of loneliness is like."

"And you do?"

"Yes, my father and I had a conversation very similar to this when I was twenty years old and about to graduate from college. I thought he had done something shady with our family trust and I called him out on it. He got angry because I was questioning his judgement, and it escalated until he said just about what you said, and I said just about what Ken said. I left that night. I left this house, graduated from college with not a soul at my graduation. My parents had barely spoken to one another or, quite frankly, to me in over a decade at that point, but they sure agreed on not coming to my graduation. I went to work, lived on my own, and was very alone for a very long time. The only thing that brought me back here was a call from my mother when my father was ill. I came back, wary of what he would say and do. He was so filled with regret and sorrow over the loss of our relationship, it was literally killing him. We worked it out, but Alicia, it was after almost two decades and he died a week after I came home. You can't do that to these kids who have already lost their parents. I know you lost your sister too, but think about this for a just a minute. Those four children are the last remaining blood relatives you have on this earth. If they leave tonight, you will be alone."

"What, you would leave too?"

"Alicia, what I did to my father and the loss I felt, I will probably never get over it. I know what it's like to lose parents with nothing but bad feelings between you. Trust me, I know what it's like to be alone all the time because your parents are too busy with their social lives, and their friends and work, to pay any attention to a lonely ten-year-old boy. You and your nieces and nephews have become very important to me. You can't do this. I care about you too, but I feel like I have to take the kids' side here. They need protection that you're not providing them it for them."

"I can't believe you would do that to me." She turned away from him at this point so he couldn't see her tears.

"Alicia, I'm not trying to do anything to you, but help you. The point is that this is not just about you anymore. That will gave you the responsibility of four children that need a lot of love and support to get over their grief and to continue to grow and learn."

"I too have had heartache in my life. Just because my parents were present in my life doesn't mean it was all sunshine and roses, Darrick. My parents virtually ignored me, too. Why wouldn't they ignore the child that was just into silly things like fashion when they had a brilliant daughter who married a brilliant businessman and was hugely success-ful? They had the grandchildren, while I couldn't attract and keep a man for longer than two weeks, according to my mother. I know what lonely is because I was lonely my whole life. They were at the events of my life, but they were distracted and always pointing out what my sister had done and how soon she had accomplished everything. I never measured up. Then, when my sister called and told me she was splitting with her husband, a miracle occurred. I got my sister, finally. She cared about what I was doing, and she wanted to see me, and she had me over to see her often. It was wonderful. Then he goes and dies in a plane crash and she has to go chasing after him again. Surprise! Your sister has been in a car accident, and now, not only did you lose your sister, but you have to deal with her four children. The reason I never had children is because I didn't want to endure all those days and nights of caring for a small child and I didn't want to do to any child what was done to me. I guess, truth be told, I don't really want to give up my career and my sister gave up so much to have kids. Her teaching career was on hold for several years, and I don't want to do that. Plus, I enjoy my life. The sacrifice gets to me. The questions when I come home and what invitations I accept if I had children. I like my nieces and nephews, but mostly because they are older now. I've suffered too, Darrick."

"Oh, Alicia, I didn't know your childhood was so lonely. You never let on that anything was ever wrong there. You made it seem like you had an idyllic childhood. I've always been a bit jealous of the family you described and your relationship with your sister."

Aunt Alicia was crying and Mr. Reynolds held her and soothed her. When she finally calmed down, he said, "We have to make this right with Ken. What in the world happened today?"

"I heard from the lawyer because I made a request for funds from the trust. The forms were to request money to cover the expense of having them here this summer and to get Ken ready for college and to pay for the nanny you and I discussed. I submitted the forms, and the lawyer called today and told me he would process the request, but now that Ken was eighteen and set up as co-executor, he had to be consulted for approval of any fund request. I had no idea he had done that, and it really made me angry. He must have snuck off and met with the lawyer and didn't even speak to me about it. I was barely given anything from my sister. I don't understand why Ken can come in now and prevent me from having the money to take care of these kids."

"I don't believe Ken snuck off and did anything to get you, Alicia. I think he was hurt by how you handled the will reading and he just had questions. Don't you think he has a right to know what his parents wanted of him?"

"I guess. Just why didn't he call me and ask?"

"I think he might feel like he asked. Remember, he said he felt you were keeping things from him."

"I wasn't. I was just upset about losing my sister and then over-whelmed about having to deal with four kids. See, I was deciding based on what I would want if I was in their shoes, not bothering to ask them."

"Ok, let's talk about this with Ken now, sweetheart."

Mr. Reynolds went and got Ken and explained a little about what Aunt Alicia had told him in an effort to help calm Ken down. They came back into the office and sat down in the chairs arranged near the desk.

"I'm sorry for getting angry, Aunt Alicia," Ken said right away.

"I'm sorry too, Ken. I let my feelings about so many other things cloud my judgement today."

"Can we start over, then?"

"Yes. Let me start, please. First, I wasn't trying to keep details from you on the day of your parents' will reading. I'm new to this parent thing, Ken, and I really thought keeping you out of the meeting would help you somehow, keep you from feeling the sudden burden I felt. I did what I thought I would have wanted if I were in your place. It wasn't an effort to hide things from you. I also didn't tell you anything about the trust while you were at school. I figured you had enough to deal with being at a new school, a boarding school at that, with your brother and sisters so depending on you, all the while being away from the home you knew, the friends you knew, and your football team, while trying to finish high school."

"I see how that might have seemed like the right decision."

"I actually intended to sit down with you next weekend when we came out here and go over everything, and then talk to the others about how the trust works. I thought summer vacation was a better time."

"I see."

"I have to be honest, Ken, I was more than a little upset about your parents' wills. I thought I would get something to remember my sister by, and better help to take care of you all than having to fill out forms and account for your every expense. No parent has to justify the money they spend on their children, but because I am merely the guardian, I have to do that in great detail. It has made me frustrated and upset."

"I had no idea that nothing was really left to you."

"You read the wills, didn't you? They boxed all the belongings of both of your parents up for storage for the four of you to go through."

"Yes, I read that. But is there something you would like to have? I know you lost someone too. I would like to help with that, at least. Also, about the letters they wrote to us. They were personal notes to each of us about what our parents hoped for us and about them being sad they were going to miss so much. There was nothing more important than that in those letters."

"Ken, that's very nice of you. Actually, there is a bracelet that was our mother's, your grandmother's, that I always loved, that she gave to your mother before she died. I would really like to have that."

"I was hoping to go through the storage items this summer before I go off to school. Can you come with us to do that and find that bracelet? I'm sure my parents weren't thinking of excluding you, just thinking about making it easier for the four of us to divide up things to remember them by."

"That's an interesting way of looking at it that did not occur to me," Mr. Reynolds added as he took Aunt Alicia's hand. "Since neither your aunt nor I are parents, it's a bit hard to see how single-minded a parent can be. What you're saying is your parents weren't thinking about anything more than their priority, you kids."

"Yes, it never occurred to me they were concentrating on making sure you four had what you wanted to remember them by. Remember Ken, I am new to this parent thing," Aunt Alicia added.

Ken laughed a little and smiled at Aunt Alicia. He now understood that what he thought was suspicion was just a woman who was missing her sister and suddenly burdened with kids she didn't intend to have; not to mention that she had never been a parent, and did not know what she was doing. He looked at her and said, "I'm sorry for what I was thinking too, Aunt Alicia. It's pretty dumb of me not to realize that you lost family, too. We have done nothing to make that easier for you or to help you deal with it, or to even acknowledge what happened to you. We were only thinking of ourselves."

After they sat thinking about what was said, Aunt Alicia added, "I found out today about this when the lawyer called and said your approval was needed for the funds I had requested. Perhaps we can see about making that easier for both of us by going over it together first and sending our approval together in the future."

"I would like that. Aunt Alicia, I have talked to Joe, Deb and Kim and we all want you to continue to be their guardian until each of them is eighteen. We don't want to burden you, but I recognize that I'm not ready, nor do I expect Deb or Joe to feel like they're ready at eighteen to take this on. And also, we may not say it, but we need you. You are our only family."

"Ken, I will again be honest. I'm not sure I would ever have had kids, but I really have grown to enjoy having you all around. I would like that too."

"So, do you have the forms and whatever you submitted so I can see it and maybe I can call the lawyer first thing on Monday and approve it?"

"That's a great idea, Ken. This request is money to cover summer travels for the four of you, spending money for each of you, food, since you eat much more that Alicia and I do here, and we were thinking about getting a nanny to be here for Kim while the rest of you are travelling to see friends. As you know, it's proven hard driving back and forth each day for your aunt and I to work, so we're thinking about staying in the city during the week and being here on the weekends. With a nanny, Kim will get to go and do things even if you and Deb and Joe are out with your friends," Mr. Reynolds said.

"This all sounds fine. I imagine I will have to sign something, though."

"Yes, the lawyer told me today that you would have to see the papers and sign them. He indicated I could provide them to you, and then we can messenger them over on Monday morning. I will go get them," Aunt Alicia said.

She went to the car to retrieve her folders and brought the papers to Ken. Ken took the papers and then stood up and gave Aunt Alicia a hug. He left the room and Aunt Alicia sat down next to Mr. Reynolds.

"See how talking things out got to the bottom of this?" Mr. Reynolds said.

"Yes, I didn't realize I had those feelings bottled up. I'm not used to having kids around, but he took it all very well once he knew what I was thinking."

"Ken is a very mature young man and cares deeply for his family."

"Yes. He's not like his father."

"Alicia, we've talked about this. Two people can either make a marriage or break a marriage. Your sister isn't completely guiltless in their breakup. Didn't she tell you she said some things she regretted and couldn't take back?"

"Yes, she did. I just can't help thinking that if he hadn't abandoned them, none of this would have happened."

Joe and Deb had made themselves scarce when Aunt Alicia had stormed in. They were pacing on the lawn off the back patio when Ken came outside.

"What happened in there?" Joe asked.

"Aunt Alicia made a request for funds from the trust and they called her today to inform her they would need my approval to release the funds. She was angry and thought I'd gone behind her back."

"So, she comes storming out here from the city and misses a big party to confront you?" Joe asked.

"Joe, I was perhaps a little wrong about Aunt Alicia. You don't have to be mad at her and try to stick up for me here."

Deb touched Ken on the arm and asked, "What do you mean you were wrong about Aunt Alicia?"

"She's not trying to get at our parents' money. She's upset because nothing was given to her to remember her sister by, and she's burdened by suddenly having to be a parent to four kids that she didn't plan on ever having kids. The trust protects us, but it makes it a real pain for her to get money to keep us in school, and for food, clothes and stuff. She has to fill out forms and give details that no parent really has to in order to get money to pay for things. Look at it from her perspective. She lost her sister and then has to work harder than she ever planned on taking care of us. I would be tense and seem angry, too."

"When you put it like that, it seems like we gave her a bad rap," Joe said.

"Yeah, we can't condemn her if we will not condemn you," Deb replied.

"Actually, I think that's a good point, Deb. We can't continue to be so angry at Joe if we're going to forgive Aunt Alicia for just missing her sister. He gets to miss our parents," Ken added.

"Joe, I was never angry at you for missing our parents, just for taking a trip in the machine alone. I don't want to know what it's like to miss a brother or sister, not right now," Deb said.

"Me either, Joe," Ken said.

"Listen, you two. I've been thinking. Clearly, it was kind of dumb to take a trip alone. I just didn't think you would try again to save our parents and I'll admit it; I was very fixated on that. I've been thinking about what you said, Ken, and I don't want to make it harder for any of you to deal with losing our parents. Can we get back to being brothers and sisters, though? I can't go back now and change things. I will meet myself again and I don't think that will go well."

"What do you mean, meet yourself again? Is there something you're not telling us, Joe? Did you meet yourself?" Deb asked frantically.

"Calm down, Deb. I didn't meet myself, but I had some symptoms that I can only attribute to the fact that I was there, in that time and space. My other self was at Harvard. I'm not sure, Mr. Brewster and I are looking into it, but we don't know for sure," Joe said.

"No, you can't go back in the machine to the same time. You and Mr. Brewster confirmed that there is not enough evidence to prove that would not have terrible consequences. Plus, I'm not sure it's a good idea to change someone's death. I'm still thinking that over as well," Ken added, "And even if you determine these symptoms you had were because you were there twice, we will not give you definitive proof by going back there again."

"I think we have proven that trying to change someone's death doesn't work, right?" Deb asked.

"Maybe. I think maybe we've been thinking about it all wrong. I have some theories brewing, and I will share them with you when I sort some things out. OK?" Joe said.

"I haven't changed my mind about this. No more trips in the machine," Ken added sternly.

"I'm working on the time passage issue, and I think we might need one more trip to confirm that calculation, but it doesn't have to be to change our parents' history if you don't want it to be," Joe added, hoping Ken would agree to the science.

"You and Mr. Brewster together are going to have to convince me that another trip is warranted before anyone gets back into that machine. And if that happens, it will be with the full knowledge of all of us and with us all there. Understood?"

"Yes. I'm just glad you are both talking to me again."

"In celebration, how about we walk into the village for ice cream? I've been dying to try that new three-flavored sundae at the Sunday Scoops, in town."

"That's a great idea, Deb. Let me just go tell Mr. Reynolds and Aunt Alicia we're leaving," Ken said, and he went into the house.

When they got back to the house, Deb heard someone in the kitchen and left the boys to go upstairs while she went and investigated. She found Aunt Alicia sitting at the kitchen island having a cup of tea. Deb asked if she would mind if she sat down and Aunt Alicia said it was fine.

"Aunt Alicia, can I ask you something?"

"Sure."

"Were you and my mother close when you were growing up?"

"For a long time, it seemed like we were, but then she went to college and we must have drifted apart."

"Why do you think that is?"

"I don't know. I guess when you get to college, you just shift somehow. Different things matter to you and you let go of all the old things."

"She didn't call you or send you notes or anything?"

"She did for a while, then she met your father."

"Ah, then she was too busy for you."

"Yes, I guess."

"I felt that way when Ken got a girlfriend. He was busy with her all the time and didn't care what any of us were doing."

"But you still had your mother."

"Yes. She was always there for me. You don't feel that way about Grandma, do you?"

"Your grandmother and I neve got along. I was always doing something wrong."

"Like what?"

"Like not making my bed, and not picking up my clothes and wanting too many clothes and needing money."

"What about with Grandpa?"

"Grandpa was always talking about his church family and all the things your mother was accomplishing in college. She was published in a renowned mathematical journal; did you know that?"

"No, I didn't."

"She was. My father talked about all the time."

"Did he ever talk about what you did?"

"No. No, I didn't seem to pick the right things to do, so he never talked about what I did."

"How do you pick the right things?"

"Well, I was always interested in fashion and drawing. Oh, and I played the violin for a long time."

"I never knew you played the violin."

"No, probably not. My father never went to any of my recitals or anything."

"Aunt Alicia, I'm so sorry. I wish you had a mom and dad like I had."

Aunt Alicia smiled at Deb, but her eyes still looked sad.

"You know something else. I watched you. At your job when you took me. I saw what you did. You knew exactly what to do with the models, the colors and the clothes. You're smart. Someone should have told you that a long time ago."

"Thank you, Deb. I have to say, I don't know the first thing about being a mother or taking care of children. You probably all see that as me not being interested in any of you, but that's not it. I think some women just don't have the gene to be mothers. I think if you're not born with it, you don't intuitively know how to be a mother. Your mother had it."

"Does that make you sad, too?"

"Not really. It's making this new situation for all of us harder, though, isn't it?"

"I don't know about that. I know that we're all much more sensitive to the feelings of others and ourselves than we used to be. Perhaps we might have behaved differently if we understood some of these things."

"I guess so."

"Aunt Alicia, can I ask you something else?"

"Sure."

"Why didn't you tell Ken and I what happened with the lawyers right away?"

"I think I was trying to save you both from more of the hurt of losing them. I thought I was doing the right thing. But, in retrospect, maybe it was more about my own feelings. I was so angry at your father. I seemed to remember a fight they had on the phone where he said he was really trying not to travel that month, but then he had to. Your mother asked him to respect Joe's wishes. That made little sense to me, but I figured your father was just being selfish. I was so elated to have my sister, finally. To feel you belong is a powerful thing, and I was angry that he took it from me. When the lawyer called with the message that I should probably bring Ken and you to the reading that your father had desired that, I snapped. I can distinctly remember thinking he had a lot of nerve setting the rules from the great beyond after taking my sister away."

"But, Aunt Alicia, you took something from Ken and I by this choice."

"Yes. I see that now. You see, I'm not a very good mother figure."

"I don't think you should be condemned for one mistake. Mom used to say that to us when we messed up."

"My mother said that your mother and I when we were little."

"So, we'll try not to condemn you, but you need to try too."

Deb got up from the island at that point and walked to the door. She turned and said goodnight, and Aunt Alicia replied goodnight back to her.

4

The next day, Mr. Reynolds and Aunt Alicia returned to the city for another party and Ryan came out to the Hamptons to spend the day with Deb. They went to the beach and into the village for dinner and Ryan ended up calling his parents and staying the night. While Deb was with Ryan, Ken spent the day with Joe, playing ball and hanging out on the beach. He had missed his brother, and the blowup with Aunt Alicia had taught Ken a lot about seeing things from someone else's perspective. What Joe did was wrong, but he couldn't blame him for his reasons. Plus, Ken was already feeling like he was abandoning his siblings by going off to college, and he had decided last night to spend as much time as he could with them this summer.

The next weekend, Kim returned from her two-week trip with her friend. She was really back to her happy self, and it was clear that she had forgotten about what happened with Joe, so Ken would not bring it up. Instead, they spent several days hearing every detail of Kim's travels, and what she and Amy did each day. By the next weekend, Joe and Deb were leaving: Deb to go spend two weeks with Ryan and his family, and Joe to his friend Todd's family in Michigan. Joe got to go on an airplane, which was harrowing for Ken until he heard Joe had arrived safely. Deb left with Ryan on the train back to New York City on Friday and they left on a road trip to North Carolina from there. Ken talked to Mary each day, and they made plans for when Mary was coming to the Hamptons. All too soon, it was the Fourth of July. Mary arrived in the Hamptons, and they were taking Kim to the parade and fireworks.

On the way back from the parade, Mary asked Kim what she liked best. Kim replied, "The floats with the girls in the long dresses. That was my favorite. Oh, and the bands. I love the marching band music."

"I like the marching band music too," Mary replied.

When they got home, the cook had made them a picnic to take to the beach to be ready for the fireworks. They went down and set up a blanket and their picnic and played in the sand and water. Later they ate and laid on the blanket, watching the stars come out. Soon the fireworks started and Kim was quiet for the first time that day. Mary and Ken held hands and watched Kim have a wonderful time. Later, after Kim went to bed, Mary and Ken sat on the back porch.

"It was a great day, wasn't it?" Mary asked.

"Yes, it was a great day. I loved having you here with me. Kim really liked you being here, too."

"She's so innocent sometimes. I loved watching her watch the parade and fireworks."

"Yeah, sometimes it catches me. She's still so young."

"When is her birthday?"

"It's at the end of this month, actually. I've been planning something big with Deb and Joe."

"Really? What are you planning?"

"Well, you know that this year I wanted all of our birthdays to be just the four of us, but you and Deb kind of botched that with my birthday."

"Sorry, I just wanted it to be special for you."

"I know. I'm kidding, you know."

"So, what are you planning?"

"Well, I wanted to talk to you about this. There is this new Broadway musical coming out this weekend, actually, that I thought Kim would like. It's called Annie. Anyway, I wanted to take her to it, but make it a really big deal. I've talked to Mr. Reynolds, and he has helped set it up. We're going to take her first to get something really fabulous to wear—that's Aunt Alicia's contribution—then we're going to use the limousine to go somewhere really fancy for dinner. Then we're going to go to the musical. Mr. Reynolds has set that part up. We have box seats. He wanted you and Ryan to come along as well. Ryan is flying up from his family's place for the weekend we're planning on, and I was hoping you could join us."

"Wow, she'll love this. Did you think about inviting any of her friends from school?"

"Oh, yeah, I called a couple of her friends' parents last week and asked if they could come too. Rebecca's, Amy's and Kathy's parents all said they would bring them here that morning. So, Aunt Alicia is hosting a dress up party at a shop in the city for them to pick out new clothes. Deb and Ryan are going with for that shopping spree, but I thought you and I would have lunch in the city and then meet up with them later in the day. We're going to some bakery that does these fabulous cupcakes, because Kim talked about wanting that for her birthday when we were at school."

"It sounds great, and I would love to spend the afternoon with you. What day are we talking about?"

"Saturday, July twentieth."

"Is that actually her birthday?"

"Yes, so it works out perfectly for my plans."

"She's going to love it. What should I get her for a gift?"

"Deb and Ryan are getting her two weeks of art classes at the Art League in the village here and Joe is making her something, since she made us all gifts. I'm still trying to decide what to get her."

"What about a charm bracelet? They're real popular with the younger girls now. You can get the bracelet and some charms and I can get her some charms to add to it."

"That sounds great. You will help pick it out, won't you? I'm not sure I'm up to picking out jewelry for a girl turning eleven."

"Of course, but you're not getting off that easy. You're going to have to come with me to buy it!"

"Oh good, I wouldn't want to miss that!"

"That's not very romantic of you, Kenneth Fitzgerald. I guess I won't be getting jewelry from you, will I?"

"Actually, now that you mention it, I have something for you."

"I was joking. Sort of," Mary laughed.

Ken went into the house and came back a couple minutes later carrying a box.

"Here. Tom Hohulin told me at graduation that it was shameful that I hadn't sealed the deal with you with something. He's sure I'm in jeopardy of losing you to some hockey player this fall when you're at Choate, and I'm at Harvard. Hopefully, this will do."

"Ken, you don't have to give me anything to make me yours."

"I was just joking with you. My friends did say all of that, but I trust you, baby. I just wanted to give you something."

Mary opened the box and found a beautiful mother-of-pearl ring. She took it out and tried it on. It fit pretty well.

"It's beautiful. Where did you find this?"

"It was my mother's. She gave it to me when I turned seventeen and told me to save it for someone special. She said she didn't care who I gave it to, as long as I could tell her that the girl loved me like I loved her, and would take care of me. I think that's you."

"Oh Ken, it's so much more beautiful now. But are you sure you shouldn't give this to Deb or Kim?"

"My mom had lots of jewelry and in her letter to me from the wills, she told me to make sure that they both had something from her collection. I'm sure they will find something equally nice. I want you to have this. We went over to the storage recently and went through some things and we got something for Deb, Kim and Aunt Alicia. It was really special for all of them."

"Thank you so much. I love it."

Mary went to put it on and wasn't sure which finger to put it on. Ken had said nothing in particular about it being a promise ring or anything, so she didn't know what he meant by it. She tentatively went to put it on her left ring finger, but as she did, she looked up at him and he didn't look so happy about that. She quickly changed it to her right hand. It fit better on that finger anyway, so she left it. She was a little disappointed he didn't really be specific about what he meant with this ring, but maybe she could coax him to be more specific.

Deb came home that Saturday, and she and Mary departed for Mary's house in Boston on the train that Sunday afternoon. Joe was home too and worked on his calculations with Mr. Brewster over the phone and played with Kim. Ken spent the next two weeks shopping for things he needed for college. He would take the train into the city and meet either Mr. Reynolds or Aunt Alicia, and come home laden down with bags of things. Marveling at how he was going to fit all the things he bought into a small dorm room, he kept at it until he had checked off all the items on the recommended list he had received in the mail. He also got a steady stream of mail from Harvard regarding his orientation, dorm mate, class schedule, and campus activities.

In no time, it was the Saturday of Kim's birthday celebration. How they had kept everything a secret all this time was a miracle, but Ken had done it. He and Deb got up that morning and made breakfast and took it up to Kim, as was the tradition in their family for birthdays. It thrilled her, they remembered. Then, Mr. Reynolds insisted they give her the family gifts before any of the festivities started, so they sat together on the porch and Kim opened her gifts. Mr. Reynolds and Aunt Alicia gave her a new bicycle. Deb and Ryan gave her the art classes. Joe had made her a collage of pictures they had taken at school, at the parties and birthday celebrations and holidays. It was framed and had shells and other things that were meaningful to Kim in it. Ken gave Kim the charm bracelet, which she adored. As soon as they were done opening gifts, the doorbell rang and Michael announced that Miss Kim had visitors. The squealing that started brought the cook running, thinking someone had been hurt. It was amazing to Ken how much noise four young girls could make. Mary and Ryan arrived and then Aunt Alicia announced their plans to go shopping. They all loaded into the limousine and headed into the city.

Ryan, Deb, Joe and Mr. Reynolds sat on a small sofa outside the dressing room at the elite dress shop while Aunt Alicia orchestrated the fashion show in back. The girls came out in dresses and the four sat there watching them preen and pirouette, clapping and cheering for each round. Eventually, the girls decided on dresses and they went to the bakery. Ken and Mary met them at the bakery, and they all had decadent cupcakes. Kim thanked Ken for remembering that she really wanted cupcakes for her birthday. Then, Mr. Reynolds had the limousine tour them around central park, and down to Battery Park. The four young girls were thrilled with dinner, but even more thrilled with the Broadway musical and the fact that Mr. Reynolds got them in to see the stars of the show so the girls could get autographs. Kim commented on the way back to the Hamptons that it was positively the best birthday she had ever had. She hugged Aunt Alicia and Mr. Reynolds and whispered to Ken that she knew he had planned the whole thing before she went off with her friends to the den for a sleepover to top off the night.

Ken left with Mary the next day to spend a few days with her before going to Harvard for orientation. Mr. Reynolds and Aunt Alicia met him at Harvard for this. While Ken was away, Kim was off doing her art classes and spending days at the beach with the nanny they had hired, while Joe wrote to Becky and Deb talked to Ryan and they thought about heading back to school. After the orientation was over, they all went into the city for a week so they could get ready for school. They went shopping for clothing and shoes and everything they would need at Choate and finished up shopping for Ken. They went out for dinner almost every night and played games and had a really wonderful time. Kim commented that it finally felt like they were a family again. This surprised Ken, but since his sister was proving to be so insightful, he figured it must be true. He was happy for the first time in a long time and felt closer to his siblings than he had ever felt. It seemed strange for Ken to be thinking about going away to college and, for the first time, being away from his brother and sisters, while still feeling this close to them. Later that week, Joe commented about this to Ken, saying he was finding it hard to think of Ken being gone after the last year they had together. Ken replied he would be sure to visit and they would never be more than a phone call away.

All too soon, it seemed, summer ended, first with the trip to Harvard to get Ken situated in his dorm room, and then for the other three to pack up and get back to Choate. Kim was very talkative the whole drive from New York to campus. She was excited to see friends and start back with Girl Scouts and get back into classes. Deb was rather quiet during the ride back, and Joe spent the time looking through notes that Mr. Brewster had sent him. When the car arrived at the girls' dorm, Kim bounded out and headed directly for her friends that were gathering near the front stairs. Mr. Reynolds got out of the car and laughed at Kim's enthusiasm, saying, "I was never that excited to get back to school when I was her age."

"She's young, Darrick. She's more interested in meeting up with her friends. It wouldn't matter where that was taking place," Aunt Alicia replied.

"I'll get us checked in with the house monitor and get Kim's keys and mine and be right out so we can get our things out of the other car," Deb indicated as she walked off at a much slower pace than Kim toward the stairs and door.

While Deb was inside, the other car arrived, driven by Michael, bringing all the kids' belongings. He and Joe unloaded the girls' bags and when Deb came out, she indicated where to take Kim's things and she started carrying her things. Aunt Alicia and Mr. Reynolds both picked up bags, and they all went first into Kim's room, where Kim and her roommate were already discussing which side each would take. Mr. Reynolds and Joe stayed with her to assist her in getting unpacked while Aunt Alicia, Michael and Deb continued on up to the third floor where Deb's room was. Once all the bags were in Deb's room, she asked if they wanted her help to get Joe situated. Joe said he was fine, and they all walked back to Kim's room to see how she was doing.

"How do you like this new room, Kim?" Deb asked.

"It's so bright in here. I love it. Amy and I are so excited to live together this year," Kim said as she pulled out all her books and put them on a bookshelf above the desk. This year, Kim was in a room with only one roommate and they had desks and shelves, so Kim could bring her beloved Little House books and all of her drawing and art supplies.

"Well, it looks like you have things under control here. Should we go over to the boys' dorm and get Joe situated?" Mr. Reynolds asked.

"I can help her finish unpacking and putting things away, Mr. Reynolds. You all go over and get Joe unloaded," Deb said as she helped Kim put her art supplies on the shelf in her closet.

"When we're finished, we'll be back to get you both so we can go to lunch before we head back to the city. Say about an hour?" Mr. Reynolds said as they all started out into the hallway.

"Sounds good. We'll be waiting," Deb responded.

Deb helped Kim finish unpacking and putting everything away in her new room. She had a new bedspread from Aunt Alicia, and Mr. Reynolds had given her a framed picture of all four of them taken in New York while they were there over the summer. Kim put that and her other treasures on the dresser and put all her clothes away. She asked Deb if she needed help and Deb said, no, that Kim should visit with Amy and her other friends while Deb unpacked and she would be down in an hour. Deb then went up to her room and unpacked. While she was hanging up clothes, Mary knocked on Deb's door. Deb was very glad to see Mary, as it had been a month since they had last seen one another. Mary helped Deb put clothes on hangers, and she said, "You have so many really great clothes, Deb. Are they all from your aunt?"

"Yes, after she and Ken sort of had it out this summer, she has been much easier to deal with. She took me into Vogue again and set me up with all these new things. The problem is, and I'm sure this might sound ungrateful, but now I have a pile of clothes that she says are last season, and I shouldn't be wearing anymore. They're in that suitcase. I don't know what to do with them and I can't just throw them out," Deb said as she put the last of the items into her closet.

"What does 'last season' mean?"

"Aunt Alicia says that each season, new fashion is introduced in Europe and here in New York and all the new trends are shown. She says that you just don't wear last season's trends. I don't know; it was never something I thought of before. But getting new clothes all the time sure seems great."

"Maybe you could give some away here?" Mary said hopefully.

"That was what I was thinking, but I was also thinking about asking at the church if they took donations or something," Deb said as she put the heaviest suitcase on the bed and opened it up.

"I think they do donations at the church. Why don't you offer some up here and whatever is left, I will help you take them to the church this weekend?" Mary said as she started touching a sweater she had admired of Deb's.

"Ok, Mary, pick out what you want first and then I'll open the door and announce," laughed Deb.

Mary picked out a few things and then took them to her room, which was next door. Deb announced in the hall that she had clothes available in her room and the girls all crowded into Deb's room to go through the suitcase. In a matter of minutes, the suitcase was half empty. Deb closed it back up and slid it under her bed. She finished unpacking books and school supplies into her desk and put her new bedspread on the bed. Mary came back into Deb's room and they talked as Deb finished putting things away.

"So, have you talked to Ken since you got him to Harvard?" Mary asked.

"Yeah, he called last night to wish us good luck at school and said he was going to call me tomorrow night and Joe later today. I'm sure he's called you too, hasn't he?"

"Yes, we've talked every night since he left my house for the orientation. He really likes it at Harvard, I think. He was talking last night about coming out here in a couple of weeks for the weekend. Joe is going to ask the boys' dorm monitor if Ken can stay on some weekends."

"He mentioned that to me last night."

"What else did he tell you?"

"Oh, I don't think he said anything else about you two. He just talked to each of us about working hard and stuff."

"Hey, I have my car here this year and I asked my parents if I could see Ken on weekends sometimes, too."

"What did they say? Can you do that, leave on Friday and come back on Sunday if a parent has signed you out?"

"Since we're seniors now, I can do that. My parents had to sign a form, but it allows me to leave campus for weekends. I won't do it every weekend or anything like that, but it would be nice to be away with Ken sometimes."

"He didn't tell Aunt Alicia or Mr. Reynolds you were going to be doing this, did he?"

"I don't know."

"Well, I think it's great that you two are so devoted to one another, and I hope you're able to see each other as much as you can."

"Thanks Deb. It means a lot to me that you approve of Ken and me."

"You have been great for him, Mary."

"So, the enormous elephant in the room. Are we going to talk about it?"

"What do you mean?"

"Oh, I don't know if you're still mad at Joe and barely speaking, or maybe how Ryan is, or maybe about the blow-up between Ken and your aunt?"

"That's three elephants, Mary, and they wouldn't all fit in this room!"

They both laughed and then Kim came up to the door and said that Aunt Alicia and the others were back a little early. Deb told Mary that she would be back later, that they were all having lunch and then Mr. Reynolds and Aunt Alicia were leaving. Deb and Kim went out and got into the car and they all went into town to have lunch at the Italian restaurant that had become their family celebration place since last year. When Deb returned, Mary sought her out again.

"Deb, so tell me your thoughts on what Joe told you and Ken, please?"

"Didn't Ken tell you about our big conversation?"

"Yes, but I wanted to hear your thoughts."

"Well, I, as you know, was very aggravated that Joe took it upon himself to take the machine on his own. So, for most of the summer, I was really just angry because he took this chance, and that something happened that I can't remember. So, that first week we were all back together this summer, Joe asked to talk to Ken and I, and we met later at night in the kitchen. Joe started by handing us both a letter describing what he did and what changed."

"Ken told me all that. He said he was having a hard time believing what Joe wrote. Do you believe Joe?'

"Here's the thing. Remember when we all went on the trip in the machine and when we came back, you and Ryan remembered a unique history with Ken and me? Well, at the time, I was sure that what I knew was the correct history because we went in the machine and we knew the before and the after. I think this is the same thing. I have to believe Joe, because he knows the before and after."

"So, you believe that when he got into the machine, your parents were together and when he got out, they had separated and died within three days of one another, but in separate accidents?"

"I think I have to."

"I tried to talk to Ken about this when he was out visiting. He didn't want to hear my thoughts on how this again proves that you shouldn't make any more trips. The impact is getting worse."

"Ken has told me he's putting a lot of thought into his ideas regarding the impact of our trips in the machine. He actually told me on the phone just before we came back to campus that he was having a meeting with the reverend at the chapel at Harvard next week."

"Well, that's good. I haven't tried to talk to him about any of this since that conversation. I was sure he was furious with me, and I didn't want to have an argument over it. He gets to have his own beliefs; I have to keep reminding myself of that. I just wish he'd told me all this."

"Is this coming between you two?"

"I hope not, but clearly we differ on this point in a big way."

"I don't think you actually differ as much as you think. I just think Ken has been put through so much with our parents' accidents and everything that has happened last year here. You just need to give him some time."

"You've talked about your family history and your grandfather. I have to say; I wonder if it took in Ken's case."

The two of them talked for a long time that first night back while Deb gave Mary some family history to help make sure she understood Ken and would be patient with him.

The next day after lunch, Kim found Deb after eating with her friends and asked if she and Deb could talk after class that day. Deb said that was fine, and they met in the main hall where they had spent so many hours last year having family conferences. Kim sat down and turned to Deb and said, "Am I still part of this family?"

"Wow, I have to say, this was the last thing I expected you to want to discuss. What gives you the idea that you aren't part of the family?"

"You and Ken, and you and Joe, and you and Mary are always in conversations, and no one has even asked me to listen in, let alone take part. Just because I was with friends this summer and wasn't always around, or you were gone, doesn't mean I don't want to know what's going on. I know I'm younger than all of you, but I have ideas and thoughts to offer."

"Of course, you're part of the family. And of course, you have thoughts to add. I'm so sorry you feel like we've excluded you. I don't want to make excuses, but here's where I was coming from all summer. You spent so much time visiting with friends, which was great. I wanted you to have that time, and do what you wanted. But we had to figure out what Joe did and how to deal with this. Ken has been deep in thought all summer trying to figure out his beliefs, and I have been angry enough that I didn't want to bring it up often."

"No one ever told me what Joe did."

"Kim, first let me say that I'm so sorry about that. I didn't realize until you said it we hadn't sat down with you at all this summer. I promise I won't ever do that again. What happened is that Joe took the machine back in time by himself. I was angry that he took that risk. I was angry because I was afraid. What if something had happened to him?"

"Where did he go?"

"He tried to go home and talk to Dad to stop them from travelling so that they would be safe from accidents."

"Did he get home?"

"He did, and he talked to Dad. That was the source of the arguments between Mom and Dad that you remember."

"So now Joe feels even guiltier than he did before, right?"

"Yes."

"Wait a minute, I thought something bad would happen if you went to a time when you existed and you met yourself."

"Well, Joe went on a day that he knew he was with Mom at Harvard and the rest of us were all going to be gone, except Dad."

"So, he was ok?"

"I'm not sure. He said he was feeling terrible when he got home and could barely walk by the time he got back to the machine to come back here. I don't know if he and Mr. Brewster have worked that all out yet."

"Is he ok now?"

"Yes. He said the symptoms went away as soon as the machine started up."

"So, what's going to happen now?"

"Ken doesn't want anyone making any more trips in the machine, and I'm pretty sure I agree with him."

"But does Joe agree? If he feels responsible for the fights between Mom and Dad, he'll want to fix that."

"Yes, but I don't have any idea about what he's thinking."

They sat for a few minutes and Kim thought about what Deb had told her. As she was about to say something more, both Joe and Amy walked up to where she and Deb were sitting.

"Kim, we're all going to work on the geography assignment over at the tables. Are you coming with us?" asked Amy.

"Yes," Kim said as she got up to leave. She looked back at Deb and said, "Thanks for talking with me, Deb. Please don't exclude me anymore, ok?"

"I won't," Deb responded.

Then Deb looked up at Joe, who had been standing there silently. He had decided that day that he was done not talking with his sister and needed to fix what was going on in this time before he fixed anything else. He said, "Will you talk to me too, Deb? I know you're still upset and I really want to fix this. I understand now that being right with my sisters and brother is as important as my desire to bring our parents back and work on computers."

"I want to fix things with you, too. I'm just not sure how to."

"Well, what can I do or say?"

"I don't know. I mean, I know why you did it. You wanted our parents back more than you wanted anything else, and you were willing to risk everything to get it."

"I was pretty focused, that's true."

"I can go over this as many times as you want, and as many times as I have in my head, and each time, I come up with more what ifs that make me so angry with you."

"Can you just forgive me?"

"You mean just let it all go and go on from here?"

"Yeah."

"That's a big thing to ask."

"Too big for family?"

This time, it was Joe's friend Becky that walked up to them. She and Joe had been exchanging letters all summer and had become close. Joe turned to Deb and asked if they could talk again tomorrow, and Deb agreed. That at least would give Deb time to contemplate whether she could just let all of this go. Deb walked back to the girls' dorm and went to her room to start homework. and was finishing up an English assignment when someone told her she had a phone call. It was Ken. They talked for a few minutes about getting back to campus and the dorm assignments and how Joe and Kim were doing. Deb told Ken about her conversation with Kim and Joe from earlier, and then she asked how classes were going for Ken. Ken made Deb promise to call him tomorrow after she talked to Joe again, and then they hung up. Just as Deb was heading back to her room, she was called back down because Ryan was in the lobby of the girls' dorm.

Deb ran to Ryan and wrapped her arms around his neck. He laughed and hugged her back and then whispered, "I was wondering when I was going to see you. We had class together, and then you seemed surrounded at lunch and then no classes together in the afternoon, and you didn't even come to find me. Should I be worried?"

"Don't be silly. I have been so busy today. Yes, all the girls were all over me asking about the clothes I brought back and had planned to give away, and that's what they were hounding me about."

"Why are you giving away clothes?"

"Well, Aunt Alicia says that the clothes she gave me last school year are not in style anymore. I don't know if that is true, and I'm sure none of the girls here agree with Aunt Alicia, and I didn't want to just get rid of them."

"Have you thought about donating them to church or something?"

"Yes, Mary and I are going to take whatever is left after some more of the girls go through it tonight, to the church tomorrow."

"So, everybody wins. You get some new clothes; the girls get new clothes and the church gets some they can give to more needy people."

"Exactly."

"None of this explains why I'm here and you didn't even come looking for me after class," Ryan said as he finally let Deb go and they sat down. He looked at her with a pouty face.

"Oh, don't be mad. I wasn't avoiding you; I was talking with Kim and then Joe. And then I saw some girls who said that you and a bunch of the guys were playing hockey or something."

"We did for a little while, but then everyone went to do homework. I came in search of you. Tell me about your conversations with Kim and Joe."

Deb told Ryan about how hurt Kim was, and how she was going to work to smooth that over, and then she explained she was at a crossroad with Joe, and his asking her for forgiveness. After a few minutes, Ryan asked, "What are you going to do?"

"I don't know."

"Well, I have to agree with Joe on this. It's about family, and you have to find a way to move on. You can't stay mad at him, and nothing you say, or that he says or does, can take back what happened."

"I know. I understand what my parents meant when they said they were angry because we worried about them now."

"Yeah, I never understood that either."

"I think it might be really good to talk to the reverend tomorrow when we go to donate. Maybe that will help me find a way to let it go."

"That's a good idea. Now, can I escort you to dinner?"

"That would be lovely."

They went to dinner and met Kim, Amy, Mary, Joe and Becky and established where they were going to eat meals this year. After dinner, the girls all went to Deb's room and went through the clothes and then she and Mary packed up what was left to take to the church. Later, Kim came to remind Deb that the first Girl Scouts meeting was the next afternoon and Deb told Kim of her plans to go to the church. They agreed to meet at dinner.

The next day, Mary and Deb loaded up the clothing they were taking to the church and drove into town. When they arrived at the church, Reverend Patrick met them and brought some help to bring in the clothing. Deb asked if she might talk to him for a moment and he led her to his office.

"It is so good to see you again, Deborah. You're a senior now, aren't you?" the reverend asked.

"Yes, this will be my last year at Choate. I have learned so much, and feel like I have grown so much since I first came here. A lot of that is because of the help you have given me, sir."

"I'm always here to help."

"That's why I wanted to talk to you. I was hoping you could help me. This summer my younger brother made me so angry. He did something very foolish that put him at risk of being hurt, and I'm having a hard time letting that go."

"It's interesting that you bring this up, Deborah. I was talking with a group here at the church just this week about parents dealing with anger when their children are in harm's way."

"That's what I was telling my boyfriend, Ryan, last night. That I'm feeling angry because of the risk he took. What did you recommend to those parents as ways to calm down when they are angry like this?"

"I reminded them to consider that they were angry because their child had done something that would mean some risk, and that worried them because they love their child. Once you get back to the love, it becomes easier to let go of your harsh feelings and forgive."

"I think I see. I know my situation is very different. Joe isn't my child."

"Maybe not, but Deborah, remember you all lost your parents, so your roles are blurry now. You and Ken have taken on some parental roles with Joe and Kim. You have to recognize that and learn to manage those feelings differently than you would as a sibling."

"Thank you, Reverend Patrick. This has helped."

"I'm glad I could give you something to think about. It's wonderful having all you students back, and I look forward to seeing you this Sunday."

"Yes, I'm looking forward to it as well."

Deb and Mary returned to campus. Deb went in search of Joe as they had arranged and found him in the lobby of the girls' dorm, waiting for her. He stood up as she walked in, anticipating an outburst from her. It surprised him when she walked up and hugged him. As she pulled away, she said, "Joe, I'm sorry I've had a hard time forgiving you. Please understand that I've been dealing mostly with worry for you, and not quite knowing how to address the parent-like feelings I have about you putting yourself in danger. I'm done with that now."

"Wow, I wasn't expecting a one-eighty. What happened?"

"I had a conversation with the reverend and it helped me to see that I was mixing my sibling ways with my parent ways."

"You're not my parent, you know."

"I know, but we all have blurry roles now that our parents are gone. Sometimes I'm going to have feelings like a parent toward you and Kim, and even Ken."

"Yeah, I get that. I feel that way about Kim a lot now."

"So now what?"

"Are you totally done being mad at me, really?"

"I'm still a little angry that you didn't see how what you were doing was going to affect Ken and me and Kim, but I'm pretty sure I can get over it."

"I would like you and Kim to come with me to Mr. Brewster's later this week, and we should probably bring Ryan and Mary along. I want to discuss the trip and what happened to me."

"Ok Joe, I'm ready to do that, but first you have to promise me something."

"What?"

"No more trips in the machine alone."

"I promise."

"I mean it, Joe. This is serious. Pinky promise."

Deb held up her right pinky, and Joe linked his pinky with hers. He laughed and said he thought this was ridiculous, but he'd do it if it made her happy. She said pinky promises were lifelong and more serious than any other promises. He said ok.

"Thank you. I'm not saying I'm ready to plan another trip, by the way. I just want to ensure you will not try to go alone again."

"I know."

"Good."

"If we're done, and back to being brother and sister, I got to go. I have a math assignment due tomorrow. Is that ok?"

"Of course, do your homework. I'll talk to Mary and Kim and Ryan and arrange to go to Mr. Brewster's. Is Friday after class going to be alright with you?"

"Yeah, that sounds great."

5

After classes ended on Friday, Deb, Ryan, Mary, Joe and Kim all walked over to Mr. Brewster's barn. It felt strange returning to the place where they had spent so much time last year, but also where Joe had done the unthinkable. When they arrived at the barn, Mr. Brewster was already inside and he had set up a little party of sorts to welcome them all back. There were snacks and drinks and he had a small gift for each of them. Once they had opened the gifts and thanked Mr. Brewster, they all sat around the table as Mr. Brewster said, "I have to say, I've so looked forward to your return. It's been a very quiet summer without you all here, even though I spoke to Joe and wrote back and forth with some of you, it's still good to have you here."

"We sure missed you, too," Kim said.

"What did you do all summer, Mr. Brewster?" Mary asked.

"Well, I worked on the restoration of the car over there, and worked in my garden and we had a lot of maintenance projects to do on campus this year. We repainted all the classrooms and replaced all the heating systems in the dorms this summer."

"Wow, so you were busy," Mary replied.

"Yes, there's not really a summer break for the staff."

"I don't want to spoil the reunion, but we came here to talk about Joe's trip in the machine, didn't we?" Ryan asked.

"Yes, we did," Joe replied.

"So, Joe, tell us," Ryan said.

"After what happened on the trip to Dallas, I had decided that none of you would ever want to try again to save our parents after the last trip, and that had me very upset. Clearly, it was foolish, but I decided if you wouldn't try, I would, so I went back to Cambridge on a day when everyone was out of the house but my father, and I talked to him. We spoke for about an hour, and I told him everything about the machine, and the math problem, and about our first trip, and I took a bunch of the documentation and showed him. Trying to change things, I told him I was doing all that so he would stay off mountains and out of airplanes long enough to get past the times he and Mom had been in the accidents."

"Since you're still students, I presume it didn't work?" Ryan asked.

"Oh, come on Ryan, I know you talked to Deb about this during the summer. Why are you making me rehash this all now?"

"I'm hoping if you hear how ridiculous a plan this was by repeating it a bunch of times, you might not try to repeat this nonsense," Ryan said.

"Listen, we know it didn't stop the accident, but what it did was sync up the times when we arrived here and our histories with you and Mary," Deb said.

"So that's one good thing. I didn't like Ken and I having different memories of our times together," Mary said.

"I thought you weren't supposed to go back to a time where you already existed. That this would cause some great catastrophe or something?" Kim asked.

"We were just suspecting it would cause something to happen, Kim. We didn't know what it would cause, or how time would work out two of any one person being in a specific space and time," Mr. Brewster explained.

"What did you discover?" Ryan asked.

"What we discovered is that it caused me a great deal of pain, a terrible headache, some weakness and blurry vision," Joe said.

"Why don't you start at the beginning, Joe," Deb suggested.

"Ok. When I landed in the machine, I was north of our house in a wooded area. I was near Fresh Pond in Cambridge Highlands. I made sure no one was around, camouflaged the machine, and started walking toward our house. It was Saturday morning. By the time I got to the block behind ours, and I was about to climb the fence between our backyard neighbor's house and ours. You know the one that was abandoned and people said it was going to be restored 'cause Robert Frost lived there? Anyway, my legs kind of gave out, and I fell to the ground. When I got up, all the bones and muscles in my limbs twitched for a few minutes, and then just really hurt. I managed to get over the fence and into the house and talked with Dad, but all afternoon the pain got worse. When I left the house, and headed back to the machine, the lake nearby was crowded with people. This caused me to hide out for a long time waiting for all the people to leave so they didn't see the machine when I started it up. During that time, my head started to hurt really bad. I think I fell asleep for a little while, and when I woke up, my vision was blurry. I realized I had to get to the machine and take off no matter the risk because I was feeling like if I waited any longer, I wouldn't make it. Crawling to the machine, I somehow got in and shut the door and started the return trip setting. It was strange, because as soon as I started up the machine, the symptoms started going away. Then I was back in the barn and Ken and Deb were there. That's it."

"So, you barely made it back here?" Kim asked, suddenly looking very alarmed.

"Kind of," Joe replied.

"Were all those symptoms because you were in a time where you already existed?" Mary asked.

"It has to be that, because none of us had any symptoms like that when we went on the first trip, and Mr. Brewster didn't have any when he did the test run," Joe said.

"Do either of you have any idea what these symptoms mean?" asked Deb.

"Well, I had a phone conversation with an old colleague of mine, and I have a theory about this," Mr. Brewster started. "I believe that the Joe that travelled through time was slowly being erased by some force that would not allow two of him to be present in the same space and time."

"If you had stayed longer, then the Joe from right now that travelled in the machine would never have come back here?" Kim asked, getting a little hysterical.

"Kim, calm down. It's just Mr. Brewster's theory. We don't know for sure if that's why Joe had those symptoms," Ryan said after he went to Kim and put his arm around her shoulder.

"We don't know what would have happened if Joe had stayed longer," Mr. Brewster said, hoping to reassure Kim.

While they all sat digesting that information, Mr. Brewster pulled out the sheets from the folder he had brought to the table and explained that these were readings from when Joe first got into the machine and hooked himself up for the return trip. It showed Joe's heartbeat being very erratic, his oxygen levels being way too low, like he had been hyperventilating, and had a very high temperature.

"Did you learn anything else about this trip?" Ryan asked.

"We believe we have nailed down the calculation of how time passes for anyone that travelled and anyone left here. It's complicated and based on some variables that appear to be linked to how far back in time you go in the machine. When Mr. Brewster went back on the first trip, time here travelled faster than when we went back to Dallas. On this last trip, because I didn't go very far back in history, the time moved almost at the same rate. But with this calculation, we can be nearly positive about how much time will pass here based on when the machine is going back to and how long it will be there," Joe explained.

"Well, that's interesting anyway. Now, at least if you try this again, we'll not have to worry about when you might be back. We'll have a good idea of when you will return by these calculations," Mary said reluctantly.

"Why would there be another trip?" Ryan asked as he looked at Joe.

"I guess we'll need to talk about that, Ryan. Since we left with that question this past school year, maybe we can decide now," Joe said.

"I think I may not have been clear, Joe. I'm trying to say, with the time passage calculation complete, there is no need for anyone to get into the machine again, is there?" Ryan said.

"I agree, and I know from Ken that he doesn't want the machine to be used again," Mary said.

"Although I didn't hear this from Ken, I had expected this being the reaction to this last trip. Joe really upset you all, and it upset me as well. If we can focus now on drafting the paper to present to the world, perhaps everyone can gain a better perspective. It should take us about a month or so, Joe, don't you think? While we are working on that, everyone can get some closure on the trip Joe made and maybe we can look at the use of the machine again with less emotion," Mr. Brewster said, hoping to keep the children from having an argument.

"I want nothing to happen to any of us, so I don't think we should use the machine anymore," Kim added.

No one spoke for a few moments and Mary got up and said she needed to get back to be at the dorm for a call from Ken. They all said goodbye to Mr. Brewster and left the barn. The next day was the first Friday night social event. They all went to join their friends in the main hall. Mary had left to go to Harvard to see Ken. Kim spent the evening with Amy and their other friends watching a movie, and Ryan and Deb spent the evening dancing with their friends. Joe went for a walk with what appeared to be his new girlfriend, Becky.

The next day, Deb went to the library to do research for a project for class, when she noticed Mr. Brewster walking toward his house in a black suit. She had never seen him dressed up and wondered what was going on. As he turned to head down a pathway to his house, Deb noticed he appeared to have been crying. She didn't even think about what she was doing as she changed course and followed Mr. Brewster. He had become very important to all of them, and she wondered what had upset him. When she arrived at Mr. Brewster's house, she wondered if she was intruding, but knocked on his door, anyway. He came to the door and said he was surprised to see her, but motioned for Deb to come in.

"Mr. Brewster, I'm sorry to bother you, but I noticed you walking through campus on my way to the library. I've never seen you all dressed up, and it looked like you were upset. Is there anything I can do?" Deb asked.

"You are such a sweet young thing, Deb."

"Are you alright?"

"Yes, today is just a hard day for me, is all. No need to worry about me, though. It will pass, just as it has each year for the past eighteen years."

Mr. Brewster sat down at his kitchen table with a handkerchief in his hand. Deb sat down and looked at him, wondering what to say. She finally said, "Mr. Brewster, you've been so helpful to all of us, and so important to Joe, as he dealt with the loss of our parents. I feel like this must have something to do with your loss. Will you tell me about it?"

"Oh, Deb, this is a long story."

"I can't think of anything else I have to do that is more important, and I have all afternoon."

"Ok, then. Abigale and I moved to Las Vegas in April of 1957. They had asked me to join the teams working on the testing at the NTS. That's the Nevada Test Site. I was part of the team of physicists overseeing weapon component design for the new ICBM missiles to be outfitted with nuclear warheads. We conducted tests for only four months. But followed that up with many months going through and reporting and re-designing and completing our assignment. We did twenty-nine tests during that time. It was hard work, and very long days. Abby was a schoolteacher, so she taught each day and then waited for me to get home for dinner each night. On weekends, we would meet friends, and go see Sammy Davis or Dean Martin or Frank sing at one of the casinos that had just opened, or we played cards at one of our houses."

"It was interesting being in Las Vegas with all the building going on. In '57, the Tropicana opened, and it was a flashy place. Abby and I went there a few times, but we were trying to have a baby, you see. So, she wanted to get rest, and it was hard for us to have both a social life and work and try for a baby. It made her sad often. The tests finished, and some teams left because they were there only to implement the tests, and we stayed so I could finish the re-design of several key parts for the missiles. It was January and Abby had a miscarriage. For weeks, we both just went through the motions. The doctors said we could try again, but we never got the chance. One Thursday night, I was working late, and Abby went with several of the teachers at her school to a dinner for someone who was retiring, and after she dropped off one teacher, she was driving home, and a car struck her car as she was driving down Las Vegas Boulevard toward our home."

"I got home that night and a police car was in our driveway. When I got out of my car, the police officer asked if I was Carl Brewster and when I acknowledged him, he said I needed to go with them, that my wife had been in an accident. They took me to the hospital and walked me down the hall to the morgue. They uncovered her and asked me to identify her. I had her flown back here because her family is from out-side of Wallingford. Her father worked at the pewter factory. We buried her here. Today is her birthday. I went back to Las Vegas, to that house, and finished the project, barely. I started drinking. It was the only way I could end the day and go home; I had to drink before I pulled into the driveway. I was to interview for a teaching position back here, but I never even went to the interview. Everything was harder for me without her. First, I lost my job, then I lost the house, and I was living with a friend for a while. All I did all day was drink. It was the worst time in my entire life. One day, my friend said I had to leave as it was getting too hard on his wife having me there. I just got in my car and drove. I ended up at the cemetery and the reverend found me there. He helped me get sober, get a job here, and put my life back together, or what was left of my life. And each year, on her birthday, I get dressed up and go to see her. I take her flowers and sit with her."

Deb said nothing at first. She got up and got Mr. Brewster a glass of water, and sat back down. Finally, she reached for his hand, sitting on the table. He looked up, and she said, "I am so sorry. I'm sorry about the baby, and Abigale and your job and your house and everything. I wish you would have had someone like Joe had you to help you during that horrible time, but I'm so glad you're here."

"You are such a sweet girl. You are like Abby, in a way. She was sweet, and always ready to help a friend."

"She must have been wonderful."

"I was the lucky one. I used to say to her I wasn't sure what I did to be so lucky, but I would not question it, because she was mine now."

"I bet that made her smile."

"Yes, she used to laugh at me often."

"What were you going to teach?"

"Oh, I was going to be a science teacher at a college near here. I guess it all works out, doesn't it? I ended up here and met Joe and Ken and Kim and you."

"Tell me more about the testing. I mean, if you can. Is that top secret or something?"

"Now, why would you want to know about that?" Mr. Brewster laughed.

"Well, I'm always trying to learn more about history, and now I know I get first-hand knowledge of a very important time in US history."

"What do you want to know?"

"I don't know. Just tell me about the tests."

"Well, I suppose we should start with the stated purpose of the testing. We were to test the tactical design of the new weapons that were to be strapped to planes and launched through missile sites. Those were the ICBMs."

"What exactly is an ICBM?"

"An ICBM is an intercontinental ballistic missile. It's a missile that is launched from one continent and can travel through the upper atmosphere to another continent."

"How does it do that?"

"The missile contains a guidance system that has coordinates for where it is supposed to go. A lot like the coordinates you give the machine to go to a specific date and geographical location."

"I see."

"We were also running tests to determine the bio-medical impact of the radioactive material and detonation."

"How did you do that?"

"Some tests were to see what the detonation did to structures like buildings and houses, so we built various buildings at specific distances from where we detonated the bombs and used different materials. Other tests were to see what the impact might be on animals and humans. So, we put pigs at different distances, had some of them covered with different materials and some behind glass panels or behind other structures to see what the impact was. And finally, we tested how troops could perform in bomb zones, in cases of accidental detonation, or if they had to go into an area after someone had detonated a bomb."

"You put pigs and people near the sites where you set off the bombs?"

"The pigs were near the bomb detonation; the troops went in after they had detonated the bombs."

"What happened to the pigs?"

"Well, some died, some had injuries and burns and some lived."

"And the troops?"

"They were all fine. Although I've heard that they have had some long-term medical issues and increased instances of leukemia."

"That's terrible. Why did you do that?"

"Deb, you have to remember we had just come out of the war. We were in a race during the war with Hitler to be sure he didn't succeed. Then we were in a race with Russia to ensure they didn't spread communism around the globe. The government wasn't trying to hurt people; we were trying to understand this new capability and how to use it safely."

"I understand the historical reference, but you know those bombs are terrible, right? We can never really use them or we will destroy the entire planet."

"Yes, we have learned many things since 1957. We don't test in the atmosphere since the treaty in 1963 and we are trying to control the stockpile."

"Sorry, I know I asked. It's just that I don't believe we should have or use or allow anyone else to have nuclear weapons."

"Yes, I'm familiar with your thoughts on it. But, Deb, we also use it as an energy source, you know. It can power so much more than coal and other sources."

"Yes, but those aren't always safe either, are they?"

"All use of energy comes with some risk. Coal can light on fire and explode."

"Ok, point taken. I didn't mean to distract you like that."

"Actually, the distraction helped."

The two of them talked for another half hour about school, where Deb was considering for college, Joe's trip and what they learned and how Ken was doing. Deb left Mr. Brewster's house and went on to the library, as she had planned. When she got back to the dorm after the library, there were several messages from Ken. She called Ken right away, thinking something might be wrong. When she reached him, he said, "I was worried about you. Where were you all day that you didn't call me back until now?"

"I was headed to the library for research and saw Mr. Brewster. I went over to his house to talk and then went to the library. And just why aren't you studying, might I ask?"

"I'm studying. I'm just doing it in my room right now because I'm waiting on a call back from my sister."

"Ok, so what did you want?'

"Well, I talked to Mary last night, and she told me about the meeting at Mr. Brewster's."

"Yes, I figured she would."

"Well?"

"Well, what?"

"Are you going to tell me what happened?"

"I'm not sure why I have to retell what Mary obviously told you. We discussed Joe's trip, what happened to him, the reports from the machine and the time passage calculation that they worked out. Then we discussed briefly that we do not expect the need for any other trips and that Joe and Mr. Brewster should start completing the reports and papers necessary to take the machine public."

"I don't want anyone taking trips, remember?"

"Yes."

"Is Joe ok?"

"Well, he's still very upset and still feels responsible for our parents separating, and I think he understands he can't fix that. I think he would want to fix it if we would support him, but right now, no one is supporting that, so it doesn't matter. He promised me he would never again try to go into the machine alone, and I believe him."

"I will be out there in two weeks, so we can all talk about that when I'm there. What did you talk to Mr. Brewster about today?"

"You won't believe this! I saw him walking through campus all dressed up in a suit, but he looked like he had been crying. He told me about his wife, and how she died and his work in Las Vegas and today was her birthday, so he goes every year to see her grave on her birthday."

"Wow, I never knew he was still so impacted by his wife's death. I mean, I know that was the bond he had with Joe. I guess that's why they're kindred spirits."

"Yeah. I was so sad for him. He really loved his wife, and they were trying to have a baby, and he lost everything. He ended up here because he lost his job, his home, and he had nowhere else to go. A reverend helped him get this groundskeeper job at Choate. He was going to be a science teacher."

"Really? I wish we could do something for him. He has been so helpful to all of us, and Joe in particular."

"I've been thinking the very same thing all afternoon."

"So, how is Ryan?"

"He's very good, thank you."

"And have you started looking at schools yet?"

"Yes, I have. I'm thinking of applying to NYU and Duke."

"Why those?"

"Well, they both have excellent history and archeology departments and they both are great schools."

"And they are both schools Ryan might consider?"

"In fact, he is thinking about both of them. Don't be mad at me for wanting to go to the same school as him, Ken. I love him and want to be with him."

"I'm not mad; I'm teasing you, that's all," Ken said, laughing.

"And I heard yesterday that the only two schools Mary is applying to are Wellesley and Harvard. Do you think that has anything to do with you?"

"I hope so."

They both laughed and talked about Joe and Kim and how things were going at Choate after the first week. Ken said that Mary was coming to see him next weekend and he would be out to see all of them a week after that. They hung up and Deb went to see what Kim was doing.

Later that evening, as Ryan and Deb were walking back from town where they had taken Kim and her friend Amy for ice cream, Deb told Ryan about what Mr. Brewster had told her that day. Ryan was surprised that Mr. Brewster had been that open, saying that he figured Mr. Brewster was so much of a recluse that he wouldn't tell anyone about his life. They talked about how sad it was and how interesting a life Mr. Brewster lived until that accident and how much he must have missed in his life.

Deb was still thinking about Mr. Brewster on Sunday after they returned from church and they were sitting in the main hall working on homework. She was at the table with Mary, Joe was on the couch with Becky reading, and Kim was on the floor working on a presentation for her literature class. She started telling Mary about Mr. Brewster and Joe heard her. He walked over to the table and listened until she was finished, and then went back to the couch. He wanted to talk to Deb, but didn't want to do it with all these other people around.

As they all walked over to the dining hall for dinner, Becky asked Joe who Mr. Brewster was. He didn't think twice when he told her about meeting Mr. Brewster while he was trying to deal with his parents' deaths and how Mr. Brewster had helped him. They had struck up a friendship, and he had included his sisters later, and they were close with him. Becky said she thought that was very nice, as she always thought he was sad for some reason. Joe told her what Deb had found out, and Becky said it was nice that Mr. Brewster had them to care for him, too. Joe really liked the idea that Becky wasn't upset about his spending time with Mr. Brewster, and they had been getting along so well.

After dinner, Joe went in search of Deb. He had spent an hour with Becky finishing up homework and wanted to discuss Mr. Brewster. After only a couple of tries, he found Deb in the lobby of the girls' dorm with some other girls working on a project for chemistry class. He asked Deb if he could talk to her, and she indicated they would be done in a few minutes if he wanted to wait. He did. After the girls all departed the lobby, Deb asked, "What's up?"

"I wanted to first be sure that everything was alright between us from the meeting on Friday. Clearly, Ryan and Mary don't want to even consider using the machine again, and I heard from Ken about it too yesterday, but I wanted to be sure you and I were ok. We made a promise, and I meant it; I will not use the machine without someone with me ever again. I just don't want to shut the door on never using it. We might find a use for it."

"While it's true that we might find a more productive use for it, I don't want you making that decision without me and the others, ok?"

"Understood. But I also wanted to talk to you about Mr. Brewster."

"What about?"

"Well, after hearing what you had to say about him yesterday, I was worried about him. And, frankly, I'm worried about us all, too. If it's taking him that long to deal with losing his wife, how long is it going to take for us?"

"I think his situation is very different is several important ways. First, we're talking about his spouse, not a parent, and while parents are important, they are not the same as a person you commit to spending your life with and that you fell in love with. And second, he had no one to help him, and we all have each other."

"Yeah, that's true. So, he told you about his wife and their life before he came here?"

"Yeah, her name was Abigale, and she was a teacher. They were trying to have a baby, but she had a miscarriage shortly before she died in a car accident. Did you know he worked on the nuclear bomb testing in Las Vegas? That is why they were living out there."

"He told me he had a team of scientists and they worked on parts of it. I never knew he was that involved, though. I was wondering why he told you all that, and not me."

"I don't think you should think anything about it. He told me because it was her birthday, and I saw him coming home from the cemetery, and he probably needed to talk at that moment. If you had been nearby, he probably would have talked to you before talking to me."

"I want to help him; I'm just not sure how."

"I know. I want to help him too. I've been thinking about it since yesterday."

"Well, if you come up with something, please let me know."

"You too."

"I've got to get back. It's nearly eight o'clock. See you tomorrow."

"Yeah, see you."

Joe was sitting with Becky the next Saturday evening while Kim was on a Girl Scout camping trip and Deb was with Ryan at a theater assignment in town when it hit him about what they needed to do to help Mr. Brewster. This made him kind of laughed to himself when he thought about it, and Becky nudged him. Joe leaned over and whispered to her he was sorry. He had drifted off in thought. As he walked her back to the dorm after the movie, she asked what was going on, and what he had been thinking about, and he promised to tell her after church the next day.

After church, while they were all walking back together, Becky kept asking Joe what he needed to tell her, and he kept putting it off. As they arrived at the girls' dorm, he told Becky that he wanted to go for a walk after he changed, if she had time. She said she did and went to change as well. Ryan, Deb, Mary, Kim and Amy all laughed that perhaps he was finally going to ask her to be his girlfriend, and then they all dispersed to finish their homework.

Becky was waiting in the lobby when Joe got back, and they left the dorm on a walk. Joe kept to the exterior of the campus so they would not be interrupted. He wasn't sure how to start, so he just said, "Becky, I really like you. I hope you know that. I would like to consider you my girlfriend, if that is ok with you."

"Joe, I like you too. Don't be mad, but I've been telling the girls all this past week that you are my boyfriend," she said as she laughed a little.

"Whew, that was harder than I thought it was going to be."

"Why?"

"I was afraid you would say you didn't want to be my girlfriend."

"Don't be silly. By the way, does this mean I have a date for the Fall Festival dance?"

"Yes, it does. Of course, you might change your mind once I tell you the rest."

Joe told her everything. How they got to Choate, finding the math formula and the prototype, working with Mr. Brewster to solve it, building the machine, and taking the three trips last year. He told her everything. They kept walking, and he eventually steered her over toward Mr. Brewster's place. She said nothing for a long time, but eventually said, "How can this be true?"

"Do you want to see?"

"Yes!"

Joe walked her to the barn and opened the sliding door. There, in the middle of the barn, was the machine, just as it was when they left last spring, and when they met a week ago to discuss his crazy trip alone. Joe showed her the formula, the notes, the time passage calculation, the machine printouts from the three trips, and everything they had done to create the machine and program. She listened to everything he said and looked over the math and the machine. She asked if they could look inside and Joe showed her the inside of the machine. As they left, Becky said, "Wow, that's amazing. I love science fiction, and I've always wondered how we could do some of the things we've done as a society, like travel to the moon, but still not mapped time and travel this way through time. And look, you've figured it out."

"Well, I wouldn't say we really figured it out, Becky. We started out trying to go back in time to change something that would trigger a change in our parents' lives so they wouldn't be in the accident. It's funny, at the time it seemed so logical, but saying it now maybe sounds strange. Anyway, we were trying to bring our parents back, and it didn't work. Each time, we messed it up more."

"But you got to meet someone that tried to, or wanted to assassinate the President of the United States! That's so unreal!"

"Yeah, it was pretty cool being in Dallas, and knowing that we changed the outcome of that day. The funny thing is, no one here even remembers it like we did. The books all tell it differently. But the point is, both President Kennedy and our parents died."

"And that's why you went back again. But closer to home, right?"

"Yeah, I thought if I could convince my father that the machine existed, and told him not to travel when the accident occurred, they would be fine. Instead, I created a huge rift between my parents and they separated and died anyway, each alone, within three days of one another."

"Well, can't you go back and fix that part? Can't you undo the last visit? Wouldn't that reset things to at least where you were before that trip?"

"I suppose, but I had all kinds of strange physical symptoms when I went back to where I already existed and lived. I don't think I could go back there again without it doing something terrible. We just don't understand that part yet."

"Well, I wouldn't want anything to happen to you. Thanks for telling me all of this."

"Yeah, it didn't feel right keeping it from you, and I wanted you to know in case I was spending a lot of time over there at the barn."

"I might help you; you know. I got a better grade in science than you."

"That would be great."

They were standing in front of the girls' dorm when she looked up at Joe and said, "Joe, you know you can't keep people from dying, right?"

"It's sure looking like that, isn't it? I was just in a terrible place last year, and couldn't image my life without my parents. It's starting to look better now. Nearly losing my sisters and brother over that last trip was harder than losing my parents, so I'm re-thinking my fixations and priorities."

"I think I believe what Mary and Deb believe, that you have some free will to change where you are in life. You can make choices that take you onto different paths, but the end is already determined. I believe that. You might go back in time and shift things, maybe extend some-one's life, but you can't cheat death, Joe."

"That's an interesting idea, Becky. Last night when we were at the movie, I thought we might go back in the time machine and try to stop Mr. Brewster's wife from being in that accident. Maybe the goal shouldn't be bringing someone back from the dead, maybe it should just be prolonging their life so that the person has a little more time."

"But Mr. Brewster might still lose his wife and end up right here as the caretaker."

"But what if we can save her long enough for him to get that teaching job, or maybe have a child with her? If not any of that, at least he could be around people that could help him when he needed it after she was gone? And maybe he wouldn't lose her."

"I don't know."

"Thanks for letting me talk through this with you."

"You're my boyfriend, right?"

"Yes, I am." Joe smiled and gave Becky a hug. They said goodnight, and Joe went back to the boys' dorm.

A few days later, Joe found Deb in the library and told her about his idea to help Mr. Brewster. He told Deb about his conversation with Becky, how he had told her everything. He explained Becky's suggestion that although they couldn't cheat death, they could trick it for a little while. Deb had the same response as Becky in that she was worried Mr. Brewster would still suffer, and they had no way of knowing when or how he would suffer. They talked about using the machine again, and Deb couldn't argue with the idea of doing it to help someone they cared about, and said she would give it some thought. She thought about it and decided to tell Ryan about Joe's plan on Thursday evening when they met in the library to fill out college applications.

"So, what do you think?" she asked.

"I think the sentiment is commendable, Deb. I know you mean well. But didn't we agree we can't stop a person's death with that machine? Why would you want to do this?"

"Because you didn't see him. He was so lost as he told me about her and what happened. If we can bring him even a little more happiness, why shouldn't we try?"

"The thing is, like you said, as we have all talked about both before and after the trips you already made, you won't know if you did anything until you get back. And what if you make it worse, like you did with your parents?"

"I don't know Ryan; I just have a feeling about this. A very different feeling than I did about trying to change things for my parents. First of all, we're not trying to bring her back from the dead and have her here, we're trying to provide Mr. Brewster some comfort, for some amount of time and maybe get him to a place where he has support after she is gone. Is that so bad?"

"No. It's a very nice thing to do, sweetheart. But will your intentions really make that much difference in the outcome? Did you tell Ken about any of this yet?"

"No, and I'm not sure I'm going to."

"What?"

"Well, he absolutely doesn't want us using the machine at all. I know that, and until this week, I totally agreed with him. We're not talking about going to someplace any of us has been, in a time when any of us existed. And we're doing it to help someone we care about."

"So, you're going to keep this from Ken?"

"Maybe."

"I don't want to sound mean here, but you know you will also have to keep it from Mary if you don't want Ken to know."

"Yes, I had thought of that. I don't like that part, but I think that might be true as well. Keeping it from Ken means keeping it from Mary."

"I want to go with you."

"You do?"

"I do not want you to get into that machine without me ever again."

"You sound so stern, Mr. McDonnell."

"I love you, Deborah Fitzgerald, and I do not want to be here, when you are somewhere and some other time in that machine again. Please say you'll let me come with you."

"I love you too."

"You didn't answer my question."

"Yes, if we end up going, you can come with us."

"It might be fun."

"Going to a different time and knowing what is going on around you and knowing you can change that is pretty cool."

"So, what would the plan be?"

"Well, I think we would just have to find Mrs. Brewster and keep her off that road that night. Shouldn't it be that simple?"

"Perhaps. Do you know what the date was and where she taught or something that would get us to her?"

"I don't know those details. We would have to get that from Mr. Brewster somehow without his knowing, and then we would have to decide where to take the machine in that area. With all the development going on and that nuclear testing, we would have to be very careful about the location."

"Yeah, and it's a desert there, not a forest or park, so it will be harder to hide the machine, right?"

"Probably."

"Well, with Ken coming up tomorrow night, I think we should table all of this until Sunday and talk to Joe and Kim when Mary is not around and see what their thoughts are. Remember, you promised not to exclude Kim."

"Good idea. I can't tell Kim before Ken gets here, or she might spill the beans."

"Sounds good. Are you finished with your paper for Duke?"

"Just about. I want to leave it for tonight and check it over tomorrow again while we're waiting for Ken."

"I want to do that too. Do you have everything ready for NYU?"

"Yes, I just have to pick up the recommendation that Mr. Wentwright is doing for me from history. So, I should have that package ready to send out tomorrow."

"I have to pick up a recommendation too, but not from history. Mr. Ahbrams told me could mail all this out for us when we have it put together. If you get me your NYU information tomorrow at lunch, I can take it over to him after class when I pick up my recommendation."

"That sounds great."

They walked back to the dorms and Ryan kissed Deb goodnight and left her to get to the boys' dorm before curfew. The next day, as promised, Ryan took both of their materials to Mr. Ahbrams, their advisor, who mailed them out.

6

During class on Friday, Ryan had a bit of an inspiration. He knew they would need more information in order to decide what to do to help Mr. Brewster. He knew Mr. Brewster might get suspicious if Deb asked more questions, but he figured Mr. Brewster would not get too upset with Ryan asking a round of questions and the idea presented itself in his physics class. He sought Mr. Brewster as soon as class was over, finding him carting a bunch of landscape garbage to the dump area at the far reaches of campus. As he walked up behind Mr. Brewster, he said, "Mr. Brewster, I'm sorry to sneak up on you, but I was wondering if you have a minute for me."

Mr. Brewster turned, smiled at Ryan, and said, "Sure, if you don't mind walking with me."

"Sure, let me help you with that," Ryan said, as he bent to pick up some branches and grass that had fallen out of the large wheelbarrow that Mr. Brewster was pushing.

"What can I do for you?"

"Well, I just was in physics class and we have to do a paper on some part of the nuclear fission discovery and evolution. Deb told me about her conversation recently with you and I was hoping I might get some information, or some books or something to help with this paper."

"Ah, I see."

"Mr. Brewster, it's not like that. Deb tells me things, and she was worried about you and was interested in the history aspect of your former profession. You know we have all become like a big family, and you matter a lot to us."

"You all have become very important to me as well. I don't mind that Deb told you. I would expect that as close as the two of you are."

"I love her."

"Yes, I know, Ryan. It makes me happy to see you both so happy together. I know I'm not your parents, but I think of you as my children, and it makes me happy to know that you've found someone like Deb and that she's found you."

"Thanks. We kind of think of you as our favorite uncle; we care about you as well."

"I do have some books and things you can borrow for your paper. Let's head over to my house and I'll get them for you."

They finished unloading the garbage and left the tools Mr. Brewster had in the shed near the dump and walked back to Mr. Brewster's house. Ryan sat down at the kitchen table and Mr. Brewster went to the office and pulled books off the shelf. He came back with several books and two folders of papers. He laid them on the table as he said, "So these are some books that contain research material published in journals and such in 1951 when the testing began. These folders contain test results from those first fission reaction tests. These were tests I worked on, so they are from much later in the process. Probably 1957 or so. This should give you what you need."

Ryan skimmed through one book and said, "Thanks so much. This is great."

They talked for a few minutes about the paper, and Mr. Brewster offered some suggestions. Ryan tried to ask some other questions and tentatively explored what Deb had told him about his wife. Mr. Brewster told him some things, like the name of the school where she worked and what grade, and what she did when Mr. Brewster was working late. He had some good leads, so he allowed the conversation to drift to Ken, Joe, Deb, and Kim.

"Ken is coming out here today, actually."

"To see you all?"

"Yes, I mean, I'm sure he's mostly interested in seeing Mary, but I know he's worried about Joe in particular, but all of them, as well."

"He's told me about his worry. We, in fact, speak quite a bit."

"Oh, I didn't know that."

"Yes, Ken calls me every once in a while. He has since this past summer."

"That's cool."

"How is Joe doing? I haven't seen him all week."

"He has a new girlfriend apparently, and I know he's also been busy with two of his classes, but I think he's doing alright. The trip, and what happened to his parents, still really bothers him. Plus, I think he might have had a bit of a breakthrough on the computer language idea he was working on, so his focus is somewhere else right now."

"He was mentioning something about that last weekend after we all met. I hoped it would give him something to focus on."

"Yeah."

"It's getting close to dinnertime. You're more than welcome to stay for dinner, but I imagine Deb might expect you."

"I'd love to stay, but I promised Deb I would meet her."

"Well, then head back to campus. It was good to talk to you. If you need anything else for your paper, come find me."

"Thanks again for the books and information."

"Sure, I'm ready to help you all whenever you need it."

"See you later."

Ryan walked directly back to the girls' dorm to meet Deb. He found her in the lobby and told her he had been to Mr. Brewster's, and asked her to hold the books and folders for him. Deb ran the materials to her room and then they all went over to the dining hall for dinner. They were all waiting in the lobby of the boys' dorm after dinner for Ken to arrive. When he got there, they were all laughing and hugging and Ken swung Kim around and they were all talking at once. Ken got Joe to take his bag up to his room, and then they all went to the main hall. They played games and talked until it was time for the girls to get to the dorm. Ken carried Kim on his back while holding Mary's hand. Everyone said goodnight, and the boys walked back to their dorm.

The next day, Ken took Mary and Kim into town for some shopping and lunch, while Deb worked on some homework. Ryan sought Joe to talk.

"So, Joe, I hear you might have had some breakthrough in your computer language or program or whatever. Is that true?"

"Kind of."

"What do you mean, kind of?"

"Well, I'm still working some details out on sub-routines."

"What are those? Are they related to the zero and one and two language?"

"That's binary language, or machine code. It's just zeros and ones."

"I thought I heard last fall that you said it was zeros, ones, and twos."

"Yeah, well, I was testing people. Wanted to know if anyone would catch that little detail. I guess you're the only one that figured it out."

"Maybe, maybe not."

"What do you mean by that?"

"Well, I heard someone commenting on the floor last year about it. I think it was Robert, from the second floor."

"Really?"

"Yeah."

"Anyway, that's not what I'm working on. I'm working on a language that is English-based that uses statements to change a program's state. It's an extension or evolution of COBOL. That's a language that uses English, but it has a whole bunch of restricted words you can't use except as commands. They developed it about ten years ago and is too heavy of a language. This language I'm working on should make the program leaner, and easier to code in, and would allow programs to do many things like typing and saving documents, and doing calculations like accounting and things like that."

"Oh, what's your language going to be called? Is it going to have a name like COBOL?"

"Not sure yet."

"Maybe something derived from COBOL, since that seems to be its starting point, but without those restricted words."

"Maybe."

"So why were there restricted words? What were they used for?"

"Well, those words had meaning for the program, so you couldn't have a statement that used the word 'run' unless you wanted the program to run something that came right after that word. It had to have specific syntax with those restricted words for the program to do its job. This new language uses syntax and routines and sub-routines to act on."

"Oh. How does that make it leaner?"

"Well, it means you have fewer lines of code to do the same number of actions and because it's in English, it's easier to learn and easier to code."

"So, can I talk to you about something else while you're working on this?"

"Not really. Can I come find you when I'm done?"

"Yeah sure. I'm going to head over to the library and sit with Deb and work on homework. Come over there when you're done."

"Sure."

Ryan went over to the library and found Deb sitting at a table upstairs. She was working on a paper with books all around her.

"This is your favorite place, isn't it, sweetheart?"

"You know it is. Libraries are a kind of paradise for me. What are you doing here?"

She stood up and hugged him. They both sat down, and Ryan suggested they move to a study room so they could talk in private. He carried all her books and set them down on the table.

"So, what's up?"

"Well, honey, you're going to be really proud of me. I came up with this great idea to start a conversation with Mr. Brewster to get more of the information you needed. See, I have this assignment in physics to write a paper on nuclear fission evolution, and I went to Mr. Brewster to see if he had some information. Don't be angry, but I revealed to him you told me about his wife. This allowed me to ask a few questions. I found out she taught fourth grade and all kinds of things she liked to do while he worked late. She went to the library to help in the kids' area every Tuesday afternoon and was in a book club with some other teachers that met every other week on Wednesday evenings."

"Wow, that's a lot of information. The important question is, we have to confirm not just the day of the week, but the date of the accident. I can probably look it up in the microfilm though, since we know the accident happened on Las Vegas Boulevard in January 1958. That's great Ryan."

Grinning and motioning like he had just won a race or something, Ryan shared he had seen Joe and he was coming over once he was done working on a program thing. He told Deb he wanted to discuss a few things about a possible trip with just Deb and Joe before they went any further. They worked on homework then until Joe came in about an hour later.

"So, what's up, Ryan?" Joe asked as he found them in the study room.

"I had a great talk with Mr. Brewster yesterday afternoon, and I think I have the information we need to think about a trip to help him," Ryan answered.

"In the machine?"

"Yeah, Joe, Deb and I talked about this last week."

They talked over the details that Deb and Ryan had learned about Mrs. Brewster's death, what they knew about the area, time-frame, and such. Then Ryan brought up that they had to keep Mary out of it or Ken would find out. They all agreed that would be best because of Ken's feelings about not using the machine. Deb expressed she didn't enjoy doing this behind his back, but she felt too strongly about helping Mr. Brewster to not do it. Joe was all for it, because he figured if they could figure this out, maybe they would do this for his parents. At the end of an hour, the only thing outstanding for them was the thought that even after this effort, Mr. Brewster would still likely lose his wife anyway, and that might mean they shouldn't do it. They decided to wait until they knew Ken's plans for the next few weeks, and whether Mary was going to Harvard anytime.

Later that afternoon, they all piled into Mary's big car and went into town to have dinner together and to see the next Star Wars movie that was playing at the in-town theater. Ken paid for everything and they all had a great time. Ken left Sunday morning after church to get back to school. He had received permission to come back for the Fall Festival dance, but that meant he would not be back for about five weeks. Mary was going to go to Harvard for the weekend in two weeks. Deb noted all this in her usual tone, but was calculating whether they could plan a trip for the weekend that Mary was away. Everyone dispersed to finish homework, but Deb went with Kim to the main hall, where she was working on a project with several kids from her history class. Deb read while they worked, but she wanted to be close, as Kim had commented on missing being with all of her siblings.

The next week, Deb pulled Kim into her room after dinner and explained the idea they had. Of course, Kim wanted to help Mr. Brewster and thought it would be great to have his wife back. She was concerned that if they brought her back, though, would that mean that Mr. Brewster would not end up at Choate? The two decided that if he could have some happiness, they were ready to sacrifice having him here. Deb thanked her for the insight, and said they would all be meeting, but had to figure out how to do that without Mary around. On Wednesday, Mary told Deb that her parents were coming up to spend the day with her on Saturday, so that ended up being the planning day. All the rest of them, including Becky, gathered in the library Saturday afternoon to discuss the plan.

"So, first of all, we can only fit four people inside the machine. That means we cannot all go," Joe said.

"I think I should stay back. I mean, this is something you all feel strongly about, and someone needs to be here in case you are successful and that barn is not Mr. Brewster's anymore," Becky said.

"Thanks Becky. I really want to go along and I figured I would be the one that got left behind," Kim said, looking down.

Deb reached over and grabbed Kim's hand as she said, "We wouldn't go without you, Kim."

"Perhaps we should come up with another place to come back to instead of the barn in case Becky is right, and the barn doesn't belong to Mr. Brewster anymore. I mean, if we're successful, he might be a teacher somewhere else and a different person might own that house and be a caretaker here," Ryan added.

"That's a good idea, Ryan. Does anyone have an idea where we could come back to? It has to be a private place that is hidden, as we stir up wind and dust and create a lot of light when we come back," Joe added.

"What about that large shed that has been out of use for a couple of years?" Ryan said.

"Which shed are you thinking of?" Deb asked.

"Well, last Friday when I was talking with Mr. Brewster, we took some landscape garbage to the dump area. There was a large shed behind there that he said was not in use and hadn't been for a couple of years. They had used it for storing the lawn mowers or something, but Mr. Brewster said when they got new equipment, it wouldn't fit in that shed, so they just stopped using it."

"That should work, if it's big enough. Let's check it out when we leave here. Also, we'll need to get the coordinates of someplace safe near Las Vegas so we can target it in the machine," Joe said.

"I think you should write Mr. Brewster a letter before we go, and mail it to him. He might not know who we are when we get back, and you will want to let him know something, won't you, Joe? I mean, I want to help him, but I don't want that to mean we can't talk to him anymore," Kim said.

"Where would we mail it?" Joe asked.

"I think we should mail it here to the school, but I'm not sure what would happen if he ends up not working at Choate," Kim replied.

"If he isn't here at all, and hasn't been here because we changed his timeline so much, they might try to forward or return it, right?" Becky said.

"I don't know where they would forward it to if they do not know who he is, but I'm sure they would return it to the return address if they had no options. Maybe we should put the Hampton house as the return address?" Deb asked.

"That's a great idea, Deb!" Kim said.

"Who's going to write the letter?" Ryan asked.

"Joe and Deb," Kim answered before anyone else could say anything.

"Alright, so the plan is to go Friday afternoon because we know that Mr. Brewster is helping at the church and Mary will be gone, visiting Ken. We have a site we think is not heavily populated to target, and then we will make our way to the school. Ryan found out they have a book fair going on the week of the retirement dinner, so we will go in and say we're visiting, and wanted to get some books. We will locate Mrs. Brewster and make up some good reason to be there. Then all we have to do is keep her busy long enough that she doesn't have time to pick up the teacher that she drives to the dinner. That will make this other teacher hopefully get a ride from someone else, and that will mean Mrs. Brewster takes a different route home. We should only be there for a few hours, but the time to get back and forth to the machine needs to be figured out," Deb said.

"It looks on the map like the walk would be about two miles from the landing site to a place we are likely to get a cab or bus or something," Kim said, looking at the map they had in the center of the table.

"It should take us what, about forty-five minutes to make that walk?" Joe asked.

"Probably," Kim replied.

"So, we're up to about six hours," Ryan said.

"I think we should plan for seven hours," Joe said.

Joe did some calculations. He looked up when he finished and said that if the theory held true and the calculation was correct, they would be gone about three and a half hours. That would mean they would be back Friday night. They left the library to walk over to the shed to see if they could get inside. The doors were unlocked and Ryan was correct; it was empty. Given the weed growth all around the shed, they figured no one had been inside for a long time. Deb and Ryan said they would get the coordinates to Joe, and they agreed they were all ready to go. They just needed to wait until Friday evening.

The week seemed to crawl by for the five of them. Finally, it was Friday, and they finished classes and got ready to go. Thursday, Becky and Joe had taken clothes appropriate for the 1950s to the barn and put them in the compartments of the machine while Mr. Brewster was still working. Friday, Deb and Becky said goodbye to Mary as she packed up her car to go to Harvard. Kim sent something she had made in art class. It was a ceramic desk stand for pens and pencils and notes. Mary left and the three girls prepared to meet the boys.

7 |

The five of them walked quietly to the barn. They went inside, and Ryan helped Joe program the machine while Deb and Kim changed clothes with Becky's help. They had mailed the letter earlier that day, and hopefully it would arrive no later than Monday, so long as Mr. Brewster was still here at Choate. Ryan and Joe changed clothes, and they climbed into the machine. Becky was going to turn everything off in the barn, and then she was going to head back to campus and wait in her room. Then she would sneak out just before the curfew and make her way to the shed to wait for them all.

The machine started; the noise, the wind and everything that meant it was ready to go started up. With all the communication equipment disconnected, Becky had no way to talk to the others inside before they disappeared. She was shocked at the wind and noise, but then quietly turned off the lights as Joe had instructed, and left the barn. She hoped the four of them were ok and that their fantastic plan worked. She went back to her room and waited.

The machine came to a stop and Joe unbuckled himself and went to look out the portal window to see if there was anyone around where they had landed outside Las Vegas. It was clear, so he helped Ryan unbuckle Deb and Kim, and they exited the machine. They found some tumbleweed nearby, and stacked it up around the machine to help disguise it, and then left to make it to the outskirts of town to locate a cab.

They got out of the cab a block away from the school. Deb and Kim decided they were going to be new residents and thought that was the best way to get into the school. So, the two of them were going to the book fair, and were going to see if they could arrive just as school was letting out, hoping to locate Mrs. Brewster. Shortly after they entered the building and went into the library, Mrs. Brewster entered with several of her students. They walked around and talked about different books and Kim made her way to tag along. After Mrs. Brewster left the kids from her class to finish making their selections, Kim said, "Excuse me, can you help me, please?"

"I would be happy to help you, dear. What is your name? I don't think I've seen you around the building," Mrs. Brewster replied.

"My name is Kim. I'm new to the area. My parents are looking at a house a few blocks from here that we might move to, and my sister and I walked over to see the book fair while they did that."

"Oh, how nice of your sister to walk you over here."

"Yes, she's always looking out for me."

"What can I help you with?"

"I'm looking for books about history. I'm just fascinated with early American history, like during the time of the pioneers."

"Well, let's see what we can find."

Mrs. Brewster held out her hand, motioning toward the table she thought would have what Kim was interested in, and Kim followed her. They walked around a few tables, and Mrs. Brewster showed Kim several books that looked like they would cover the subject Kim was interested in. While they looked, they talked a bit.

"So what grade are you in, Kim?"

"I'm in sixth grade, ma'am."

"Oh, my goodness, forgive me. My name is Mrs. Brewster. I am the fourth-grade teacher here."

"It is nice to meet you, Mrs. Brewster."

"You said your family was moving to Las Vegas?"

"Well, I guess so. My father works in construction and is going to be working on one of the new big hotels here."

"That's nice. We go sometimes to those big hotels to see singers and have dinner."

"I didn't realize they had shows and restaurants. My father doesn't talk about what happens when he's done building much."

"Does your mother work, Kim?"

"She's a high school math teacher, but I'm not sure if she is going to work here or not."

"Perhaps she will start teaching again next fall when the new year starts up."

"Maybe."

"How old is your sister?"

"She's a senior in high school. Her name is Deb."

"Is that short for Deborah?"

"Yeah."

"Well, with you in sixth grade, and your sister in high school, I won't have the pleasure of having you in my class. Do you have other siblings?"

"I do, a brother, but he's a sophomore in high school."

At that moment, Deb walked up to them.

"Mrs. Brewster, this is my sister, Deb. Deb, this is Mrs. Brewster. She teaches fourth grade here."

"It's nice to meet you, Mrs. Brewster. Thank you for helping my sister."

"It was a genuine pleasure to talk with her. I don't want to keep you two, and I am sure your parents will be looking for you soon."

"Probably, but they asked us to be busy for an hour to allow them to see a house. Could I trouble you for a minute, Mrs. Brewster?"

"You are not in trouble are you, Deborah?" Mrs. Brewster asked because of the look on Deb's face.

"Oh no, I just was hoping you could tell me something about the high school, and what the kids are like, and a little bit about the schools and the community. We've moved a few times, and it's always hard to get to know a new area."

"I am sure that must be hard for you, being a teen and all. I've had to move around quite a bit as well. My husband is a scientist."

"Wow, is he working on the testing here? I read about that in the newspaper."

"Yes, he works on the testing. We've been here for a few months."

"That must be so fascinating. I really want to explore archeology, but anything that clearly is going to make history, like this testing, certainly will, interests me."

"Well, how about we go back to my classroom and we can talk there?"

"Let me buy these two books first. Will that be alright?" Kim asked.

They waited for Kim to purchase her books, and then the three of them walked down the hall from the library and went into Mrs. Brewster's classroom. They talked for nearly half an hour when another teacher came into the room.

"Mrs. Brewster, I didn't realize you were still working with students. I can come back if you like," the other teacher said.

"These aren't students, Miss Halloway. These are two new residents of Las Vegas that wandered into the book fair while their parents are viewing a house for sale nearby. They're quizzing me on schools and the community. We have a future archeologist and a future history teacher, perhaps, here in my classroom."

"How nice."

"Yes. Were you ready to go to the dinner? I'm not sure I am going to be ready for a bit."

"Well, I need to go over and help get some decorations set up. If you're not ready, Mr. Schmidt is ready to go, so perhaps I can ride with him instead? Also, he indicated he would be happy to take me home as well. Would that be too much trouble to change plans for you? It would allow you to visit with your new friends and it might give me a chance to get to know the new single teacher. You mentioned I should try to, and I know I hesitated, but he invited me again."

"Not at all. I will see you at the dinner then."

"Thank you. Bye, and welcome to Las Vegas, girls."

The girls said thank you and Miss Halloway left. Deb then apologized for keeping Mrs. Brewster, who said there was no need to apologize. They continued talking for several more minutes and then Deb said they should probably get back to their parents. They thanked Mrs. Brewster for her help and time and left the building.

"Wow, do you think that was enough to change things?" Kim asked.

"I sure hope so. It couldn't have worked out better with that Miss Halloway getting both a ride there and a ride home. Now surely Mrs. Brewster will go home a different way tonight. I think we can call this mission accomplished!"

The girls met Ryan and Joe and then hailed a cab to get as far out of town as possible. They still had to walk about two miles to the machine. It was getting dark when they got close to the machine and they noticed several cars near it. Ryan told Deb and Kim to wait behind some thick bushes while he and Joe crept closer to see what was going on. There were about five vehicles backed in together to form a circle of sorts. A bunch of older teenagers were making a fire in the middle of that circle and were pulling coolers and bags out of the trunks of two of the cars. Ryan pulled Joe back, and they slunk back to where Kim and Deb were waiting.

"It looks like they're planning a barbeque and beer fest over there," Ryan said in a whisper.

"What are we going to do?" Deb asked.

"I don't know. Joe, any ideas?"

"Well, we can't sneak into the machine and start it up. It will blow them all around and they might get to the machine before we can get it going and out of here. There's no lock on the door. I do not know what would happen if someone opened the door while it was running the program."

"Great, so we're stuck here?" Kim asked.

"I think so. We'll have to wait them out."

Since they knew it was going to be a while before these boys left, they all walked back and found a little shack of a restaurant and had some hot dogs and chips. The owner of the place said he set this stand up a few months ago to take care of the people that went out to watch the testing. Joe started asking him all kinds of questions. "Did you have this place when they started doing all the tests last summer?"

"Set up about July when they were in full swing of the tests. They've been naming all the tests and called this one Plumbbob. Not sure how the name got out, but we figured it out by late June. I think someone said they saw every test and there were twenty-five or thirty of those," the owner replied.

"Why did they need to do so many?" Joe asked.

"Seems to me I heard they did some tests with pigs out there and then they had a whole bunch of troops from the army out there in the fall. I think they might have been testing what the impact of the bombs were or something."

"Why pigs?" Kim asked.

"I read in the paper they used pigs because their skin was most like humans, and their organs were a lot like ours. They used them first before they started putting live people out there when the bombs went off."

"Wow," they all said.

"Yeah, one night, as I was building this place, they came through here with a truck full of pigs that had some suits on or something. It looked like they had clothes on. I asked the driver about it. He said they put different material on the pigs to see if anything would stop the blast."

"Did he come through here after the test or before?" Joe asked.

"Before, why?"

"I just wondered if the suits you saw were the ones that survived the blast or if they hadn't been in the blast yet."

"Oh, yeah, gotcha."

"Thanks for the dogs and the talk, sir. We enjoyed it," Joe said as they got up and put their wrappers and cups in the garbage can.

"Where are you young folks headed, anyway?"

"Oh, we are visiting some family near here and took the girls out for a walk and they got hungry. It's late, so we should get back before we worry our folks," Ryan added as he started ushering the girls away.

"Yeah, you be safe walking out here. You never know when they're testing and who is driving around out here."

"Thanks," Ryan said as they walked away.

As they walked back, the four talked about what the owner had said and wondered about why they needed all the different tests. They got quiet when they neared the machine. The girls again hid in the bushes while the boys walked up. The cars were still there, but the boys had all basically passed out from too much alcohol. Joe ran back and got the girls and they climbed through the tumbleweed they had piled up and got into the machine. Joe made sure the readings would put them in the shed and not the barn, and they started it up. They never knew if they woke up any of those boys. No one tried to get to the machine, so they thought they were safe. When the machine came to a stop, and they climbed out, they found Becky there, looking very anxious.

"My gosh, I'm so glad you made it back. You're two hours later than you expected. I don't know how we're going to get back into the dorms this late without getting caught."

"We'll figure it out," Joe replied as he hugged Becky.

"What happened?" She asked.

"We got back in plenty of time to the machine, but the place we picked to land had become a hangout for teenage boys by the time we got there. We had to wait until we could get to the machine and get out of there without notice."

"Did they leave?"

"No, they all had too much to drink and fell asleep. If one of them woke up from the noise or wind, I'm sure they would think it was the beer making them see and hear things."

They all laughed as they hurried back to campus. Ryan and Joe helped the girls get into the back door of the girls' dorm without notice, and then they went back to the boys' dorm, where they had to climb through a window to get in as the doors were locked. They sneaked past the younger boys sleeping in the room they had climbed into and up to their rooms undetected. The next day, all four of them met just outside the dining hall and had breakfast. There were many of their friends there and several asked Deb why she had missed the movie and games last night. Ryan jumped in and said he had wanted a little girlfriend time and they had gone for a walk. That seemed to satisfy Deb's friends. Joe and Becky were not having as much luck.

"What do you mean you went to the library on a Friday night?" asked his friend Tim.

"Well, Becky and I were working on a project I'm hot to finish, and we went to the library instead of game night. What of it?"

"Oh sure, you and Becky were in the library working on a Friday night. Yeah right!" Tim replied.

"Were you hiding in the study rooms? Maybe you were studying Becky, huh?" joked Mike from Joe's math class.

"No man, and don't joke about my girlfriend like that!" Joe said, getting a little angry.

At this point, both Becky and Kim walked up. Becky was smiling because that was the first time she had heard Joe refer to her as his girlfriend, but Kim was busy thinking. Just as they walked up, Kim said, "Actually, Mike, they went to work on that project of Joe's 'cause I wanted to read last night. You jugheads might not understand this, but sometimes girls are more interested in books than boys, and sometimes big brothers are good to their little sisters."

"Oh yeah, like Joe is going to give up his Friday night to babysit his little sister!" several of the guys said.

"Maybe it was because I asked him to. What do you think of that?" Becky said as she put her hand in Joe's.

Becky, Joe and Kim walked away at that point. They sat down and Joe thanked Becky for the save and apologized for the jokes they were making. Kim punched Joe in the arm and asked what about her save? Joe replied he doubted helping his little sister was much of a save, but he thanked her for the effort. Ryan and Deb joined them and asked if they had been questioned. They said they had, but had deflected the issue. Kim said it was because she said Joe was taking care of her, and they all laughed. Ryan suggested that they all head off campus today to keep others from questioning them, and in case something big was about to break because of their trip. They agreed nothing could be known until they found out about Mr. Brewster, and for some reason, none of them wanted to walk over to his house, or what had been his house, to see. So, the four of them walked to town and watched a movie and had lunch and then returned to campus. They all went to the bowling alley that night for the school function, and because of the action, didn't get questioned much by any of the kids.

On Sunday, Deb talked to Aunt Alicia and Joe talked to Mr. Reynolds, as had become their habit this year. Everything seemed normal until they were sitting in the main hall doing homework when Ryan came running in and called them all to a corner. He reported he had been playing hockey with some of his teammates from last year when one of them talked about having a huge assignment to finish for physics. None of that seemed unusual until Ryan said he asked which teacher gave such a huge assignment and the friend said, "Mr. Brewster." He said he was sorry he got assigned to that teacher, instead of the one that Ryan had. They were all speechless when they heard this. No one knew quite what to do when it occurred to Kim that there had to be a faculty directory somewhere. Deb said, "Yes, there is a directory. It's in the lobby of the dorms. Let's get over to the girls' dorm and look him up."

They gathered up their books and went to the girls' dorm. Deb went and asked at the main desk for the faculty directory and brought it into the lounge where they all had sat down. She opened it to the page where Mr. Brewster was listed and sat it down in the middle of them all.

"Oh my gosh, it's him!" cried Kim.

"He looks so different with a suit on. I don't think I remember him with a suit on, ever," Joe said, a little quiet.

"I know you all went back to Las Vegas to keep Mr. Brewster's wife from dying, but why don't you remember he is a teacher here?" Becky asked.

"I kind of remember having him for science last year," Deb replied. "This is the time when we remember the old and the new timelines, isn't it? We know he was the caretaker when we met him originally, but now we have memories of him as a teacher. Becky, only the people that went into the machine know the old and the new, but the new comes to us slowly."

"Joe," Becky asked, "Is this true? How could this happen? No, wait a minute, I think I have it figured out! When you told me about your trip last spring and how you had physical symptoms, I remember thinking that it was interesting that forces of space and time took some time to realign everything and know you were in that place twice. Maybe that's why you don't remember the new timeline after a trip in the machine! Maybe it's taking some time for the re-alignment."

"That's probably on the right track. We should look into that," Joe replied, smiling at Becky.

"Read what his bio says," Ryan added.

"It says he came to Choate in 1970. He became a teacher in August 1958 after completing work with the NTS in Las Vegas. He taught at Amherst College until 1969. His wife died that year of cancer and he and his son moved to Wallingford so that he could join the Choate faculty. He has a son named Thomas."

"So, we know his wife didn't die in that car accident," Joe said.

"And we know they had a child, and he got to teach," Kim said, smiling.

"She died anyway," Deb said.

"Yes, but it looks like it didn't drive him to drink and basically check out, like it did in the original history we know," Joe said.

"You have to give Joe that," Ryan replied.

"Now all we don't know is how he will react when he gets that letter from us," Deb said.

"Hey, I wonder what Ken remembers of Mr. Brewster. I mean, now that we have changed his history since he didn't go with us. He won't remember the old history, will he, Joe?" Kim pondered.

"Well, as long as things remain as they had been for our past travels, since he didn't go with us, and wasn't there when we left and we didn't tell him anything about this, he won't know what we know anymore."

"Is that I why I don't remember him being anything but a teacher?" Becky asked.

"When Joe went on a trip alone that night while he was still gone, Ken and I had vague memories starting to pop up. We wrote a bunch of things down, but by morning, we didn't remember what we wrote. For you, Becky, you were there, so you would remember some of the old and all the new timelines, but once a day had passed, the old timeline would start to disappear. Since we didn't really talk about the old and new timeline on the way back to campus, and then everyone just went to sleep, you would lose the old timeline," Deb said.

"Should we call Ken and see if we can get him to tell us how things are going with Mr. Brewster?" Kim asked.

"No, I don't think that's a good idea, for now," Deb replied to Kim's question.

"I wonder if anyone noticed your departure from Las Vegas? What if one of those boys saw you?" Becky said to no one in particular.

"I'm going to the library to check out the microfilm!" Deb announced.

Ryan said he would go with her and Kim, Joe and Becky returned to the main hall. A short time later, Deb and Ryan returned and reported that, in fact, one of those boys woke up and reported seeing strange lights take off from out in the desert where the boys had been. He said the lights disappeared almost as fast as he saw them. Most people thought the kid was crazy, but a few thought perhaps the nuclear testing had drawn aliens. For a period of time between their trip and the end of above-ground testing, there was a group of people that spent many nights watching the skies for alien spacecraft.

After Deb told them all this news, the four of them waited to see what Mr. Brewster would do once he got the letter, which would arrive at his office the next day. They all went back to the main hall and finished homework, wondering what tomorrow would bring.

8

Getting through classes on Monday was murder for Deb, Ryan, Joe, and Becky. They all expected to have Mr. Brewster or the school dean or some other authoritative person grab them by the arm and take them off at some point. The four of them talked about it at dinner after surviving the whole day and no one heard a word. Joe was prepared to go over to Mr. Brewster's supposed house and see if he lived there, but Ryan talked him out of it. Deb did talk to Ken after classes on Monday. He apologized for not calling on Sunday, but after Mary had been there all weekend, he said he had a lot of homework to finish. He asked how they all were and what they did that weekend. Deb said they hung out, saw a movie, and played games. No huge homework, but it was gearing up at Choate.

The fall dance was the next weekend and Ken was coming to Choate to take Mary to the dance. He had classes cancelled for Friday, so he was coming out on Thursday night. He had got a hotel room in town, and was taking Kim and her friends to dinner Friday night, and making a big deal out of it because they were still too young for the dances. Deb thought that was a great idea. Ken wanted to make it a surprise, but when he contacted his old counselor, he was told they would need permission from parents, so he sent notes to the girls after he had all the required forms into the school. Ken then asked Deb if she would take Kim and her friends into town to get dresses. She said she would. Deb asked about his weekend with Mary, and he gushed about her. It was obvious they were destined to be together. Nothing was said about

Mr. Brewster or the machine. Ken asked about Joe, and Deb replied he seemed to be doing better, which was true, but she thought that might be more about Becky than Joe addressing his feelings.

The entire conversation got Deb thinking that maybe she needed to check with Joe, so she asked him if he could meet her at the library Wednesday after dinner. He said he would. Monday evening, with no one asking to see them about the machine and Mr. Brewster still not reaching out, Deb spent the evening planning and organizing the girls for the shopping trip. This ended up being more of an effort to calm the girls down than to make plans and made Deb barely get her homework completed that night. She awoke rather tired, and when she went into the science classroom on Tuesday, she had forgotten all about Mr. Brewster.

"Miss Fitzgerald, I have a note here requesting you to present yourself in Mr. Brewster's office today at 3:30 p.m. I am uncertain what this is regarding. However, I can tell you I delivered the same message last hour to your brother, Joseph," Mr. Baumgartner, the chemistry teacher, indicated as Deb walked in and sat down at her desk.

"Thank you, Mr. Baumgartner."

Because Deb had classes all afternoon, she did not have an opportunity to check in with Ryan, Kim, Joe or Becky and therefore, wondered if they too had been summoned to Mr. Brewster's office that day. She went to the third floor, where the teacher's offices were, and found them all waiting in the hall near Mr. Brewster's office.

"What's going on? I got this note in my physics class with Ryan?" Mary asked Deb as she walked up.

"I'm not sure."

"This seems really strange that he would summon us all like this. Why didn't he just invite us all to the barn?"

"I'm not sure Mary," Deb said.

Just then, Mr. Brewster opened his office door and motioned for them to all come in. They filed into his office and waited.

"I received a letter yesterday afternoon here in my office. Which one of you would like to explain?"

"I will, Mr. Brewster," Deb answered.

Deb looked at each of the others and then turned again to Mr. Brewster. Then she said, "Mr. Brewster, we wrote you the letter because we hoped that our attempt to change your history was successful, and we weren't sure if you would remember any of the things we did and the time we spent with you. We wanted you to know what was going on."

"A year ago, when we all arrived here at Choate, you befriended Joe. He was, of the four of us, really struggling the most with the deaths of our parents. You two were kind of kindred spirits at that time because you were just a caretaker here at Choate. You told me once that you had kind of checked out until you found Joe. Joe had found a bunch of old mathematical formulas and papers, and a prototype in the building that is not used anymore behind the main hall. He brought them to you, and the two of you worked on them, and solved the formula. You found the formula showed how to bend time and travel through it. The prototype was a machine that could be programmed to do this time travel. You and Joe finished programming the machine mechanicals, and you and Ken built the machine. Last spring you went in the machine as a test and met your father the day he was to marry your mother. You never knew him because he was killed on Normandy Beach. Then later, the four of us went into the machine and went to Dallas to stop President Kennedy from being assassinated. We determined, well, I determined, that this event was the start of my father's business with his partner Mr. Davis, and if we could impact that, we could stop our parents' plane crash. We stopped the assassination that day, but President Kennedy was killed a few weeks later. Our parents didn't die in a plane crash, but in a different accident. We spent several long days talking about whether we could impact a person's life enough to change when and how they died, and whether it was right to do that. Through all of that, you were so supportive of us all and helped us, and looked out for us when we tried this machine, and you have come to mean so much to all of us."

Deb paused and waited in case Mr. Brewster had questions. When he did not, she continued, "This fall, I found you one Saturday in a suit walking through campus and I followed you. We sat at your kitchen table and you told me about your wife, and testing the nuclear bombs in Las Vegas. You told me she died, and that you didn't get to have any children because of her miscarriage and her accident in the car on a night you were trying to finish up testing. We decided we would try one more time to help someone we cared about; Joe, Ryan, Kim and I went back to 1957 to that Thursday night. We met your wife at her school, talked to her for a while, and kept her from driving Miss Halloway home, which kept her from that car accident. That one change, changed the course of your life, clearly for the better. You became a teacher like you planned, and you have a son, and we are so happy about that. We wrote the letter because we have discovered with these trips that anyone that is not travelling, and anyone that is not standing there when the machine leaves and comes back, remembers nothing but the new time-line we create by changing something in history, and those of that did travel and were there, lose some of the old timeline over time."

They all waited as Mr. Brewster looked at each of them. Finally, Mary could wait no longer and said, "What are you talking about, Deb? Mr. Brewster has been a teacher here since I came to Choate. He helped us, but he's always been a teacher."

"It seems you changed some part of history, but not my connection to you all. I was there for the formula solving, and the machine building, and the trips, just as a teacher, not a caretaker."

"You went back into the machine?" Mary practically screamed.

"Yes, Mary, we went back into the machine. We wanted to help Mr. Brewster," Deb replied.

"Ken specifically said no one was to use the machine again, did he not?"

"Yes, he said that."

"I thought we had decided it was not good to go into the machine, that we should not make trips because it was not right to attempt to change God's plan?"

"Mary, we agreed to discuss it all further, and as you might remember. We didn't all agree with your ideas about why it didn't work when we tried to save our parents." Joe stood up as he said this.

"You are so selfish, Joe!"

"He did this for someone else, Mary. Perhaps a review of the assumptions is in order," Becky said, defending Joe.

"Let's all calm down. Mary, I was there when we all gathered to discuss the fact that the attempt to save Ken's parents was unsuccessful, and we all needed to search our feelings and listen carefully to one another. I believe Joe was struggling with his grief and he did, perhaps, incorrectly tie his efforts with the machine to his grief. However, we do not need to attack one another while we sort through this latest trip, now do we?" Mr. Brewster said, trying to keep the kids from fighting while he sorted this all out.

"We need to tell Ken. He needs to know about this," Mary said.

"We will tell Ken this weekend," Mr. Brewster confirmed.

Deb and Joe looked at each other and silently nodded, confirming they would have each other's backs when it was time to tell Ken.

"To be clear, in the original timeline you all understood, I was a caretaker here, and not a teacher. Is that right?"

"Yes, Mr. Brewster. You had lost your wife to a car accident in Las Vegas in 1958 when you were finishing up testing with the NTS. She was driving home after dropping off a fellow teacher, Miss Halloway, when she was hit head on. She had a miscarriage in October 1957 right after you all arrived in Las Vegas, and after she died, you became so despondent. You started drinking and your friends in Las Vegas couldn't save you. You wandered around the country for a couple of years and ended up here. Your wife was buried close to Wallingford because her family was here. They found you in the cemetery looking for her grave by a reverend, and he got you this caretaker job," Deb said, trying to fill in details of their past.

"That sounds pretty grim. And likely, what would have happened had I lost her like that?"

"That's why we used the machine, Mr. Brewster. We wanted to improve your life, and we knew the only way to do that was to stop that accident, even if it meant she was only going to be with you for a little while longer," Joe added.

"We knew we were taking a risk. Especially after the attempt to save our parents and Joe's impulsive trip last spring," Deb added.

"It seems to have worked out better this time, however," Mr. Brewster pondered.

"What do you mean?" Mary asked.

"Well, to start with, I am a teacher here, not a caretaker. I taught at Amherst College when we moved back here after we completed the testing. We have a son; his name is Thomas. He is in college and will probably be done with his bachelor's degree this spring. He is training to be a doctor. Wants to concentrate on cancer treatment, since his mother died of cancer."

"When did she die?" Mary asked.

"In the winter of 1969."

"I'm so sorry," Mary said.

"I am too. I miss her every day, but I had many good years with her, and she was a wonderful mother to Tommy, and we were happy."

"What is Tommy like?" Kim asked.

"He is thoughtful like Deb, and insightful, like you, and smart like Joe and caring and a born leader like Ken. I am so proud of him."

"He sounds wonderful," Kim said.

"Mr. Brewster, you aren't angry at us for meddling in your past, are you?" Deb asked.

"No, I'm not angry. As I think this through, I should thank you all. You gave me my will to live back, my wife back, and I have a son.

The only reason I have all this is because you all came into my life and because of the trip you made Friday night."

"And all we did was talk to Mrs. Brewster about books and Las Vegas and stuff. Then Miss Halloway came into the room and said she needed to go early to the retirement dinner to set up and she would arrange a ride with someone else. Said that the other teacher had said he would take her home too; I think she might have wanted to do that, anyway. She mentioned something about wanting to learn about the new single male teacher," Kim said.

"Barely anything," Ryan added.

"Maybe that's why it worked," Joe thought out loud.

They all sat with their own thoughts for a moment when Mr. Brewster looked up and said, "So, where is the machine? When I went to the barn on Sunday evening, I was so worried about what happened. I was expecting one of you to talk to me Monday and when no one did, I was getting worried. Then I got the letter."

"When we came back from 1958, we landed the machine in the old landscaping shed at the other end of campus because we weren't sure if the barn was still going to be yours when we got back. We didn't want to land it there and cause any trouble," Joe replied.

"Pretty smart of you to plan for what you would come back to," Mr. Brewster reflected.

"How will you get the machine back to the barn now, though?" Mary asked.

"We're going to have to start it up and move it back there," Joe answered.

"Let's address that later this weekend," Mr. Brewster said, "after we talk to Ken."

"Are we ok then, Mr. Brewster?" Deb asked.

"Yes, we're ok. Why don't the six of you head back to your dorms and go on with your evenings? I will check in with you, Joe, tomorrow," Mr. Brewster said.

The six of them all got up and walked out of his office and out of the building. When they got outside, Mary continued her tirade.

"How could you have agreed to do this after everything we talked about last spring and all this summer? And how could you have done this when I was gone and not told me so I could talk you out of it?" she asked as she stood in front of Deb.

"Mary, I think you might want to let me explain some things to you."

"I don't know how I can trust you now."

Deb looked at Ryan, who understood she needed help. Ryan said to the others, "Why don't we head back and everyone work on homework until dinner. We'll all meet at the girls' dorm to walk over around 4:45. Is that ok?"

Deb agreed, and she and Mary walked a short way over to a bench and sat down. Deb started, "Mary, I'm sorry you feel this way. Let me explain."

"Why Deb? Why, after all our talks, me taking you to the reverend, why did you agree to do this? I thought you understood that God's plan should not be messed with and this machine was wrong from the beginning."

"Listen, I know we talked, and you got to express your point of view and I listened. But you apparently never listened to me!"

"I listened, but I thought you understood!"

"Do you hear yourself? Like your way, and your feelings are the only thing that is important here? You are my friend Mary, but you do not get to tell me how to feel, or how to act. And just because you are with my brother, it does not mean you have any say over me!"

"You spend a little bit of time with Joe and now you're on his side."

"This is not about sides. It's about how he and I, and even Ken, are processing the loss of our parents, which, by the way, you have no way of ever understanding, as your parents are alive and well. And how each of us is resolving that loss with our faith. Into all of that, this discovery happened and we are trying to figure out that, too."

"Then what changed?"

"I changed. I saw Mr. Brewster, and he was so heartbroken, and I just knew I had to help him. This wasn't Joe; it was my idea."

"Then why not tell me, unless you were sure what you were doing was wrong, and you didn't want Ken to find out?"

"I didn't tell you because I knew there were risks and I at least listened to you and understood your position. I knew you didn't want any of us to use the machine. We have failed now twice to save our parents, and I still wonder about trying to change history. But I had to do this. I knew I would only save her for a little while; I knew God was going to take her when He was going to take her. We were just hoping that the accident wasn't really meant for her, and if I gave her another chance, I could help Mr. Brewster. You see, I hoped that God's plan really wasn't for Mrs. Brewster; it was for the man that was going to hit her. She just got in the way."

"You purposely planned this for the weekend I was at Ken's, didn't you?"

"It's true. We knew Ken had told us not to use the machine, and once I convinced Ryan that we had to try this, we knew telling Ken would mean he would try to stop us. Telling you would be telling Ken. I'm sorry, Mary. I don't want to lose you as a friend, but you have acted pretty badly today, too."

"How?"

"Well, this business about how you told us already like you are in charge, and your way is the only way. If I learned one thing from talking to you and to the reverend, it is that everyone has to reach their faith on their own. You can't force it. And you are definitely trying to force your faith on all of us today."

"No, I'm not."

"Oh yes, you are."

"I'm so angry, I can't see straight!"

"I know you are. And you have every right to be angry about me keeping this from you. I just didn't know any other way."

"If you had asked, I would have kept your secret."

"Really? From Ken? You don't believe that, do you? You don't expect me to believe that?"

"Ok, I probably would have told him, and he would have rushed back here."

"And it would have already been done. We were only gone for six hours."

"And that is supposed to make this alright? That you weren't gone long?"

"No, I'm just saying that you would have found us already back."

"I suppose you want me to wait to tell him until this weekend?"

"I would prefer to do that in person. And like you just said, you'd keep my secret, right?"

"I don't know if I can deal with you right now at all."

"I'm trying to meet you halfway. You haven't even done that. You still think it has to be your way."

Mary stood up and walked away. She turned and said, "I need some time to think this through."

Deb let her walk away and sat there for a few minutes. She bent her head and cried. Then she got up and decided that she was pretty mad at Mary, and she stalked back to the girls' dorm. She went directly to the phone booth and called Ken.

"Hi."

"Hey little sister, what's up?"

"I need to talk to you. Is this a good time?"

"You sound very upset. What's going on? Are Kim and Joe ok?"

"Yeah, they're both fine."

"Is something going on with Ryan?"

"No, he's fine too."

"Then what's wrong? You are kinda scaring me now."

"Promise me you won't go off the deep end?"

"I will do my best."

"So, we wanted to wait until this weekend, but Mary is pretty upset, and I'm really upset, and I'm sure it can't wait that long. A couple of weeks ago, I found Mr. Brewster returning from the cemetery and he was really upset. I went with him to his house and he told me all about the testing in Las Vegas and his wife. Remember me telling you about that? Anyway, after talking to Ryan and Joe, we decided to try to help him, and we took the machine to Las Vegas and kept his wife from being in a car accident."

"You what?! After I told you that no one was to use that machine again?"

"I know, Ken, but please listen to me. It wasn't about our parents; it was to help someone else. And you won't believe what happened. We did it! She didn't die and they have a son, and he is a teacher and he is so much happier."

"Of course, Mr. Brewster is a teacher. I had him for physics last year."

"I know you don't remember, but in our original timeline, Mr. Brewster was just a caretaker here."

There was silence on the phone for a few minutes.

"Are you mad?"

"I'm trying not to be."

"I'm sorry we didn't tell you."

"Is Mrs. Brewster still alive?"

"No, she died in 1969 from cancer, but she was a teacher and a wonderful mother, and their son is trying to be a doctor to help cancer patients."

"Why is Mary upset?"

"Well, because we didn't tell her, because we knew she would tell you. What I didn't know was how mad she was going to be. Today, she yelled at me. She said that she thought I understood from our talks that this was wrong. It was like we had to believe what she believes and do it her way. It made me very mad, too."

"What do you mean?"

"I don't know. She said things like 'I thought you understood,' and stuff."

"Yes, presented that way, I can see how it would make you mad. Are you sure she said that? That exact thing you had to believe as she did and do it her way?"

"Yes. You know she feels strongly about her faith, and has always thought our trips in the machine were wrong, well now it's not just about that, it's about the fact that she thinks we did something we shouldn't and that we kept it from her just because she disagrees with us."

"Yeah, she has been a little pushy with me too about her faith. I've always managed to pass it off, though."

"Well, I'm sure you're going to hear from her, and I wanted you to hear my side before you were so mad you couldn't listen."

"Is that what you're worried about? That I wouldn't believe you, or listen to your side?"

"Yeah."

"Listen, I love Mary, and she's important to me, but you're my sister. I may not like what you did, and I may be angry at the way you did this, but I will always be here for you. You believe that, don't you? Haven't we learned at least that much over the past year?"

"I don't know. I figured you loved Mary more."

"Oh Deb."

"I'm sorry, but I have to go. We're meeting for dinner, and I don't want to be late."

"I get it. I'm going to think about this more and may call you later. Is that ok?"

"Sure. Sorry about making you mad."

"It's alright. I'm trying to keep an open mind."

"Thanks. Bye."

Deb walked alone over to the dining hall and met Kim and her friends Rebecca and Amy; Joe, Becky and Ryan were already there. Kim mentioned Mary had already gone in with some other girls, so they went in and sat down. After the reverend finished prayers and the announcements were read, Ryan leaned over and asked Deb what was wrong. She shook her head to show that nothing was wrong, but he persisted, "I know something is bothering you, and you've been crying, sweetheart. Tell me what it is."

"Things got pretty heated with Mary after you all left, and I'm still upset about it. Can we talk about this later?"

"Yeah, if that's what you want."

They all finished eating, and Kim and the girls went off to a Girl Scout meeting. Joe and Becky went to the main hall to meet friends for group projects and Deb and Ryan left for a walk.

"Are you ready to tell me?"

"She was so mean. She just kept coming at me with the business about how she thought I understood and had agreed with her that God's plan could not and should not be messed with. It made me so mad, like it was all her beliefs and her way!"

"I know. It surprised me at her reaction in the office, and then when we got outside. I know she feels very strongly about her faith, but I don't get why she doesn't respect how anyone else feels."

"She is so sure she's right, and the rest of us have to agree with her. I don't know. Did we make a huge mistake by doing this?"

"I was worried about that too, but look at how this turned out. Look at Mr. Brewster; he's a teacher and happier, and has a son and you heard him. He said it seems to have helped him."

"Yeah, but he doesn't even remember how he was in our timeline. He doesn't really have anything to compare it to, does he?"

"Well, not really. But we do."

"She said some mean things too, and it seemed like she was trying to tell me she wasn't sure we could be friends anymore. She thinks we lied to her, and did it on purpose so Ken wouldn't find out. I guess she's right. We kept this from her. I just knew she would fight us and tell us we were violating some rule of faith. She never really wanted us to use the machine. I think she just went along because Ken said it was ok. Now that he has concerns, she feels like she can rule over all of us."

"I'm so sorry, babe. Is that why you were crying?"

"Yeah, that, and I called Ken."

"You did?"

"Yeah. I told him what we did. I explained how angry Mary got, and how I was worried he would believe her only and not listen. I didn't want it to be about sides, but I was afraid he would be mad at us."

"And what did he say?"

"He said he was trying to keep an open mind, and he had seen Mary's pushy side about faith. That was always Ken's biggest argument for the machine. He didn't agree with the greater plan thing. It was the one thing they had issues about."

"Yeah, I know losing your parents has really tested his beliefs."

"I guess she was kinda pushy with him, too."

"Did he say that?"

"Not specifically, but kind of. Then he tried to reassure me he would always support me, even if he didn't agree with what I did, and he agreed to wait to discuss this all further when he gets here this weekend. But I'm sure Mary is going to call him."

"Well, at least you got to present your side, and hopefully he will keep that open mind."

"Yeah."

"Feeling any better?"

"A little. Let's go to the main hall and work on homework together. Is that ok?"

"Sure, I don't mind what we're doing, as long as I get to be with you."

"Thanks, you really helped."

"That's what I'm here for, baby."

They laughed and walked back to campus, got their books, and went to the main hall. Joe saw them and could tell Deb had been upset, but said nothing. He was kind of deep in thought himself about their trip in the machine. He wanted to sort it out before he talked to his sister.

9

The next day, Mr. Brewster found Joe as he was leaving the science and math building just before lunch. He asked Joe if he would walk to the dining hall with him, and they started in that direction. They talked about the machine, a plan to get it back to the barn, and what they did with the last trip. Joe talked to Mr. Brewster about why this trip seemed to work when the others failed, and he presented his theories. Mr. Brewster also said that he had decided he was glad that the kids had tried to help him the way they did, and he would not dwell on what had been, or what might happen now. He was going to count his blessings from his life and move on. Joe agreed that seemed the best way to deal with it. He was glad Mr. Brewster was still a part of what they were doing, and he told him so. Mr. Brewster said he was glad as well.

Meanwhile, Deb was wondering why she hadn't heard from Ken again last night, as he said he was going to call. She realized just after lunch why she hadn't heard from him. Mary confronted her coming down the stairs in the girls' dorm.

"So, you went and told Ken all about what you did, I see."

"What do you mean, Mary?"

"I talked to Kenny last night, and he told me he already knew about your little secret."

"Yeah, I called him yesterday afternoon after you and I fought. I was upset and needed my brother. What of it?"

"You did that on purpose to get him on your side!"

"No Mary, that's not what I did. You were right, and I was upset and wanted him to know because I knew we were wrong for not telling him and you. I apologized to him and I want to apologize to you as well for that. However, I do not apologize for going on the trip, and what we did. That will probably make you mad, and I'm sorry if you don't agree with it, and I'm really sorry if that means we can't be friends, but you will not tell me how to feel and what to do!"

Deb stalked off to class before Mary could say anything else. Luckily, they didn't have many classes together this semester, so she didn't have to see Mary again until dinner. Mary again sat with other girls, and ignored Deb and the others. Even Joe commented she was going a little overboard at this point, but there didn't seem to be anything any of them could do. Maybe Ken arriving the next day would help.

Ken arrived on campus after driving to town and checking into the hotel. He first went in search of Joe, as he knew Joe got out of class first on Thursday afternoons. He found him just as he got to the boys' dorm, and the two hugged and entered Joe's room. They talked for about an hour. They went over what Joe said to Deb earlier in the year, and how he promised to never take the machine alone again, and they talked about this latest trip. He said he understood why they wanted to help Mr. Brewster, and he was really glad it worked out the way it did. Ken remembered nothing about their original timeline with Mr. Brewster, so he asked Joe a lot of questions about that and agreed by the end of the hour that this trip might have been a success while the others had failed. He said if Mr. Brewster was as happy as Joe said he was, then maybe he had been premature to say they should never again use the machine. They talked about Joe's theories about why this trip worked and the others didn't. Ken agreed that the likely reason was that this was a tiny, simple change and not a dramatic one, like Dallas, but neither of them had a good theory why Joe's trip home, which was a simple change, was not a success.

The two found Ryan as they left Joe's room, and the three of them walked over to the girls' dorm. On the way, Ryan told Ken that Mary and Deb weren't talking, and Deb was pretty upset still. Ken said Mary was upset too, and he was hoping to help them patch things up. Kim, who spotted them first, jumped into Ken's arms. Ken lifted her up and declared that she had grown at least two inches since last he saw her, and they both laughed and laughed. Kim went and got Deb and Ryan said he had plans to play some hockey, so he left after Deb arrived. Then Ken said he wanted to take them all for a ride. They left and went into town to the burger place and ate an early dinner. Once they all had food, Ken figured it was a good time to get it all out on the table.

"Ok, I was more than a little angry when I first heard about what you three did. I'll admit it."

"We weren't trying to make you mad. We just wanted to help Mr. Brewster," Kim said pleadingly.

"I know you were just trying to help."

"We changed things for the better for Mr. Brewster, Ken," Joe said.

"Yes, it appears you did."

"So, what are you mad at?" Deb asked.

"I'm angry that you didn't tell me. I'm angry that you didn't include me in the decision process. Remember earlier this summer, Deb, when you were mad at Joe for the same reason?"

"We didn't tell you because you were adamant that we were not to use the machine again," Deb said.

"Does that make this ok? Did it make it ok for you when Joe kind of did it for the same reason? And how do you know I wouldn't have changed my mind? You didn't even give me a chance."

"No, you're right."

"I don't know, Ken; you were more than just saying that we shouldn't use the machine again. It was pretty forceful. You remember, you said 'do you hear me?'" Joe said.

"I know. That's what I said. And maybe I was wrong about that."

"You think you were wrong?" Joe asked.

"Yeah. I might have been wrong. Look at what you did. You saved Mrs. Brewster from that car accident, she taught, they had a child and

Mr. Brewster is a teacher now, not a caretaker. It sounds like you did a good thing. Maybe my order to not use the machine was more about us not seeming to be able to accomplish what we wanted to, rather than about what was right for us and the machine."

"Like, maybe because we changed something very small, and it was to help someone else, it's ok?" Kim asked.

"Yeah, maybe that's why it worked out on this trip and didn't on the two other trips when we were trying to change something big and save our parents."

Deb added, "Perhaps it's a combination of this, and the fact that the accident Mrs. Brewster had been in wasn't her time to die. Remember, the other driver left a note and wanted to take his life? Our visit took her out of that situation that she was merely a casualty of?"

"That would make both you and Mary right, wouldn't it?" Kim asked.

"Sounds like it," Ken added.

"Mr. Brewster would like us all to come over Saturday morning before we have to get ready for the dance and talk about things. Is that alright with you?" Joe asked.

"Yeah, I think that's a great idea. But first we have to fix things with Mary."

"I don't know how you're going to do that. She's really mad, and not talking to any of us," Joe said.

"Well, she and I have talked every day this week, and she has this idea that our using the machine is messing with God's plan and we need to stop. I need to convince her to be more open-minded about it, or at least to remind her that ditching her friends, even when they do something you don't agree with, is not cool," Ken said.

"Good luck with that," Joe said.

They all went back to campus and Ken asked for Mary at the girls' dorm front desk. She came down and saw Ken there with Deb, Joe and Kim, and wasn't sure what was going on. As she approached, Joe said he was leaving to finish homework and both Deb and Kim left as well.

Ken and Mary walked out of the dorm and toward Ken's car. Mary was silent and hadn't even greeted Ken. He was worried he would not be able to fix this, but said, "You're quiet. And no hug or anything. What's up?"

"I didn't realize you were already here. You wanted to see your sisters and brother before me."

"Oh, Mary, please understand. I have a responsibility to them. I needed to make sure they knew I was not mad at what they did."

"Not mad at what they did? They lied to you and to me."

"They didn't lie; they withheld."

"Same thing."

"Perhaps. But I have learned something this week about being the oldest, and being kind of like their parent. You have to stand by the people you love, even when they do things that make you angry and that you think are wrong. You have to forgive them when they make mistakes and respect how they feel."

Mary was stunned by Ken's words. She got into the car. He walked around and got into the driver's seat and they drove off campus. After a few minutes, Ken pulled into the town square and parked the car. He turned and said, "Nothing more to say?"

"What you said hit me. It hit me harder than anything we talked about this week or anything that Deb and I said to each other. Have I been wrong?"

"Mary, you get to feel how you feel. You get to believe what you want to believe. But you have to let me and Deb and the others feel and believe how we want to as well. You should not expect us to believe like you, just like you don't have to believe like us."

"I just feel like I need to help you see the truth about how there is a plan, and God is taking care of you and your sisters and brother."

"I know that's how you feel, but Mary, I'm not there yet. I'm still dealing with the loss of my parents; with the new situation my family finds itself in. This machine didn't create these questions. The questions were there; the machine is just giving a unique voice to them."

"If I don't talk to you, how can I help you get there?"

"I have to ask, Mary, what if I never get there? What if I never believe what you believe? What if I always believe from now 'til the end of time, that although there might have been a plan for my life, set by God, my choices, and my path is mine to direct? Is that going to come between us?"

Mary sat there, thinking for a long time. Ken started to worry that her answer was going to be the end of their relationship. This had him in a panic. Finally, she answered, "Ken, I know we're not the same people and that your life has differed from mine. But shouldn't we agree on some basic things if we are going to spend our lives together?"

"Yes, I know we have to agree on some things. But I thought we did."

"Well, we've talked about where we want to live, and what we want to do with our lives, and about kids and family. Is this faith question going to be something we need to agree on?"

"It doesn't feel like it to me. Does it to you?"

"I don't know. I don't want it to."

"I don't want to lose you."

"Me either. I feel like it must be what you said about forgiveness. Acceptance and forgiveness."

"Can you have some patience with me and the fact that life has made me question my faith?"

"I want to. I'll try."

They hugged and talked some more, and then Ken drove Mary back to campus. He talked for a minute with Kim about plans for Friday and then he found Deb. He asked if she would walk over to the boys' dorm with him so he could talk to Joe and Ryan. They talked on the way about what he said to Mary, and Ken encouraged Deb to try the forgiveness route with Mary. He asked that she reach out to her tomorrow. She said she would think about it and left him to talk with Joe and Ryan. He explained the same things to them, and then said goodnight. He headed back to his hotel so he could finish his homework.

Later that night, Mary knocked on Deb's door. When Deb answered, Mary stood there for a minute and then stepped inside. She turned and looked at Deb and said, "I'm sorry for the things I said to you earlier this week. It was wrong of me to expect you to believe what I believe and for me to say what you did was wrong."

"I'm sorry too. You are my best friend. What you think matters to me, and I do care about what you feel and believe."

"I know. You just need space to feel how you want and believe what you want."

"Yeah."

They sat down and Mary asked Deb to start at the beginning and explain everything. Deb started with her talk with Joe, where he promised to never get in the machine alone again, and how they had talked about what they had learned from the previous trips. She told her about seeing Mr. Brewster and the time they spent at his kitchen table and all they talked about. When she got to the end, Mary said, "I can see now why you wanted to do this. I can see it all clearly. It was so kind of you to want to help him. And I have to admit, this time it worked. You made his life so much better."

"Yeah. That's strange, isn't it? We tried twice to bring our parents back and couldn't do it, and this time it worked. What do you think that means?"

"I don't know."

"I've been thinking that it must be that the accident wasn't really Mrs. Brewster's time to be called to heaven. She was maybe collateral damage, and we saved her. I have read over newspaper reports. There was still an accident on that street that night. But the man that hit her originally ran into a hotel or casino sign."

"Maybe you're right. Maybe that makes it all make sense. It really wasn't her time, so you could bring her back, and it was your parents' time, so you can't fix that."

"It's making it easier to think of it that way, anyway."

"I'm so sorry. I hadn't even thought that doing this for Mr. Brewster and being successful would bring up so much of the hurt over your parents. How is Joe taking all of this?"

"He seems to be off somewhere in thought. Or maybe it's just young love with Becky."

They laughed and hugged and decided all was forgiven.

On Friday, Mr. Reynolds and Aunt Alicia surprised everyone by arriving with a large van filled with dresses. Aunt Alicia was beside herself to help all of Deb's friends find a perfect designer dress for the dance. The girls were in absolute heaven, and while all that was going on, Mr. Reynolds took Joe and Ryan out for dinner and to play pool at the bowling alley. Ken had told them about his plans to take Kim and her friends on a big night out, so everyone was off having fun. With all the dresses picked out and ready to go for Deb, Mary, Becky and several of the other girls, Aunt Alicia took the girls to dinner since the boys were all out. Later that night, after dropping all the kids off at campus, Mr. Reynolds and Aunt Alicia went to the hotel. They were going to stay to take pictures of the dance preparation before leaving to go back to New York.

After Ken had taken the girls out for breakfast in the morning, he brought them all back to campus. He was exhausted, but he knew the girls all had a wonderful time. Not wanting to stir things up further, he checked in with Mary and then Deb and discovered that they had patched things up the night before, so he was happy, but tired. Ken then went to confirm with the boys about the dance that night and left again; he told them all to get some rest and get cleaned up for the dance. The boys were all meeting in front of the boys' dorm and then going over to get the girls. Mr. Reynolds and Aunt Alicia went to the girls' dorm around three in the afternoon to take pictures of the girls in all their dresses. Kim left shortly after they were done taking pictures to join the other younger kids for pizza dinner and movies in the main hall.

The boys arrived, and more pictures were taken before Mr. Reynolds and Aunt Alicia left to go back to New York City. They all walked over to the gymnasium for the dance and everyone had a wonderful time. Ryan was so glad that Mary and Deb had figured things out and were trying to get along, but he was certain there was still a strain. At some point, he told Ken about his concerns, and Ken said he would talk to Mary later. At the end of the dance, Ryan took Deb outside and told her he wanted to have a few minutes alone. He asked if she was really ok, and she said she still felt distant from Mary, but hoped it would improve. Ryan agreed. It looked somewhat strained and said he hoped they could all get back to where they were again soon.

The next day, after church services, Ken prepared to head back to Harvard. He spent a few minutes with each of his siblings, re-affirming that he was thinking over the use of the machine, but encouraged Joe to proceed with preparing it for public release. He told Kim how much he enjoyed treating her and her friends and Kim said he was the best brother ever for what he did that weekend and for her birthday. Deb told Ken she was glad he was no longer angry, and they talked about the parenting roles they had encountered lately, and how to manage that with each other, and Joe and Kim. Then Ken said goodbye to Mary. He had midterms in two weeks and said he was going to be very busy so he would not see her or his siblings for three weeks. It disappointed Mary, but she had plans with her parents the next weekend, so she was going to be gone, anyway.

Classes progressed that next week, and Mary left for the weekend with her parents. Joe spent the next Saturday with Mr. Brewster, going over his new computer language and how to utilize it for the machine. They had yet to get it back to the barn, and they did it that day. Joe got in it at the shed and programmed it for the barn at the same time. They used this to test a theory that you could not return the machine to the exact time it left, but surprisingly, that worked. With further calculations, they determined the reason for the same time trip had to be because of the short time of the trip. They documented that test and then Joe sat in the barn most of the day working on reprogramming the machine with his new language.

Deb and Ryan located Joe at the barn, and asked if he wanted to go to town to eat dinner at the Burgers and Shakes, their regular spot, with them and he agreed, as he had become a little blurry-eyed with the programming. He told Deb and Ryan all about what he was doing and although Ryan was interested, Deb hadn't the foggiest idea what they were talking about.

"So, tell me again how this language differs from the, what did you call it, COBAL?" Ryan asked Joe.

"COBOL is really the first higher language for programming. This means it allowed English language and not operate solely in machine language or the translation of a language into machine language. It uses certain words to act as action words for the program to start a process. Because of this, those words are locked and cannot be used for anything else. It's also a very heavy language, because it takes a lot of lines to do simple tasks because of those locked words. However, it is very stable and can deal with administrative tasks and numbers with high accuracy," Joe explained.

What's your language going to do to improve this?" Ryan asked.

"First, it will not have all those locked words. It's a procedural language so it will do many small processes quickly, and second, it's going to work on a smaller computer that can fit on a desk and not take up half of a room. This will allow individuals to have computers to do things other than games and simple typing documents," Joe explained.

"Like each person would have a computer? That would be totally cool. But what would we do with it?" Ryan said excitedly.

"Well, you could do your homework on it, or manage your bank accounts or input an enormous set of numbers and do all kinds of calculations and analysis," Joe thought out loud.

"That would be totally cool," Ryan said, even more excited now.

"That's what I am hoping for," Joe said.

"So, what are your plans to get this out there? I mean, are you going to pitch it to that partner of your father's, or are you going to do something with Harvard or what?" Ryan asked more seriously.

"I haven't decided. I'm going to use the new language to streamline the machine and test it there, and then write up a paper and talk to Mr. Davis," Joe pondered.

At that, Deb looked up and said, "What do you mean reprogram the machine and test it? Test it how?"

"Don't have a fit, Deb. I'm not talking about travelling alone. I want you all to participate," Joe said, holding his hands up.

That seemed to calm Deb down and they continued to talk for a while and then went to see what was going on in the main hall where activities were going on.

On Sunday, Ryan went with Joe to the barn and talked with Mr. Brewster while Joe worked more on the programming. It would take Joe a while to complete this new program, which he announced while they were all at the bowling alley three weeks later, with Ken after his midterm exams. Ken was very excited about what Joe told him, and he said he wanted to talk to Mr. Davis about this and get Joe in touch with Mr. Davis. Joe said they had already been communicating via mail for a while now. Deb watched all of this and thought it was one of those parenting kind of moments and hoped Ken would understand that Joe was ready to do this on his own.

It seemed like it was nearly Thanksgiving break in no time. They all prepared to go home for the few days off, which meant they were going to the Hamptons. It was strange that they had all thought of that place as home. When it was time to go, Michael picked up Deb, Joe and Kim and they loaded their things into the car, while saying goodbye to friends and Ryan and Becky. Ken had arrived earlier as Harvard was off the entire week of Thanksgiving, but the others only had Wednesday through the weekend off. It thrilled Ken to see his siblings and was ready to spend some time with them. They spent Thursday on the beach and playing games. Mr. Reynolds had planned a more traditional Thanksgiving this year, which included them all sitting together for the meal. Aunt Alicia even sat with them as they again watched movies after dinner.

Friday, Ken and Joe went into the city to meet with Mr. Davis. After Joe had corresponded back and forth regarding his new programming language, Mr. Davis had asked if they could get together over this break from school. When Joe and Ken arrived at the offices, Joe commented they were bigger than he remembered. Mr. Davis greeted them in front of their father's old office and took them inside.

"Joe, I've been looking forward to hearing more about this language, and working with you both to get this launched, but first, tell me how you and your sisters are doing this year at school," Mr. Davis said as they sat down.

"Mr. Davis, we're all doing pretty well. Kim is growing up fast and Deb has already applied to schools. How was your Thanksgiving, sir?" Joe replied.

"We had a lovely time yesterday. Thank you for asking. I am glad your sisters are doing so well. It's hard to believe that Ken is already in college and Deb is about to be."

"I'm nearly halfway through my first year at Harvard. Time is certainly whizzing by," Ken said.

"Indeed, it is, and seems to move faster each day. Well, how about we get down to business so you two can get back to your vacation?"

"Well, this new language really is what I would call an improvement on COBOL. It is a plain English language without the restricted words of COBOL, but also is a fresh approach utilizing subroutines that contain the executable parts of the program and statements to change the program's state. I think it is will be leaner than COBOL because of this, and with more flexibility, which will allow it to personalize the computer usage," Joe explained.

"It's this idea that intrigues me the most. What do you mean by personalizing the computer usage?" Mr. Davis asked.

"The flexibility and the ability of the statements and routines to do so much will allow it to operate as a document manager, like a typewriter, like an accounting book, and probably so many other things. If it can do all of those things, it will be valuable to individuals at work and at home. That is how it gets more personal. Computers won't just be for big companies and the government and schools; they will be for everyone."

"That would mean households and elementary schools and any kind of business would need a computer, wouldn't it?" Mr. Davis asked.

"Yes."

"That's the idea I was telling you about, Mr. Davis, when I first contacted you about Joe's project. We could build and market personal computers," Ken said.

"What each computer would need is an operating system, something at its core that allowed programs to run and managed. Then there could be programs that specialized in different functions, like for documents or for accounting books," Joe explained.

"What we will need to determine is the specifications of these personal computers, what engineering they would require, and then how to package both the computers and these programs," Mr. Davis mused out loud.

"I have some testing to finish and then we need to determine a prototype for the first personal computer before we can get to the marketing efforts, I think," Joe said.

"What have you done toward this end, Joe? This seems like a sound approach to proving out your program language and determining the feasibility of the idea."

"I am nearly done with the language, I think. Then I will need to document it, run a few tests by setting up a program and then we should think about loading it onto a currently available computer and then possibility cutting down the size of that computer and re-testing each time."

"I also think we need to understand what the power requirements and space requirements will be. Joe, how can we do that?" Ken asked.

"I think if we take apart a current computer and determine its parts and then start to either make them smaller in size or find alternatives that are smaller to provide the power and storage of data, that might be the best place to start," Joe answered.

"Joe, do you still have contacts at the Harvard lab? Perhaps they would assist on some of this," Ken said.

"I also have contacts at MIT. That is where we have done several partnerships in the past when we are working on design and prototyping," Mr. Davis added.

"Would it be ok if I took the lead in trying to contact Harvard first, and then if that doesn't work out, Mr. Davis, we can use your contacts," Joe said.

"That sounds fine. This is your project, Joe. How about if we talk again in a week to see what progress you have made?" Mr. Davis said.

"Thanks. I'm usually done with classes at about three-thirty. How about if I call you the week after we get back to school in the afternoon?"

"Any day, but Monday at that time would be fine."

"Great. Can we maybe look around and see the product room today before we go?" Joe asked.

"Sure. I can have someone show you around while I talk with Ken a bit."

Mr. Davis opened the door and asked someone to escort Joe to the product room. Joe left, and Mr. Davis and Ken sat down again.

"Ken, I have put together a plan for your summer internships. I have it here in the folder. Why don't you look at this for a minute and I will be right back?"

Ken took the folder and looked through the papers that had goals and departments, responsibilities, and mentors for each summer. He was just about finished looking them over when Mr. Davis returned. They talked over the plans and made a few adjustments, which Mr. Davis said he would document and then send a final copy to Ken at school next week. They then went out into the lobby for Ken to wait for Joe to return from the tour. When Joe got back, Ken and Joe said goodbye to Mr. Davis and left.

On Saturday, Mr. Reynolds decided it would be a good day to spend with Kim, so he took her down to the harbor and they went out on a small boat for most of the day. Kim talked about her parents and how things had changed, and Mr. Reynolds told Kim all about his childhood.

"Did you meet a lot of famous people?" Kim asked after Mr. Reynolds told her about her father being appointed to the mayor's office.

"Yes, I met many famous people. It would surprise you how many people want favors from those in politics. My meetings with these people were only in passing, however. No one really talked to the young kid standing near his father. Sometimes I felt like I was just there for the picture taking part of the events."

"That seems a little sad, Mr. Reynolds," Kim said.

"Well, it was nothing like what you all had with each other. I had no siblings."

"I like that part the best about my family. The fact that I have Joe, Ken and Deb to help me and do things with me makes me really happy. I don't think any of us would have survived losing our parents without having each other."

"I imagine that's true. I know there were many times when I wished I had a brother or sister."

"I bet there were some advantages to being an only child. My friend Rebecca is an only child and her parents give her so much. Sometimes it seems like they give her everything she asks for."

"Sometimes that isn't the best way to take care of someone."

"You're probably right. Do you miss your parents?"

"I miss my mother a lot. We were always very close. But she was a lot like your aunt in some ways. She liked to be where all the parties were and all the important people."

"I think it's so cool that Aunt Alicia gets to meet all those models and famous fashion people. It would be great to get to do that, but sometimes I like it out here, just with us. What about your dad?"

"Well, my father and I had a very hard time getting along once I was a teenager. He wanted me to be something I didn't want to be, and we fought about that all the time. I left as soon as I could and made my own way. We only mended those fences later, when he was very sick. I didn't really have enough time to fix things with him and spend more time with him, and that is what I regret. I don't think I miss him, but that is because I didn't really feel like I had him much in my life."

"Wow. I couldn't imagine my life without my mom and dad. Well, before last year."

"You're all very lucky, Kim. You had time with your parents and you have each other now."

"And we have you and Aunt Alicia now."

"Yes, you do. Now, how about some ice cream before we head back to the house?"

"Won't that spoil dinner?"

"Maybe, but every once in a while, you have to spoil a little dinner, don't you think?"

"I really like you, Mr. Reynolds. You're funny and you take good care of all of us."

"I really like you too."

They made their way back to the pier and went for ice cream before returning to the house. When they arrived home, they found Ken and Joe just returning. They all went in together and found Deb in the family room.

"Where is Ryan?" Mr. Reynolds asked.

"He had to get back to the city for a dinner with his parents," Deb replied.

"And how about your aunt?"

"She is upstairs on the phone, I think."

"I'll go check on her then."

"How was your day with Mr. Reynolds?" Deb asked Kim as she sat down.

"We had a lot of fun. We went out on a small boat and I got to see New York from out on the water. That was cool! And then we got some ice cream. What did you do?" Kim replied.

"Ryan and I went into town and I started my Christmas shopping and we got some lunch."

"What about your meeting, Joe?" Kim asked.

"It went pretty great. I'm writing a note to the professor at Harvard right now to see if I can work with someone there on the computer language and Mr. Davis is helping me get started on the personal computer ideas. That wasn't something I was thinking about doing, but both Ken and Mr. Davis think it's a great way to jump into the personal computing market and help the introduction of my language," Joe said excitedly.

"What is personal computing?" Kim asked.

"Well, it's a smaller version of a computer that you can have on your desk at home to do papers, balance your checking account, play games, probably all kinds of things."

"But we have typewriters for papers and practically everyone has a calculator. Why would we need another thing that does the same thing?"

"The thing about personal computers, Kim, is that's all-in-one place. You won't have to have a typewriter, calculator, game console for your TV, and all the other ideas that are going to be created from this one idea."

"Will it have Space Invaders?"

"I don't know what system Space Invaders were invented on, but I'm sure we can convert it."

"That would be cool."

Just then, Ken walked into the room and announced that Mary was coming over. She was taking the train, and he was leaving in a few minutes to go get her.

"Is she staying all weekend?" Kim asked.

"No, just tonight. She is going home later tomorrow afternoon to get ready to go back to school on Sunday."

"I think we should have a game night and get out all the old games."

"We can think about it."

Mr. Reynolds and Aunt Alicia came down the stairs carrying bags with them. The kids all looked at each other and just knew what was about to happen. Aunt Alicia came in and told them they had to get back to the city for a big fashion party. She said she would contact Deb as usual on Sunday evening at the dorms, and to enjoy the last night of break. They left and Ken left to get Mary. The cook came in and told them all that dinner would be in an hour and that they were having pizza since they had had left over Thanksgiving dinner for lunch today. That night, they played board games and had fun. Mary was still a little distant from Deb and Joe, but they had fun.

That Sunday, after they all returned to Choate and Ken was back at Harvard, Ryan and Deb were working on homework in the lobby of the girls' dorm, awaiting Aunt Alicia's call. When she called, she asked Deb what they should plan for Joe's birthday, which was about a week away. Deb told her that Joe had mentioned that he had been in contact with someone at Harvard regarding his computer ideas and they had asked that he come to see them the next weekend. Deb suggested they do something near Harvard so that Ken could join. Aunt Alicia said she would set up a dinner and would have Mr. Reynolds arrange for a car to pick them all up that Saturday morning and take them to Cambridge.

Later in the week, Deb called both Ken and Aunt Alicia. She called Ken to discuss the gift she wanted to get Joe, and he thought it was a great idea. He made some arrangements with the professor at Harvard that Joe had worked with for years and called Deb back to tell her he had it all arranged. When she called Aunt Alicia, it was to request that Mary, Ryan and Becky be allowed to come with them. It was the last Saturday before hockey season really started for Ryan, so it worked out that he could come along. Aunt Alicia said that was fine, so Deb invited them all to come with. Saturday morning, Michael arrived with the limousine and they all departed for Cambridge to meet Ken for the celebration. Ken and Deb had pulled together several boxes of computer parts. That is what they were giving Joe for his birthday. They thrilled Joe with it. Ryan gave him several books he had spoken about over the past couple of months, and Mary gave him some games. Aunt Alicia and Mr. Reynolds gave him new clothes. Joe was very embarrassed when Becky said she was glad he finally had some decent clothes to wear. Becky said she was giving him his gift the next day when they were together. They had dinner at a steakhouse near Harvard and then Michael took the kids back to Choate. Mr. Reynolds and Aunt Alicia took all the computer parts back to the New York City apartment as that is where they were to spend Christmas break at.

On the way back to Choate, Deb asked Joe how his meeting with Harvard went.

"It was really great," Joe replied.

"Well, what did you discuss?" Deb asked.

"We talked about the language development and then we spent most of the time going over the next steps. I'm going to be providing them some information soon and they gave me someone at IBM to contact about tests that need to be conducted to verify the language."

"Did you tell them about your attempt to reprogram the machine to try it there?" Ryan asked.

"No."

"Why are you reprogramming the machine? I thought you were done with that," Mary said.

"Mary, we had to get it back to the barn, remember?" Joe said, trying to prevent her from getting too agitated.

"Oh."

"So, what are you going to use for your testing?" Ryan asked.

"Well, it seems I now have all the parts I need to build a computer of my own. I think I'll be using that."

"That will allow you to not have to discuss the machine, right?"

"Yeah, I hope so," Joe said.

10

A week later, Ryan and Deb were sitting in the main hall on Saturday afternoon after the hockey game, where Ryan had scored two goals and got hit with the puck and was now sporting a black eye. They were studying for finals, which were coming up in two weeks. Kim was sitting with her friends reading for their latest book report when Mr. Reynolds walked up to Deb and Ryan.

"Didn't mean to startle you. I was hoping to get the three of you together for a little meeting if I could," Mr. Reynolds said as Deb looked up and panicked a bit.

"Is everything ok? Is Kenny ok?"

"Yes, sorry, he's fine. Your aunt is fine. I just wanted to talk to you all."

"I'm not sure where Joe is right now, but Kim is over there with her friends."

"I actually found Joe at the boys' dorm. He was getting back from the library or something. He is waiting there for us."

"Oh, ok, let me get Kim."

Deb got up and went over to where Kim was and pointed back at Mr. Reynolds and told her he asked to meet with them, adding that nothing was wrong with Ken or Aunt Alicia before Kim could get worried. Kim began packing up her things.

While they waited for the girls, Ryan asked, "So what's up, Mr. Reynolds?"

"I'm sorry, Ryan. This isn't supposed to freak everyone out. I want to talk to the kids about what is going on with me and their aunt. It isn't anything more than that."

"Oh." He smiled and held out his hand. "Should I congratulate you?"

"Perhaps." As he laughed, he grasped Ryan's hand. "What happened to your eye?"

"Oh, just hockey. We had a game earlier today."

"Hope the other guy looks worse."

"I got hit with a puck that some dude slapshot down the ice. No big deal. Scored two goals and stuck it to them."

"At least you won the game. Put some ice on that, and maybe it won't look so terrible tomorrow."

"Thanks Mr. Reynolds, but it doesn't really hurt, and truth be told, I've learned something. If I have these injuries from hockey, Deb takes real good care of me!"

"Your secret's safe with me," Mr. Reynolds said conspiratorially.

Just then, Deb returned and started packing up her books and things. She looked up and asked if they needed to drop them off first.

Mr. Reynolds replied, "No, you can bring them along. This will not take a really long time."

Mr. Reynolds and the girls got into his car and they went to the boys' dorm to get Joe. Then they went into town to Burgers and Shakes. After they ordered and were sitting in a big corner booth, Mr. Reynolds said, "Let me start with the fact that I didn't mean to scare any of you today. It really didn't occur to me that someone appearing suddenly would be reminiscent of the notification of your parents. I just really wanted to have you all present when I asked your permission."

"Permission for what?" Kim asked.

"Well, you know I have been with your aunt for over a year now, and I have become very fond of all of you during that time. I'm ready to make a commitment to your aunt and doing that means I have to make a commitment to all of you. I want your permission to ask your aunt for her hand in marriage, and that would mean we would all become a family."

"Wow," Kim said.

"Deb and Joe, you both look a little freaked out. What are you thinking?"

Deb answered first, "Sorry, I was just letting this sink in, I guess. If you really love Aunt Alicia and want to marry her, I don't think we can stand in the way of that."

"What I was hoping for was that we would move on as a family together. I want you all to feel you have a family to count on, not just a place to spend your school breaks with an aunt that was told to care for you and her boyfriend."

"What exactly are you thinking we would be?" Joe asked.

"This isn't what I was expecting, Joe. Certainly this wasn't supposed to make you angry. I expected that we would be a family."

"What I was asking was, well, like, what are we supposed to call you now?" Joe asked to clarify what he was thinking.

"Oh, I see. Joe, I'm not trying to usurp your father's place. I would never do that to you. I have no plans to adopt any of you or anything like that. How does Uncle Darrick sound for what to call me now?"

"That would be ok, I guess," Joe said.

"Does Ken know about this yet?" Deb asked.

"He does. I spoke to him yesterday before I came out here."

"What does Aunt Alicia think you are doing? Does she know you are out here to see us?" Kim asked.

"I'll have to admit, now that it looks like we might become family, that I lied to your aunt. I told her I was working late last night and then had to spend some time with clients today."

"I think that's ok. I mean, you don't want to her to know you are doing this, right? How exciting that this is a secret for her," Kim said as she reasoned out the lying part with the exciting news.

"You will help me keep the secret, won't you, Kim?"

"Oh yeah! But when are you going to ask her?"

"I was planning to ask her on Christmas Eve. That was something my mother always wanted for me, to ask the woman I wanted to marry on Christmas Eve."

"It sounds like Kim is on board. What about you Joe?" Deb said.

"I think this would be ok. I mean, if you love her and want to be with her, I think it would be nice for Aunt Alicia to feel like she has a family. After what happened this summer with Ken, I think this will help her," Joe said.

"I think this is great. But I guess we can't call you Uncle Darrick until after you ask Aunt Alicia, can we?" Kim said.

"No, you're going to have to wait on that."

"Can we eat now?" Joe said, to lighten the mood.

They all laughed.

After Mr. Reynolds dropped them off, Deb called Ken.

"Ken, we just had a visit from Mr. Reynolds."

"Yeah, he was here yesterday. I was trying hard not to be mad at him since I have finals next week, but when he told me what he wanted, I totally stopped being angry."

"But weird, right?"

"Maybe. I kept wanting to ask him what he sees in her I don't, but held my tongue."

"Kenny! I thought you were done being mad at her after the big fight this past summer?"

"I am, but that doesn't change the fact that she has some crazy personality quirks. I mean, remember how she sat us at the table when we first went out to his house in the Hamptons? And she is always ready to jump for a party."

"Yeah, but I wonder if some of that is the fact that she never felt accepted in the family. Remember how she said she always felt she was invisible when she was growing up? I wonder if the parties and the attention validate her in some way."

"You're probably right. So, what did Kim and Joe have to say about being asked for their permission?"

"Kim was ready to jump right in. She is totally ready to just move on at this point. Joe got a little panicked at first. Mr. Reynolds framed it like we would all be a family now and I think Joe took it that Mr. Reynolds wanted to become 'dad.' When Mr. Reynolds explained it, Joe was ok."

"I figured he might have trouble with this. What was the verdict on what we were going to call him now?"

"Uncle Darrick."

"Sounds good."

"Well, listen, I know you have tests so good luck this week. Are you going out to the Hamptons as soon as you are done?"

"No, I'm coming out there for the weekend, then I am going into the city. Mr. Reynolds told me that is where they will be and I'm meeting with Mr. Davis and some other people at the firm. I will be back to get you all at the end of that week and bring us all back to the city. We're going to be there for break."

"Oh, that will be fun. Then I can see Ryan."

"I'm probably going to spend some time with Mr. Davis during break too, so being in the city will make that easier," Ken said.

"Great. Well, good luck on your tests and see you next week. I will let Kim and Joe know you are coming out. I suppose you will talk to Mary, so I don't need to tell her, right?"

"Yeah, I talk to her almost every day."

"She got upset on the way back here when we were talking about Joe reprogramming the machine."

"Yeah, I heard about that already."

"Oh."

"I'm trying, Deb. She is just very adamant about her beliefs. She is struggling with us not seeing it as she does."

"She's really distant with me still, too."

"Can I ask you to keep trying, Deb? For me? She means everything to me and I'm trying to help her as much as she's trying to help me."

"Yeah, I'll try, for you."

"Bye Sis."

"Bye."

Deb went down to the main hall, where Saturday night activities had already begun. She found Ryan talking with Joe and Becky, and Mary was there. Deb walked up and said she had called Ken. Mary looked at her expectantly, but Deb didn't elaborate.

"Did Ken think it was ok?" Ryan asked her.

"Yeah, he said he kept wanting to ask what Mr. Reynolds saw he didn't, but he kept quiet."

"Right!" Joe said, laughing.

"Did Ken say anything else?" Mary asked.

"Yeah, he's coming out here next weekend after he finishes finals and then will be back to get us all to go to the city the next week when we are done with our finals."

"Oh, yeah, he told me he was coming out too," Mary said.

Deb wondered what that was about, but she said nothing. Deb and Ryan and Kim walked off. Kim and her friends had entered a board game tournament, so Deb and Ryan took them over and watched as they got started. Then they left to go meet up with some friends for some dancing.

"What is going on between you and Mary now?" Ryan asked Deb during a break from dancing.

"I'm not sure. Clearly, she talks with Ken all the time, but she doesn't want to tell me anything about that. Yet, she seems to get angry when I talk to Ken and wants to know what we discuss. I don't want to cause trouble between them, and it's Ken's choice who he is with, but I thought she and I were better friends."

"She was very upset in the car too when we were talking about the machine."

"Yeah, she told Ken about it. He wasn't mad at us and he knew we had to get the machine back to the barn, but I thought Joe was not done programming it, so that couldn't have been the test."

"You know what? I really don't want to talk about Mary right now. I want to just be with my girlfriend."

"Sounds good to me," Deb answered with a smile.

11

Just before the end of the last week of classes at Choate, Mr. Brewster found Joe as he was walking out of the science building and asked him to stop by later that day at the barn. When Joe arrived around 3:30, Mr. Brewster was sitting at the worktable.

"What's up, Mr. Brewster?"

"Joe, I was looking over the new program and that error you mentioned last week, and I think I might have found the problem and even corrected it."

"Great."

The two looked over the printout that Mr. Brewster had laid out on the table and Joe agreed that the fix Mr. Brewster proposed would solve the problem, but he made one other minor adjustment in one subroutine of the program to accommodate the change Mr. Brewster made. Then they loaded it back into the machine and fired the systems up. All the pre-checks seemed to be fine.

"Now all we need to do is test it," Joe said.

"Listen, I'm going to do that test. I don't want anything to happen to you."

"I don't want anything to happen to you either," Joe said exaggeratedly.

"How about we move it from here to that shed you had it in before and then move it back right away?" Mr. Brewster proposed.

"That's a good idea. When do you want to do it?"

"How does this Saturday morning sound?"

"Ken is going to be here, but I bet he'll want to see this, too. I will call him and check, and then let you know tomorrow."

"Sounds good."

"Thanks. This really helped me. You sure figured out the language quick."

"You made that easy. This is a brilliant design for a programming language, Joe. You're going to revolutionize the computer industry. Think of what it will mean for scientific research. You will be able to store and analyze large amounts of data quickly. I can't wait to see what the applications of this will be."

"I never thought of that. Wow, another whole new way to use a personal computer."

"A personal computer?"

"Yeah, that is my other revolutionary idea. A personal computer. Small enough and affordable enough that anyone can own one and do all kinds of things on it."

"Which do you think will be bigger? The time travel or the computer?"

They both laughed.

After dinner, Joe called Ken and told him about the program change and the fact that they wanted to test it on Saturday. Ken was ecstatic about the use of Joe's new programming language, but was fearful of the test. They discussed it further and Ken said he would be there.

At the end of that week, Ken came to Choate for the day on Saturday. He had originally planned to be there the whole weekend, but ended up spending Thursday and Friday with some of his friends from Harvard. He went directly to the boys' dorm and found Joe, and then the two of them went to Mr. Brewster's.

"Hey Mr. Brewster!" Ken called as they got to the barn.

"Hey yourself! How was your first semester at Harvard?"

"It was great. I've met so many people, and the classes were good, tough, but good."

"And your finals this week?"

"I think I did ok. Find out in a week or so."

"I'm sure you did fine."

"So, another test, huh?"

"Yeah, we got the reprogramming all finished and corrected the last problem the other day. Mr. Brewster found it," Joe said.

"For some reason, I'm more worried about this test than anything else we have done. Seems weird, but that's how it is," Ken said.

"What? Ken, don't you trust my work?" Joe asked.

"No, it's not about that. It's just, you know, we had this thing working and I'm worried that something will happen. Joe, I don't want you jumping into the thing today. I'm not trying to be bossy, but I want nothing to happen to you, ok?"

"I have already told Joe that I'm doing the jumping today," Mr. Brewster interjected.

With that, the three of them looked over the settings for the trip and Joe completed putting all the coordinates into the machine. Mr. Brewster got in and turned the communications on. They talked about what the readings looked like and decided they were a go for the test. The machine started, the noise and wind started, and then, with a flash of light, the machine was gone. Then suddenly another flash of light before the wind even died down, and the machine was back.

Mr. Brewster shut the systems down and climbed out of the machine. Joe was jumping around, cheering that not only had the new program worked, but they had successfully moved the machine forward and back to the same location and time. He went into the machine and started the printout, and they all sat down at the table.

"Well Joe, now you have proved your programming language and that the machine can move forward and back. Great job, little brother!" Ken said, patting him on the back.

"Not only that, but we have moved the machine back to the same location and same time as it left, with no adverse impact to Mr. Brewster or us!" Joe exclaimed.

"Yes, the test went smoothly. We will have updated all the documentation we have prepared, Joe, and then you have some decisions to make," Mr. Brewster said.

"What decisions are those, Mr. Brewster?" Ken asked.

"Well, whether he's ready to announce his time travel ideas to the world, how much of it to release right now and how to do that. I have explained to Joe that before he can release any of this, we will need to submit several copyright requests to protect him and prepare some more documentation."

"Joe, what are you thinking?" Ken asked.

"I'm kind of thinking that I would prefer the machine not to be the focus of the new language as the driver for release. This needs to be independently tested and have some other people test it and release that separately. I'm also not sure if I want to release this as a tested time travel machine and theory or just the theory. Most importantly, I want the focus with the new language to be on the new personal computer, not the time machine."

"Lots to think about, but I agree on not linking the language and the machine or time travel. I've been wondering, with what happened to you on your solo trip, if we even should ever talk about the machine publicly," Ken said thoughtfully.

"Yeah, I'm hoping to have some time to really think it through over our break, and I've been thinking the same thing. There could be huge implications if governments or wealthy people or just more than a few people had access to a time machine," Joe said.

"Not just that, Joe," Ken reflected. "We did so much research and planning. If someone got into a machine and just traveled to somewhere else, without all that research, they would really mess things up."

"So, we will talk again after the Christmas break and get started accordingly and I agree with these concerns, but Joe, it's your invention, you should get to decide," Mr. Brewster said.

"Mr. Brewster, is your son coming here for the holiday, or are you going to his place?" Ken asked.

"He is coming here with his new serious girlfriend."

"Does he know about the machine and what we have done?" Joe asked.

"No, he has seen the machine here in the barn, but I have told him it's a project with one of my students for science class."

"Sorry about making you keep secrets from him," Joe said.

"You're going to find later in life, Joe, that parents don't tell their children everything. It's just not good parenting to be completely honest with your children. And besides, this is your find, your creation, and that makes it yours to release."

"You're like our Yoda, Mr. Brewster—wise and always ready to provide counsel." Ken laughed.

Mr. Brewster didn't appear to the understand Ken's reference to the Star Wars character, but Joe did and he laughed along. They finished closing the machine up and then Ken went to find Mary and Joe went to meet Becky at the library. When Ken got to the girls' dorm, Mary was in the lobby area with several other girls.

"Where have you been? Did you just get into town?" Mary asked.

"No, I met Joe first thing. We had something we had to take care of."

"Oh. Are you all done with him?"

"Yeah, just needed help with something related to his new programming language."

"Did you see Kim and Deb yet?"

"I kind of expected them to be here with you."

"Kim is in her room, writing a paper that is due on Monday, and I'm not sure where Deb is."

"Mary, are you and Deb getting along?"

"Yeah, sort of. It's hard though. I feel like we are in some sort of competition for your attention."

"Has Deb made you feel that way?"

"Not really. It just seems like since we had the issues with the machine this fall, she doesn't tell me when she calls you or if you sent her something."

"We better go somewhere and talk about this."

Ken led her outside, and they left for a drive, parking at the Wharton Brook State Park. They got out. It was snowing, and the area was quiet and peaceful. Ken waited for Mary to say something, and when she didn't, he said, "Mary, Deb has told me she senses a distance between the two of you since the argument you had over the machine. Do you feel that way, too?"

"Yeah."

"Where is this competition thing coming from?"

"Well, she won't tell me when she talks to you, and sometimes you only want to be with them and not me, and you don't include me and you see them first, like today."

"Mary, they are my younger siblings. I'm obligated to take care of them."

"They have your aunt, don't they? Isn't she their guardian?"

"I promised my father, and if that isn't enough, he asked me to in the letter he left for me."

Mary stopped and sat down on a bench. She said nothing for a long time. She just looked out at the water that was nearly frozen now and then looked over at Ken. Finally, she said, "I know you feel obligated, but I thought we had something special and we would share everything. I thought Deb understood you and I were planning our lives together and everything you did mattered to me."

"Everything you do matters to me, too. And we do have something spccial."

"Then why doesn't she tell me about your phone calls and why don't you tell me about them?"

"Mary, you like theater, right?"

"Yeah, so?"

"Yeah, so, I don't really like theater. But that's ok with me. You get to like to do things that don't interest me. Just like I'm sure you don't want to play football with the guys when you come to visit me at school."

"This is different, Ken. We're not talking about things you like to do that I don't, and things I like to do and you don't. We're talking about your sister and how you put her before me sometimes."

"I guess it's hard for you to understand since you are an only child, but Mary, they're my sisters and brother. You and they are in totally different ball fields. I love you and I love them, but this shouldn't be a competition. You are first in my heart, but you share space there with Deb, Joe, and Kim."

"Why, if we share space, can't you tell me what you talk to Deb about, then?"

"Why is it only my conversations with Deb that you care about? Why don't you care I talked to Joe three times this week? Or that I sent Kim two letters in the last couple of weeks?"

"I don't know why it's only Deb that I care about."

"You sound jealous," he said, chuckling a little.

"Are you laughing at my feelings?"

"No, sweetheart, I'm chuckling over the fact that you're jealous, and maybe it's a little sweet that my girlfriend is jealous, that's all. Sorry."

"It's not funny."

"Listen," he said, as he pulled Mary closer and put his hand under her chin and raised her head so he could look right into her eyes, "you are the only one I want to kiss, the only one I think about each night and the only one I want to live with after college. Just you." Then he kissed her.

"Well, that makes me feel better."

"How do we help you not feel jealous of Deb and not be so distant from her? Because, honestly, sweetheart, I think it's your jealousy that is creating the problem with Deb, not anything she is doing."

"Can you tell her to just tell me about her calls and letters and stuff with you?"

"Mary, are you listening to what you are saying?"

Mary got up and turned away, then turned back to Ken and said, "Why won't you just do this thing for me? I thought you loved me!"

Ken got up too. "Mary, honey, listen to what you are saying. What if Deb or anyone asked me to tell them everything you and I talked about? Would you like that?"

"That stuff is between you and me. It's private and I don't want you sharing it."

"Don't you think Deb might feel the same way? What if she has secrets from the world that she only trusts to me? You want me to break that trust, but not the trust between us?"

"No, I don't want you to do that to me. Have you already done that? Have you told Deb what we talk about?"

"Certainly not. That is private stuff between me and the woman I'm planning to spend my life with."

"I don't know why this matters so much to me, or why it bothers me so much."

"You have no reason to be jealous of my little sister."

"But you're going to always keep secret what she tells you on the phone. So much for wanting to spend your life with someone and loving someone."

"Come on, Mary, you are sounding like a pouty child. I don't keep secrets from you and I tell you I have talked to her, just not every little detail of what we discussed."

"And no matter what I say, or how many times I ask you to do this for me, for our relationship, you will not do it, will you?"

"No, Mary, I'm not changing my mind on this. My father and my grandfather always told me trust and integrity are all you really have to bank on in this world. You do not break promises, you do not betray trust, and you keep your word. If you say you will do something, do it. Unless Deb tells me it's ok to share what she tells me, I am not, ever, going to betray her trust. Just as I will never betray yours."

"It sure seems like I am being asked to accommodate something that is important to you, over something that is important to me in this relationship."

"What do you mean by that?"

"Well, you know I feel strongly about faith, about listening to God, about trying to live in the word of God. You don't share that same feeling. Now there is this. You won't betray her trust and I'm asking you to share everything, and I mean everything, with me. Are you ever going to let me win an argument?"

"Win an argument? That's what this is about? Who's winning our arguments? Mary, in relationships, no one wins an argument. That's not what this is about. I'm really sorry that the first two things we argued about were things that are such a big deal to both of us, and things we both feel strongly about. I think that speaks to all the things we agree on that you are not giving us credit for. But that is the reality of the situation. You know, I could throw this all back at you. Why are you even asking me to change? Don't you love me? If you do, shouldn't you love me for who I am, not who you think I should be? Why are you judging my love as only whether I follow your directions?"

"Now you think I don't love you?"

"Well, Mary, it sure seems like you have this idea in mind of the man you wanted to spend your life with and on two important issues. I fall short."

"That's not true. You are everything I ever wanted."

"Except where these two things that you have said are very important to you are concerned."

"I guess so."

They started walking again in the car's direction. Just before they got into the car, Ken kissed Mary again and asked, "Are you going to overlook these two things? Or are they so big for you that you can't get past this?"

"I don't know. All I know is that I don't want to lose you."

"How can I help you decide if you can get past this?"

"I don't know. Honestly, Ken, I think we should just table this for now. I have finals to study for."

"Ok, I'll get you back then."

They drove in near silence. When they arrived back at the girls' dorm, Kim was outside with Joe, and when she saw Ken, she ran over and hugged him. He picked her up and commented about her growing more and asked about her paper.

"It's all done."

"Great."

"I'm going to study," Mary said.

"Ok, can I check in with you later? I was thinking about taking everyone to town for a burger and maybe skating if everyone needs a break from studying."

"I'm not sure. Let me know when you're ready to go and I will let you know."

"Ok, bye sweetheart."

"Bye."

"Is she ok?" Kim asked.

"Not sure."

Just then, Ryan and Deb walked up, having been at the library, and Deb said, "Hey Kenny, how were your finals?"

"Good. Glad they're over though."

"Yeah."

"Are you all done studying?"

"Pretty much. But right now, I feel like my brain is fried, so we're taking a break. Joe, what are you up to?"

"Also taking a break. Was just waiting for Becky to come down. We were going to walk into town for a burger."

"How about we all go?" Ken asked.

"Sure, if you're buying," Joe said, laughing.

Becky came out, and they all walked to town and got lunch and then went to the skating rink and roller skated for a couple of hours. Ken said he wanted to see if Mary was around, so they headed back to the girls' dorm. When they got there, someone told them Mary had left with two girls to go see a movie. Kim said she was going to a Girl Scout Christmas party and went to get ready. Becky said she had more studying to do, but Joe said he was done. So, Joe, Ken, Deb and Ryan went to the main hall to play games. After several games of pool, they decided they had had enough and Ken went back to the girls' dorm to see if Mary was back. She wasn't, so he went back to the boys' dorm with Joe and Ryan. Ken left early Sunday morning to get to New York City. He didn't see Mary again, but left her a note at the girls' dorm.

Finals week at Choate was cold and snowy. Deb called Ken twice to see how he was and to ask about Mary. Ken told her they had argued, and he hadn't heard from her since the call they had on Sunday evening. Deb reported Mary was not looking that great and was avoiding her again. Ken asked about Ryan's hockey team and Deb said they were again in the playoffs so they would have games over break, but they hoped to see each other in New York. Friday finally came, and Ken arrived again with Michael. They all packed their things into the trunk and went to the New York apartment. Joe was thrilled with the setup that Mr. Reynolds had put together for him to work on the computer and said so. Mr. Reynolds had converted two bedrooms so that Kim and Deb could each have their own rooms. Everyone was pleased with the arrangements.

During the few days before Christmas, they all went Christmas shopping and baked cookies and went to look at all the shops in the evening. When they weren't shopping, Joe worked on his personal computer build, Kim read books and drew, Deb visited with Ryan and Ken had several calls with Mary. She had apparently done poorly on her finals because of their argument and her parents were angry with her, and probably with Ken. She had been told she could not see Ken during the break as punishment for her poor grades. It didn't help their situation, but there was nothing they could do about it.

Deb was up early on Christmas Eve and went to the kitchen in search of a muffin or something to eat. She found Ken sitting at the table with his head in his hands.

"What are you doing up so early?" she asked him.

"Couldn't sleep."

"Is this because of whatever is going on with Mary? You want to talk about it?"

"I didn't think I wanted to talk about it, but maybe that will help. You just have to promise me you won't tell anyone about this, even Ryan."

"Ok."

"Remember the Saturday I came to campus to see you all? It started then."

Ken told Deb about the argument, about Mary being jealous and wanting to know everything he and Deb talked about. He told her about how that impacted Mary's grades and how angry her parents now were.

"Wow. I did not know that was what she was so upset about. She never once said anything to me about being mad at you and me talking. I guess she was a little weird whenever she heard I talked to you, but she never said she was angry or anything."

"Yeah, wow."

Ken then told her about how Mary wasn't sure she was going to get past this and how it was now the second big thing that they had issues with.

"What are you going to do?"

"At this point, there's nothing I can do. Her parents won't let me see her, and she is so upset she doesn't want to talk to me. You guys go back to Choate before I have to be back, so I guess I will try to talk to her when it's time to get you all back to campus."

"I'm so sorry, Ken. Honestly, I don't feel like I did anything, but I will certainly be more aware of how I come across to her. There was a couple of times when I mentioned to everyone that you and I talked and she was pretty insistent to know what we talked about, and once or twice I was a little irritated at her reaction, but I will try to not make this worse for you. I will try hard to not react to it, if she ever spends time with me again, that is."

"Thanks. Maybe you could try to call her today? Would you do that for me?"

"Sure. Is it ok if I ask her if she's mad at me about something? As long as I don't tell her what you told me?"

"Sure. Maybe you'll learn something she hasn't told me."

Deb finished her muffin and left, saying that she needed to get ready to go meet Ryan. A short time later, Mr. Reynolds entered the kitchen and found Ken in much the same state.

"You look like you're carrying the weight of the world on your shoulders, buddy. Want to unload a little?" Mr. Reynolds asked.

"Nothing big is going on, Darrick. Just had some trouble with Mary that I can't seem to resolve."

"Ken, I'm sorry, but I came to the kitchen a little bit ago and heard you talking to Deb. Not wanting to interrupt, I left you alone, but I heard you had a big argument with Mary. I'm sorry, Ken. But I have to say, when two people love each other, and want to spend their lives together, there are some basic, core concepts that are probably good to agree on. Having a difference of opinion on faith and on what you share and don't share with one another are two critical issues. I think the only things that might outweigh your issues are kids, parenting styles, and money management."

"The faith issue I imagine I will get around at some point. I mean, my grandfather was a pastor. Losing my parents really tested my ideas about a loving God and everyone having some path set or getting direction from God. How can those things be true when I lost my parents long before we were all grown up? How can that be the plan from a loving God? But I know at some point I will reconcile my life events with my faith."

"Tested you, has it?"

"To say the least. But really, I have gained a lot too. I would never in a million years be close to my little sister if this hadn't happened to us, and look at Joe. He would never be about to do all this with computers.

So maybe Deb is right, maybe the plan for us was always going to mean we were going on without our parents."

"You know, when my mother called me to tell me I should come home, that my father was dying, I wondered about the same thing. How do you reconcile the teachings from Sunday school with life events? After he died, as I was standing at the grave watching them lower him into the ground, I was thanking God that I had the courage to talk to him and correct the huge wrong that had stood between us for so many years. I thanked God for giving me the will or the guidance or whatever He gives to alter my course while I still had the courage to do it."

"You know Deb says that after meeting with the reverend at the church at Choate, free will allows us to fork off the road, and even get so far off the road, it no longer looks like the plan God started for us. I guess maybe we all have a way back to our plan if we want it."

"That's certainly what they teach in church, don't they? Forgiveness and mercy."

"Yeah. Hey, so can I ask you something?"

"Sure."

"Last year, on Christmas Eve, we wrote a note to our parents here. We left it near the fireplace where we had the stockings hung. When we got up the next morning, the note was gone. Deb and I didn't do it, and I know that Joe and Kim didn't do it."

"Is there a question in there?"

"Did you take it?"

"Yes. I went out to the living room well after your aunt and I went to bed and found it. I read it and it really touched me. You all pouring out your wishes to your parents on that first Christmas without them. It reminded me of my loneliness during my childhood. It helped me to understand you all much better. In fact, it was that night I started thinking about marrying your aunt."

"Do you still have it?"

"Yes, it has become one of my most treasured possessions. You all have become very important to me. You have become the family I always wanted."

"Darrick, you aren't marrying my aunt just to ensure you keep the four of us in your life, are you?"

Laughing, he said, "No, I know to an eighteen-year-old, your aunt looks like she has no appeal, but trust me, she does. You and your sisters and brother are just a bonus as far as I am concerned, and a happy one. I always wanted kids, but knew at my age, having some was becoming unlikely."

"Well, we are excited about it, both for you and her, and for us."

"Glad to hear it."

Just then, the cook arrived and started making breakfast. Ken left the kitchen to go shower and get dressed and Mr. Reynolds returned to the room he shared with Aunt Alicia. Deb left after breakfast to go meet Ryan, where they exchanged gifts, and then Ryan came back with her to see Kim and Joe, and Ken. He brought gifts for them, too.

Later that evening, Mr. Reynolds and Aunt Alicia went out to a dinner with friends and to a party. The kids all figured that tonight was when he was going to pop the question, so it was hard for them to settle down. They all went to bed fully expecting to be woken up by the news. No news came. When Kim got them up around seven, they all wondered what had happened last night. They made breakfast because the cook was not coming in until later. Mr. Reynolds appeared first in the kitchen, with Aunt Alicia coming in shortly after him. Ken noticed that Aunt Alicia did not have an engagement ring on, so he wondered what had happened, but didn't ask. Mr. Reynolds asked what they did last night while they all ate the eggs and French toast that Kim and Deb had made. Joe told them he finished his first version of a personal computer and Mr. Reynolds asked him a bunch of questions. When Kim could take it no longer, she asked if they could open presents. They all went into the living room and Kim passed presents around. Everyone was pleased with the gifts they received, but it was strangely quiet. Mr.

Reynolds announced he was ready to see the personal computer, so he, Ken, and Joe went into the room where Joe had been working. Kim went to try on her new clothing and to set up the painting easel that Mr. Reynolds had given her, along with paints and several canvases so she could start a painting. Aunt Alicia went into the kitchen and Deb felt compelled to follow her.

"Aunt Alicia, are you ok?"

"I suppose so," she replied as she poured herself some more coffee.

"Do you want to help me carry my new clothes to my room and tell me what you think as I try them on?"

"That would be lovely. I didn't think you really liked all the fashion fluff, though."

"To be honest, Aunt Alicia, I know I don't come off like other girls, like I care about makeup and clothes and jewelry, but that's only because I never thought I fit in or looked pretty or anything."

"I felt the same way when I was growing up, Deb. And now look, I am in the fashion industry."

"You're also beautiful and sometimes I think you belong on the other side of the cameras, Aunt Alicia," Deb said somewhat solemnly.

"You're sweet, Deb, but I'm way past a chance to be a model."

They gathered up the clothing and jewelry and things and went to Deb's room. Deb stepped into the attached bathroom and began trying on clothes and modelling for Aunt Alicia. They were laughing and having fun when Deb came out with the last outfit on and found Aunt Alicia standing at her window looking out over the park and crying.

"Aunt Alicia, I know I'm not older and all, and we aren't exactly life-long friends, but you really look like you could use someone to talk to. Can I help?"

"Oh Deb, I think I may have messed everything up."

"What are you talking about?"

"Mr. Reynolds proposed to me last night."

"Oh my gosh, that's wonderful!"

"Not really. I freaked out, and couldn't answer him and then when I did, all I could say was that I needed time to think about it."

"Oh."

"Now you see what I mean?"

Deb moved all the clothes that were scattered on her bed to a chair and turned back to Aunt Alicia and said, "Why don't you come over here and sit down and tell me what happened?"

"We were having a wonderful evening. The dinner was wonderful, the party and everything. We were headed back here and Darrick suggested a ride in the park. It was snowing, and the trees were covered, you know, all white and quiet. It was picturesque. Then he said some wonderful things, about how I made his world complete and how he loved every quirky thing about me, and wanted to make us all a family. He pulled out this box from Tiffany's and I was stunned."

"Because you're not sure if you love him?"

"Oh, no, I love him. I love him more than anything in my life."

"Then what happened?"

"I just sat there for a long time. I couldn't say anything."

"What did Mr. Reynolds do?"

"He got more and more upset. I mean, I could see his face falling, but then he sort of got it together and asked me if I was really that surprised."

"He was trying to give you an out for not answering right away?"

"I think so. So, I said, yes, I was surprised and asked if it would be ok if I thought about it for a day or so."

"And then you came home?"

"Yes, and he slept in another room."

"Oh."

"See, I really messed it up."

"I don't know, Aunt Alicia. Maybe he was just hurt that you weren't as excited as he was or something."

"Yeah, maybe. But now I don't know what to do."

"Do you want to marry him?"

"Yes, he is exactly what I always dreamed of for a husband. He is successful, smart, funny and kind and he always does nice things for me. He takes such good care of you and your brothers and sister. I don't know what freaked me out so much."

"Aunt Alicia, Ken told me about your argument last summer, when you talked about how hard things were for you when you were growing up and how you felt like you were overlooked because of my mother."

"He did?"

"Yeah. I'm pretty sure Ken told me only so that I might understand how it must feel from your perspective."

"And?"

"Well, maybe the fact that Mr. Reynolds started his proposal with the idea that we would all be a family, and that isn't such a happy memory for you. Maybe that is why you freaked out."

"Not all of my childhood was bad. I had a great relationship with my sister, your mother. At least until she got married and then later when they split up."

"Well, I know, from what I have been through, that my ideas about family are definitely not the same as they were before."

"Yes, but I always wanted a family that was close and happy together."

"Don't you feel like we are happy?"

"Now I do. Not at first."

"No, not at first, but I think that was two things, a misunderstanding about what you were thinking and suddenly losing both of our parents. I think we all value you and Mr. Reynolds a lot."

"Yes, I can see that. I probably wasn't very understanding about what you kids were going through at first, any more than you were understanding about what I was going through."

"So, what are you afraid of?"

"It seems too perfect?"

"Yeah, but listen to how that sounds."

"You are way too much like your mother."

They both laughed and Deb hugged her aunt. Then she asked her, "Now what are you going to do?"

"I don't know how to fix this."

"I have an idea."

Deb went to Kim's room and found her setting up her art supplies in the corner of her room by the window. She told Kim what had happened and what she was planning to do to help Mr. Reynolds and their aunt. Kim thought it was a wonderful idea and left to go sit with their aunt. Deb then went to the room where the boys were and asked to talk to Ken. Ken left the room and the two of them went back to the living room. Deb told him about what Aunt Alicia had told her and then she told him about her plan. Ken thought it was a good idea, and he went back to convince Joe and Mr. Reynolds to leave the computer.

An hour later, they were all walking in Central Park. It was still snowing, and the trees were covered. It was like walking in a Winter Wonderland. At some point, Deb directed Kim to head out into an open area off the pathway to build a snowman. The other three followed, and soon Mr. Reynolds and Aunt Alicia were alone. Just before Deb left, she whispered to Aunt Alicia to tell Mr. Reynolds why she freaked out.

"I have something to say, Darrick, and I hope you will hear me out," Aunt Alicia said.

"Alicia, what in the world would make you think I wouldn't hear you out?"

"I know I hurt you last night."

"Well, I don't know if I would use the word 'hurt,' but ok."

"Darrick, you are the most wonderful man I have ever met. You are smart, funny, handsome and you are so good to me and have been so good to my nieces and nephews. I freaked out last night because I was worried that things were too perfect and that something bad was going to take it all away from me. And frankly, the idea of an instant family scares me, since neither one of us exactly has a Norman-Rockwell-like upbringing. That is the only reason I didn't answer you right away and the only thing I needed time to think through."

"And what changed today?"

"Well, the fact that you didn't throw me out today, the fact that you slept somewhere else and that scared me, and talking to Deborah. It was like talking to my sister. She is so calm and reasonable and mature. She helped me acknowledge my fears and realize they were silly."

"I would not throw you out."

At that, Aunt Alicia got down on her knees and looked up at Darrick and said, "Darrick Reynolds, I love you more than words can say. Will you please marry me?"

Mr. Reynolds looked down at her and smiled. He got down on his knees too and took the box out of his pocket. He handed it to her, and she put the ring on her finger. They hugged. Just then, they heard the kids whooping and hollering.

"It appears we have an audience," Darrick said.

"Yes, well, I expected them to be surreptitiously watching. This was Deb's idea. After I spoiled your proposal, she suggested I propose to you."

"I will have to thank her later for the best story I will ever have to tell people."

They laughed, got up off their knees, and motioned for the kids to come back. Kim yelled they needed to come and check out their snowman. After they had admired the work, the kids had done, and the kids congratulated their new Uncle Darrick, they all walked home. After they enjoyed dinner, Joe showed them his new personal computer. Kim played some games on it, and Deb tried to use the document manager, but it had some issues. Despite that, they all marveled at what Joe had accomplished.

12

Ryan joined Deb and the others for New Year's Eve since there was a break in the hockey games, and so did two of Ken's friends from Harvard, since he couldn't see Mary during the break. They all had a good time playing games, watching movies and waiting for the stroke of midnight. Fireworks went off somewhere they could see from the windows in the living room. Kim said it was the best New Year's ever.

The next Sunday, they all loaded up in one car with Michael driving another car loaded down with their belongings and headed to Choate. Ken drove his car with Joe, and the girls rode with Uncle Darrick and Aunt Alicia. When they had unloaded all the belongings and gotten Kim, Deb and Joe situated, Uncle Darrick, Aunt Alicia and Michael departed to get back to the city. Kim went to find her friends, Joe went to meet up with Becky and give her the gift he had bought her, and Deb and Ryan went for a walk. Ken went in search of Mary. He found her coming out of the library.

"Hi," he said as he approached her.

"Hi."

"Can we talk?"

"I guess so."

"Mary, I'm so sorry about our argument, the issues you had with finals week, and not being able to see you all of break."

"My parents were furious."

"I can imagine. Do they hate me?"

"No, they think this is all me, actually. They think that I have become too dependent on you and that I need to wait to get more serious about you until I am finished with college."

"Is that what you want?"

"No. I've missed you so much."

"I've missed you too."

"The argument we had seems so petty now. I was jealous of Deb and your close relationship with her. It drove me crazy. We had that big fight and then I bombed all my tests. Well, not all, but most of them."

"Did it impact your grades?"

"Yes, of course. I got two A's and four B's. The B's were all because of bad test scores. My father wants me to go to those teachers tomorrow and ask if I can retake the exams. I'm not going to."

Mary stopped walking and turned to look at Ken. Then she said, "I don't really know why my father was so worked up. My grades were not that bad, but after getting straight A's for so long, he went crazy and my whole break was terrible. I spent most of the time going over our fight, what I was upset about, and I could barely remember what the big deal was, except that I was being weird about your sister. If I could, I'd want to go back and do all of this all over again and keep it from happening this way."

"You want to hop into the machine and have a do over?"

Mary laughed and moved closer to Ken when she said, "I don't know if I am ready for that, but I sure wish I could fix this."

"You have." Ken put his arms around her and gave her a big hug and kissed her. She held onto him for a long time.

"I have a lot to fix with Deb too, don't I?"

"I'm not sure. She mentioned when I told her we had an argument that you had seemed very distant from her and she wasn't sure what that was about."

"I know I was, because of this freaking out I was doing, but I'm going to fix it."

"I think she just wants her friend back, so I'm sure she will be willing, too."

They walked up the stairs of the girls' dorm and went inside. Mary said she had Ken's gift up in her room. Ken left to get his gift for Mary and came back to the lounge in the girls' dorm. They spent some time talking about their breaks, and Ken told Mary about Mr. Reynolds and Aunt Alicia and everything Deb did to help them. Kim came in at that point and told Ken she was going to dinner with her friend and her friend's family. Deb and Ryan returned from their walk, and Joe and Becky appeared. Ken suggested they all go get some dinner, and they piled into Mary's car and went into town to Burgers and Shakes. Later, Ken went with Joe and Ryan to the boys' dorm for the night. The next day, Ken went back to New York.

Classes resumed, and Mary and Deb had three classes together. Mary hoped this would help her repair things with her friend. Ryan was in two of Deb's classes as well, so they were all excited about their schedules this final semester of school. Joe and Becky had most of their classes together, so they were happy as well. Kim, on the other hand, didn't have any classes with her best friend, but she was holding it together with the words from Deb that three girls from her Girl Scout troop were in her classes.

After about a week, Kim was situated with both her best friend and her new friends. They were walking back to campus after church services on Sunday when Kim mentioned to Deb that she was still very troubled about their parents' separation and what Joe did. They went off to Deb's room to discuss it and Deb said at the end that she needed some time to think things over before they could talk again.

Before Deb could figure out whether it was a good idea to discuss the things Kim brought up with Joe, or even Ken, Joe had the biggest news ever. He received a letter from the staff at Harvard and at IBM who had been testing this new language and personal computer plans. They all asked if they could schedule a meeting with him to go over their testing and ideas. Joe wasn't sure what to do, so he came to Deb to figure out plans. He found her walking back from the last of the playoff hockey games with Kim and Mary. After confirming that they had won, he said, "Deb, how can I arrange this meeting with all these people and be in school?"

Deb told the others that she needed to talk with Joe and they went into the main hall while the other girls continued on to the girls' dorm. When Deb and Joe found a table and sat down, Deb said, "Well, first I think you should contact Mr. Davis and see if he can assist in any way. There is an office there and meeting rooms you should be able to use. I mean, you want to do this in cooperation with Dad's company, right?"

"Yeah, I do. That would solve where to meet. Do you think they would all meet at one time rather than having to have two meetings?"

"That's something I think you should propose back to them all. Once you know you can use the offices, then you have to arrange to get to New York. Then you will have to contact Aunt Alicia and get her to set that part up and excuse you from school for a couple of days. That should be all you need, right?"

"Yeah, I think so."

"So, start with Mr. Davis and then go to Aunt Alicia, and while you're waiting for confirmation from everyone, you might want to check in with your teachers to see which days would be best for you to miss. Remember, they asked you for the meeting, so don't be afraid to set it around your class schedules a little bit."

"Thanks Deb."

"Any time. I wish I could be there."

"You can't miss any time of your last semester, and anyway, this stuff is way over your head."

"That's true, but it would be cool to see you stand in front of all those smart people and go over your inventions."

"I wish Dad was here."

"I know. This is when I find I miss them most. When something happens that I wish we could share with them."

"Me too. It's funny how I go days without even thinking of them now. I never expected to get to this point."

"Actually, I never thought you'd get to this point either, but I'm glad you are."

"Why glad?"

"Mainly so you don't have to hurt so much all the time. I know it was hard for you, and harder still after last spring. I'm just glad you're happy now and seem better."

"This language and personal computer project have helped keep my mind off it, I suppose. And all the activities here at school have helped."

"And Becky?"

"Her too."

"When you're done with this meeting, we need to talk, though. Kim has been pretty upset still and brought it to me a few days ago."

"We can talk now. I mean, I don't want Kim to be upset."

"No, let's hold off until your meetings are done. I need to think it through some more too, anyway."

"Ok, then I'm going to go try to reach Mr. Davis. Thanks for the help."

Joe walked off and called Mr. Davis, who was thrilled with the progress Joe had made, and said the meeting space was at his disposal. They talked for a bit about the personal computer and Joe's plans for that, and Mr. Davis was pleased that Joe wanted to turn the design plans and his notes over to Mr. Davis to complete the design and start planning for production and release. Joe was hoping to get it out before the summer, so Mr. Davis asked Joe to mail all the materials to him to get started right away. Armed with dates, Joe contacted the professor at Harvard and Jeff Hansen, the person at IBM who was heading up that team, to propose a full collaborative meeting, and they all agreed that was the best plan. Once they had decided on a date, Joe confirmed with teachers that he could be out for a couple of days, and Aunt Alicia completed the process to sign him out. It was agreed that Michael would come and pick Joe up and bring him to the city where he would stay with Aunt Alicia and Mr. Reynolds, and that Mr. Reynolds would accompany Joe to the meetings and then get him back to campus.

A week later, Joe met with Mr. Davis and the design engineers, along with Ken, to discuss the personal computer plans and then Joe spent the day going over feedback, notes and release plans for the new language. During that time, the teams decided they would call the new language "C" because it was based somewhat on COBOL but simplified and shorter. They gave each team a specific section of the paper to write and they planned to get it all to Joe and Mr. Davis to compile and clean up for a final full team read and release. They also decided at the meeting that they would complete the paper sections in the next two weeks, with a final read-through and release set for February tenth.

When Joe got back to campus, he made a beeline for the main hall, hoping he would find Deb, Ryan, Mary, Becky, and Kim all there. Everyone was there but Kim, as she had a Girl Scout meeting, but he gathered them all at a table and started going over what had happened.

"It was the coolest thing. First, the design team had come up with a cleaner prototype of the personal computer and full design plans. We went over. Ken was there, and he offered a few suggestions that were superb ideas. We all agreed on a plan and signed off on it and they are starting production next week."

"Wow, that was fast!" Ryan said.

"Yeah. It totally surprised me, but Mr. Davis said it was because I had written such good notes."

"This is so exciting. Is your name going to be on the computer?" Becky asked.

"No, we are going to call this computer Sinclair 1000."

"Is that significant in some way or just made up?" Mary asked.

"Well, Sinclair is the name of a model that my father and Mr. Davis made of a personal aircraft when they first met. I thought it was a good idea to name the first computer in honor of their first project. Mr. Davis thought it was a great idea."

"I do too," Deb said.

"So, when does it come out?" Ryan asked.

"We are trying to time the release of the first shipment of personal computers with the release of the paper on the code. So, mid-February. The marketing team at Fitzgerald and Davis are working on a plan and the sales team has started to sell it already to business supply stores and other places."

"Do we get a discount on one?" Becky asked.

They all laughed and Joe said he would see what he could do to get everyone a new computer as soon as possible.

"What about the language meeting?" Deb asked.

"That was totally cool. Everyone around a table talking about the language I wrote and their testing methods and what they had tried. They asked me all kinds of questions and really listened to me. It was great having all those really smart people looking to me for answers."

"Joe, we always knew you were going to be smart and do great things. I don't know why you're so surprised by this," Deb said.

"It's always cool; the first time people take you seriously. Joe, I totally get it. It was kind of like that for me in hockey. When everyone around you realizes you can do something, they can't and they look to you for your knowledge," Ryan added.

"Yeah, that's what it was like," Joe said.

"Did you have to tell them about the machine and that you pro-grammed it with the new language?" Becky asked.

"No, in fact, they suggested that any testing I did outside of the use on the personal computer should not be included in the paper. Jeff Hansen said that would taint the evidence. He said you always want the independent testing only. It worked out great because I'm totally not ready or not even willing at this point to let the world know about the machine."

"I think that's a good idea. Given how much it has made just us struggle, what do you think will happen if the world finds out you can travel through time and change things?" Mary said.

"I agree, Mary. We're not ready for that," Deb said.

"When is this paper going to be published?" Becky asked.

"By mid-February too. We have each team—the IBM, and the Harvard teams—completing sections of the testing report and then we are going to combine it all into a single paper and the entire team will review that, and then we publish."

"Where do you publish something like this?" Deb asked.

"Jeff Hansen is going to submit it to the professional symposium that publishes a journal and Harvard is going to put it out in their annual Science and Technology Journal. Mr. Davis is talking to both teams about a press release as well."

"Wow, Joe, this is a big deal. You are going to be published before you're even out of high school. Your name is going to be on all this stuff somewhere, right?" Ryan asked.

"Yeah, I get first billing on the publications and Mr. Davis is submitting the copyright on the computer design with my name and the company's name on it."

"Does that mean you get paid?" Ryan asked.

"For the computer sales, yes, I will get a royalty payment. For the language, probably not. We are presenting it as public knowledge. It's a language to program other things in, not really an entity in and of itself."

"Still, if your personal computer takes off and becomes popular, you could make a lot of money," Ryan said.

"Enough about that. How was the game?" Joe asked, to deflect some of the attention that was getting to him.

"Oh man, you missed a great game of hockey. We were back and forth each period scoring, so by the last few minutes we were tied. It was impossible to get the drop on them, and then one guy from the other team must have decided he'd had enough and took a swing at Dave with his stick. It turned into a huge brawl on the ice. At the end, they had two players in penalty and that was all we needed. We scored in the last few seconds of the game and won!"

"Great way to end the season. Sorry I missed it."

"He had his whole fan club there," Becky said.

"Yeah, that was cool. Deb, Mary, Becky, Kim, a bunch of the guys from the floor and my parents and grandparents were there. It was great."

"And no black eye this time?"

"No, but have I got an epic bruise on my right side!"

They laughed some more and then everyone went to finish their homework. Everyone was proud of Joe and said so, and he looked very happy. Later that evening, before curfew, Deb asked Ryan to come over to the girls' dorm. They sat in the lobby area and Deb presented him with a special gift.

"This is for your championship win and the end of your high school hockey career. Since you told me there wasn't a hockey team at NYU and this would be your last competitive season, I thought we should commemorate it with something special."

Deb handed Ryan a box that was wrapped in plain paper, the color of the hockey team, with a ribbon that was the other color. He held it for a moment.

"You didn't have to do this, you know," he said.

"I know. I wanted to. I know you didn't want a big thing, and you told your parents not to plan anything, but this is a big deal for you and I wanted to give you something. Aren't you going to open it?"

Ryan tore into the paper and opened the box. There was a very nice watch in the box. He looked at for a few minutes and then looked up at Deb and hugged her. He whispered in her ear, "Thank you, it's really great. But mostly, thank you for knowing that I didn't want something big, but wanted something."

She whispered back, "You're welcome."

He took the watch out and put it on, when she stopped him and turned it over. On the back was an engraving that read 'To my champion on and off the ice. I love you. Deb.' He hugged her again, gave her a kiss and said, "I really love you, Deborah Fitzgerald."

"I love you too, Ryan McDonnell."

While all the computer and language activity were going on with Joe, several other big things were happening. First, Ken had decided that he had to fix what he felt he did to mess Mary up. During that first weekend back for everyone at Choate, but before Ken had to be back at Harvard, he contacted Mary's parents and asked if he could see them. He didn't tell Mary before he went. When he arrived at the Rollins' house, he was very nervous. Mrs. Rollins greeted him and brought into the living room of their home. Mrs. Rollins went to locate Mr. Rollins. When he came in and they sat down, Ken began, "Mr. and Mrs. Rollins, thank you for seeing me. I don't mean to impose on you both, but I really felt I owed you some explanation about what happened. You see, Mary and I have something special. I love her. I want to spend my life with her, with your permission, of course. But I want her to have time to be sure about what she wants. That's why we are waiting to do anything until after she finished college."

Ken paused in case they had anything to say, but when they didn't, he continued, "I don't know what all Mary has told you about me, but we, my brother and two sisters, came to Choate after both of our parents had been killed in terrible accidents. I was raised in a household that had faith and lived that faith. My grandfather was a pastor. I grew up believing that God loved us all and if we believed, we could live a happy, healthy life. Then my parents were killed, and I questioned everything about my faith and everything about what I had been taught. As you know, Mary feels strongly about her faith. It's one of the things I love about her. Her strong convictions. Just before she had finals, she and I had a quarrel about the question of faith, all that I was struggling with, and it kind of came down to the question of whether or not we could form a life together, if there was a path for us, while I was in such turmoil, and while she had such strong convictions. That is why she had a hard time during finals week. It was really my fault."

He waited for what seemed like hours and finally, Mr. Rollins spoke.

"Ken, we appreciate your coming here today, taking responsibility, explaining the argument you had, and what is surely a painful and difficult thing for you to discuss still. We know you have powerful feelings for our daughter and that she feels the same for you. But we think this speaks to both of your maturity levels and the need for caution in your relationship. The fact that you can have such a profound difference in ideology, and the fact that you both thought it was a good idea to discuss that difference on the weekend before one of you had critical tests to take, tells me you are not ready for a more serious relationship."

"Mr. Rollins, I did not go to Choate that weekend to start a fight with Mary. We were talking, and it just led there. I would never do anything to mess up her hopes and dreams for her future. I know she has things she wants to accomplish, and I want to support her every way I can in her goals."

"We know you do, dear," Mrs. Rollins said while looking at her husband.

"The thing is, Ken, we don't want either of you to interfere in each other's dreams. There is plenty of time for you to join your lives together later, after college, and we want Mary to focus on her education as she finishes this last semester at Choate and moves on to college at Wellesley."

"Are you asking me to not see her?"

"No, certainly not. We just want you to slow things down a bit. That you came here tells us you care deeply for Mary, and it speaks to your character that you would come here and face her father over this and take responsibility. Can you both just focus on school and not so much on seeing each other every weekend?" Mrs. Rollins said before Mr. Rollins could respond.

"I believe we are focusing on school, ma'am."

"As Mrs. Rollins has said, we want you to slow things down. It is incumbent upon you, Ken, to control this and make sure she sees clearly your support of her education," Mr. Rollins added.

"I don't want to sound disrespectful, sir, but I think I have been supportive of Mary's education. To be clear, by slowing down, do you mean you want us to see each other less or is there some other concern you have?"

"Well, she has told us she wants to go to Harvard nearly every weekend this semester. We think that is too much."

"I wasn't aware that she was telling you that. We didn't see each other every weekend last semester. I had tests at different times and class projects and we only saw each other about once a month."

"Well, that certainly changes things, as we thought you were either spending the weekend at Choate or she was at Harvard every weekend."

"No, sir. Our schedules are different, and my midterms are not the same week as hers. Our finals are not the same week, so there are at least those times when we don't see each other for a few weeks straight."

"I think it would be acceptable if you maintain a once-a-month schedule for visits. That allows you to see one another while not removing the focus from school. Does that sound acceptable to you?"

"Yes, sir."

"One other thing. I know that college differs greatly from high school, even boarding school. I hope you are not pressuring her, Ken."

"I think I know what you are trying to ask me, sir, and I can assure you, I respect Mary too much and respect the two of you too much to do that. You may not know this, but I have two younger sisters. I treat Mary the way I want my sisters to be treated by any young man they may be dating."

"That's good enough for me," Mr. Rollins said.

"Thank you for listening to me and for being so understanding."

"Thank you for taking responsibility and coming here to face the music, so to say," Mr. Rollins said as he stood up to escort Ken to the door.

Mary's parents walked Ken to the door and said goodbye. It was a brief visit, but one he was glad he made. He didn't tell Mary about the visit until he was back at school after Joe's big meetings and asked Mary to come and see him that weekend. She hesitated because of her parents, and that is when Ken told her about his visit. Mary was surprised and asked Ken what her parents had said and how they had acted. Ken gave her all the information she asked for, including the request to not pressure her. She thought that was weird and commented that it was probably awkward for him, but she said that she appreciated him doing that. Given what he said, she said she would love to see him and was planning on coming to see him Friday night.

Mary went to Deb's room right after she spoke to Ken that night. When Deb beckoned her into the room, Mary said, "I just spoke to Ken. You will not believe what he did."

"What did he do?"

"He went to see my parents' last weekend before he went back to school."

"What for?"

"Well, to apologize for having a fight with me before finals week and messing me up."

"He didn't tell them about the machine, did he?"

"No way. He said the issue was about his questioning his faith and my strong conviction on my faith and that we had inadvertently arrived in a conversation at a place where we wondered if we had a future with such primary ideological differences."

"Wow, what did your parents say to him?"

"Well, they thanked him for the courage to come there and take responsibility, and they asked him to slow things down with me."

"How embarrassing."

"Yeah, can you imagine?"

"Well, if they were mad at him before, at least now they know he's going to take responsibility for you."

"True. And they said it was ok for us to visit each other, but to keep it to once a month."

"You can always go see him once a month and then have him come here to see all of us. That way, it's not just to see you, and it won't count on your once-a-month thing."

"Good idea. I was wondering if you would let me borrow that great blue dress for this weekend?"

"Oh, yeah sure. Do you want it now?"

"Yeah, if you don't mind. I'm going to pack tomorrow so I can leave Friday as soon as classes are over."

Deb got up and pulled the dress that Mary asked for out of her closet. She said, "Have you received your formal acceptance letter from Wellesley yet?"

"Yeah, I got it yesterday. How about you?"

"I got accepted at UNC, Duke and NYU."

"Wow, that's great! All three of the schools you were looking at."

"Yeah. I'm pretty excited. I'm debating now between Duke and NYU."

"Where is Ryan going? Has he received his acceptance letters?"

"Yeah, he got into NYU and UNC, but hasn't heard from Duke yet. Although, he didn't really want to go to Duke. He wants to stay in New York 'cause that's where his parents are, but he's torn about it. His grandparents are in North Carolina, and that has a real chance for him."

"Are you making your decision based on his decision?"

"No. I was planning on that last year when we took the ACT and SAT, but now I really want to go where I can get the history and archeology degree I'm looking for."

"No offense, but you should go where you need to go for your dreams."

"Yeah, that's what Aunt Alicia and Ken are saying, too."

"So, if that's the only thing that matters, then where?"

"NYU."

"Great! Then we can visit some times. You won't be that far away."

"Yeah, and if not during the year, the breaks for sure."

Mary got up to leave and Deb told her to have fun this weekend and say hi to Ken for her. It was great now that they seemed to get along again. Now, if only she could do something about what was troubling Kim.

That weekend, while Mary was away visiting Ken, Deb and Ryan took Becky, Joe, Kim and one of Kim's friends to the skating rink and out for dinner. Ryan noticed that Deb and Kim were whispering to each other several times and that afterward, each time, Deb looked sad and was distant for a while. When they got back to campus, there wasn't enough time to ask Deb what was going on, so he waited until the next day. Sunday after church, Kim went with the Girl Scouts to do some charity work. Joe and Becky were working on a class project, and Deb and Ryan did homework in the library.

Ryan found a study room, and they sat down and began working. He wondered if she was going to tell him what was going on of if he would have to ask. He waited a while and then said, "What were you and Kim whispering about yesterday?"

"Oh, nothing much."

"Sweetie, it can't be nothing. Every time you got done whispering with her, you looked sad and barely talked to anyone for about fifteen minutes. Why won't you tell me what's going on?"

"I'm not trying to keep anything from you, Ryan. It's just that she's upset. She's been upset for a while about our parents separating and what happened when Joe made his secret trip back to Cambridge last spring. It keeps coming up for her and she is having trouble getting past it because she knows something one of us did caused it to happen."

"That's not nothing much. Again, why were you keeping this from me?"

"Well, technically, I'm telling you now, so I'm not keeping it from you anymore."

"That's not funny."

"I'm sorry. It's just that I didn't know what do to do about it and then when I got this crazy idea, I didn't want to tell anyone 'cause it really is a crazy idea."

"Does Joe know about what is going on with Kim?"

"No. I told him I needed to discuss something with him, but I wanted to wait until after his big meetings and now I think I'm going to wait until after the release."

"Are you hoping that Kim will get over this or something else?"

"Well, I'm kind of hoping that Kim can get past this, but if not, again, I know that the only thing that will fix this is this crazy idea, and I don't want to distract Joe before his big release."

"You're thinking about going back to Cambridge, aren't you?"

"Can you think of another way to fix this, other than going back there and changing what Joe did?"

"Tell me what your plan is."

"Well, since I wasn't there, all I know for sure is what Joe told me."

"You remember Joe telling us he wasn't well and that he and Mr. Brewster theorized it was because he existed in that timeframe and then went to it. If that's true, Joe definitely can't go back again. That would make a third instance of him in the same time and space," Ryan added.

"That's right. That means I would have to go and just find Joe and stop him from talking to our father. Like catch him before he leaves the machine, so he never gets home," Deb said.

"But then you would run the risk that you would get sick because you exist in that space and time too," Ryan said.

"Joe said he didn't start to feel bad until he was there for six or seven hours. So as long as I could do this and be back before then, I think I would be ok," Deb responded.

"No way," Ryan said, sternly.

"What do you mean, no way?" Deb asked.

"I mean, if your crazy idea involves you going alone, no way," Ryan declared.

"Ryan, I want to fix this. I want Kim to be better, and frankly, it bothers me a great deal that we caused our parents to separate right before their deaths, too."

"What I mean is not alone. I have to go with you. It is a crazy idea, but I understand why you want to do it. My going with you. That's the only way I will support you in this," Ryan said.

"Ryan, you are being autocratic, aren't you?"

"I love you and I'm not letting you get into that machine, and go back to your home where you might have problems we can't define or prevent without me. If that's autocratic, then so be it."

"You're kind of cute when you act all worried about me, you know that?"

"That's not funny, and you are not changing the subject. Promise me you won't go alone," Ryan said.

"Listen, Joe and I already made a pinky promise no one goes into the machine alone. I will not break a pinky promise. That's the worst kind of bad luck."

Deb got up and went to where Ryan was sitting and wrapped her arms around his neck and kissed him. She smiled, but he was still frowning. She kissed him again, and then said, "I promise, if I decide this crazy idea is the only way, I will bring you along."

Ryan stopped frowning and pulled Deb onto his lap and kissed her again. Then he said, "Thank you, I think. I'm not sure I should trust you on this. I mean, you kept this from me. When did Kim first tell you she was upset?"

"Just after we got back to campus. I wasn't keeping it from you. I was just thinking it over and trying to come up with a way to help Kim not feel so bad. Then I started thinking that maybe Kim was right, that it was very wrong what Joe did to them, and I wanted to undo what he did and not just find a way to help Kim. All of this thinking led me to this crazy idea."

"Did you tell Kim you wanted to do this?"

"Not yet."

"She's going to want to come with, you know."

"I know. That is a big problem. I don't want anything to happen to her, and I know she is going to want to see our father if we get her that close."

"So, it's perfectly alright for you take this risk, but not your sister?"

"Of course."

"I'm going to have to watch you like a hawk, aren't I?"

"I don't need watching."

"Just remember, you promised to not go alone."

"I know. At the risk of making you frown again; I'm going to change the subject. Have you made a decision about which school you are going to accept yet?"

"Yeah, I'm thinking about NYU. I know that is where you really want to go, and I can't stand the idea of only seeing you on breaks for the next four years."

"I wasn't wanting to do that either, but, Ryan, if you really want to be in North Carolina, I think you should go."

"No, I've already informed my parents. They actually like the idea, so it's decided."

"Great! I can't wait, can you?"

"I'm getting excited about it now that I have decided."

"Me too. Now, back to homework."

They finished up and met everyone for dinner. After dinner, Deb called Aunt Alicia and told her she had decided on NYU. Aunt Alicia was very excited to have her close by, and Uncle Darrick said he was happy for her and knew she would enjoy it. Then she called Ken. He was excited too, because this meant Deb would be close enough to see. Deb asked how things went with Mary and they talked about what each had done over the weekend. Deb didn't mention Kim or her plans for using the machine.

13

Deb had planned on asking Joe and Mr. Brewster to discuss the issues that Joe had on his trip to Cambridge later that week, but when she saw Mr. Brewster in the hall after a class, he said excitedly that his son and his son's girlfriend were coming home this weekend for a visit. Mr. Brewster asked if Deb and all the others would mind coming over on Saturday to meet his son, as he had spoken about them often, and Thomas wanted to meet them all. Deb replied she would arrange for them to come over and left it at that. This meant the conversation about the problems Joe had had would have to wait.

That Saturday, as arranged, Deb, Ryan, Joe, Becky, Mary, and Kim walked over to Mr. Brewster's house. Deb knocked on the door and Mr. Brewster came quickly to open it. Then he ushered them all into his small living room. There sat Thomas and his girlfriend, whom he introduced as Brittany. Mr. Brewster introduced all the kids to Thomas and Brittany and then announced that Thomas and Brittany were getting married. At that Deb said, "Congratulations. I can see your father is very proud."

"That he is," Thomas answered with a big smile on his face.

"This is the best news I've had in a long time," Mr. Brewster added.

"It's great to meet you all. Dad has never really spoken of students here at Choate, so it surprised me at how much he talks about you all."

"He's been very helpful to Joe," Deb answered.

"In what way?" Brittany asked.

"I'm not sure if Mr. Brewster, well, your dad, told you about us. We came here a year ago after our parents were both killed in accidents. It was a very hard time for Joe, and your dad sort of took him under his wing and helped Joe through a tough time."

"What brought you and Joe together, Dad?"

"I recognized in him the profound loss of a loved one and thought I could offer some outside counsel. We discovered we share a love of science and math and research, and it has blossomed from there," Mr. Brewster explained.

"Well Joe, that kind of makes us brothers, if you don't mind, anyway."

"That's cool. Thanks for sharing him with me," Joe said.

"Dad tells me you're a big inventor, Joe."

"Oh, I don't know about that."

"Come on, Joe, don't be modest. Joe here is about to make lots of cash on a new personal computer and has developed a new language for computers that will revolutionize the industry," Ryan said as he grabbed Joe by the neck.

"What's a personal computer?" Brittany asked.

"It's a smaller version of a computer that can have programs on it for you to write papers and letters, compile data and numbers, play games, things like that," Joe explained.

"Isn't that what a typewriter and calculator do now?" Thomas asked.

"They do, but this new computer will allow you to store that finished paper, or set of data, and use it repeatedly," Mr. Brewster added.

"Yeah," Joe said.

"Someday everyone will have one of these personal computers on their desks at home, and we will do homework on them, do research on them, do everything on them. Joe is going to be famous," Kim added, standing up.

"Well, I guess I picked one great guy as my chosen brother, huh?"

"Thomas, your dad tells us you are studying to be a doctor for cancer research. Can you tell us about that?" Mary asked.

"I lost my mother too, when I was about your age, Kim, and it had a profound impact on my life. She was very sick in the end, and I knew as I watched her then that all I wanted to do was find a way to stop that kind of pain from happening," Thomas said solemnly.

"It's really nice the way you have turned your tragedy into something positive," Mary said.

"Well, you have to, don't you? Find something to occupy your mind and focus on so you can get past that loss. At least that's how I did it."

"I did it with your dad's help. He talked to me and listened and understood," Joe added, just as solemnly.

They spent a couple of hours talking about Thomas' research and his plans and how Brittany was a researcher, too. She did her research on animal behavior in the psychology department. When it got close to dinnertime, the kids left and headed back to campus. After dinner, they all went to the main hall for the Saturday night movies and games.

"You've been quiet since we left Mr. Brewster's," Ryan whispered to Deb while they were watching the movie.

"We're watching a movie; we have to be quiet," Deb whispered back, smiling.

"That's not what I meant."

"Do you want to get out of here?" she asked.

"Yeah, let's go for a walk."

"Ok, but a short one. It's freezing out there, and I think it's still snowing."

"You're such a softy."

"Thanks a lot, what a great boyfriend you are!"

"I'll keep you warm."

They walked for a bit and then Deb said, "I've been quiet because I've been thinking. First, did you notice Thomas?"

"Of course, I noticed him. We sat and talked with him for a couple of hours."

"No, I mean how he looks."

"I don't get what you mean."

"He is the absolute copy of Mr. Brewster's grandfather from that picture we found in the library of him when he went off to war."

"Oh, I knew he looked familiar, but I just figured it was because he looks like a younger version of Mr. Brewster."

"If we went back to the library and looked that picture up again, you would see they could be twins."

"I wonder if Mr. Brewster notices it?"

"He remembers going into the machine and meeting his father, but I don't know."

"You have to go to the library tomorrow, right? Why don't you look up the picture again and get a copy of it and take it to Mr. Brewster and remind him?"

"That would be nice."

"So, what else are you thinking about?"

"What makes you think I'm thinking of anything else?"

"Only because I know you, and have been dating you for over a year now."

"Oh, is that all? Yes, I have been thinking about what happened to Joe and deciding if we should go back to Cambridge and do something about our parents. I was thinking about it when we were sitting in Mr. Brewster's living room. I mean, we did a tiny thing and changed things for him. He had his wife for many more years and they had Thomas and look at how happy Mr. Brewster seems. I think the key to changes we make in the machine is they have to be small ones, nothing as dramatic and stopping an assassination, just minor changes, like delaying a teacher."

"What about what happened to Joe? He almost didn't make it back."

"Yes, I know. I'm still trying to figure that all out. I wanted to sit down with Joe and Mr. Brewster and go over it, and had planned to do that this past weekend, but then Mr. Brewster had his son visit and I haven't set it up yet."

"Maybe this is something you and I should do with Joe and Mr. Brewster?"

"Maybe, but Kim gets so upset when we don't include her and I don't know how to talk about what happened to Joe without talking about my plan to go back to Cambridge and I have a feeling that Mr. Brewster will not support me on this."

"What if we put it to them as simply a follow up since we had some questions from the first time we discussed it all?"

"That might work, but if that's what we are going to do, I think it should wait until after Joe's release in two weeks."

"That sounds like a good idea. Ready to head back? I'm sure the movies are just about over and we need to get Kim and her friends back to the girls' dorm."

"Yeah, let's go. Besides, I'm freezing!"

"Well then, first come here and I will warm you up."

Deb came closer and Ryan pulled her to him, wrapping his arms around her. They held each other for a few minutes and whispered back and forth. Then they headed back to the main hall just in time to gather up the girls, Joe and Becky and Mary, and head out.

On a freezing Monday, two weeks later, the press release went out from Fitzgerald & Davis announcing the release of a new computer, known as a personal computer, for retail and business purchase. By the end of that day, the buzz was so great that Mr. Davis called Joe and told him they had requested a press conference to ask questions about this new product. Mr. Davis wanted Joe there. Joe indicated they could only release him from school if Aunt Alicia contacted the school. Mr. Davis suggested he plan it for the afternoon on Friday so that it would interfere the least with Joe's classes. It was all arranged by Tuesday afternoon and Ken was driving over to get Joe and both of his sisters to meet Aunt Alicia and Mr. Reynolds for the press conference in New York. Kim was very excited and chattered the entire way to the city. Ken was trying to patient with her, but his patience was running thin. He too was nervous about today and was overjoyed when Aunt Alicia and Darrick greeted them and took Kim by the hand. They found seats just behind Joe, who was in the front row, and sat down.

Mr. Davis was at the podium and he asked that everyone be seated so they could begin. The cameras were flashing and all the press people were behind the row that Deb and the others were sitting in.

"First, let me say, thank you all for coming today and allowing us to do this on a Friday afternoon. We have brought you all here because of the profound number of questions you have presented to us. To answer your questions, I have gathered the designers and the creator of this new personal computer, as I am woefully under-informed about what this new product is all about. With that, I will introduce first the young man that is responsible for the creation of this new product, and the son of my late partner, Joseph Fitzgerald."

Mr. Davis motioned for Joe to come up to the podium. Joe got up on the raised platform and moved the microphone down a bit. He looked first at his family and then out to the crowd. He turned to the others sitting behind the podium and motioned for some of them to come up as well.

"Since you have questions, perhaps we can start with those and forgo any comments from the team," Joe said, looking out at the crowd and feeling very nervous.

"Can you tell us about yourself and how you came to invent this new device, Mr. Fitzgerald?" the first reporter asked.

"Sure. My name is Joseph. My father is Mr. Patrick Fitzgerald, a founding partner of this company. I currently attend school at Choate Rosemary Hall in Wallingford, Connecticut."

"How old are you?" that same reporter asked.

"I'm sixteen."

"And how did you come up with this computer design?" he asked.

"Well, my mother was a professor at Harvard University and I spent quite a bit of time there working with the staff in the computer department. There, I learned a lot about COBOL and Assembler language and how computers work using these early languages. I started thinking that if computers could be smaller and work on a language that was much easier to program in, they could have many more uses outside the university research labs. I mean, NASA has rooms full of computers, but you certainly can't have one of those in your house."

The group laughed, and Joe continued, "Over the last year, I started working on a language that is in English, is simple in design, and doesn't block the action words to make the program run. That is how we came up with 'C,' which these guys behind me helped finish and test. While I was working on that, I came up with this idea that if the programming was smaller, it could fit on a smaller device and that would be more practical for everyday use. Last fall I started trying different parts and came up with a crude first version that these other guys from my father's company designed and put together."

"So, you would say your parents inspired you to create this language and computer?" a reporter from the back asked.

"Definitely. Everything I've done has been in tribute to my parents," Joe replied.

"Are they here?" a third reporter asked.

"No, as Mr. Davis noted, my parents are both dead. They were killed in accidents last year."

After a few minutes' pause, another reporter asked, "Can you introduce these other players to us?"

"Sure, to my left are the design team from Fitzgerald and Davis. They include Matt Jones, Tim Rhoades, and Steve Findlay. My brother, sitting out there, Ken Fitzgerald, also helped with the design. On my right are the guys from IBM and Harvard that helped with the new language and the testing. The head of the testing team is Jeff Hansen. The others are Mike Childers, Ben Adler, Mark Donnelly, and Professor Thomas Smithers."

"What type of programs are going to run on this new computer?" another reporter asked.

"The guys here from IBM have created a word processing program. It will let the user create reports, documents and letters, and save them to the computer's storage drive. There is also a program that will allow you to enter data in a table and run processes and calculations against it. The team from Harvard has created a game program that lets the user play different versions of solitaire. That is all the first release will have, but with the simple programming tools that can be obtained from IBM, Harvard and Fitzgerald and Davis, more sophisticated users can create programs all on their own."

"How much is it going to cost?" a man in the back asked.

"Well, it comes with the machine, a screen, and a keyboard. It will cost $900," one designer chimed in.

"There will be other versions offered soon that have more storage capabilities and that will probably come with other standard programs," Matt added from next to Joe.

At that point, the reporters asked Matt several other technical design questions and then they asked about the word processing and data management tools developed by IBM and Jeff came to the podium and answered those questions. Then they asked many storage questions that both Matt and Joe fielded.

The questions continued for a few more minutes, and then there was a request for the full team to stand for photos. Joe motioned for Ken to join them. He hesitated and then Mr. Reynolds pushed him to go up and join Joe.

While they were taking pictures, Mr. Reynolds commented, "Joe seemed to relax as the questions went on, and he did an excellent job."

"Yes, he seemed very professional. It impressed me with his not using slang and being so professional in his speech," Aunt Alicia said.

"He looks really nice in that suit too," Kim said as she took some pictures with the camera she had brought along.

"This is so cool. He is so young and has done something really great. I wish Mom and Dad were here to see him," Deb said.

"Yes, your parents would both be very proud of him. I wish your mother could see you all, and how you are all doing so well in the things that matter to you. Look at you Deb, you are about to graduate and head off to college at NYU," Aunt Alicia responded.

"I'm sure they're here, watching this impressive accomplishment," Mr. Reynolds added.

"I miss them so much, especially on days like this," Kim said, looking down at the floor.

Mr. Reynolds wrapped his arm around her and said, "I know, I miss my mother too when great things happen. Like when your aunt agreed to marry me and you all became my nieces and nephews?"

"Is that a significant moment for you?" Kim asked.

"It is going to go down as one of the greatest. I can't think of anything I'm going to be prouder of than being her husband and your uncle."

"When is this next significant event going to happen, Uncle Darrick?" Deb asked, smiling.

"Your aunt hasn't decided, but I was thinking we do it over your spring break at the Hampton house. What do you think of that?"

"I think that is a great idea. Is Ken going to have the same break as us?"

"I asked him, and he does this year."

"Aunt Alicia, what do you say about this?" Deb asked.

"I'm still deciding. Darrick wants a small wedding with just you all and a few of our friends. I was really thinking of a bigger event."

"If that's what you want, Alicia, I will do it. This is your big day, so just decide and we can start planning," Mr. Reynolds said as he looked fondly at Aunt Alicia.

At that point, the boys came back to where they were sitting, and Mr. Davis followed.

"It went wonderfully, Joe. I'm so proud of you. You did a wonderful job answering questions and were very professional," Mr. Davis said.

"Yes, Joe, we're all very proud of you and so glad we could join you on this monumental day. I know, however, that this is just the beginning, and only the first of your big press conferences," Mr. Reynolds said.

"Joe, you looked so cool up there. This was really cool!" Kim said as she got up and hugged Joe.

"You looked great in your suit and sounded so grown up," Deb added.

"Joe, we're all so proud of you," Aunt Alicia added.

"Thanks everybody. I'm really glad you were all here. It really means a lot to me. I was pretty nervous at first, so seeing you guys helped," Joe said.

"We might have been able to see that you seemed a little nervous at first, Joe, but no one else saw it, I'm sure," Ken added.

"Mr. Davis, do you think we covered everything we needed to?" Joe asked.

"Indeed, I do. The sales people were at the back and they said to me while you all were having your pictures taken that they were thrilled with how this went and they intend to use these stories when they are out selling and they plan to get quotes into the marketing material. They think this will really boost sales. Which I am happy about," Mr. Davis said, smiling.

"Well, that's good. I know little about sales, but I want to do my part to make this a successful venture for Fitzgerald and Davis," Joe replied.

"Mr. Davis, we are headed out for dinner to celebrate Joe's accomplishment, and to celebrate Ken's birthday, which is tomorrow. Would you like to join us?" Mr. Reynolds asked.

"That would be wonderful. Thank you so much for thinking of me. Let me just be sure the news people are out of the building and speak to the teams and I will be right with you."

They gathered their coats and headed to the hallway to wait for Mr. Davis to join them. Then they all went to the restaurant that Mr. Reynolds had made reservations at and had a great steak dinner and toasted Joe's big day and Ken's birthday. Mr. Reynolds and Aunt Alicia presented Ken with a really expensive looking watch. Deb gave Ken a really nice leather portfolio to hold notepads and a briefcase for when he started working at Fitzgerald & Davis. Joe said his gift was being shipped to Ken at Harvard, but he wrote on the card that Ken was getting a first edition computer for school. Kim had found a picture that was taken the Christmas before their parents died and created a painting of the picture for Ken. Ken commented how her skills as an artist were improving all the time and how he was going to hang this picture in his dorm room.

After dinner, they all stood in the street, saying their goodbyes. Ken was going to drive Deb, Joe, and Kim back to campus and spend the weekend with them and Mary. Aunt Alicia and Mr. Reynolds were heading back to the New York apartment and Mr. Davis was heading home. They all congratulated Joe again and wished Ken a happy birthday and Aunt Alicia said she would call on Sunday.

They got back to campus really late. Ken took the girls first to their dorm and asked Deb to tell Mary that he would see her tomorrow. Then Ken and Joe went back to the boys' dorm, where Ken was going to sleep. The next day, Kim had an all-day Girl Scout event and so Ken asked all the others if they wanted to go bowling and see a movie and have dinner in town. They all agreed on that plan, but Deb suggested they end the evening with dinner so that Ken and Mary could have some time together. Mary whispered her thanks to Deb as they were exiting the dining hall from breakfast. They got Kim ready and off on her Girl Scout event, and the others all walked into town and went to the bowling alley. They bowled several games and had some snacks. Of course, Joe won all the games they played. Then they went to see the matinee of Close Encounters of the Third Kind playing at the town theater. When the movie ended, the girls stayed in town and walked through some shops while the boys went back to campus to pick Kim up for dinner.

On the way back into town, Joe asked Kim what they did today. Kim replied, "Today was a badge event day. We each got to pick a morning activity and an afternoon activity to earn a badge."

Ryan asked, "What did you pick to do?"

"I did a baking and cooking badge for the morning and a pet care badge for the afternoon."

"What do you do for a baking and cooking badge?" Ken asked.

"We went to the bakery in town and got to see how they make bread, cookies and pastries and we each got to make and decorate cupcakes, and then a nurse from the hospital came and talked to us about nutrition and meal planning and stuff like that. Then for the pet care badge, we went to the veterinary clinic. We learned about what the vet does to check dogs and cats and what they need vaccines for, and what foods they can and cannot eat. Then we learned about caring for other kinds of animals like fish and mice and stuff. We got to help with the dogs and cats that were being boarded at the veterinary office. It was really fun."

"Did you get your badges today?" Joe asked.

"No, we get those in a few weeks when we have a badge ceremony at our meeting."

"Who sews on your badges?" Ken asked, concerned that she wasn't getting the support their mother would have provided.

"I do it. I got my sewing badge last year, so I know how to sew by hand and with a machine now."

"Oh, that's good. So, which one did you like better today?"

"I really liked the vet visit. It seemed so cool taking care of the animals and making sure they were safe and stuff. I don't know. I've been thinking for a while that I want to be an artist, but maybe now I want to be a vet."

"I'm sure you'd be a good one," Ryan said.

"You have time. You never know what will happen in the next few years to change your mind about what you want to be," Ken added.

They got to the Italian restaurant where they had celebrated so many occasions last year, and the girls were already seated inside. They all had dinner together and then walked back to campus. Deb, Ryan, Joe, Becky and Kim all went to the main hall for Saturday activities, while Ken and Mary got into Ken's car and left campus again to spend some time together.

In the main hall, the four older kids went to play pool and Kim went to meet her friends to watch a movie. While they were playing pool,

Joe and Ryan talked about the movie they had seen and the possibility of UFOs and aliens and how cool it would be to figure out a way to communicate with another race. Deb and Becky got a little tired of the UFO talk and wandered off to find some refreshments and talk to their friends until the pool game was over.

Meanwhile, Ken took Mary to the ice cream parlor. Afterward, they went for a drive and ended up at the same park they had argued at before finals.

"I wanted to come back here so we could have some happier memories of this park. I know it's one of your favorite places," Ken said.

"Thanks. I'm glad we're here."

They walked up to the lake, and the moon was shining brightly on the ice and snow. Mary brought the gift she had for Ken's birthday and she handed it over to him while they stood by the lake. Ken opened the box and in it was a beautiful cross on a chain.

"I know you don't wear a lot of jewelry, but this was something special that was my grandfather's that I wanted you to have. He wore it every day and said that it kept his heart true during the war. He was a soldier in World War II."

"Wow, Mary, are you sure you want me to have this? I mean, this is probably something that is important to your family."

"I want you to have it."

"Are you sure?"

"Aren't we going to be a family someday?"

"That's my plan."

"Then keep it. Maybe it will be a source of inspiration as you sort through your faith questions."

"This really means a lot to you, so I will wear it every day, too. Thank you for understanding that I need some time to sort my feelings out. That really means a lot to me, too."

"I love you, Ken. I love everything about you, even your questions, even our differences, even your doubts."

"I love you too. Everything about you. Even when you are jealous."

"Well, I'm glad you love that. I look back on that now and I don't like how I acted. But enough about that."

Ken took the chain out of the box and handed it to Mary to put on him. He hunched down so she could reach and she put it around his neck. He turned back around and hugged her. They stood like that for a long time and then Mary said she was sorry, but she was getting cold. They got back in the car and talked for a while about how often they hoped to see each other for the rest of the year, how to see each other over the summer, and all the times they would visit during college. Ken couldn't remember a time he was as happy or a time when he felt as at home as in those moments with Mary that night. They drove back to campus and met the others as they were heading back to the dorms. On Sunday after church services, Ken left to get back to Harvard.

That afternoon, Mr. Brewster found Kim in the main hall working on a project with her friends and asked where he might find Joe. Kim said she thought he was in the library doing research for a history paper. When Mr. Brewster arrived at the library, he found Deb and Mary there working on a project for their English class. Deb told him she was pretty sure Joe had walked back to the dorm with Ryan. When Mr. Brewster finally arrived at the boys' dorm, he found Joe with Ryan playing a board game in the lobby area.

"Joe, there you are; I've been searching for you everywhere."

"Sorry, Mr. Brewster. I was at the library, but we got done a little bit ago and Ryan wanted to play a game. What's up?"

"What's up? What a question, my famous young friend."

With that, Mr. Brewster reached into the briefcase he was carrying and pulled out several newspapers. In each, was a story about the young genius who had written a revolutionary new computer language and had developed a new computer that was going to take over the business world. The three of them read over the different stories and occasionally read something aloud for the others. They laughed and Mr. Brewster said Joe could keep these copies, as he had purchased several copies at the newsstand that day.

"So, the press conference was a success!" Mr. Brewster said.

"Yeah, it was pretty cool. I was really nervous at first. It helped that Ken, Deb and everyone were there so I could look at them instead of all those strangers there to hear what I had to say. But it worked out ok. Mr. Davis said I sounded very professional."

"I'm very sorry I missed it. But I know there will be others in your future, so hopefully I can make it to one."

"I wish you could have been there, too. You were a big help to me. Not just in this project."

"That's nice of you to say, but Joe, this was all you. Your dream and you made it happen."

"Now I get to say I know someone famous!" Ryan said.

"Yes, you do," Mr. Brewster added.

"Let's not make such a big deal out of this, huh?" Joe said, looking embarrassed.

"Never be ashamed of your accomplishments, Joe. You did this. Remember last year when you were talking about finding your place, in your family and at this school? Now you have. Don't downplay that," Ryan said.

"Precisely. Joe, why don't you and Becky and Deb and Ryan see if you can stop by some afternoon this week? I haven't sat and talked with you in a while and I want to check in with everyone."

"Sure, Mr. Brewster, I will check with Deb tonight at dinner and let you know sometime tomorrow. Would that be alright?"

"Yes, I will see you tomorrow. Enjoy the papers. You earned it."

14

A few days later, the four of them sat around the worktable in the barn once again. Mr. Brewster brought several copies of the papers and a recent addition to the stories about Joe, Life magazine, which had an article in it about Joe's invention and how technology was coming, whether or not the world wanted it. They all laughed about the doomsday implications from the magazine about how this new personal computer was going to be the downfall of society as it was known. After another round of raving about Joe's press conference and inventions, Mr. Brewster said, "It's so good to have you here. I've missed our regular sessions around this table working through things."

Deb used this as an opportunity to explore what happened to Joe on his trip to Cambridge and said, "As long as we are talking about past sessions around this table, I have a few questions about what happened to Joe on the trip he made to Cambridge. Can I ask them now?"

"I think that would be ok. What do you think, Joe?" Mr. Brewster replied.

"Sure. Why now though, Deb?"

"Oh, no reason. I was just thinking about the machine and how much we have learned and how we seem to have stopped thinking about it with your other impressive feat this past month."

"Ok, what are your questions?" Joe asked, wanting to deflect some of the attention, as it was getting a little embarrassing.

"Well, here's the thing: you said you felt queasy and light-headed and dizzy just after you left the house that day to go back to the machine.

Was that because of how long you were there, or was it all of sudden these things started, or did they build up over time?"

"The headaches started shortly after I arrived home. In fact, that started just after I hopped the fence into our backyard. The queasiness started after about an hour when I was going over notes and printouts from the machine. The dizziness didn't start until after I had gotten about a block from our house and was headed back to the machine."

"Did other symptoms occur while you waited to get to the machine?"

"The headache got way worse. I think I might have blacked out for some period, because I was sitting in the bushes waiting for some guys who were fishing to leave when I realized it was dark all of a sudden. The headache was nearly unbearable at that point, and my muscles seemed weak, like it was hard to stand and walk. You know, like when your arm is asleep and tingly and you can't seem to make it do what you want it to do, but then you see it doing what you planned?"

"Yeah, I know what you mean. That happens to me sometimes when I get really clocked on the ice," Ryan said.

"Yeah, then when I got in the machine and turned everything on and started up the program, the symptoms went away."

"Wow, Joe, do you think they would have gotten worse if you hadn't made it to the machine?" Becky asked, looking worried.

"I would suspect the symptoms would have worsened if he had not made it to the machine, but we have no actual way of knowing what that might be or if it would have incapacitated him," Mr. Brewster added.

"To hear you talk about this, it makes me wonder if you'd stayed longer if you would have made it back at all," Deb said, looking over at Ryan.

"What do you think might have caused these symptoms? Do you have any idea?" Ryan asked.

"Well, based on the printouts from when Joe strapped himself into the chair in the machine and it could read his vitals and such, all his readings were very erratic," Mr. Brewster replied.

"Erratic how?" Deb asked.

"For instance, his heartbeat was up and down and seemed to stop for long periods and then start back up suddenly at a rapid rate. His breathing was all over the place as well. When he first strapped in, he was breathing heavily, but then his breath seemed to dwindle down to a short, shallow rasp," Mr. Brewster said.

"What would cause that?" Becky asked.

"We think—but keep in mind this is theoretical at this point—there is something about space and time rules that will not allow the same entity to be present more than once. The accepted theory this is based on is that we believe there is a finite amount of energy in the universe and Joe, being there twice, added his energy of the second Joe, which put the universe out of whack. We also think that the entity, or in this case, the Joe that was supposed to exist in that time and space, would be the dominant entity. So, we think what was happening was that this 'rule' of time and space was working to reconcile the conflict of two entities," Mr. Brewster tried delicately to explain a complex scientific theory as well as reduce the blow for everyone about what he and Joe thought might be happening.

"You mean erase the second instance of you, don't you?" Deb asked, with a shocked look on her face.

"Basically, yes," Joe said.

"Joe, but you seemed ok when you first arrived and after about an hour, the symptoms started. Is that because this time and space rule you are talking about was figuring out there were two of you in that time and space?" Deb asked.

"Yes, that is what we think. There must be some amount of time when we travel and bend time and I jump into this time where I already existed, where the balance in the universe or whatever, doesn't know I'm there, and then when it figures it out, it tries to correct it," Joe said.

"And that time it takes for this universal balance or whatever to figure it out is about an hour?" Deb asked.

"Well, we're only speculating on that. We do not know about how long that would take. We're fairly certain this must be what was going on, as none of you had any of these symptoms when you went to Dallas, nor did I have any of these symptoms when I went to Iowa. In both cases, everyone travelled to a time and place where they didn't already exist," Mr. Brewster explained.

"We didn't have any of these issues when we went to Las Vegas either," Ryan said.

"So, it is safe to conclude that whatever happened and however long it takes to happen will only occur when anyone goes to a time and space where they already exist," Joe concluded.

"I'm not sure I want to ask this, but is there any way to prove any of this?" Ryan asked.

"The only way is for someone else to get into the machine and go to a time and space they already exist and see if they have the same symptoms," Joe said.

"That doesn't sound like a good idea to me," Becky said, reaching for Joe's hand.

"Do you have any other questions, Deb?" Joe asked.

"No, that was scary enough, thank you. Remember your promise, no trips alone in the machine ever again. I think that goes for all of us. No trips in the machine alone. From now on, any trips, at least two people have to go, in case something like this happens," Deb said.

"What if I had gone with you? I existed in that time, but not in that specific space. What I mean is, I was at Choate on the day you went back to. If I had been with you, would that have happened to me, too?" Ryan asked.

"That's an interesting question, Ryan," Mr. Brewster said, as he grabbed his chin in thought.

"My suspicion is that you would have to exist in both the time and space. So, if we went back to say, North Carolina, to the town where your grandparents live, and you were visiting, say the Fourth of July two years ago, I suspect the symptoms would happen to you, but not me. I existed in that time, but I was in a different space, in Cambridge," Joe thought out loud.

"So, by space you mean actual space, like a city or house or something?" Becky asked.

"I think so," Joe replied.

"That's an interesting hypothesis, Joe," Mr. Brewster said, still holding his chin in thought, then he said, "This hypothesis would imply there is some unit of time and space, that exists independently of other time and space units where the energy is finite. That is a significant variation on the current theory. The current theory understands the entire universe as one space and time unit. According to that theory, if Ryan went with you to Cambridge, he would exist twice and would experience the same kinds of symptoms."

"Again, there would be no actual way to test this without a trip to a space and time where one of us existed and one didn't, right?" Ryan asked.

"Yes, that would be the only way to confirm Joe's theory," Mr. Brewster said.

They all sat there thinking about Joe's theory for a few minutes, not saying anything. Then Mr. Brewster said, "This is what I was missing, an intellectual debate about a question and theory!"

"I missed it too," Deb said, but then she said, "Oh, by the way, Mr. Brewster, I have something for you. Remember when we were researching for your test trip to Iowa? When I went to the library to look up some things and found your father in a news article about soldiers from that area that went to the war and were lost at Normandy? I found his picture. I went over to the library and looked it up again and copied the picture. You have to look at this. Your son, Thomas, looks exactly like your father in that picture!"

Deb pulled the picture out of her purse and handed it to Mr. Brewster. He looked at and then looked up at Deb and around the room. He looked back at the picture and said, "I never realized the resemblance. You're right, Deb, he could be my father's twin brother. Thank you so much for this. I have told Thomas stories about my father since he was a little boy. He loved them. He will surely love knowing he looks just like him."

"I hope so. I was so shocked when we met him at your house and it took me some time to figure out why. It was because I remembered this picture."

"Thank you, Deb."

"Sure."

"This has been exactly what I needed today. Thank you all for coming. Please bring Kim the next time you come. However, it is getting close to the dinner hour, so you all better make your way back to campus."

"Thanks Mr. Brewster," Ryan said.

"Can I keep this magazine, Mr. Brewster?" Joe asked.

"Of course, I purchased it for you to have. Take all three copies, in fact. I'm sure Ken would like to see it, and probably your aunt as well."

"Thanks."

"I'll see you all tomorrow in the science building. Come on back soon."

The kids made their way back to campus. Later that night, Deb told Mary about the picture and that they had discussed what happened to Joe and about his theories on the trip and about the magazine that Joe was in. Mary thought the magazine was really great. She said she was sorry she missed that big event and she worried about the machine and anyone trying to prove Joe's theories. Deb assured her they had no plans to do anything like that, so she didn't have to worry. They were so glad things were right between them and neither wanted anything to change that again. Mary thanked Deb for sharing what happened and being so honest with her.

That Sunday, when Aunt Alicia called Deb, she had much news to report. She began with news about the wedding, saying, "We have made a few decisions. First, as I have always wanted a winter wedding, and we want all of you kids here. We are going to have the wedding in New York during your Christmas break. How many people will be there is still to be decided. Darrick still wants to keep it smaller, but we'll see. I'm trying not to focus on that right now."

This brought them to the other bit of news, as she said, "I have an interview on Tuesday with Grace Mirabella. I just might be the next editor of the fashion trend section of the magazine. It would be a huge promotion for me and a considerable raise. I'm rather nervous to meet with her for this interview."

"I'm sure you'll do great, Aunt Alicia. Whenever I watched you at photoshoots and those meetings last year, you seemed to always know so much and were always first with ideas. I'm so excited for you. You totally deserve this."

"I hope you're right, dear. Anyway, I will need you to be my maid of honor, and I'm planning to ask Kim to be a bridesmaid. Darrick is going to ask Ken to be his best man and Joe to be a groomsman."

"Kim will just love this. So will I."

"Well, hopefully by the time you are here for spring break we will have some more decisions made and we can make a trip to look at dresses for you two. It might be hard to find the right style for you and Kim at the same time, but we'll figure it out."

"I'm sure you can find just the right look, and I totally trust you to pick it out."

"Goodness, you are such a boost for my ego today. Thanks for that!"

"Any time. Good luck on Tuesday. I'll be rooting for you all afternoon."

"Please tell Kim and Joe I said hello. Oh, by the way, I almost forgot, Darrick said that Joe was in the latest Life magazine. Can you believe it?"

"Oh, yeah, we saw that. The teacher that Joe is close with, Mr. Brewster, bought him several copies of it when he saw it."

"Well, Darrick and I already bought three or four copies. It's so fun to watch Darrick parade around and praise his genius soon-to-be-nephew!"

"You know, last year, Joe was so worried that he would have nothing to make him special. He told Ken once that he felt like he didn't fit in with our family. Ken was athletic and popular; I was some history genius and Kim was going to be this great artist. What was he going to be? Now look," Deb commented.

"Yes, now look. You are going to have to work pretty hard to surpass him with your archeology career plans. Perhaps it's time to consider a different path?"

"As much as I love the clothes and things you've given me and shown me, I still really want to work in archeology somewhere. Who knows, maybe Kim will become a fashion designer and you can feature her in the trend section of Vogue?"

They both laughed and said goodbye with that positive note. Tuesday evening while working with Ryan on a project, Deb remembered that this was interview day, and she rushed back to the dorm to call her aunt.

"Hi Aunt Alicia, I just called to see how your interview went."

"How thoughtful you are, Deb. It went really great."

"I knew it would."

"We talked about her vision for the trend section and I offered several ideas for changes and she seemed to really like them. She said she would have a decision by the end of the week."

"I know you'll get it."

"Keep that thought, and prayers might help too."

"I definitely will add it to my nightly prayers. Call me Friday when you find out?"

"Sure. When are you done with classes?"

"I finish at three, so I will be back to the dorm by three-twenty."

"I'll call you Friday. Thanks for calling Deb. You're a doll."

"Well, goodnight, Miss Editor."

"Goodnight."

Deb was glad she had called. Things had really changed with Aunt Alicia since the blowout with Ken over the summer and her admitting her issues with their mother's death. Again, Deb thought that fixing what happened when Joe went to Cambridge would help because it would hopefully stop the separation and maybe Aunt Alicia would not be so angry with their father.

The next day, Deb reported to Kim and Joe about the wedding plans. She didn't add the part about what roles Kim and Joe would play, but she said it was going to be that Christmas break. Kim was very excited. She said she knew exactly what she was going to make as a wedding gift and she couldn't wait to start it this summer when school was out. Later that day, Deb found Ryan after class and asked him if he had some time to talk. He suggested they find one of those music practice rooms in the main hall where they could be alone and they walked over there. They sat at the piano. Ryan waited for Deb to tell him what was on her mind. He looked at her expectantly and raised his eyebrows.

"I've been thinking about going to Cambridge and trying to stop Joe from what he did," Deb finally blurted out.

"I figured you were."

"Is that why you asked about you going to a place where you didn't exist in a time you existed?"

"Yes. I told you if you ended up doing this, you were not going alone."

"You know it's a risk for both of us."

"Yes, but you're not going alone."

"Is that all you're going to say?"

"No, tell me about your plan," he said, laughing.

"Well, here is what I've been thinking. If you and I go back and meet Joe just before he goes into our house, tell him what will happen if he does it, and take the magazine about his personal computer and show him, he will know that it's a bad idea. He will get back to the machine he came in and we will get back into the machine we came in, and we will all end up back here. No one will be there long enough for symptoms to start and our parents won't separate."

"Well, I have a couple of questions. First, how are you going to convince the Joe from last spring, that still really wanted nothing more than to get his parents back, that seeing his father is going to hurt, not help that situation? Second, we didn't ask about the machine being in the same space and time. What do you think will happen when that occurs?"

"Well, for your first question, I know that what really bothered Joe was that we made it worse with the trip to Dallas. If I tell him how he makes it so much worse with this trip to Cambridge, I think that will stop him. And I think showing him what he has to look forward to might help. As to your second question, I'm not sure I thought that through. We'll have to ask Joe about that."

"This seems simple enough. I mean, you said that you think the trip to Las Vegas worked because we made a very simple change. Meeting the other Joe just before he goes home and telling him what it will do, that seems simple enough."

"I really want to do this. It will help Kim so much and now that Joe is doing so much better, I hate to think that Kim is going to struggle for a long time because our parents separated."

"I imagine none of you like the idea that the machine caused this rift for your parents. Well, even though the machine can't really do that."

"You know what I meant."

"Yes, sweetie, I do. I know this is important to you. Have you thought about where you will land the machine? I mean, I'm pretty sure, even without talking to Joe, that you can't simply land the machine next to the other version of it in that park he goes to."

"The house behind ours was vacant when we moved out. It had been for several years. Joe goes into the backyard and climbs over the fence into our backyard. I was thinking about landing the machine in that backyard."

"It makes quite an entrance, you know."

"Yeah. I know, but this backyard is heavy with trees and shrubs and very overgrown because of its abandoned state. I think it will be alright, even though it's in the middle of our neighborhood of houses."

"We should talk to Joe about this."

"Yeah, probably, but I figured if I couldn't talk you into it, I probably had no chance of talking Joe into it."

"I don't know about that. Are we planning to bring anyone else in on this?"

"You mean like Kim, Becky, Mary and Ken?"

"Yeah."

"I don't know. I mean, I did promise Kim that I would not exclude her, but I'm doing this primarily for her. She will wake up the day after we do this and never know that our parents separated in one of these timelines. We will erase it from her memory. I like that idea. But I also promised Ken that we wouldn't use the machine again without him knowing. I just know he will not like this idea if he hears what we heard about Joe's theory about his symptoms."

"And if you don't tell Ken, you can't tell Mary."

"Yes."

"I'd like for someone here at Choate to know that we're doing this, in case we really have issues. Should that be Becky or Mr. Brewster?" Ryan asked.

"I have this feeling that Mr. Brewster will try to talk us out of it, even though I think he is the person who should know."

"Well, we probably should have Becky involved somehow. She seems to really be good for Joe and I wouldn't want to mess that up."

"Yeah," Deb said and then sat for a minute, thinking.

"How about this? We talk this over with Joe and see what he thinks about the machine being in the same space and time, and then if he thinks it should be ok, we talk to Mr. Brewster and get his take on it. If he really doesn't want us to do it, we're going to have to rethink this," Ryan offered.

"We could always sneak it out like we did before."

"Really? You want to do that again?"

"Not really, but if that is the only thing stopping us, I'm not sure."

"Who knew I had a girlfriend that was such a risk-taker and so ready to break the rules?"

"Generally speaking, I'm not like that at all. It's just something I feel down deep that I have to do."

"Why?"

"I don't know. Maybe in the big picture, you know, big cosmic picture, I don't want it going down for all eternity that my parents split up because they couldn't both buy into the idea that their kids figured out how to travel through time. Maybe I just want to right what seems to be a huge wrong. They were so much in love. I can remember thinking when I was little and I would watch them be playful and kiss and hug and hold hands, that all I ever wanted was a husband like that and a life like that."

"Sweetie, I have to be the bad guy here for just a minute. Your parents argued over whether they both believed this fantastical story that Joe told your father. Your mother decided that something must be wrong with Joe and had him go through all those tests and things. Then, because they couldn't agree on this, they separated. What makes you think if you fix this, that something else won't come between them?"

Deb looked at him and started to cry. He reached for her as she said, "I don't know."

"I'm so sorry. I didn't want to make you cry."

"I'd like to think nothing would do that, but you're right. Maybe their marriage wasn't as strong as it looked to the little girl watching them. Maybe in the few months after Joe went there, if he hadn't gone there, something else might have come between them. I don't know."

"Maybe it was just this thing. I mean, your mother was a math professor. You know, numbers don't lie. They stay the same, always. Maybe the idea that Joe had figured out how to travel through time, even though it was based on math, was too much for her to comprehend.

Maybe it was that hugely crazy idea that caused the rift to start because your father believed and your mother couldn't."

"Where did you hear this numbers don't lie thing?"

"My father said it once. I remember it. It seemed funny at the time, but it's true. Numbers don't lie. They live by a constant rule."

"That makes some sense. I remember my mother was always so practical. She thought fancy anything was a waste."

"See. That's probably it. I mean, in the timeline before Joe went to Cambridge, nothing was going on between your parents. I mean, nothing out of the ordinary, right?"

"No, in the timeline just before they died in the avalanche. They were together and happy in all the memories I have of them."

"And before that, the first timeline, the one before any trips in the machine, they were fine then, too, right?"

"Yeah. We had such a fun day just before we went camping and they died in that plane crash."

"So, it seems to me that if we remove this huge thing that your mother couldn't wrap her head around, it should put them back in the right place, with their marriage as strong as you remember."

"I don't know."

"You don't know if you want to do this now?"

"No, I think I still want to do this. I'm just not sure it will fix things with my parents like I was before."

"I'm sorry."

"No, don't be sorry. One thing this machine has taught me is that we have to face the possibilities and the reality we end up with."

"So, we talk to Joe?"

"Yes, and we make one more pinky promise. This is the very last time we use the machine to do anything to our parents' timeline."

"I'm ready to pinky promise that."

"You are the best boyfriend, Ryan. Did anyone ever tell you that?"

"Oh, all my girlfriends have said that."

Deb playfully punched him in the shoulder as she said, "All your girlfriends. Just how many girlfriends have you had?"

"Only one. Only you."

"Oh."

"Did I take the wind out of your jealous fit?"

"First, it wasn't a fit, and second, I am not jealous!"

"Oh yes, you were. For a minute there, you were jealous, thinking that I had lots of girlfriends in my past."

He was laughing. She laughed too.

"Maybe I was a little jealous, but it wasn't a fit."

"I'll concede on the fit part."

"Thanks."

"Come here."

Deb sat back down, and Ryan pulled her close and kissed her. They hugged for a few minutes and then left the music room. They found Kim, Mary, Becky and Joe in the lobby of the girls' dorm.

"We were looking for you," Kim said.

"Sorry, we had a couple of things to talk about. Ready for dinner?" Deb asked.

"Yeah, let's go."

They walked over to the dining hall. Kim tried to get both Deb and Ryan to tell her what they were talking about. Ryan finally whispered to her he had just needed some alone time with his girlfriend so he could kiss her. That made Kim laugh and start singing the kissing song. On the way back from dinner, Deb asked Joe if he could meet her and Ryan in the library after classes the next day. He agreed. However, they didn't end up talking until early the next week. Ryan had to help a friend after classes that next day, and Joe was busy finishing a paper after that, which he didn't finish until late on Sunday. Friday, before Deb took Kim and her friend into town to pick up a few things, Aunt Alicia called. She was ecstatic. She had gotten the promotion. Deb congratulated her and said she knew she would get the job. Aunt Alicia didn't talk long; she and Uncle Darrick were headed to a party that night and she had to get ready, but Deb thanked her for calling.

On Monday of the next week, the first week of March, Ryan, Deb, Becky, and Joe sat at a table in one of the library study rooms. Joe had asked if Becky could be there, and Deb said that was fine.

"Right after we got back after Christmas break, Kim came to me and told me she was really struggling. That although she thought things were better here, she couldn't seem to stop feeling bad about our parents splitting up and it felt like it was going to be something that would be with her always," Deb started.

Joe looked down. He knew that going back to Cambridge was a mistake. Well, he knew that now anyway. He said, "I'm sorry every day that I made that trip. I know it hurt all of us, even you, Ryan. In so many ways. I wish I could take it back, Deb, but I can't."

"Listen, I'm not trying to make you feel bad or blame you. Kim wasn't struggling with losing our parents at the end of last year, when you still had issues, and when you took that trip alone. She knows about it, in terms of your going and what you did, because we told her. She just can't let it all go now. Frankly, it really bothers me, too. I mean, our parents were always so perfect together and it bothers me that something we did with the machine messed that up."

"We didn't do it, I did."

"Joe, hear her out?" Ryan asked.

Joe nodded and Deb continued, "I've been thinking about this a lot. I mean, we went to Las Vegas and made a tiny change and it ended up really helping Mr. Brewster, so why can't we do that here? Why can't we do something to just stop your trip?"

"Like, what are you thinking about doing?" Joe asked.

"Well, what if Ryan and I go back and land in the backyard of that vacant house behind ours and we stop you from going in and meeting Dad?"

"I mean, I guess that would work," Joe said thoughtfully.

"Joe, remember your state of mind last spring? All you wanted was to fix things for your parents. Remember you said, all you wanted was to bring your parents back to the world of the living? Are you sure you will listen to us if you meet us in that backyard?" Ryan asked.

"I don't know."

Deb answered, "I think I have come up with a way to convince you. Remember the letters our parents wrote Ken gave us from the lawyers? My letter speaks to the fact that I was not to blame you for what happened to our family. I'm thinking I will bring that version of the letter with me and show it to you. I'm also going to bring the newspaper clippings of our parents' deaths, where they died separately. Would that convince you that your trip did something bad and you shouldn't go into the house?"

"Maybe, probably."

"I hate to bring this up, but remember the talk we just had on how you can't be in the same space and time as another version of you? Won't that mean Deb will have symptoms?" Becky asked.

"If my theory is correct, yes," Joe replied.

"So, isn't this too big of a risk?" Becky asked.

"Deb, are you doing this just for Kim?" Joe asked.

"No, I'm doing it for me and for you too, Joe, and for Aunt Alicia and all of us."

"Why for Aunt Alicia?"

"Remember the blow out with Ken last summer? She said she was so angry with our father for leaving the way he did, but she was glad to have our mother back in her life? That is how it will help her."

"But if we do this, and set things back to what they were, she might not have our mother back in her life."

Deb thought for a minute and then replied, "I used to put notes on Mom's car sometimes and she used to put notes in my bag and lunch. Maybe I will put a note on her car? I mean, when you told me the date, I started thinking that was when Mom's car wasn't working and it was sitting in the driveway."

"Yeah, she and I took the train that day to Harvard," Joe said.

"I have another question: We know there is a risk that Deb will have symptoms if we do this. You think I won't because that wasn't a space I occupied. But what about the machine, Joe? Doing this will mean that the machine will exist in this time and space twice," Ryan asked.

"I hadn't thought about that at all, to be honest and remember, you not having issues is my theory. Mr. Brewster said that was not the current scientific theory. According to that theory, you will have symptoms too," Joe said.

"I think that means we do not know what might happen. I know I'm ready to take the risk because I don't want Deb going alone, and I think your theory might be more correct than the going scientific theory, but if a person can't exist twice in a specific space and time, can a machine?" Ryan asked.

"I don't know. Given the theory, I would have to say no. Something might happen to make one machine not work," Joe pondered.

"Do you think it would matter if one machine arrived at one time and took off at a set time and the other machine landed and took off at different times? Like if you arrive at eleven a.m. say, and Ryan and I arrive at noon, and you leave at eight p.m. and we leave at two p.m. Would that make it ok?" Deb asked.

"So, you're saying if we powered the machines up at different times, would that allow them to exist in the same space and time? Excellent theory, Deb," Joe said.

Deb, who had been thinking about Aunt Alicia, said, "Maybe that will be fine. I really need to put a note on Mom's car. I don't want to take Aunt Alicia's memories of our mother being back away, even if it means fixing our parents' marriage. Is there a bigger risk for me if I run around to the font the of the house to leave this note?"

"I can take the note. Then the only risk is someone thinking I'm breaking into your mother's car, since I will look like a stranger on your block," Ryan said.

"While you are thinking about that, have you thought about whether we are telling Ken and Mary about this?" Joe asked.

"Well, I know for sure Ken will not want us to take this risk if he hears all the stuff you went through in detail, and if he hears your theory. He will think this is a terrible idea," Deb said.

"And again, if we don't want Ken to know, we can't tell Mary, and we know that didn't turn out well. You almost lost a friend over it," Ryan said.

"Not to change the subject, but if Joe's theory is correct, Deb will have symptoms and the only one that supposedly won't have symptoms is Ryan. Ryan, are you going to handle both Joe and Deb if trouble happens?" Becky asked.

"We know Joe gets back. So, if we stop him from spending the day with his father, perhaps he won't have as many symptoms. Also, I've been thinking, if we manage to stop him, and he gets back to the machine faster, maybe he won't have to wait so long, and maybe he won't even have that blackout," Ryan said.

"That might work," Joe said.

"How about if I go with you and Deb and then when we see Joe, I go back to his machine and come back with him? That way, someone is with him if he does still have issues," Becky said.

"I'm not sure about that. I'm not sure if that will work if you travel in one machine to that time and space and another to get back to where you belong," Joe said.

"Why does it matter as long as I get back here?"

"Remember, you and Joe were not really dating at the time he went. If you come back with him, you are coming back to the end of last year. I think that is a bad idea. Then you would exist twice in the timeline here," Ryan speculated.

"Yeah, that is probably a correct assumption, Ryan. I come from last spring and return the day after graduation. Becky, you can't come back with me."

"Hey, how about this? What if I go with Becky and you back to your machine and get you into it and off and then we both come back and get into the other machine with Deb?" Ryan asked.

"Why add another person to this at all?" Deb asked.

"Don't you want me to help?" Becky asked.

"No, it's totally not that. I'm just working on the assumption that we were successful in Las Vegas because we kept it simple. I think we should keep it as simple as possible here too," Deb said.

"Oh, ok."

"I can always go with Joe and make sure he gets back and into his machine and then come back and go with you, Deb," Ryan said.

"I was only thinking about this to make sure Joe gets back with no issues, and maybe we prevent his blackout while you fix this thing with your parents," Becky said.

"It's a good idea, but I agree with Deb about this. Keep it simple and I think that means you have to sit this trip out, Becky, sorry. And I wanted you to be here in case any of these trips back had any issues," Ryan said.

Joe, who had been rolling the different issues around in his head this whole time, said, "I'm going to talk to Mr. Brewster about this, I think."

"Joe, we're not sure we should tell him, either. I know he's going to talk us out of this," Deb replied.

"Well, I can frame the discussion with Mr. Brewster as a follow up to our other discussion when you asked all the questions about my symptoms. Hey, is that why you asked all the questions? Anyway, I can put it to him that I was contemplating what would happen if the machine was taken twice to the same space and time and see what his thoughts are."

"That seems like a good next step, Joe," Ryan said.

"Then that's what we'll do," Deb said.

"When are you going to talk to Mr. Brewster, Joe?" Becky asked.

"I think I will go see him tomorrow after class."

"Can I come with you?" Becky asked.

"Sure."

"Are we done for now, then?" Ryan asked.

"I think so. I will check in with you two after we talk to Mr. Brewster tomorrow, and we can decide what to do next. Does that sound good?" Joe asked.

Deb and Ryan agreed to the plan, and they departed the library study room. The next day, Becky and Joe walked over to Mr. Brewster's after class and found him in the barn working on the old car that he had been trying to restore for over a year now. Joe put the question to him and he came and sat down at the table. After he sat there for many minutes, rubbing his chin as he did when he was thinking through a problem, he said, "I agree, Joe. If the theory is correct, it would follow that the machine and all that energy could not exist twice in the same space and time. However, I wonder how that can be true since each time you travel back here, the machine is technically for a few seconds existing in two space and time locations."

"When we were talking about this, Deb suggested that maybe if the machine were not powered up at the same time when the machine existed twice in the same space and time, that it might not matter," Becky offered.

"That is an interesting hypothesis," Mr. Brewster said.

"Is there some way we could test this?" Joe asked.

"I don't think so," Mr. Brewster replied.

"What if we sent it into the future like thirty minutes and then brought it back, and then sent it again into the future in the middle of that future to a different location, but close by, and sent it right back," Joe suggested.

"That might work, so long as whomever was in the machine didn't leave it. We know for sure that a person being in the same time and space continuum is a problem. You didn't seem to have issues once you were back in the machine and you powered it up," Mr. Brewster said.

"How about if we use the shed and the barn as locations and plot out the course and see if we can see any problems?" Joe asked.

"That seems like a place to start. Why don't you go through it and I will go through it separately and we can compare notes?" Mr. Brewster asked.

"Good idea. How about if I come over Saturday to go over what we plotted?" Joe said.

"Sounds like a plan. Excellent theory, good question. Let's work it through."

The kids left and went back to campus. Joe found both Ryan and Deb and said he had talked to Mr. Brewster and what their plan was.

15

That Saturday, Joe sat down with Mr. Brewster and went over their theories about the machine being in the same space and time. Everything that Mr. Brewster had researched indicated that other scientist agreed with the theory that an organic life form could not exist more than once in the same space and time continuum, but the thoughts were mixed on inanimate objects, like the machine. They combed over the printouts from the five trips and saw a pattern where the machine seemed to not exist at all while it was in the time bending and transfer mode. There was no real sign that led them to a solid conclusion on whether the powered-up machine might have issues if it existed elsewhere in that space and time continuum. Unfortunately, they also knew the only way to test it was to have it happen.

While that discussion was going on, Deb was walking back from taking Kim to spend the day with Amy's family, stopped off at the boys' dorm, and asked for Ryan. He was just coming down the stairs and they went out for a walk.

"I have decided the note is the right way to get some information to my mother."

"What were these notes about, the ones you and your mother sent?"

"Mostly little ones, like in my lunch or I would leave them in her briefcase. Sometimes they were longer, like when my mother wanted to make sure she conveyed some piece of what she called 'wisdom' for me to hold on to until later. It sometimes was a way for me to tell my mom about my feelings without having to say it to her directly. It helped to start conversations."

"Well, then I guess that would work."

"Here's the thing. I was thinking about leaving it under the windshield or on the seat if it's unlocked. How are we going to make it more plausible for you to be in front of my house and messing near my mother's car?" Deb asked.

"How about if I bring a bunch of sheets of paper and if anyone sees me, I will only put it under the windshield and then do the same at the neighbor's house, so he thinks I am advertising or something?"

"That might work."

"What are you going to say to your mom in this letter?"

"I'm going to say that I had called Aunt Alicia about some school project that I thought she might help with, and while we were talking, she opened up about missing her sister and not feeling like they were a part of each other's lives. I will say that thinking about that made me think about me and Kim and I wouldn't ever want Kim to feel like I was not part of her life and that I think my mom should fix this."

"That seems plausible."

"Then it's a plan."

"So, when are you thinking we are doing this, anyway?"

"I'm not sure. I want to find out what Joe and Mr. Brewster come up with, and then we need to decide."

"With spring break only a week away and midterms next week, I'm not sure we can pull this off before break."

"I know. I was thinking the same thing."

They arrived at the main hall and went inside to see who was there and what was going on. They noticed Joe and Becky sitting at a table talking and walked over to them.

"What did you figure out, Joe?" Deb asked.

"Nothing great. We know for sure that the experts agree organic objects cannot exist more than once in a given space-time location. I proved that with my trip to Cambridge. But we are not really sure about the machine. We learned that while the machine is in its program and at the point where time is bending and it is transporting, it doesn't seem to exist as we know an object to exist in any space and time. That was a revelation, anyway."

"There's no way to test this?" Ryan asked.

"Nothing short of making a trip to a place the machine already is and seeing what happens, it looks like," Becky said, a bit forlorn.

"We think there might be some safeguard if we do not power the machine up at the same time from both instances of it. We don't know that for sure, but it seems to feel right," Joe said.

"Now what?" Deb asked.

"I'm not sure, but I feel like we know what can happen to us, and the machine has performed really consistently so far," Joe pondered.

"You think we should do this, anyway?" Becky asked.

"Yeah, I do," Joe said.

"I do too," Deb said.

"I'm still deciding," Ryan said.

"One thing more, though, before we set this in motion. Joe, you have to pinky swear this is the very last time we are doing anything to fix our parents' lives. Never again are we trying to intercept their plans, so avalanches and plane crashes and stuff don't happen. Whatever the outcome of this trip is, we just learn to live with it, whatever it means," Deb said with total seriousness, holding out her pinky.

"Not this again. You're going to make me pinky promise, in front of Ryan and Becky?"

"It's the only way. This is only the second time I've asked, and it probably will be the last time where this machine is concerned."

"Ok," he said, holding out his pinky. Then Becky held out a pinky and Ryan did too, and the four of them locked together with pinkies.

"It's official. This is a 'for all time' pinky promise," Deb announced, and they dropped pinkies.

At that they all decided some studying was in order for midterms and separated to their rooms. The next week was busy with tests and preparation to head off for spring break. At the end of the week, Ken showed up with Michael to gather them all up and say goodbyes to Becky, Ryan, and Mary. Fortunately, they all had permission to visit, and all three of them were staying Wednesday through Friday at the Hampton house. Ken told them all that Aunt Alicia had an enormous party to attend that Friday night. Apparently, now that she was the trend editor, she was getting all kinds of important invitations, so Aunt Alicia and Uncle Darrick would not be out to the Hamptons until Saturday afternoon. Aunt Alicia would be returning to the city on Monday morning for the week, but their new Uncle Darrick had arranged to work a little from home to be there with them all week. During the ride, Ken and Joe talked about the computer and the new updates that Ken had heard from the Fitzgerald and Davis team. There had been several new programs offered, and they were working them into the standard design. One was to draw pictures on the computer, and the other was a game system that took all the old Atari games and put them into a computer program. Kim was excited about that. She laughed when she remembered Joe saying he wasn't sure they could play those games. The Fitzgerald and Davis design team were mailing copies of these programs to Joe at the Hampton house, and Uncle Darrick was bringing a new version of the computer home with him tomorrow. That would give Joe time to mess with these new programs, and he offered Kim a chance to play with the drawing program and the gaming program.

Deb said little the entire trip from campus to the Hamptons. She was tired. Studying for midterms had kept her up late this week. She wanted to finish her final semester of high school on a high note. She heard some kids from her literature class talking about how they didn't feel the need to try hard, now that they had gotten into their first pick of colleges. Deb didn't understand this. Why would you want to stop working just because you thought it was a done deal when it might not be? Didn't they understand that if they bombed their last semester, the college might change their mind?

Ken noticed Deb was quiet and asked her if she was ok when they arrived at the house. She said she was just tired, but he persisted, asking if Kim was ok, if Joe was ok, if Ryan was ok and if things were ok with Mary. When Deb answered yes to all of his questions and he still looked like he would persist, she said, "I'm just tired, Ken. I was up late every night this week studying so I could finish strong and I'm tired."

Ken asked Joe about it and Joe said he didn't know if anything was bothering Deb. Ken thought he sounded evasive, but he didn't press Joe like he had pressed Deb. He had a great idea, though; he would do something with Kim first thing in the morning and try to find out what was going on.

The next morning, Ken was up before Kim. She found him in the kitchen making cinnamon rolls. Kim loved cinnamon rolls, so she was very excited. After they ate, he suggested they take a new kite out and see if they could fly it down by the water. Kim thought that was a great idea, so they headed down to the beach.

After Ken had tied on the string and the long tail to the kite, and while he and Kim were trying to launch the thing, he asked, "How is Girl Scouts going?"

"Great. A few weeks ago, remember when you were in town after Joe's press conference? We did that badge day? Then we did a cookie sale. Then we had a badge ceremony where I got three new badges. Just after we get back from spring break, we are able to camp again."

"Is that your favorite part?"

"I love the camping trips!"

"And how are things with your classes going?"

"Good. I got two A's last week on papers in history and English. My favorite class is the art class, but we are learning all kinds of things in history and science."

"Do you have any of your friends in your classes this semester?"

"No, not my old friends, but I made some new friends, so now I have a whole bunch of friends."

"That's great. You sound very happy. Are you happy?"

"Most of the time."

"What do you mean?"

Just then, the kite took off and Ken motioned for Kim to let out more string. She did, and it went way up in the sky. She was really enjoying this and told him so.

"Are you going to answer my question?"

"I'm thinking."

"Thinking about what?"

"How to tell you without worrying you like I worried Deb."

"Ok, now I'm worried anyway, so just tell me."

"I think of Mom and Dad a lot. I think about the fights they had, and the night Dad left, and how sad it made me, and then first Dad dying in that plane crash, and then Mom having that accident. It just makes me so sad that they had all these issues and ended up dying alone. And we did that to them."

"Kim, we didn't do that to them."

"Well, just because Joe was the only one that went in the machine on that trip doesn't change the fact that we were all involved."

Ken sighed and said, "You're probably right."

"I think about it all the time, actually. Way more than I was doing before Joe went on the trip home. I'm pretty sure it wouldn't bother me if the fights and Dad leaving hadn't happened."

"I see. And you told Deb about this?"

"Yeah. She said she was going to come up with some way to help me and she has. We have looked at pictures, and she has helped me with homework and spent time with me. She bought me some new books in town. But she can't really fix this, I know."

"And how do you think this worried, Deb?"

"Well, she said it bothered her too and other times she said she was so sorry this was bothering me, and I heard her tell Ryan that she feels so totally helpless to fix this for me."

"That's a lot to worry about."

"Yes, it is. Sometimes I feel bad, I told her."

"Kimmy, you should never feel bad bringing your troubles to any of us. We will always be here to help you."

"I know, but I worry about you all, too. Like last year when Joe was so upset all the time and then lately when they were all meeting and whispering about things again."

"Whispering about things again. What are you talking about?"

"Well, a few weekends ago, they all met at the barn to talk about things while I was with my Amy's family for the day. I asked Deb about it later and she said they were going over what happened to Joe in more detail and what the machine printouts said and making sure they thought through what happened on that trip."

"Is Joe feeling alright?"

"He seems ok to me. That's what I thought when Deb told me what they talked about, but I watched Joe like a hawk that week, and he seemed his normal self."

"Enough about that. I'm sorry you're feeling bad, but just like it took some time to get past losing Mom and Dad, it will take some time to get past this part, too."

"I know. Hey look, the kite is way up there. I wish I had brought my camera to take pictures of this."

"I can hold it and you can run and get it."

"No, that's alright, maybe next time."

The kite eventually came down, and they walked back up to the house. By that time, both Joe and Deb were up and they all went back down to the beach to play and collect shells. They had a glorious afternoon, just the four of them. Just before dinner, Aunt Alicia and Uncle Darrick arrived. They all ate together and during that time, Aunt Alicia went over the plans for the wedding. She asked Kim to be a bridesmaid, and Uncle Darrick asked both Ken and Joe to stand up with him. It excited them all about their roles in the wedding. Aunt Alicia said they would probably look for dresses as soon as school was out this summer. After dinner, Ken grabbed Joe, insisting they go for a walk. They headed down to the beach and as soon as they got there, Ken started in on Joe. "So are you feeling alright?"

"Of course I am. What's wrong with you?"

"Kimmy told me you had a big conference at the barn a couple of weeks ago to go over the details of what happened to you on your trip back home. Are you having some residual symptoms?"

"No. The barn meeting was actually Mr. Brewster's idea. He said he missed our little debates and thinking aloud sessions at the barn and invited us all over. After we talked for a bit, Deb just asked a few questions. That took us deeper into the theory of why I had symptoms and the idea that a person cannot exist more than once in a given space and time continuum. We looked at the machine reading printouts and talked through some theories. Some are more wild than others. It was nothing."

"You're sure you're alright?"

"I'm better than ok. I mean, really man, I have this personal computer thing, the language, Becky, I'm about to finish my junior year of high school, my aunt is about to get married to a pretty cool guy that seems to want us around more than she does. What could be wrong?"

"Then why is Deb so quiet? And why did no one tell me Kim had been upset for at least a few months about our parents separating and fighting and dying alone and everything?"

"Well, Deb just told me about that recently. She said she didn't want to interfere with my release and press conference and stuff. Quite frankly, I'm glad she waited. That's the only thing that's bothering me. That I went on that trip alone and couldn't see what you could see so clearly—that keeps me up some nights. All I wanted to do was bring our parents back and what I ended up doing was making it as bad as I could."

"Is anything else bothering Deb? Are she and Ryan ok?"

"As far as I know. Have you seen them together lately? It's kind of gross the way Ryan takes care of her and sometimes fawns over her and they seem to have some private joke most of the time. YUK!"

Ken laughed at that. "Ok, so they're doing fine. Given what you just said, are you and Becky doing fine?"

"Yeah sure. We just don't really have that kind of relationship, I guess. I mean, I've kissed Becky and we hold hands and stuff, but we don't fawn all over each other the way Ryan and Deb sometimes do. I never expected to see Deb act like that with anyone."

"I guess I will have to talk to Deb."

"Where is all of this coming from?"

"I was out this morning with Kim flying the new kite that Darrick bought and was asking her how things were going. She basically told me everything was great except because she has, for months now, been upset about our parents and the new reality and feels like it's all our fault."

"She didn't do anything. I did it."

"Well, in her mind, since we all signed off on the machine and travelling through time, then we are all partly to blame. I'm not sure I totally disagree with her logic. I was pretty upset hearing that my baby sister has been struggling and none of you told me."

"Sorry, man. I didn't know until a couple of weeks ago. Deb kept it from me, too."

"I guess I'm going to have to have a talk with her now."

"If you're looking for someone to holler at about not telling you something, then yes, Deb is your new target. I just figured she didn't tell me because she knew I felt guilty, knew this would make me feel worse, and waited until after the release. Maybe she was waiting until this week to tell you when she could do it directly with you. Maybe she's not guilty of anything. Consider that."

"I'll consider it."

"At least give her a chance to explain before you start yelling at her. Remember, you said you wanted to wait until after you finished college to take on having full responsibility for us all? One full semester of college does not constitute finished, brother."

"College doesn't change the fact that I feel responsible for you all. It doesn't change the fact that Deb and I had an understanding that we would help each other, help you and Kim."

"Well, at least now, I think I have proven I can manage without such a close mom and dad. Wouldn't you say?"

Ken could tell that Joe was getting a little mad. He said, "I'm not saying you need parents to watch over you, and I'm not trying to be your parents. It's just I promised Dad. I promised him I would look after you all. I don't enjoy thinking something is going on that I don't know about. It means I can't help you three."

"Well, at least try to be calm when you talk to Deb, huh?"

"I am calm."

"Yeah right."

"Maybe I'm not totally calm. I won't talk to her until I calm down."

They walked back to the house and found Deb had already gone to bed, so had Aunt Alicia and Uncle Darrick. Ken and Joe said goodnight to Kim and told her not to stay up too late, and they both went to bed as well.

The next day, Darrick chartered a boat, and they all went sailing. They fished and looked at all the enormous houses and lay in the sun. Joe and Ken both caught fish that they brought home for dinner that night. As they were getting up from the table, Darrick pulled Ken into the hallway and asked, "What's wrong with Deb? She's been so quiet."

"I know. I'm not sure what's up, but I'm going to find out tonight."

"Would you rather I speak to her or your aunt?"

"No, I want to do this."

"Ok, but let me know what she says, please. I want to make sure she has what she needs. She seems to carry the burden of managing all of your feelings in the last year. I worry about her."

"I will keep you posted."

Just then, the girls returned, and Ken told Deb he wanted to talk to her. They went out onto the back porch.

"What's up?" Deb asked.

"You tell me. You've been quiet since I picked you up on Friday. For two days, you barely talked to anyone. Even Darrick has noticed."

"I told you I'm just tired. Midterms took a toll on me."

"Deb, you and I both know that's not all of it. I talked to both Kim and Joe. Kim told me that everything was great except for the fact that she is regularly upset about our parents splitting up and then dying alone and she knows it's all of our fault. Joe says he is carrying tremendous guilt over it and you kept what was going on with Kim from him, probably because of his guilt and his release this spring. What I want to know is why you kept it from me and what else might be going on."

Deb sat down and looked up at Ken. "I didn't tell you because you had all that going on with Mary at the end of the semester and over break and Kim didn't tell me until we got back to school in January. I kept it from Joe because of his big release, and I knew he felt guilty already."

"It doesn't matter what I had going on, Deb; you should've told me one of my sisters was in trouble. In fact, you both were. Kim because she was upset, and you because you have been carrying this around for months."

Ken sat down too.

"Of course it matters. You needed to fix things with Mary. Not worry about Kim or I, having sleepless nights over what happened last spring."

"Did it matter to you when Kim told you? Wasn't that when you were on the outs with Mary, too? You had something else going on. You were applying to colleges and waiting to hear. Why does my issue matter, but not yours?"

"Ken, I'm sorry. You're right. I had things going on, and so did you, and so did Joe, and I should have told you both right away. But to what end? We can't fix this for her."

"Is that why you asked about what happened to Joe? You were trying to figure out if we could go back and fix this?"

"I don't know. Anyway, when we went over it and Joe and Mr. Brewster reviewed research and sort of played it out with their formulas and things, they're not at all sure the machine can be there twice, let alone any of us. Joe was really having issues. He blacked out, and they have determined that they think what was happening was the higher universal rules were kicking in and reconciling the fact that there were two Joes in that space and time and the universe or whatever was trying to correct that by basically erasing one Joe."

"That's what the big meeting was about?"

"No. We went there because Mr. Brewster missed our regular Saturdays in his barn. We talked about his son and the wedding they are going to have and then I just asked Joe because I had been thinking about what happened to him because I was thinking about what was going on with Kim."

"That's what Joe said."

"What do you think? I'm lying to you?"

"No. But clearly, Deb, you've decided that you need to be everyone's counselor and you're forgetting one truth we all acknowledged last year. We are in this together. That means we don't keep things from one another," Ken said emphatically. Then he added, "So, what have you come up with to help Kim?"

"Well, we've looked at a lot of pictures from when she was little and everyone was happy, and I told her that what happened last spring was not what our family was about, it was what was in those family pictures. Our trips in the machine were somewhat misguided, Joe's especially. I've talked to Ryan about this. He thinks the reason that Mom had so many issues with this is because of her math background. She just couldn't make the leap that Dad seemed to do easily and they let it come between them."

"That kind of makes sense. Did you explain that to Kim?"

"Sort of. She's still only eleven."

"But way smarter than she ever seems to let on."

"That's true."

"She told me you were being very supportive."

"I'm glad she feels that way. I feel like I have done nothing to help her at all."

"Is that why you are so quiet lately?"

"I don't know. I feel like there should be something I can do to help her I just haven't thought of. Something I could say or do that would turn this around for her."

"No luck?"

"Everything I come up with seems silly or is not likely to help. Did you ever have a problem and wonder if the plan you come up with to solve it, although it might work, doesn't seem like a great idea?"

"You mean like, does the end justify the means?"

"Yeah."

"Sure. Remember about a year before Mom and Dad died when you all were out doing something and I was down the street at Mike's house? Dad came home, and we were in the backyard and he asked me what was up? Well, we had come over trying to get my bike 'cause we wanted to go for ice cream and ride by a girl's house and we couldn't get into the garage. I tried to get in through that window over Dad's work-bench, but I broke the frame and then couldn't even fit through the window. Anyway. We stayed in our yard and played football and then the next day I had another friend, Joey, come over and help me fix the frame of the window. I never told anyone. We fixed what I broke, but I never told Dad."

"I'm not sure it's the same thing. Also, I can't believe you lied to Dad."

"Well, I did figure out a way to fix it without having to tell anyone. I found the means to fix it and felt, at the time at least, like my ends, having the window fixed, justified the lie and the secret repair."

"I suppose. Do you think sometimes it's ok not to tell people what you're doing then? If you can take care of it?"

"I don't know. I'm sure if Dad found out what I did, I would have been in trouble and in that way, what I did was wrong whether or not

I got caught. But I don't know if you have to tell people, like those in your family, absolutely everything."

"Then why are you mad at me for not telling you everything? I don't know though, hearing you say it makes it seem kind of wrong."

"Is that why you've been so quiet? Did you do something you don't want to tell me about or have me find out about?"

"No, I'm just worried about Kim."

"Is Ryan pressuring you to do something you don't want to do?"

"What do you mean?"

"You know, is he pressuring you to go further than you want to? Like to second base or something?"

Deb laughed. Then she said, "Of course not. Ryan is the perfect gentleman. We've talked about it. We do have very strong feelings for each other, but we both really want to go to college and I really want a career, and you can't have those things if you accidentally end up pregnant. No, I swear, it's just that I'm worried about Kim."

"Ok, ok, just know that I will kill him, no matter how much I like him, if he ever pressures you."

"Enough with the big brother macho stuff!"

"Hey, by the way, Kim told me you bought her some new books. What are they?"

"Well, she finished all the Little House books, and she is getting a little older, so I took her to the bookstore in town a few weeks ago and let her pick something out. She ended up with a Nancy Drew book."

"What in the heck is a Nancy Drew book?"

"It's a series of books about a young girl that solves mysteries. Kim liked the idea of a teenager being smart and figuring things out. Said it reminded her of our working on the machine. "

"It's a series, so we might get her more of them for her birthday and stuff?"

"Yeah."

"That's cool."

"Mary went with us and she also got her a book that day. I'm not sure if it's a series, but it's called Anne of Green Gables. Anyway, that was Mary's childhood favorite, so she has two different stories to read now."

"Is this part of your plan? To interest her in other things?"

"Yeah. Was this all you wanted to talk about? What I was so quiet about?"

"Yes, I was worried."

"Done being worried?"

"Hey, Darrick noticed it too. He was going to talk to you as well. I just told him I would try first."

"Oh, well, if you tell him, be sure to not include the part about how Joe and I really feel guilty that the time travel in the machine created the problem for Kim. That it's the splitting up and dying alone our parents did that has Kim upset."

"No kidding. Very funny."

They went inside and sat down in the family room, watching television for a while. The next day, Aunt Alicia and Ken went into the city. Kim and Joe, and Deb went with Uncle Darrick into town and did some shopping. By the time they got back later in the afternoon, Ken was already back from meeting with Mr. Davis about his summer internship with the company. They ate dinner and played games. Tuesday, the kids went to the beach because Uncle Darrick had some work to do, and on Wednesday, Mary, Ryan, and Becky all arrived. They had a lot of fun picnicking at the beach and walking around town and Uncle Darrick chartered another sailboat and they went on a long cruise on Thursday. Friday, Mary, Ryan and Becky left and Uncle Darrick went into the city for a big party with his firm that Aunt Alicia was joining him for. They returned Saturday afternoon and helped in the preparation to get everyone back to school. Sunday, Aunt Alicia and Michael took the kids back to Choate, while Uncle Darrick took Ken back to Harvard.

16 |

Deb was still conflicted about making the trip back to Cambridge for many reasons. First, she knew she would have to keep it from both Ken and Mary. Second, there was an enormous risk something terrible would happen to her or Joe or the machine and trap someone there. Finally, what to do about Kim? She didn't tell Ken that this was what was troubling her throughout spring break, but Ryan knew.

Deb was holed up in the library doing research for a big final history paper when Joe and Becky and Ryan found her later that week in the early evening.

"Here you are. We've been looking for you all over," Joe said.

"I'm pretty sure I told all of you that was going to be in the library tonight. Kim was doing something with her friends and I have to get busy on this paper. What's up?"

"We wanted to talk about the trip to Cambridge," Joe said as he sat down at the table Deb was at and moved some books out of the way.

"More importantly, we wanted to see if this trip had you so quiet for the last few weeks," Becky said.

"I'm not sure we should do this trip in the machine."

"What? What happened? I thought you had decided this was a good idea?" Joe asked, shocked.

"I don't know. Maybe the risks are too great."

"You mean the machine being there twice? I've been thinking about that and I feel like it will not be as a big a deal as I originally thought.

I mean, there's more than one house and one car at the same time on a block."

"But never the same car twice," Ryan pointed out.

"So now you are doubting it too?" Joe asked.

"I don't know that I ever thought it was a great idea. I was just supporting you all because Deb wanted to do this."

"Why don't we sit down and Deb, you can go through what is causing you to change your mind or doubt or whatever," Becky added.

Ryan and Becky sat down and looked expectantly at Deb.

"Well, first, I don't think it's a good idea keeping this from Mary and Ken. He was furious the last time we did a trip and didn't tell him and it almost cost me Mary as a friend. Ken and I had a conversation over break about whether the ends justified the means. I think this is absolutely true here. Does fixing the situation between our parents and probably only putting them back to dying in the avalanche justify the risk and lying?"

"I would just like to point out that if we succeed, they will never know we did this trip and we don't have to tell them," Joe said.

"Joe, you're talking about keeping a secret from Ken, Kim and Mary for our whole lives," Deb replied.

"I know. But isn't that point with Kim? She's upset about what happened with our parents and if we fix this, she doesn't have to be upset, and never even has to remember there was a short time in our parents' timeline when they were separated."

"True, but that gets right back to my point. Does the end justify the means?"

"I remember talking about this in my English class last semester. We were talking about a book and the teacher asked us to discuss this point. If you end up with something positive, that helps people or makes it right for even one person, does how you did it, how you accomplished it, even matter?" Becky said.

"I think if you cross a line, even if it's your line about honesty or something, you might have gone too far to accomplish something," Ryan said, looking at Deb.

"What about helping me? I know that my feelings, and my stubbornness last spring created this problem, but the fact that I think every day about what I did, the guilt I carry, does that matter at all?" Joe asked.

"Yes, this trip might help you too, matters to me. But what about the risk?" Deb asked.

"Risk of the machines not working, or do you mean to you?" Joe pondered.

"Both," Ryan replied.

"Well, as I said, I'm not sure the machine is going to have any issues. And as far as Deb is concerned, if you limit the trip to a shorter time period as we have discussed, I'm not sure she will have any symptoms at all."

"But you don't know that for sure, right?"

"No, Ryan, this is science, and in science, something is theory until you test it and prove it. We know for sure if you spend ten hours as a second instance in the same space and time, you begin to have symptoms; it is unclear how little time you can do that and not have symptoms. We also have never had the machine in the same space and time location twice. There is that, you know, the benefit of this test will teach us even more about the time travel process."

"I'm not prepared to lose Deb to further the science of time travel."

"I'm not either, but that is not a risk."

"But, Joe, you really do not know, right?" Deb asked.

"As far as you are concerned, yes, I think we have ideas. We have a clear understanding that a person going to the same space and time will have issues within the ten hours. We don't really have verification when they start, and therefore, what amount of time would be safe."

"My last point is about Aunt Alicia. You remember, she got close to Mom again after our parents separated. She will not like not having that. We would take that away from her," Deb said, to finish up her points.

"I thought you said you were going to write your mother a note to make her see that she needed to reach out to Aunt Alicia and repair things?" Becky asked.

"I was planning on doing that, but that means Ryan has to risk going to the front of our house and putting a note in or on our mother's car and that is a risk, too."

"Ok, so what do you want to do? Scrap this trip? Not fix things for our parents?" Joe asked.

"Here's the thing, whenever I think this over, whenever I get to the end of this list and think about the ends justifying the means, I can't get past the fact that I think it does. I think the end justifies these means," Deb said somewhat to herself.

"How about if we talk through the specifics of the plan and see if there is anything that increases the risk or that causes you any concern?" Becky asked.

"That sounds like a good idea," Ryan replied and he took a piece of paper from Deb's folder and got ready to write things down.

"First, we need to determine the coordinates for the backyard of that house," Joe started.

"I've done that on a map I found in the library," Ryan responded. "I have those coordinates in my room on a fresh sheet of paper."

"Great, then next we need to figure out a time we want to go to there," Joe said.

"Well, we want to time it around your visit, right? So, we can get there before you get to that backyard, but I want time for Ryan to go around and leave the note for Mom, but not too much time," Deb answered.

"I set the time on my trip to ten in the morning," Joe said, "and I'm pretty sure I had the machine powered down within fifteen minutes and took about thirty-five or forty minutes to walk to that backyard. I was in the house by eleven."

"So, if we want to keep it safe and make sure that we don't have both machines powered up at the same time, we would want to set this trip to get Deb and I there at ten-thirty. I can walk around and leave the note and we can wait for you in the backyard," Ryan offered.

"That should be good. We don't want you hanging around too long in front of our house," Deb said.

"Then, as soon as we finish talking, while I'm walking back to my machine, you guys take off and set your time to the time you left. I think you should get away from the barn right away, because I am not sure what is going to happen after that," Joe replied.

"What if we can't convince you to abandon your plan and go back to the machine?" Ryan asked.

"Well, I expect if you show me the letters and the news clippings of their deaths, I will believe you. I'm not expecting that I'll fight you."

"I don't like that at all. We don't want to have no one there and later find out there was some issue. Plus, I thought you were going to be in the barn with me on the day they make the trip?" Becky asked.

"Yeah, that's right, I keep forgetting that my trip was before this trip," Joe said.

"What are we going to tell Mr. Brewster?" Ryan asked.

"I think if we plan this for the weekend after next, we will be ok and won't have to tell him, because Mr. Brewster told me he was going to be gone for an engagement party for his son or something related to the wedding that weekend," Becky said.

"That helps. Now the only question is, how will we know Joe doesn't have any issues when he gets to his machine? I mean, if his trip was last spring, we won't know until we get out of the machine here from this trip. In fact, if it works like it did from the Las Vegas trip, it wasn't until after we went to sleep that night and got up the next day that the changed memories hit us," Ryan said.

"That's true. That is the one thing we haven't really researched or thought much about, why and how the memory shift occurs after we make a trip. We didn't remember Mr. Brewster was a teacher until the next day, even though we saw him in the directory," Joe pondered. "I'm going to have to look at that data this week."

"Maybe you should talk to Mr. Brewster about this?" Ryan asked.

"I can help you this week; I don't have much classwork," Becky said, "and we can easily ask for Mr. Brewster's help if we just tell him we were talking about how strange it was that when you got back from the Las Vegas trip, you didn't remember right away that he was a teacher and not a caretaker."

"That sounds like a plan. I was also talking to Jeff from IBM, and he was telling me about a new version of walkie-talkies that they got from NASA that work over space. Of course, I asked if he could get me a set. I wonder if that would work while you are guys are powering up your version of the machine and then while I was powering up mine 'cause you would already be back here," Joe added.

"It's worth a try, right? When is he sending a set?" Ryan asked.

"He already sent them, so I should have them this week."

After a few minutes of silence, Joe said, "This sounds like a plan. Get me the coordinates so I can prepare the machine. That is, Deb, if you've decided to go ahead now?"

"I want to do this. There is no denying that. Can I reserve the right to ask to talk about it again before the day we pick to go?"

"Yeah, I can agree with that," Joe said.

The next day, Becky and Joe went to Mr. Brewster's classroom just before lunch and asked him about meeting with them that afternoon about the memory issue they had noticed and confirmed. He agreed willingly, saying he was happy to help and was ready for a new challenge. When they got to the barn after their classes, Mr. Brewster was already there and had some cookies and drinks out for them all. As they snacked, Joe filled him in what they were trying to solve.

"So, we noticed after our trip to Las Vegas this past fall that there was some lag in our memories. Here is what I mean. None of us realized when we got back from the trip, until the next day, that you were a teacher here and not a caretaker. We, in fact, went to look it up in the staff directory after we got back to the dorms and were concerned about the results of what we did. When I went to Cambridge last spring, Deb and Ken said they didn't have any memory of the change in our family situation until after they woke up the next day, but it was before I got back. Also, Deb said she had some hazy memories that were from the other timelines that seemed to disappear by the time we got to the Hamptons later that day, after I got back. And, when we went to Dallas, we didn't have a memory of the avalanche until the next day either."

"That's very interesting, especially the part about Deb having hazy memories of the different timelines for a short time. It's almost as if the space-time continuum was catching up and erasing memories," Mr. Brewster postured.

"That's what I was thinking, too. So, I started yesterday when we were talking about this, to plot out the machine time to transmit and come back, and what memories were present when."

Joe pulled a chart out of his bag and laid it across the table. It had the three trips charted out with times, who went and what was remembered at what time. There was an obvious pattern that an entire night had to pass before the fresh memories solidified for both the people in the machine and those that were aware of the trip but not in the machine. Mr. Brewster added on the Las Vegas trip what he remembered doing the day they left and the day they returned, but he indicated he woke up the day they returned, thinking he had vague memories of taking care of maintenance on campus. They spent the next hour trying to put some mathematical formula to the pattern in relation to the bended time but could not quite get it worked out. Mr. Brewster said he wanted to play with it a bit, think it over, and he held onto all the documents. He agreed to check in with the kids next week or even after he got back from Boston, where his son and Thomas' fiancée were expecting him for an engagement party and wedding planning day.

At dinner, Joe reported what they found and that they might want to make the return time for Deb and Ryan's later in the evening, but he was still considering that. Ryan suggested it wouldn't really matter one way or another, so long as they understood they would not have memory of whatever they changed until they got up the next morning.

They agreed and set the date for the trip as the next Saturday. Mary would again be at Harvard, visiting Ken and Kim was excited about the first weekend camping trip she was going on and was leaving Friday afternoon.

All that next week, Deb was anxious about the trip and the consequences of their "means" to the end. Mary noticed her acting strange and on Wednesday pulled her aside, walking to lunch and asked her what was bothering her.

"It's nothing really," Deb replied.

"It can't be nothing. You've seemed edgy all week."

"I'm nervous about the end of the year, and graduating, and going to NYU, and I haven't heard who my assigned roommate is going to be. What if we don't get along? Stuff like that."

"Oh, so nothing major?" Mary said, kind of laughing.

"Yeah, nothing major."

"It's nothing with Ryan, is it?"

"No, we're doing great."

"Ken told me you were worried about Kim. That she's been pretty upset all year about your parents splitting up and she has wrapped that all up with the machine trips and their dying alone and all."

"Yeah, I didn't tell anybody because I didn't want to stress Ken out. I didn't want to mess up Joe's big release, and I wasn't sure what anyone could do to help."

"That's what Ken said. Is she still upset? I mean, I see her with her friends and she always seemed pretty happy."

"That's what she says. She says it hits her at different times, and I've taken the approach to distract her and tell her that time will help. It's working, sort of."

"By the way, how is Joe's release going?"

"Wow, you wouldn't believe what he told me recently. So far, there are at least fifty schools, companies and people who have submitted programs for certification by the design teams and IBM. MIT has picked it up and put money toward future development, and the computers are actually selling."

"That's great. He is so smart and so deserves this. I'm also glad to see him focus on something other than the machine and trying to bring your parents back."

"Yeah, he's pretty focused on the personal computer and new language right now."

"And Becky!"

"Yeah, and his girlfriend, Becky. This one seems to be sticking better than last year."

"She's a really great person. And smart like him, so they should do well together."

"Yeah. So, are you done being worried about me?"

"I think so."

They laughed and went into the dining hall for lunch. Deb thought perhaps she wasn't done being worried about her when she got back from the library and found a note that Ken had called. She called him back and the first thing he did was start down her worry list.

"You know, I didn't hear who my roommate was going to be until after school was out. I don't think it's any big deal that you haven't heard yet. And don't worry, we have all summer to get you ready and talk to that person, and it will be fine."

"Yeah, Kenny, I know that."

"How is Kim doing?"

"She's doing fine, I guess. This week she is focused on the weekend camping trip, so she is pretty distracted and happy."

"Well, that's good. And how is Ryan?"

"He's good."

"Has he heard who his roommate is going to be?"

"Not yet."

"See."

"Ok, I get it."

"Listen, the last month, the teachers really start to lighten up a little. You don't have to worry. You're going to finish great. And graduation is a piece of cake. It's going to be all about gifts and celebration."

"It just means a lot to me to finish strong."

"You will. What's your grade point average right now?"

"Well, it's three point nine."

"So, what are you worried about? That's half a point higher than mine was."

"I'm just trying to keep it there, and maybe make it three point nine five."

"Relax, little sister, you have this in the bag. You're such a better student than I ever was."

"Thanks. By the way, what are you planning to do with Mary this weekend?"

"There is some play that she wants to see and then dinner and a movie on Saturday."

"Oh, that sounds fun."

"Should be. But it's always great when she's here."

"Aw, aren't you a romantic guy?"

"Ok, cut it out. I was calling to check on you, remember?"

"Yeah, well, I'm fine. How about I call you on Sunday evening?"

"Sounds good. Have a good weekend."

"You too. Bye."

"Bye."

Deb was glad she got out of that call revealing nothing and hoped that he would not be too angry with her if he found out what they were planning on doing this weekend. That Friday, Deb said goodbye to Mary, then helped Kim get her camping gear downstairs and to the van for the trip. She said she would see her on Sunday and to have fun. Then Kim was gone for the weekend, too.

17

That Saturday morning, Deb, Ryan, Joe, and Becky met at the dining hall for breakfast and then headed over to the barn. Joe and Ryan spent a few minutes setting up the coordinates for the trip, and Joe went over how to set up the return trip. They also tested and stored one walkie-talkie so they could try to communicate. Finally, they put the news clippings of their parents' deaths and the letters in the storage bins in the machine. Since they weren't going back far in time, no special clothes were required. When everything was ready, Ryan and Deb got into the machine and started it up. The noise started, the wind and then the bright light and the machine was gone. By the calculations Joe had done, he expected the elapsed time for Ryan and Deb to be gone was one hour, and the elapsed time for Joe and Becky back at the barn was just over an hour.

Ryan was anxious about what would happen when they began their shut down in the backyard. He was concerned that if there was going to be a problem with two versions of the machine, it would happen right then. Also, he was very concerned about Deb. When the process shut down and he switched off the machine, he felt nothing. The metal of the machine was no hotter than it was during the trip to Las Vegas, and he figured everything was fine. He was happy about that. He switched on the walkie-talkie right after he powered down the machine and tried to communicate with Joe but could get nothing. Deb checked, and they managed to end up in the backyard of the vacant house behind their home. That was good. They were actually in a brilliant spot, under some cover of trees, so no one would see the flash of light when they arrived and left. She opened the door and stepped out. Ryan came out and asked her how she was feeling.

"I'm doing ok. I feel kind of queasy, like we do during the transition in the machine. It rarely lasts this long, though."

"Really? That went away for me both times once the machine powered down."

"It did for me too in the Dallas trip and Las Vegas trip."

"Maybe that is the start of symptoms. I'm going to get around the block and leave the note for your mom. Stay close to the machine in case you need to step inside and power up. Joe said that helped when he was here."

"Do you feel anything strange?" Deb asked.

"No, everything feels the same as when we went to Las Vegas," Ryan replied as he headed toward the gate.

"Be careful."

"I will. Be right back."

With that, Ryan took off to get around the block and leave the note Deb wrote to her mother. There were no issues getting around and onto their street, and he walked right up to her car and found the driver's door unlocked. He placed the letter on the seat and went to leave. He was thinking everything was going great when he turned to head down the street and someone called from behind him, "Hey, what are you doing there with the Fitzgerald's car?"

"Oh, sorry, I know Ken from school and he asked me to drop off an envelope with study notes from a class. He missed it for training sessions all this week for the big game and I said I'd help him out. He told me to leave it in this car and not leave it on the front porch, so just following directions," Ryan said.

The guy looked a little skeptical, but he shrugged his shoulders. Then he said, "I thought the big game was in two weeks."

"Yeah, it is, but they had some morning sessions or something."

"Oh, the coach is really trying to keep them on track, I suppose."

"Yeah, I suppose. I don't play football. I play hockey."

"Oh yeah? I didn't think they had a hockey team at the high school?"

"No, they don't. I play in a league."

"At Penderson's arena then?"

"Yeah. Well, have a good afternoon. I have to get home and help my dad around the yard, sir."

"Good day for yard work."

"Yeah."

Ryan took off before the man could question him about anything else. He hoped this brief encounter didn't cause any trouble. He got back to the yard where Deb was waiting just as Joe showed up in the same yard.

"What are you two doing here?" Joe asked.

"We're here to stop you, Joe," Ryan said.

"Stop me? What do you mean, stop me?"

"Joe, you can't go do what you intend to do. You can't talk to Dad; you can't show him the notes and printouts you have there with you. It causes Mom and Dad to fight and split up and they still die, they just die separately. Dad is in a plane crash and Mom dies in a car accident going to where they took Dad's body," Deb said and then she kind of looked like she was going to pass out.

Ryan grabbed her and held her up as Joe said, "That can't be true. They can't die, anyway. And what is wrong with you?"

Ryan handed Joe the newspaper clippings that showed how each of their parents died. Joe read them and looked up.

"How does this happen?" Joe asked.

"Joe, your dad is going to believe you, and your mother doesn't. They fight; she has you taken to a bunch of doctors, and by the time that dust settles, your father leaves the house. Then he calls you and tells you he has to go see a customer and the plane crashes. Your mother races to the hospital they brought him to and gets hit in an intersection. She lives about a week but never regains consciousness," Ryan said.

At that point, Joe doubled over for a minute. Deb asked, "Are you ok, Joe?"

"No, I feel terrible, like my insides want to come out."

"We talked about these symptoms. When you make this trip, you start to have issues when you are with your dad, and they get worse. Nothing this bad, though. You and Mr. Brewster determined there is something going on to reconcile the space-time continuum that doesn't allow two instances of you to be in the same space and time, something to do with finite energy and you being here twice adds energy. There must be something more to this, and it must be worse when more than one of you is here," Ryan said.

"You're for real, aren't you?" Joe asked as he stood up.

"Yes Joe. The good news is you were right about your theory. It matters if it's the same space and time, since I'm not having any symptoms. So right now, go back to your machine and we have to go into ours. You said when you were discussing the symptoms that it got better once you were in the machine and you powered it up. We will immediately power up. Go fast because you get delayed getting back because of people milling about where you have the machine near that lake. But we can't have both machines powered up at the same time," Ryan said.

Deb leaned on Ryan. He looked down at her and asked if she was ok. She replied, "No, it's getting worse."

"Joe, get back to your machine. Get into it as soon as you can. Just know that I am going to get this one fired up in the next ten minutes. See you back on campus," Ryan said as he ushered Deb toward the machine door.

"Do you need any help to get it configured or anything?" Joe asked.

"Joe, just get back to your machine as quickly as possible!" Deb said.

Joe left, and Ryan got Deb into the machine and buckled in. He then set about powering up the machine. The powering up part worked, but then lights starting flashing and the printout started spitting out sheets pretty fast. He stopped the startup process and checked the printouts. They were registering issues with Deb as he buckled her in. He turned to ask her what was wrong, and she passed out. He checked the print-outs again and noticed an issue with the machine processing. The coordinates they had entered earlier were not the same. He stopped the processing of the machine and went to the place where Joe and he had set up the coordinates and tried to re-enter them like they did yesterday. The machine was taking the barn coordinates, but it kept trying to set the date and time to Joe's original trip. Ryan was in a genuine panic now because Deb had not come to and he had no way of knowing if Joe was back yet. Only about ten minutes had gone by. Did he dare leave Deb to be sure Joe got out ok or should he keep trying? He had no idea what to do.

Ryan sat down in the seat he had been in when they made the trip here and tried to think it through. Just then, a garbled noise came from the walkie-talkie. He tried it and he faintly heard Joe's voice saying something. He couldn't make it out, but he pressed the talk button and said as clearly and as slowly as he could, "Joe, the machine lost the coordinates for the date and time in our machine. It will not take the setting at this point and keeps setting the date and time to your trip return settings."

After a few minutes, he heard faintly if that was the case, they would have to wait until Joe left in his machine. Ryan answered he was not sure Deb was going to make it that long, and the symptoms were worse for both Deb and Joe. He was figuring the symptoms were worse because they were both here twice. There were no more answers from the walkie-talkie. Ryan focused on trying to help Deb. He found the thermos of water in the storage compartment and tried to get her to drink some, then he put some on the bottom of his t-shirt and patted her forehead with the cool, wet shirt. She seemed to respond to that coolness and opened her eyes. He kept saying her name, and she said nothing for several minutes, just looked at him in a bewildered state. Finally, she said, "How long was I out?"

"About ten minutes. How are you?"

"I have a terrible headache and my vision seems a little fuzzy."

"Ok, I'm going to unbuckle you and I want you to lean your head forward, kind of putting it between your knees. That might keep you from passing out again."

He unbuckled her and helped her put her head down. "How is that?" he asked.

"I think it's better. I'm keeping my eyes closed. Why are we still here?"

"The machine lost the coordinates for the return. It keeps reverting to the date and time of Joe's return."

"Now, what are we going to do? We can't go to that date and time, then there will be two of us there."

"I know. Believe it or not, Joe could speak to me through the walkie-talkie. I was able to tell him what was happening, and he said we might have to wait until Joe leaves for us to leave."

"How will we know?"

"I was thinking I would go check on him, but that would mean I would have to leave you here and also, I'm uncertain I could find him, if he had to hide or blacked out like you just did."

"Ryan, you have to go check." Deb picked up her head and asked for paper and pencil. She drew Ryan a map to the park area that Joe had landed his machine and the likely route he would take to get back there.

"Sweetie, I don't want to leave you."

"You have to. If he doesn't get back, we don't get back. We have no other choice."

"I have a bad feeling about this."

"Just go, Ryan, and get back as soon as you can."

Ryan kissed her, told her not to keep her head down for fear she would pass out and fall out of the seat and hurt herself. He sat her on the floor of the machine and leaned her against the storage bins. He said he would be back as soon as he could and left the machine.

Ryan followed the route Deb had written and didn't see Joe anywhere. After he got to the lake, he got close and saw the machine and went to it cautiously and looked in and Joe was not there. Beginning to retrace his steps, he heard a moaning in the bushes. He went to the sound and found Joe lying on the ground. He had fallen, probably passed out, and put a pretty serious gash on his forehead. Ryan took off his shirt and ripped it to make a bandage and wrapped it around Joe's head. By this time, Joe was fully conscious but said his vision was terrible. Ryan managed to get Joe into the machine, turned the power on, checked the settings, and put Joe into the seat. He buckled Joe in and told him to hit the button to start the process, and left the machine. Ryan stood there for a few minutes, but the machine didn't start the processes. He rapped on the door and Joe looked over. Ryan yelled for Joe to start the systems up. Joe got his arm to the button, but it took forever and looked like it was painful. Ryan wondered how he was going to get Joe out so he could return to Deb, when suddenly the noise started and the magnetic field started to form and it threw Ryan away from the machine. He hit a tree and everything went dark.

When Ryan woke up, he was lying on the ground about ten feet from where the machine had been. The machine was gone, but he wasn't sure how long he had lain there. Ryan ran as best as he could back to where Deb was and found her breathing very shallow and rapid, and she would not wake up for him. He basically poured water on her face and still she did not wake up. He shifted focus and went to reprogram the settings. The correct settings seemed to hold steady. He turned, lifted Deb's limp body and put her into the seat, and buckled her in as tightly as he could. He sat down, buckled himself in, and started the processes. The noise, bright light and queasiness came and then it was quiet. He looked over at Deb. She was still not waking up. Ryan was really panicked now. He unbuckled, turned the machine off and unbuckled Deb. He opened the door, then turned to lift Deb out of the machine. Joe and Becky looked horrified as they saw Ryan carrying Deb's limp body. Joe pushed all the papers off the table for Ryan to put Deb on the table. He laid her out and then told Joe to get the printouts and any more that the machine could generate.

Joe came out of the machine with pages of printouts, and he started pouring over them. Ryan told Becky to find the hose on Mr. Brewster's house and bring a bucket of water to them, and then he went searching around the barn for some rags. Joe looked up then and said, "Man, the back of your head is bleeding!"

"Is it? It's kind of long story. We should wait for Becky and hopefully for Deb to be awake."

Becky returned, and they put the wet cloth on Deb's forehead and on her wrists. Becky checked her pulse and Ryan monitored her breathing, which was settling down a little and became deeper. They didn't know what else to do, so they waited, each thinking that maybe with a little bit of time, she would slowly get better. They waited almost an hour before she finally opened her eyes. She said the bright light was hurting her so Joe ran and turned off the barn lights and opened the far door so they would have some light to help her by. After a few more minutes, Deb said she wanted to sit up, and Ryan lifted her off the table and set her in a chair. Deb closed her eyes for a minute, and Ryan panicked again. Then she opened them again and said, "So, what happened?"

"Where do we begin?" Ryan asked.

"Well, let's start with this. We expected you to be gone a little more than an hour and you've been gone for four hours," Joe said.

"What does that mean in terms of how long we were gone or in our elapsed time?" Ryan asked.

"You had to have been gone for over six hours."

"Geeze. I lay there for a long time. Much longer than I thought," Ryan mused out loud.

"What are you talking about?" Deb asked.

"So, let's start at the beginning. We got to the backyard ok. We were under some cover of trees, and that was fine. I checked the return settings, and they seemed fine at that point. Then I went around to leave the note for your mother that Deb had written. I got kind of caught by your neighbor who asked what I was up to and I told him I was leaving some class notes for Ken, who was called to early morning training sessions for the football team. Anyway, when I got back to the machine and Deb, you were just walking into the backyard. We told you what we were doing there. You didn't believe us at first. We showed you the newspaper clippings and the letters and you started to believe, but then you and Deb both started having more severe symptoms. Deb was light-headed and nearly passed out. You, at one point, doubled over. Anyway, you decided we were right, and you were going to go back to your machine and get back to campus. I got Deb into the machine, but then she passed out. I tried to start up the machine, and it didn't work. The machine wouldn't take the settings and kept resetting itself to the date and time of your return last spring. Then you talked through the walkie-talkie and I told you what was going on and you told me to wait until you had left."

"Yeah, that was the craziest thing. I heard crackling and tried to speak into it, and then you responded. We are definitely going to have research that a ton when this is all over," Joe said.

"You told me through the walkie-talkie that we would have to wait until the other machine left so we could set the correct date and time. So, Deb told me I had to make sure you got off and then we could leave. I didn't want to do it, because she was having so many issues, but she insisted. So, I went to where the machine was, and you weren't there. I found you under some bushes. You had blacked out. So, I got you to your machine, started it up, verified the settings and got you into your seat. I told you to start the procedures, and I buckled you into the seat. You didn't start it, though. So, I went up to the window and knocked and you looked over at me. I yelled for you to push the button and you looked like it physically hurt you to reach out. But you did it. Unfortunately, I was standing there and when the magnetic field formed, it threw me about ten yards from the machine and into a tree. I woke up some time later and raced back to the other machine and Deb and found her barely breathing and unconscious. I could get the settings into the machine and started it up. Then we were here."

Becky again checked Deb's pulse and said it was almost back to normal. Deb said she felt weak, but better. Becky then looked at the back of Ryan's head and cleaned it up and told him to hold a rag on it for a bit to make sure it didn't start bleeding again. Joe was looking over the printouts and taking notes. After a few minutes Becky asked, "Where in the story did you lose your shirt, Ryan?"

"Oh that. Well, first I wet the end to help Deb, then when I found Joe and he had a big gash on his forehead, and it was bleeding pretty badly so I took off my t-shirt and ripped it to make a bandage for Joe's head."

"We better get back to campus so you can get a fresh shirt," Deb said, smiling at Ryan.

"Let's wait a little while longer until you are feeling stronger, ok?"

They talked about the printouts and put everything back the way it had been, so Mr. Brewster wouldn't suspect anything. Becky returned the bucket, and they checked the hose and put all the papers back on the table and rags back where they found them. Then they slowly walked back to campus. Deb said she wanted to lie down for a bit. Ryan asked Becky to go sit with her in her room and the boys returned to their dorm. Joe and Ryan talked again about what happened, and Joe took more notes.

At dinner time, the boys went back to the girls' dorm and asked for Becky and Deb. They came down the stairs and Deb looked much better. They went to dinner at the dining hall and then went to watch the movies in the main hall. After the movies, Ryan walked Deb back to the girls' dorm and asked Becky to keep an eye on her. Deb and Becky agreed Deb would not lock her door and Becky said she would check on her before she went to sleep and helped Deb get ready and into bed.

The next morning, Deb woke up feeling much better. She was in the bathroom finishing showering when Becky came in and asked how she was.

"Feeling much better today. Thanks a bunch for taking care of me last night."

"No problem."

"What's wrong Deb? Why did you need taking care of?" one girl from the floor asked.

"Oh, I wasn't feeling well yesterday, was kind of light-headed and Ryan was a little worried about me and Becky was my guardian angel last night. No big deal and I'm better today," Deb answered.

"That's good," the girl answered as she left the bathroom.

"Are you about ready to go to breakfast and church?" Becky asked.

"Yeah, just have to get dressed. Give me five minutes."

They were just getting to the bottom of the stairs when Ryan and Joe came into the lobby of the girls' dorm. They all walked out as Ryan asked, "How are you doing today, sweetheart?"

"Better."

"Did you wake up with full memories of everything?" Joe asked.

"Yeah, and it appears to have worked, huh?" She said, "Except for my being sick, you falling and opening up your forehead and Ryan here getting a big knot on the back of his head."

"All except for that," Ryan said.

"Yeah, we're back to them dying in the avalanche and our coming to school here at the same time as the timeline after the Dallas trip. They didn't split up. Did things change for Mom and Aunt Alicia?" Joe asked.

"Yeah, I think so. I mean, I remember her being around more and her and Mom doing things together. The fight she had with Ken is a little different. It's more about Aunt Alicia being upset about not getting anything in the will now, not about losing her sister. She is just upset about not having her for long."

"What about Joe's trip in the spring? How has that changed?" Becky asked.

"Wow, has that changed? I mean, Joe still takes off and misses the dinner the night of graduation, but he's back by the time we all got up the next morning. Now, though, he is very evasive about why it was a quick trip and why nothing changed. Now I guess we know why. You couldn't plant the seed this trip was needed or it might not have happened that way and Ken would have known we were doing another trip and would have tried to stop us," Deb told them.

"I didn't actually have full memory of the changes in my trip last spring until after you both left yesterday. I told Becky about some of it yesterday. It was strange the way my memory seemed to change as your trip yesterday unfolded," Joe replied.

"I wonder how Kim is going to be when she gets back today?" Deb mused as they entered the dining hall.

"Are you even going to be able to tell? I mean, if she isn't worried about your parents splitting up, will she even bring anything up?" Ryan asked.

"I'm going to spend some time with her this afternoon when she gets home and try to get a read about how she is. I will bring none of that up. Just see how she is feeling about our parents and see what she says."

"That's a good plan."

When Kim got back, she saw the note that Deb had taped to her door. She went and knocked on Deb's door.

"What did you need?" Kim asked.

"I wanted to see how much homework you had and if you wanted to walk into town with me and maybe get another one of those books."

"That sounds fun. I have a little bit of homework."

"How about you come back when you are done and we can leave, then?"

"Sure."

Kim returned about an hour later, and they left. As they walked, Deb asked, "How was your camping trip?"

"It was great!"

"Tell me about it."

"Well, Friday when we got there, we unloaded all of our gear and brought everything into the cabin. Then Mrs. Johnson, the troop leader, gave us our chore assignments. I had to do fire setup on Friday, breakfast cooking on Saturday morning and Sunday clean up. Then Anne and me went..."

"Anne and I."

"Really? Anne and I went outside and found some small sticks and dried grass and gathered some wood and started the fire. We got it started and then set the cooking grate over it. We sat there as the cooking crew started cooking the hot dogs and baked beans and sang songs. Then we all ate and sat around the fire for a while longer. Saturday, I got up, and we did the breakfast cooking. We had pancakes and scrambled eggs and sausage. While we cooked, everyone got ready and the clean-up crew swept the cabin and cleaned bathrooms. Then we ate and when we were done, we got ready while the meal clean crew did dishes. Then we worked on a tree and plant badge. The ranger was there, and he talked about the different trees and plants that were found in the area and on the grounds and gave us some pamphlets on trees and plants. We had to look for different plants and trees and take notes about what was around them and how they were growing and stuff. We stopped for lunch and finished in the afternoon. At night, we had dinner and had a badge ceremony and we all got our tree and plant badges. Then we had s'mores and told stories around the fire. On Sunday, we had breakfast and cleaned the cabin and bathrooms and then went on a hike and then we left."

"Wow, busy trip, but it sounds like you had fun."

"Yeah, it was a lot of fun. I enjoy camping."

"I do too."

"Do you think we could do that as a family sometime?"

"I don't really think Aunt Alicia is much of a camping type of person, do you?"

"Nope. But it would be funny to watch her try, wouldn't it?"

"Shame on you Kimberly!" Then Deb leaned down and whispered, "Yes, it would!"

They went into the bookstore and Deb bought Kim two books from the new series she was reading about Nancy Drew. As they walked back to campus, Deb asked, "So, Kim, I was looking through my things yesterday and found the necklace that Mom gave me for my thirteenth birthday. I was thinking a lot about her yesterday and missing her. I wondered if that happens to you ever or if you are kind of always thinking about them still."

"I think about them still, but it's not like every day or anything like that. Just sometimes, like when I am lying down to go to bed, sometimes I catch myself wanting to yell out for them to hurry to come to my room to say goodnight."

"Yeah, kind of like when I found the necklace."

"Yeah, kind of like that, but it doesn't happen as often as it did last year, and I don't compare teachers to Mom and Dad like I did las year. And I think it's better now that Aunt Alicia is better and we have a new uncle, or practically."

"Yeah, remember last year when we used to talk about this, and I would say that it was supposed to get better with time? Do you think it has?"

"Yeah, I think it has. I really like that we're all closer now. I don't think I would be talking to you like this or going to the bookstore with you if Mom and Dad were still here."

"Maybe not. That would have been my loss, though."

"Thanks."

"Does it bother you still we changed how our parents died?"

"I don't think so. Remember when you got done talking to the reverend, and you said that maybe this was how it was supposed to be? Well, I've been thinking that it probably wouldn't matter how many times we made trips in the machine. If it was supposed to be like this, with our parents gone, we probably could not change it."

"You're right. The reverend told me he believes that when it's time for God to call you to heaven, it doesn't really matter about free will and your choices and path."

"Yeah, I think I believe that, too. I think that's why we could change things for Mrs. Brewster, because it wasn't her time, she just got caught by someone else's time. And why that nice lady, Mrs. Kennedy, almost died and her husband died? Because it was his time, and not her time."

"Yeah."

"Is it ok to still miss Mom and Dad?"

"Of course it is, Kimmy. Any time and for how long you need to or want to. We don't want to forget them. But I think the idea is to hold them in our hearts, the wonderful memories and remember everything they taught us and be the best we can be. That is how we honor them and keep them going."

"I like that."

"Me too."

18

At lunch later that week, Joe asked Deb how she was feeling. She said she was better, and it must have been a twenty-four-hour thing because she woke up on Sunday feeling fine. She asked what Joe was doing after class and said she wanted to talk to him. When they met later, Deb asked if Joe was planning to tell Mr. Brewster about their trip and he said he wanted to, but wasn't sure how to handle the issue of Ken, Mary, and Kim not knowing about it. Deb asked if she could help Joe talk to Mr. Brewster about this, and Joe said that was a good idea. After dinner that night, they walked over to Mr. Brewster's house and knocked on his door.

"What are you two doing out this late?" Mr. Brewster asked as he motioned for them to come into his kitchen.

"We were hoping we could talk to you," Deb said.

"Of course, sit down here at the kitchen table and tell me what's going on."

"Well, we need your help to sort out some things," Joe said.

"What things?"

"Mr. Brewster, we used the machine last weekend when you were gone visiting your son and his fiancée. We took the machine back to Cambridge to stop Joe from talking to our father last year," Deb said, and then sighed heavily.

"Is that why we had to sit down and talk about Joe's symptoms recently?"

"Partly. I really wanted to know what happened to Joe, but yes, we had been thinking about this trip when I asked."

"Is everyone ok with your parents now?"

"Yes, but we had issues. That is what we need your help with," Joe added quickly.

"Let's start at the beginning, shall we?" Mr. Brewster asked.

Deb went through the entire history of their plans, discussions, and how it started with Kim being upset. When she finished, she looked up at Mr. Brewster and waited.

"I can see why you want to talk this through. Who knows about this trip?"

"Ryan and I, Joe and Becky. That's it."

"I'd like to look over the machine printouts before we talk about it more. That way I can be up to speed. How can we do that if Kim and Mary don't know?"

"I'm not sure."

"Why don't you want them to know? Now that the trip is over, doesn't being honest matter more?"

"Well, we know telling Kim will just erase all we have done to fix things for her. I mean, the trip was to help her," Joe said.

"Perhaps it will help her even more. And you aren't trying to say that this wasn't also for you, are you, Joe?"

"No, it helped me, too. It undid what I had done between our parents."

"And we have promised each other that there will be no more trips that attempt to change our parents' deaths," Deb added.

"Why that promise now?"

"Well, Mr. Brewster, I've gotten to where I agree with Deb on this. The machine seems to work when we make small changes, but no matter what we do, we can't change it when the higher power, or God, or whatever decides it's time for a person to die. And in our case, it's become clear to me that all we accomplish, all we do, we need each other and the only way that happens is if our parents are gone."

"It's good to hear you say that, Joe. I've been worried about where your head was on this lately."

"Yeah, it feels pretty good to be calm."

"Let's see if we can't come up with something before the end of the week. I will let you know."

They got up to leave and thanked Mr. Brewster. The next day, Mr. Brewster came up with something. The science department had been working on a very large experiment and they needed several students to help with some tasks. Mr. Brewster sent around notes that he needed Joe, Becky, Ryan and Deb for the project on Friday at three p.m. They showed up in the room as requested, on the notes he sent to their various classrooms.

"Nice way to get just us to a meeting, Mr. Brewster," Ryan said as he set his books down.

"I thought this was the best way to get you all to a meeting without you having to face questions from Mary and Kim."

They sat down at the table where Mr. Brewster had already spread out the printouts and notes.

"What are the points of contention here?" Mr. Brewster asked.

"Well, we're trying to figure out two things. First, why were the symptoms worse when there were two of us there, and two, why did the second machine seem to be stuck on the return settings of Joe's machine until after he left?" Ryan said.

"What about the fact that Ryan didn't have symptoms at all, while you and Joe did?" Becky asked.

"On that point, it appears you have preliminarily proven Joe's theory that there is not a universal overarching energy limitation, that it looks like it is a space and time unit of some kind," Mr. Brewster started.

He continued, "On the other points, the printouts that monitor your vitals from the machine show that both Deb and Joe were in terrible shape when they finally got into their chairs in the machines. Joe's vitals were showing signs I can only presume were organ failure. Deb's are less clear because she was not in the seat long enough, but I can only presume from what you've told me she was in the same or worse shape since she and Ryan were in that time and space longer than Joe was."

"That's what I was afraid of," Ryan said as he looked at Deb.

"I think that what this means is that the timeframe in which a person can be in the same space and time is much shorter if more than one of us is there," Joe said.

"Clearly, we only have this one instance to prove that theory, but Joe, I would concur and we can't test it further. I think along with your rule that no one goes alone in the machine, and you no longer intend to do anything to bring your parents back, you should no longer go back to any space and time where you already exist or have been to in the machine."

"I agree, Mr. Brewster, and I agree. We cannot test this further. But what I'm not able to figure out from the machine printouts is why, when my version of the machine was not powered up, the one Deb and Ryan were in kept reverting to the return date and time setting of my machine," Joe said, shifting gears.

"The machine printouts reveal the settings that Ryan entered, and when he is executing the save command, it saves as yours. I don't have an explanation for it," Mr. Brewster said.

"Could it be that like the universe or whatever was only allowing one instance of Joe and Deb, it will also only allow once instance of the machine, even though they were both there, until Joe's left, the other one could not get back without going to the original date and time?" Becky proposed.

"What if it's because we really are only talking about one machine? The reason I couldn't execute our date and time until Joe left was because without Joe being back, there was no machine for Deb and I to get into?" Ryan offered.

"The data supports that theory," Joe responded.

"Yes, it does, but again, we would have to test that again, and I'm uncertain that is a good idea," Mr. Brewster said, somewhat thoughtfully.

"What do we do then?" Joe asked.

"What do you want to do? Are you suggesting you need to answer every question raised by the machine's use?" Mr. Brewster asked.

"Joe, Mr. Brewster is right. I think we need to leave these two areas as open questions in your research about the machine and time travel. I don't want to test them, and I don't think it's wise to test them," Deb said.

"Maybe, I mean, yeah, I guess we're going to have to just leave these as questions," Joe said.

"I know that bothers you, Joe, but I think we have to," Ryan said.

"Ok, then I guess we're done here," Becky added.

"It appears so," Mr. Brewster said. "Unless you want to talk about the decision to keep this from Ken, Mary, and Kim?"

"For now, that's the plan," Deb said. "Do we need to do anything on your project to keep your cover?"

"Yes, actually, I need some help to set up the experiment. Ryan and Joe, if you could assist me in unboxing the items and setting them on the counter, and Becky and Deb if you wouldn't mind, I've made copies of the worksheets, if you could spread them out and collate them, I would appreciate it."

They got busy and set up everything for Mr. Brewster, thanked him for keeping their secret, and left his lab room.

Two weeks later, it was Deb's eighteenth birthday. Aunt Alicia was in Europe for a big fashion show, so Mr. Reynolds came and picked Deb up on the Friday just after her birthday and took her to New York for dinner and a Broadway show. He also bought her a car, which he said he was having brought to campus for the last month. As he brought her back to campus on Saturday, she thanked him for the special treatment and for the fantastic time and the show. Ken was there; he had come over from Harvard to spend Saturday with them. He took everyone to town, where they did some shopping, had dinner and went bowling. Joe even let Deb win several games. After they finished bowling, Ryan took Deb for a walk and gave her his gift. He handed her a small box. She opened it and looked up at him. "What is this?"

"It's a traditional Irish promise ring, called a claddagh. It signifies my intention to promise myself to you for all time."

"It's beautiful Ryan."

"I called Ken and Mr. Reynolds; you should know that. I told them my intentions of giving this to you and that for me, it was kind of a pre-engagement thing."

"You did?"

"Yeah."

"I don't know what to say, or maybe what I should say here."

"Well, is your confusion because you're not sure of a formal response or because you aren't sure you feel the same way about me?"

"No, no, Ryan, I love you. I plan to spend my life with you. Well, if you ask me to, I guess. It's that this seems like a formal Irish thing, and I didn't want to mess it up for you. Of course, it seems like I did that, anyway."

Ryan hugged her and said, "You didn't ruin it at all. That's all I wanted to hear. I love you, Deborah Fitzgerald, and I promise myself to you."

"I promise myself to you, too."

Ryan put the ring on Deb's finger, and they walked back to campus. Ken was waiting for them at the girls' dorm, sitting in the lobby with Mary and Kim. He looked at Deb and then at Ryan and both were smiling, so he figured it went well. Ryan and Deb walked over to them, and Ken grabbed Ryan in a quick hug. Mary looked a little confused, and Deb held out her hand. She looked at the ring and wondered what the big deal was. Ryan told her that being Irish, it was a real promise ring. Then Mary understood. She was a bit jealous, but she said nothing.

This all came to a head the next weekend when Mary was a little short with Deb as they prepared to go to the dining hall for lunch on Friday. Later, on the way out of the English and history building, Deb pulled Mary aside and asked her what she was mad at.

"I'm not mad, I'm just jealous. You and Ryan seem to be making progress in your relationship, and Ken and I seem to be in a holding pattern."

"I don't think that's what's going on."

"It probably isn't. Maybe I'm just trying to control this weird jealous thing that's been going on for so long. I mean, you're my friend. I'm sorry."

"Mary, you don't have to apologize. Listen, this was an important thing to Ryan because of his Irish heritage. You know, they did not preach us to about our Irish heritage. Our father didn't really feel tied to the Irish side of his family. So, of course, it wouldn't occur to Ken to do anything like this and you remember, your parents asked him to slow things down and let you get through college. Ken told me that. He will not go back on that commitment."

"Yeah, I suppose."

"You don't doubt his love for you, do you?"

"No. We have been through so much though, and the pressure my parents put on him, I just hope we get through the next four years."

"You will. Now come on, my friend, let's go get our homework done in the main hall."

19

In early May, in their last class on a Friday afternoon, Mary received a note from the main office asking her to come to the office immediately. She left and Deb, who shared this class with her, worried that something was wrong. Deb rushed back to the dorm to find Mary packing clothes.

"What's going on?"

"My grandmother is very sick. My mother called and said my father was on his way here to pick me up."

"Do they know what's wrong with her?"

"She's been kind of sick for a while now. They spent all last week doing all kinds of tests. My mother wouldn't tell me anything more."

"Oh, Mary, I'm so sorry. Can I help you?"

"No, I'm just about packed."

"Will you call and let me know you're ok?"

"Yes. Hey, can you call Ken and let him know I'm heading home and won't be able to come and see him this weekend? He's expecting me. It was going to be one of the last weekends we saw each other before his finals. Well, except for the dance."

"I will call him."

"Thanks. Tell him I will call when I can."

Just then, a girl came up and told Mary her father was there. Deb walked her down and said goodbye to Mary and that she hoped her grandmother was ok. Then she called Ken.

"Do you think I should go to their house?" Ken asked.

"I don't know. I got the impression she might be at a hospital and she didn't tell me which one. She said she would call you and me both when she knew more."

"I'll wait until I hear from her then. What are you guys doing this weekend?"

"Oh, just the usual. Kim has a Girl Scout thing tomorrow, and Joe and Becky are going to her family's house. Ryan and I are going to go to the main hall movies and stuff."

"I hope this gets resolved with her grandmother by next weekend. The spring formal is next Saturday."

"Yeah, I hope so too."

"Do you have a dress?"

"Oh, you should see it. Aunt Alicia picked it out, and it's perfect. It's white with pink flowers all over it. I love it!"

"Well, that's great news. I can't wait to see you in it."

"I'll call you if I hear from her, and you call me if you hear, ok?"

"Yeah. Tell Joe and Kim I said hello and I will see them soon."

"Bye."

"Bye."

Deb didn't hear from Mary until the next day. She was in her room finishing some homework when someone came and said Mary was on the phone. Deb ran to the phone.

"Mary?"

"Yeah, sorry, I didn't call last night. We went directly to the hospital."

"That's ok. How is your grandmother?"

"Not good. They figured out what was wrong with her. She has cancer."

"Oh my gosh, Mary. I'm so sorry. What are they doing?"

"They can't do much for her. She has breast cancer, but it has spread throughout her body. They are just trying to keep her comfortable."

"Oh, Mary. I'm so very sorry."

"They think she won't live more than a couple of days."

"What can I do? Do you want me to come there? Did you talk to Ken? Is he coming there?"

"I talked to Ken earlier. He's on his way here. You don't have to come. It's fine."

"Tell Ken to keep me updated and you call any time for anything?"

"Yeah. I will."

Deb found Ryan, and they went back to the girls' dorm and Deb called Aunt Alicia to let her know what was going on. She was very supportive of Deb and said she would do whatever Deb thought was best. Over the next three days, Ken called Deb each day and Mary called on Tuesday during lunchtime to tell her that her grandmother had died. Arrangements were being made, but she would not be back to school that week. Later, Ken called Deb to tell her that the services were going to be on Saturday. They all agreed to skip the dance and go to the services. Aunt Alicia and Mr. Reynolds came to campus and got Deb, Ryan, Becky, Joe and Kim to go to the services and returned them on Sunday morning. Ken left from the services to get back to school. His finals were that next week. Mary returned Monday evening, and she asked to sit down with Deb as soon as she got back to campus. They went into Deb's room and Mary sat on the bed.

"Deb, my mother said the doctor said that this kind of cancer might be hereditary. That means I could get it later. I'm so scared."

"Mary, I did some research last weekend when you and Ken were at the hospital. I looked all kinds of things up at the library with Ryan. It can be hereditary, but there is no guarantee. Also, wasn't she your father's mother? I think that lessens the chances that you will get it."

"You're sure?"

"According to all the medical journals and things we looked at, you have a higher chance of inheriting it if it is in your mother's family than if it is in your father's family. At least that's true for breast cancer."

"Deb, I have to ask you something. Something I never thought I would ask of you."

"I'll do anything to help you, Mary, you know that."

"I want to go forward in the machine to see if this impacts me. I want to know before I commit myself to Ken."

"Mary, what are you saying? Are you sure?"

"Yes, I'm very sure. This has been all I've been thinking about since the ride from campus to the hospital, when my father told me what was going on. I have to know, or I can't possibly marry Ken. I shouldn't marry anyone if this is what ends up happening to me."

"Remember what happened to Joe when he made the trip last year? Remember how he started having symptoms, and we determined it was probably because you can't have two instances of yourself in the same place and time? You can't go forward and be there twice."

"He did it. He had symptoms, but he didn't die from it."

"Mary, I'm sure this is going to make you furious at me, but a month ago Ryan and I went in the machine and went back to Cambridge to intercept Joe on his trip."

"Why would you do that?"

"Because in the original timeline, Joe goes to the house and talks to our father and convinces him he has travelled from the future and it causes such problems for our parents that they separate. They die anyway, just in two different accidents. This causes Kim to have all kinds of issues—you know how sensitive she is. We went there and met Joe and told him about what happened and we stopped him. The issue is that the symptoms got worse when both Joe and I had two instances of ourselves in the same space and time and we barely made it back. I came back unconscious and Joe barely made it out of there in his version of the machine. Remember the huge gash he had in his forehead when we left campus last spring for summer break? That was because of the trip we made."

"I think at some point I might be mad at you, but all I can think about is knowing if this is going to impact me. Can we talk to Ryan and Joe, and maybe Mr. Brewster about this?"

"Yes, we can talk about it. Should we wait until this weekend when Ken is here?"

"No, I don't want him to know about this."

"Are you sure?"

"Yes. First, I'm sure he'll say it won't matter. He will want to be with me, anyway. Second, he will try to stop me from doing this, and I don't want him to be there when I find out."

"Ok, if you're sure."

"When can we do this? Tomorrow?"

"I will try to see Mr. Brewster in the hall tomorrow and we can alert Ryan and Joe and Becky tomorrow at breakfast or lunch or something."

"That sounds good. Thank you, Deb, for doing this for me."

The next day, they all met at the barn after classes. Mr. Brewster indicated Thomas was due to arrive tomorrow, so they would have time to discuss whatever was bothering Mary. As they sat at the table and listened to Mary describe her situation and her desire to know what was in store for her future, everyone was silent. Joe was the first to speak. "Mary, I'm confused. You were the one who said we shouldn't use the machine again, and especially for our own purposes. Are you sure this is the answer?"

"I didn't understand then, Joe. I didn't understand what you were going through, missing your parents and wanting to use the machine for your own benefit to resolve some terrible emotional issue. Now I do," Mary said.

"What about the powerful feelings you have about not wanting to mess with God's plan, Mary? Won't going forward and finding out if you could get cancer be messing with that plan?" Ryan asked.

"Probably. But again, now I see what you all were feeling and meaning," Mary said pleadingly.

"Mary, I know this must seem scary, but what are you hoping to do by knowing? What will it change?" Kim asked.

"I will know not to put your brother through the terrible ending I just witnessed for my grandmother. The medical issues were so many, and cost so high, and loss is something I may never get over. I can't do that to him. So, if I know in advance, I can keep him from having to deal with all of this."

"It's going to break his heart anyway, if you break up with him now or he loses you later to cancer," Kim replied.

"Mary, remember when we were sitting here last fall after the trip to Las Vegas? Remember when Mr. Brewster said he was glad he had the time he had with his wife? He was glad they got to have Thomas and his childhood together?" Ryan asked.

"Yeah, so?"

"Would you want to give that up even if you know it might end earlier than you wanted it to?" Mr. Brewster asked. "That's what it came down to for me. I didn't want to give up the time I had with my wife and even if I didn't like the fact that you all went on that trip without telling me, I am thankful every day for what it gave me."

"I need to do this. Just like you all needed to save your parents and Deb how you needed to help Mr. Brewster."

"How about we shift gears?" Ryan said, "Let's talk about the logistics of getting this done. We can't just put you in the machine and send you to a point in the future hoping you would know where you lived at that time, and even if we could do that, we know from Joe's trip that the universal rules will not allow two of you in the same space and time."

"How am I going to know where I will be and at a specific point in the future?" Mary asked.

"If the universal rules won't allow Mary to be there twice, who's to say that Deb and Ryan don't live down the street from Mary and Ken in the future and if you all went, you all would be there twice? Remember, we said no more trips alone," Kim said.

"It's true we don't know where she will be at a point in the future, but we can make some assumptions. We know she is going to Wellesley, and we know she is studying journalism. Mary, have you and Ken talked about where you might live?" Deb asked.

"How about I ask a more fundamental question? Is there some way the doctors can determine with any certainty that you carry whatever is necessary to give you this cancer?" Mr. Brewster put forward.

"No, I asked that. The doctors said that they were working on something that would allow them to know if someone was likely to get breast cancer or if there was some marker or something to show they had the hereditary link, but they haven't found a means to test for it yet," Mary replied.

"Maybe we should ask Mr. Brewster's son; I mean, he is studying to be a doctor to research cancer, isn't he?" Kim asked.

"He is, but I'm not sure he will know in detail how to test for this and when a definitive test might be available," Mr. Brewster said.

"He'll be here tomorrow; should we ask him?" Deb asked.

"We can," Mr. Brewster said.

"So, we might get some insight from him, but we haven't answered the question of who should go," Becky said.

"I'll go," Mr. Brewster said. "Mary will recognize me, but it is not likely we will be in the same space and time in the future, so there will be no risk to my being there."

"What about our deal of no trips alone in the machine? That applies to you too, Mr. Brewster, doesn't it?" Kim asked.

Just then, Thomas, who had arrived a day early and found them in the barn and quietly entered, said, "What kind of trip in what kind of machine?"

They all turned and saw him standing just out of the light near the side door of the barn. Mr. Brewster got up and went to him and hugged him as he asked, "What are you doing here today? I wasn't expecting you until tomorrow."

"I decided to surprise you, but I guess I am the one that is surprised."

"I think perhaps you kids ought to head back to campus while I explain some things to Thomas. I will be in touch tomorrow."

They all got up to leave. Deb and Ryan wondered out loud as they left the barn if it was a good idea to tell Thomas about the machine and what they had been doing, but given they had brought Mary, Ryan and Becky into it, they decided Mr. Brewster had to decide this.

While the kids were eating and doing homework, Mr. Brewster was fixing dinner and talking to Thomas.

"Why did you come early? Is everything alright?"

"Yeah, Dad, I just wanted to surprise you. I'm done with tests and really wanted to have a few days with you before we went back for my graduation. That's really all that's going on; at least until I heard you all talking about you getting into a machine and going somewhere, and it didn't seem like you were talking about a car."

As they ate their dinner, Mr. Brewster started from the beginning about meeting Joe, and how distraught he was, about Joe's finding of the formula, their working together, the building of the machine and testing. He told Thomas about the trip to meet his father, about the kids going to Dallas and the latest trips to Cambridge. Mr. Brewster left out the trip to Las Vegas. When he was done, he waited for Thomas to say something.

"That's what that contraption in the barn is? A time machine?"

"Yes."

"Can you show it to me?"

"Sure, let's go have a look."

They went back to the barn and Mr. Brewster showed his son the machine. He turned it on, showed him the printouts, the notes and formula.

"Ok, I believe you. I always knew you were a fantastic scientist. So why are you the one going on a trip and what is it for?" Thomas asked.

"Well, Mary's grandmother just passed away from cancer. Undiagnosed breast cancer that had spread throughout her body. She is in an absolute panic about what her future might hold because the doctors have told her there is some proof that this type of cancer has a hereditary component. Now, Mary wants to go forward in time and see if there is a test or has been a test and find out if she has the chance of having this cancer before she commits to Ken. She wants to save him from the pain of losing her."

"Dad, I know every day that I miss my mother, and that I would give anything to have her here with us. But if she had some way to know that she was going to die of cancer and not married you, or not tried to have me... that makes me sad. She was so happy while she was with us, even at the end, when she knew her time had come. Did you explain this to Mary? She will not want to spend what life she has avoiding people just to save them the pain of losing her."

"I know. We were trying to make her see that. Then we talked about you, actually. Thinking you might have some insight into what tests might be coming or something that these doctors didn't know."

"Well, I know we are trying to map the genetic code. To determine what each thing on the string of chromosome does, what it plays a role in determining. I'm sure if we can do that, we can determine if any of those chromosomes mean you will or won't have cancer. That's actually what I hope to work on."

"How far away do you think that is?"

"I can't say. It could be two years; it could be two decades."

"That's what I was afraid of."

"I know that I'm going to work in a research hospital and have been assigned to the cancer research department. So, at some point in the future, we might have an answer for her."

"That would be wonderful, but like you said, she can't live her life in fear of that."

"Why do you need to go into the future, Dad?"

"There is a paradox in time travel that we have discovered that will not allow there to be two instances of a person in a given space and time. Scientifically, it makes sense as there is a finite amount of energy allowed in the universe and having two of someone would be double the energy for that person and the universe will try to correct that."

"But you likely will be around for many years to come. How will it not impact you?"

"There is a correlation to space, almost an exact geography of space, that allows two of you to be in the same time, but not in the same close space. Ryan went to Cambridge, and he was fine because that was not where he was located in the time the machine went to. But Deb lived near where the machine was located, so she had issues."

"So long as Mary doesn't live near Wallingford, then you would be ok then? Is that what you mean?"

"Correct."

"How will you know where to go to find Mary in the future? You don't know where she will end up living."

"We know for sure where she will be for the next four years. She is headed to Wellesley for college this fall."

"But after that, you have no way of knowing, right?"

"She has told us she always believed she would live somewhere near either Boston or New York, as she wants to pursue a career in journalism."

"That's a pretty extensive area to search for someone."

"Yes, but as we have been talking about this, I have come up with a plan."

"What is it?"

"Well, if I am talking to you right now about making this trip in the machine, it is already part of our future selves' past. So, if we could jump forward, say ten years, we would remember having this conversation. I could, knowing this, allow our present selves to know something, say that happens tomorrow, from the future."

"If you say so, Dad. That sounds very farfetched and very science fiction to me. Not to mention confusing."

"It works like this: Imagine you wake up tomorrow and you are thinking about how you wanted to surprise me, but you were surprised instead. If I had gone ahead one day, I would have known you came early, and I could have told the kids that I couldn't meet with them, and they wouldn't have been here and you would have found me alone today."

"I think I see."

"I need to ponder this some more, I think."

"Let's go back inside, then. I'm pretty tired from my tests this morning and my drive here."

They went in and prepared for bed, but Mr. Brewster stayed up very late that night, considering this new theory. The next day, he found Joe exiting the science building at lunchtime and asked if he could walk with him to the dining hall. Mr. Brewster explained his new theory, and Joe thought it had merit. They agreed to talk later that day, and Joe told the others. They all assembled again at the barn after classes, and this time, Thomas joined them.

After Mr. Brewster explained his theory, they all sat for a minute and pondered what impact that would have. Ryan was the first to come up with something and he said, "Does this make sense? Mr. Brewster, let's assume this is still your house. You could put into your head tonight to leave us a note about where Mary was living at some point in the future. In the future, you could look her up and contact her and tell her you needed to know how to reach her for this trip and she would tell you. You would put that in the note so we could see it, say tomorrow and know where to send the machine into the future. Have I got that right?"

"Yes," Joe responded before Mr. Brewster could. "Everything we discuss right here today is already in our memory of ourselves in say five years. We will remember this conversation; we will remember planning to make this trip to see Mary."

"Will I know the day you coming and everything?" Mary asked.

"Yes, you will have the entire trip, any conversations we have there and anything that happens already in your memory in the future, even if we don't know yet what those conversations might be," Mr. Brewster said.

"Do we have to make the trip at all? Couldn't you just send some sort of note now and not have anyone go?" Kim asked.

"No, without the trip now, she would have no memory of it later. Let me try to explain in terms of a simpler event. Kim, do you have memory of what you got for your twelfth birthday yet? No, because that hasn't happened yet, right?"

"Right," Kim said.

"But if we right now jump into the machine and meet up with you as you arrive here for school next fall, will you have memory of what you got for your birthday?"

"Yes, because it already would have happened at that point in time."

"Exactly."

"Oh, now I get it!"

"So, Mr. Brewster, you're going to contact me in the future and ask where I live and how to reach me, and I'm going to tell you at that point in the future, then you are going to write a note in the future, which we are going to find here in the barn? How is that going to work?"

"I believe I am going to have to ask Mary where she is regularly and put it somewhere each year, and then we will have to find it here in the barn. Because this is all happening in the future, and we don't have memory of it yet, we will have to search it out," Mr. Brewster said.

"So, whatever it is, it's already here, right?" Ryan said.

"Yes."

"What are we waiting for? Let's look around!" Ryan said, getting up and switching on the big lights so all the barn was lit up.

They all started looking and, after checking everywhere they could think of, they were about to give up, and then Thomas went over to the old car that Mr. Brewster was forever working on and opened the glove compartment. There was a piece of paper and on it was written the year and an address for each year in the future. It started the year Mary graduates from college and went on for seven years. Thomas brought it back to the table and looked at it in awe.

"It worked," Thomas said. "It actually worked."

"So now we know where I will be. What is the plan?"

"We pick one of these years, and I would suggest as close to the date that Mr. Brewster marked each year as possible, and we find a place close by to determine a location for the machine to go to and then we figure out when to do the trip," Joe said.

"I want to go with you, Dad," Thomas said.

"Why?" Mr. Brewster asked.

"Because I want to see what this is like, and also, I think I can help. I can quickly assess the advances and we can know right away, even before we go find Mary, if there has been some medical advancement that will allow us to determine her risk."

"It's actually not a bad idea, Mr. Brewster," Becky said.

"How will you determine if the time we pick will work to test Mary or whatever?" Deb asked.

"Well, I will have to locate a lab or library or something when we get there," Thomas answered.

"Why don't you just pick the last date on the list? That way, we can be sure to know something?" Mary asked.

"I'm not so sure that will work. First, we don't have any way of knowing when this medical advancement might take place," Joe pondered.

"Plus, don't you want to find out as soon as possible, Mary? If we go too far into the future to be sure we catch the medical advancement, we might be too far out for you to save things with Ken," Deb said.

"You're right Deb. So do the research, then find me, and if the means do not exist to test me, just jump to the next date on the list," Mary said.

"Then maybe it would be better to find someplace where we can send the machine to do this research first and then go find Mary to discuss with her. That way, if there is no point, because the medical research has not advanced, you come right back and we go again. Or wait a minute, why can't we set up several locations and date and time settings and if you find that the first one there isn't enough medical advancement, you just get back in the machine and go forward more?" Joe asked.

"Will that work, Joe? Will they be able to set that up in advance or will we just have to record it somehow and they adjust the settings each time if they have to jump forward again?" Ryan asked.

"I think we can record it and just show both Thomas and Mr. Brewster how to reset the program," Joe said.

"We've never tested the machine going to point A, then on to point B and on to point C before returning home. Do you think there will be any issues with that, Joe?" Mr. Brewster asked.

"Effectively, does the machine care about the settings? Does it care that you go to a setting, then come back here, or will it just look at each setting as a distinct end point?" Becky asked.

"You're probably right, Becky. The machine's program doesn't care whether you jump to another point forward or back, or just come back here. It's just a setting for the program. I think it will be fine, Mr. Brewster," Joe said.

"What are the next steps, then? It seems like we are going forward with this and Mr. Brewster and Thomas are getting in the machine," Deb said.

"Don't we need to take these addresses and see what is there now? Find their navigational settings and see if they already exist as a house or apartment or whatever? Then we need to see if we can find a hospital or library or something nearby for Thomas to research, right?" Ryan asked.

"That sounds like a plan," Becky said. "Deb and Ryan, you're the research experts. Can you do that?"

"Sure. We can work on that this weekend," Deb said. "we only need to worry about what will change in the future to make the locations right or wrong to land the machine."

"Concentrate on parks, or other kinds of protected areas that are close enough for Mr. Brewster and Thomas to travel to and from for the machine landing sites. That way, they won't change much," Joe said.

"Remember, Ken will be here, and I don't want him to know about any of this," Mary said.

"Mary, may I ask why you don't want the young man you have spoken about as your intended husband to know about your fears and your desire to use this machine to find out?" Thomas asked.

"It sounds terrible, doesn't it? He will try to talk me out of doing this, I know. I know he will probably tell me it doesn't matter, and I know this looks very hypocritical. I have been criticizing everyone for using this machine at all, let alone for personal gains and here I want to use it to find out something in my future."

"Can I just say, that I'm glad for every single moment I had with my mother, and I would do it exactly the same way if I could know in advance that I would lose her when I was twelve years old," said Thomas.

"That's how I feel too. I'm so glad for every moment I had with my parents, even knowing that I had to lose them," Kim said. "Mary, don't you think Ken will feel that way?"

"I'm sure he'll feel that way, but what about what it will cost him? Can't I want to save him from that pain?" Mary asked.

"Mary, in truth, Thomas' mother said frequently that she wished more than anything she could save us from the pain that was coming, but, dear, she always said that if not having the time with us was the only way to save us, she would have to choose to put us through it," Mr. Brewster said kindly.

"This is important to me. I didn't fight you all this hard when it was important to you."

"Mary, don't worry. We may not understand your reasons, but we know this is important to you and just like when I said I was going to do this for Joe, even with my reservations, I'm going to do this for you," Deb said.

"We better get back. We have only enough time to race over to the dining hall if we want dinner," Becky said.

"I'll drive you in my truck. Everyone climb in the back," Mr. Brewster said.

20

Ken arrived the next afternoon. Everyone was excited to see him. He took everyone out for pizza and then they went bowling. The next day, Kim was doing to an event for Girl Scouts and Joe and Becky had a big class project to finish, so Ken asked Deb and Ryan if they would mind if he spent the day with Mary. They said that was a great idea and while Ken and Mary went off, Deb and Ryan went to the library. It was a very productive day at the library and by the time Deb and Ryan left to go have dinner and then hang out in the main hall; they had everything they needed for all but one address on the list. They told Joe when they saw him and Becky at the dining hall they were ready and Joe said he would have time Monday after the class project to look at it.

On Monday, they were all concerned when they didn't see Mr. Brewster all day. They all went to the barn right after classes and found him there with Thomas. When they asked why he was not in classes, he said that he had arranged it with the school to be out so they could do this trip and used the fact that his son was there as the excuse. They sat down and Deb and Ryan went over all the information for each date and address, and they set coordinates for each as they went. Because there was no way to know if the medical advancements had been made, each trip forward, Thomas would determine if there was a way to assess Mary's risk and if there was a way, they would locate Mary and complete whatever screening. If not, they would go forward to the next date and location on the list. They determined they would start the first trip with the final year of college for Mary, hoping they could have this all resolved before she graduated. She liked that idea and they all agreed to the plan. Mr. Brewster said he would like to leave sometime tomorrow, and they agreed for them to go at lunchtime. Joe and Ryan would come over to assist with the settings, recordings of future settings, and get them off. They made a decision that the kids would not come to the barn and wait, but go on with classes and such, and Mr. Brewster would contact either Joe or Ryan when they returned.

The next day, Joe and Ryan were there to make sure they had all the recorded settings and knew exactly how to change the settings and run the machine. Thomas and Mr. Brewster carried along some changes of clothes, identification, and money in case they needed to get cabs or something. Joe and Ryan waited until the machine disappeared and then they went back to campus.

"It's really noisy, isn't it?" Thomas asked as the machine powered up and started running the program.

"Yes, it's a bit of a shock at first, but you'll be ok."

"If you say so."

All at once, everything got quiet. Mr. Brewster checked outside and found it safe, and they left the machine. They hailed a cab outside what was an abandoned shipyard. They went directly to the Wellesley library where Thomas looked up information in medical journals and checked different sources.

"It doesn't look like we have anything more sophisticated than mammograms here in 1979. We're going to have to go forward. There appears to be some promising research noted in this journal, so maybe two years."

"Let's get back to the machine, then."

They went back to the shipyard and got into the machine. Mr. Brewster set the program with settings from the information logged for 1981. He started the program up and buckled in. When the noise settled down again, Thomas said, "I guess you get used to it, and it goes pretty quickly, too."

They were on one of the islands near Manhattan. Mary was living in New York City now. The island was one large cemetery, so no activity, and they happily landed in a shed. They hitched a ride from someone leaving the cemetery to Queens, where they rode the train into Manhattan. Thomas headed directly for NYU hospital and went to the front desk, showed his student badge, and gained access to the research library. They spent about three hours there. After exhausting all information, they left and went to a diner for some dinner. It was about six at night. They got a cab back to the cemetery island and got back to the machine.

"Where to now?" Mr. Brewster asked his son.

"One more year should do it, Dad."

Mr. Brewster set the machine for one year in the future, which would be at the exact same place, but he adjusted the time to be the next morning. When the machine stopped, they were fourteen hours and one entire year ahead of where they had been. They found the cemetery caretaker who agreed to take them to Queens. From there, they returned to Manhattan and found a place for breakfast before returning to the hospital. They again returned to the research library, and Thomas found what he needed right away. He was right. During the last year, they had found a marker that could test for a breast cancer marker. A simple blood test would determine whether there was a predisposition for breast cancer. They left the hospital and hailed a cab to the address where Mary lived. They were worried about Mary being gone for work, but when they climbed the stairs to her apartment and knocked on the door, she answered.

"Hello Mr. Brewster, hello Thomas," she said, beckoning them into her apartment.

"You have a lovely place, Mary," Thomas said.

"Thanks."

"Where's Ken?"

"He lives downtown in his own apartment. We aren't really together right now. We talk pretty regularly and he keeps trying to convince me to reconcile, but I've been waiting for you," Mary said.

"Well, Mary, we have good news. There is a blood test now that will show if you have the marker for breast cancer. All we need to do is contact your doctor and ask for the test and go have it. Once the results are back, we will know for sure," Thomas said.

"Is there a name for this test?"

"There isn't a specific name. I would suggest you explain your family history and say that because you are about to get married, you want to know and ask for the CA 15.3, the Tru-Quant and the CA 27.29 marker tests. These will tell us if you have the predisposition marker for breast cancer, and whether you have cancer present in your system right now," Thomas said.

"I will call the doctor right now."

Mary went to the phone on the wall and dialed her doctor's number. She asked to speak with the nurse and told her just what Thomas had told her to. The nurse said she understood Mary's concern and would speak to the doctor and get back to Mary as soon as she could. Mary relayed the information and asked if she could offer either of them anything. They said no; they had eaten, but Mr. Brewster said he was getting exhausted. Mary offered him the couch to lie down and took Thomas into her kitchen. They sat at the kitchen table.

"How many trips have you had to make to get here?"

"Two prior to this. We went to Wellesley, then here and then one year later here."

"Oh, that's not too bad."

"No, but we moved this last trip forward to the next morning in terms of the time we went to. That's why Dad is so tired."

"Well, it might be a while before I hear from the doctor. If you would like to rest too, there is that recliner chair out there."

"That sounds great."

Both men slept for about two hours, and just before lunchtime, the phone rang.

"Hello."

"Yes, this is Mary."

After a few minutes, Mary responded, "Thank you. I will be there first thing in the morning, then."

Mr. Brewster got up and went to the kitchen, where Mary was sitting.

"Did the doctor approve the blood test?" Mr. Brewster asked.

"Yes, I go first thing tomorrow."

"Good."

"I need to go into the office for a bit. Will you two be ok to stay here? I'm sorry you will have to wait until tomorrow. The doctor told me they could tell us the results within a couple of hours, though."

"We will be fine here. I think we should get a hotel room for the night, though. Is there one close by?"

"Not in this neighborhood. But the test is scheduled for first thing tomorrow, so perhaps we can meet near the hospital. I believe there is a hotel near there."

Mary got the phone book and looked up the hotel. There was one just down the street from the hospital, and Mr. Brewster called and got a reservation. They agreed to meet Mary the next morning and, rather than staying at her apartment, in case Ken showed up, they left and went to the hotel.

After a restful sleep for Mr. Brewster and Thomas, they met Mary and walked down to the hospital. They waited while she got the blood drawn and then went to have some breakfast while Mary went to the office for a short time. She agreed to come back at eleven and get them to find out the results. When they met back at the hospital, they walked to the lab and asked for her results. A nurse ushered them into a small room and asked to wait. Just as the technician came into the room and pulled out a piece of paper, a nurse came to the room and notified Mary that Ken was there and was very upset. Apparently, he had called Mary's office at the newspaper and they told him she had gone to get test results at the hospital. Mary left the room and said to Mr. Brewster as she left, "Please don't let him see you. Can you sneak out down the hall and get back to the machine without me?"

"Yes, Mary. Do you want to see these results?"

The technician moved the paper across the table, and Thomas got a good look at the results. Mary said she couldn't now, but she would check back when she could. She left the room. The technician asked what their relationship with Mary was and they replied they were just friends trying to help a friend. The technician said she couldn't leave the results with them since they weren't family. It wasn't really necessary because Thomas had seen the results. They left the office.

They made their way down to the street and hailed a cab to the cemetery island. There was a funeral going on and there were cars milling about the shed where the machine was hidden. Mr. Brewster made them wait a couple of hours to leave. They set the machine for the return trip to the correct date and time and started it up.

While all this was going on, the six young people attended class, went to meals, and did homework for two days. At the end of the first night that Mr. Brewster and Thomas had been gone, Mary went to Deb's room.

"What are you doing?"

"Just finishing my last English assignment. You?"

"Just sitting in my room worrying and thinking."

"Mary, you can't worry so much about all of this. I hate to say it this way, but it's going to be what it's going to be. All you can do is formulate a plan once you know."

"I've been thinking about what you said when I got back to campus and told you I wanted to do this. About making a trip to Cambridge to stop Joe. What was that all about?"

"Well, Kim was very upset. She hated the fact that we did that to our parents and hated the fact that they separated and died separately, basically alone."

"What are you talking about?"

"So, when Joe originally went to Cambridge last spring, he talked to my father. He told him everything and my father believed him. My father even agreed to stay away from planes and mountains. The problem was, my mother didn't believe any of it. She thought something was up with Joe and she made him see doctors and shrinks and they fought so bad about it that my dad left. Then he had to go on a trip and the plane crashed and my mom went racing to where they had taken my father and she was in a car accident."

"Wow."

"This is what upset Kim. So, we decided we needed to fix it. Ryan and I went in the machine and went to intercept Joe. We were successful, so you all that didn't know about this trip just lost all memory of that timeline and woke up the day after this trip and only remembered the timeline where my parents died in the avalanche. We did it primarily for Kim, but Joe kind of wanted to fix what he had done."

"Why didn't you tell me or include me?"

"To start with, you really didn't like our using the machine at all, remember? Also, we didn't want Ken to know, and telling you meant Ken would know."

"Didn't we go through this already? I told I would not if you asked me not to tell him."

"Well, I didn't think that would work."

"Wow, Deb, don't you trust me?"

"I was wrong not to tell you."

"And you didn't tell Kim either, did you?"

"No, she was on a camping trip and we figured it would be much better if she just lost all memory of our parents separating."

"Have you told Ken yet?"

"No."

"Do you intend to?"

"I don't think so."

"Deb, tell him."

"What about you? Are you going to tell him about this trip to find out if you're going to have cancer in the future?"

"That's different."

"How? Trust is trust, isn't it?"

"I guess so. Trust is trust regardless of who the parties are and honesty is honesty, regardless of who is involved."

"I spent a lot of time struggling with this. I even, in a roundabout way, talked to Ken about it. About whether the ends justify the means."

"What do you mean?"

"Well, if you do something a little bad to make something good happen in the end, does the happy in the end justify whatever you had to do to get there?"

"I see. Yes, that is totally the question."

"Not always, I'm afraid. Sometimes the price you pay on the honesty and trust might be too high. I almost lost you as a friend over it last time. And Ken was furious for a long time over it."

"Trust goes both ways, you know. If I had trusted you more, maybe you wouldn't have thought to keep it from me."

"Maybe."

"Well, I'm going to get some sleep. See you in the morning."

Mr. Brewster and Thomas returned to the barn late on Wednesday evening. They decided to printout the statistics from the machine and go over the test results and contact the kids the next day. The next morning, Mr. Brewster called the office and asked for a note to be delivered to Ryan in his science class to contact Mr. Brewster after classes that day. Ryan received it just before he went into his last class of the day. After his class finished, he found Joe and then Deb. They agreed to meet at the girls' dorm and walk over to the barn together. Deb told Mary, Kim and Becky at the dorm and they all changed quickly and were waiting for Ryan and Joe. Everyone was quiet on the way over to the barn, each thinking about what might happen.

"It's going to be ok. You don't have to worry. Ken will take care of you no matter what," Kim said to Mary as she took her hand.

"That's what I'm afraid of, I think," she said in reply.

They went into the barn, and Joe went to get Mr. Brewster and Thomas from the house. When they were all assembled around the table, Mr. Brewster spread out all the printouts on the table.

"Well, what should we cover first? The stops we made or elapsed time or what?" Mr. Brewster asked.

"My gosh, Mr. Brewster. Did you find out about Mary? That's way more important. Tell Mary what you found out."

21

AUTHORS NOTES

As with any work of fiction, authors do take some license to use information to help tell the story. I am guilty of this as well. However, I would like to take this moment to give credit where credit is because of those people, dates, accomplishments and events.

Choate Rosemary Hall is an actual boarding preparatory school in Wallingford, Connecticut. It was founded as Rosemary Hall for girls in 1890 by Mary Atwater Choate. Later, a boys' school was added, the girls' school relocated and then returned to the original location. It became a co-ed school in the 1970s. President John F. Kennedy, and many other famous people attended throughout its history. Several of the buildings named here are actual buildings at Choate. However, the inclusion of younger children Kim's age and various aspects of the schedule, buildings and activities are my creation. You can learn more about this wonderful school at: www.choate.edu.

The atomic testing referred to here during the time travel to Las Vegas in the 1950s is all based on fact. The site was known as the Nevada Test Site (NTS) and it was located a mere 65 miles north of Las Vegas. The Atomic Energy Commission and this testing were established by President Truman in 1950. The first test at this site was on January 27, 1951 and was the detonation of a 1 kiloton bomb. Operation Plumbbob was conducted from May 28th to October 7th, 1957. It included 29 tests and was one of the longest and most comprehensive test series. It is true that these tests came to be much like a spectator sport with people travelling out of Las Vegas to watch. During the testing, pigs were used to determine the potential impact to humans because their skin is much like human skin. The last atmospheric test was conducted in Nevada on July 17, 1962. On August 5, 1963, the United States signed the Nuclear Test Ban Treaty that prohibited nuclear detonation in the atmosphere, in water and in space. Many eminent scientists, mathematicians and military men and women worked tirelessly in an effort to protect the United States, serve their country and advance scientific understanding. All references to Mr. Brewster being a part of this testing are fictitious.

Las Vegas was a booming city in the 1950s. During the period from 1952 to 1957, new casinos opened all the time. This time marks the opening of the Sahara, the Sands, the Showboat, the Riviera, the Horseshoe and the Tropicana. Also, during this time, many great entertainer legends spent time at these casinos. Becoming known as the rat pack, men such as Dean Martin, Frank Sinatra and Sammy Davis Jr. performed. References to these places, streets and names are based on fact, but Mr. and Mrs. Brewster being there are fictional.

The language created by Joe in this book is an actual language. Computer language began with what is called Machine Code. It was a binary language composed only of 0 and 1. Later languages such as Fortran were created to allow flexibility of a programming language, but contained conversion back to binary. In 1959, COBOL was created. This language was based on English syntax, but has what are referred to as reserved words. These reserved words are used by the language to execute so they cannot be used in any other way. This made the language long and hard to maintain. Between 1969 and 1973, the C language was created at Bell Labs by Dennis Ritchie and Ken Thompson. This language was considered an imperative procedure language and used statements to change the program's state. It was a much simpler design and more agile than COBOL. The C language has been universally adopted and has evolved into a premier business and industry language for programming. Joe, being the inventor, is strictly my doing for this book.

The concept of "personal computers" first appeared in November 1962 in an article of the New York Times, where the vision of computing was seen as a world where everyone could master personal computing. It was not until 1977 that the first pre-assembled personal computers hit the market. The Apple II, the PET 2001 and the TRS-80 were the first to sell in a retail environment as a personal computer or microcomputer, as they were called back then. Of course, now we know every child has a tablet in school and most homes have at least one computer. Joe was not the inventor of these devices. His credit with the invention is fictional.

Time travel is theoretical. The theory of bending time has been in academia for many years. The idea that time is not a linear concept, but a plane that can be bent with magnetic fields and energy, is widely recognized as a valid theory. What is known about two people being in the same space and time continuum and what one would know if you jumped forward in time are also mainstream academic theories. I have used this information to make assumptions and create the possibility that time travel can be accomplished, but to date, no machine has ever been created and no actual live tests have been documented of time travel.

Vogue magazine has been in production since 1892. It became the premier fashion magazine later in the 1960s. Grace Mirabella was, in fact, the editor of Vogue during the time of this story. Several of the people and places mentioned related to Vogue are factual. However, Aunt Alicia being employed there and her activities are fictional.

Little House on the Prairie is a book written by Laura Ingalls Wilder. It is one of a series of books chronicling Ms. Wilder's and her family's life in the 1800s. This series was a favorite of mine growing up, so I had to include it here.

Nancy Drew is a series of books written by Carolyn Keene. They were very women-empowering stories before empowering women was something we spoke about and cared about. My version of this collection of books contains a copyright of 1954, as such, they might seem outdated to young people now and hard to relate to, but they were a pre-teen favorite of mine so again, I felt I had to include them.

Annie, the musical, first came out as a comic strip in the summer of 1924. It then became a popular radio show in the 1930s. This spun into several film productions and became a Broadway musical in 1977, a year after it is noted here as the birthday event for Kim.

Robert Frost did, in fact, live in Cambridge, Massachusetts for the last two decades of his life. His home was restored and listed on the National Register of Historic Places in 1982. It is located on Brewster Street.

The Wharton Brook State Park is an actual park near Wallingford, CT. This park opened August 1, 1919 and was the precursor to modern highway rest stops. It has evolved over the years and offers fishing, picnicking, swimming, and several footpaths. Unfortunately, in 2018, a small tornado transitioned into a microburst and caused extensive damage to the park, causing it to close for the rest of the year. It re-opened in January 2019.

Breast cancer is the most common cancer in women worldwide. The first reference to breast cancer comes in a papyrus text that dates back to 3,000-2,500 B.C.E. Here are some major milestones in breast cancer research:

1882: William Halsted performed the first radical mastectomy. This surgery will remain the standard operation to treat breast cancer until into the 20th century.

1895: The first X-ray is taken. Eventually, low-dose X-rays called mammograms will be used to detect breast cancer.

1898: Marie and Pierre Curie discover the radioactive elements radium and polonium. Shortly after, radium is used in cancer treatment.

1984: Researchers discover a new gene in rats. The human version, called HER2, was found to be linked with more aggressive breast cancer when overexpressed. This cancer is called HER2-positive breast cancer and is not as responsive to treatments.

1995: Scientists can clone the tumor suppressor genes BRCA1 and BRCA2. Inherited mutations in these genes can predict an increased risk of breast cancer.

The testing for breast cancer, especially with a blood test, as used in this book, comes much later than I make it happen here. We must complete the genetic code mapping and then complete the research to determine where these cancer markers are. Thankfully, this blood test is now available and with drugs available to reduce the risk, more women survive every day from this disease.

Other references to movies, dates, events in the book are occasionally adapted for use in the story and do not represent actual release dates or actual dates when certain events took place.